Salad Days

By

Allie Cresswell

[Those were my] salad days,
When I was green in judgment.

Anthony & Cleopatra

by

William Shakespeare

DAY FAMILY TREE
George Day m
Wilhelmina
Trevor m
Lucille
Isobel m
Victor Bracewell
Eric m
Hester
Verity
Grace
Prudence
Erin
Jack
Katherine
Karen

PART ONE
1964 - 1966
Chapter One

My earliest memory is of you, Arthur. You and I were children, running across the garden at Granny's house. I don't know if we were running together towards some specific place—the orchard maybe, or the hen run—or if I was chasing you. Your fat little legs were pumping like pistons. You wore a blue sailor suit and your feet were bare. The sun on your hair made it look like copper wire. Then you stopped, and I cannoned into you. We both went headlong into the rockery. You weren't hurt but you opened your mouth into a big square maw and began to yell. I'd split my lip on a sharp rock and blood was trickling down my chin, but I didn't cry. I never cry.

My father came running and scooped us both up, not caring about the blood that dripped onto his good shirt. He carried us to the terrace where the grownups were having tea. My sisters—sour and sulky in flounced frocks and white bobby socks—looked askance at my grubby dress and messed up hair. My mother jumped up and wiped the blood from my mouth with one of Granny's best embroidered napkins, making sympathetic mewing noises in the back of her throat.

She said, 'Poor Prue. Let me take you indoors to get cleaned up.'

Your mother took a sip of her tea and looked fixedly at a tub of petunias as though you were nothing whatsoever to do with her. Your father stood at the end of the terrace and read a newspaper with intense attention, seemingly deaf to your cries. It was Granny who finally took you off my father and carried you into the house. I expect she gave you a sweetie from the jar she kept on the top shelf of the dresser. I needed two stitches, but you weren't hurt at all.

It was 1964, the summer before I started school, so I was nearly five years old. You would have been just three.

It's strange, isn't it? That my first memory is of you. Or maybe it isn't very strange at all.

Chapter Two

Although my first really vivid memory is of you, Arthur, I am also oddly conscious—from some intuitive pre-knowing—of a time *before* you; a happy well of contented being that exists dully in my subliminal memory and ended the day we fell into the rockery. Your coming disturbed the subterranean ebb and flow that carries infants through their early years—sleep and wake, food and play, the murmur of a mother's song, the low rumble of a father's chest, the familiar smells of bed and blankets, milk, rusk and Johnson's lotion. You yanked me forcibly from that vague jumble of benign impressions into searing consciousness. The shock of sudden pain, not to mention the first taste of my own blood—appalling proof of my mortality—coloured my feelings for you.

First, you were a boy. My parents already had two girls before me; looking back, I can appreciate that they can't have wanted another. But it wasn't until your advent that I began to suspect their disappointment in my sex. You were made so much of by my grandparents. You and Jack—their only grandson— were accorded privileges the rest of us girls were denied. My sisters and girl-cousins didn't seem to mind. But *I* did. I resented you, and resentment— ferrous and salt, like the blood that filled my mouth that day—has been the predominant flavour of my life ever since. I am dogged by a gremlin that speaks umbrage into my ear. I am quick to suspect people, and in pursuit of having my suspicions proved correct I am prone to sneak and pry. In fact, if I say so myself, I have become rather expert in being clandestine … I am here, after all, with you, where I have absolutely no right to be, but no one suspects a thing. And in a strange way that's down to you, Arthur.

I wonder if you knew at the time—or came to realise afterwards—what misery you caused me in the beginning.

My first day at school was soured by the knowledge that when I went afterwards to Granny's to show her my *Janet and John* book and my drawstring plimsoll bag you would be there—for no earthly reason—and that while I had been at school *you* had been at Granny's with all the toys, the whole house and garden and the entirety of Granny's attention all to yourself.

Some inkling told me that you didn't belong, and I was to have that suspicion confirmed when I eventually found out—by dint of dogged interrogation, some shameless eavesdropping and an entirely spurious family tree project supposedly set by my teacher—that although you were a cousin of Jack and Erin's you weren't a cousin of mine or the twins. Neither your mother nor your father was Granny's child—as my father, Uncle Eric and Aunt Isobel were. My aunt Isobel was married to Victor Bracewell. Your mother was Victor's sister, so not a relative to us in the proper sense at all. You were connected—I could allow that—but only tangentially. You weren't *real* family.

Nevertheless, your parents joined the rest of us at Granny's on a regular basis as though they *were* family, as though they *belonged*. You were there for the big occasions—Christmas, the traditional Easter egg hunt, and our annual summer picnic in the cove—and also 'on the off-chance' or 'because we were just passing' on days that I was sure Granny really had other things to do and didn't want visitors. After a while, your parents made no pretence of just happening by. They were *always* there. Had they nothing else to do, I wondered, as a knock on the door interrupted my cosy baking session with Granny in the kitchen? Did they not—as *my* parents did—work? Could they not see that while Granny ran round making tea and serving scones she had work to do elsewhere? Of course, she was too polite to say anything, and I must say that she masked what I thought must have been her real feelings to appear absolutely delighted by these impromptu visits. Good manners are imbued in the Day family along with mother's milk. We avert our eyes and change the subject and gloss over the rudeness of others with inane references to the weather. Maybe, if we'd been less polite, your parents wouldn't have been able to take such outrageous advantage of us.

One late spring morning, when I was out with Granny in the woods looking to see if the bluebells were in bloom, we heard a cuckoo call. Granny explained how the adults lay their eggs in the nests of other birds, and how the cuckoo chicks evict all the other eggs, and I thought, 'Just like Arthur,' but I didn't say anything. Even then I knew that there were times when it didn't do to say aloud all the thoughts that clamoured in my head.

Instead, I set myself to frustrate your attempts to oust the rest of us from Granny's nest. I gave you neither inch nor quarter. It was a big determination for a little girl but then I have always been characterised by fearlessness and grit. I expect my parents rued the day they named me Prudence! Pandora would have suited me much better. I indulged every evil impulse in the box: envy, greed, hatred, pain. I'm ashamed now to think of it, but do you remember the little Lloyd Loom rocking chair in the corner of the parlour? That had been my own preserve until you arrived. I once wrenched you from it so forcibly that your arm bruised. As was usual for you, you went wailing to Granny and I got told off. It didn't occur to me that Jack had been obliged to yield that chair to me, or that twins Katherine and Karen had been evicted for him, and before that my younger sister had usurped Erin, and before all of us my older sister had been forced to watch the seven of us take the place that had originally been hers. It was the same story with the little blue trike, the musical box and the faded quilt that had been my favourite comfort in times of illness. They had been mine but now, apparently, were yours. Oh! And the little bed by the window in the attic. There were seven little beds until you came, each with its own crocheted throw painstakingly made by Granny; but then—when *you* came—an eighth was added, shoehorned in beneath the little round window. There was a lovely view of the woods from that window, and in the springtime swallows nested in the eaves just there. How I fought you over it, sometimes literally tussling amongst the covers until we both fell asleep in a tangle of sweaty arms and legs, top-and-tail, neither one of us prepared to yield to the other.

Before you came, I was the youngest and, as it turned out, without you I'd have remained the baby of the family. My anger threw me into tantrums that frightened me, their iron fist squeezing paroxysms from me and shaking me until my teeth rattled. The adults looked on aghast. No other child in the family had displayed such appalling behaviour, but neither their dismay, disappointment nor their attempts at discipline did anything to quell the attacks. Their failure to see what was so clear to me—and my inability to articulate my outrage—only compounded my frustration. I rarely slept well, kept awake by boiling outrage. Throughout those early years, my stomach was curdled with a hot, caustic jealousy. I began to find mealtimes difficult. I couldn't eat because of the ball of acrid ire that was my permanent companion, to such an extent that my mother took me to the doctors to see if there was something seriously wrong. I was diagnosed with dysphagia—difficulty swallowing—and Mum was advised to ensure my food was cut up into small pieces. My other symptoms—rage, insomnia and a general sense of bleak despair—were not addressed.

I was miserably unhappy but couldn't explain why. You had pushed in and suddenly I was the "big" girl. My ears shrivelled to the constant refrain of, 'Oh, let Arthur have it. He's only little.' I decided that if *I* couldn't have a thing, neither could *you*. So, yes, it was me who cut through the seat of the little rocking chair with Granny's sewing scissors, and me who buried the quilt in the compost heap and me who smashed the musical box to smithereens by dropping it down the stairs. I contrived to be far away from the scene of these crimes when they were discovered. No one ever suspected me at all. They suspected *you*, but for the sake of politeness you were never accused and certainly never punished. The rules were different for you, and I just couldn't understand why.

The only reason I could come up with was the fact that your mother was married to Henry Glenister.

Chapter Three

Now, the Days were a perfectly nice, ordinary family, born and bred in the county, hard-working and respectable. My grandparents—George and Wilhelmina, but Ina to her friends—were admired because they had built up their market garden business, Salad Days, so successfully on the thirty-acre holding that had been in the Day family for three generations. People liked that it was a family concern, with my father, my aunt and my uncle being absorbed into it one way or another as they came of age. We children were given chores as soon as we were big enough to hold an egg basket or pick a blueberry and place it in a trug rather than straight into our mouths. But we still needed outside help. Mick Pullman—horribly scarred both physically and psychologically from a bullet to the face sustained at Ypres—was a fulltime employee. So was Bradley Fox, though crippled with rheumatism from long immersion in the watery trenches. Mrs Gibbs did Granny's cleaning and ironing for years. At apple-harvesttime every child in the village could be sure of a few shillings for a day collecting windfalls. In remoter rural areas like ours, that counts for a good deal. Families who put down deep roots, who provide a local service and steady employment, are going to be respected, and if they do rather well—make money and live off it comfortably—no one will begrudge them their success. That was the Days. They had done well through their own hard work, but they had no airs and graces. Granny did her stint at the tombola at the summer fête, Grandad would stand anyone a pint in the village pub. They used local tradesmen and never darkened the doors of national chain stores where there was a home-grown alternative. Their children attended local schools, Scouts and Girl Guide packs.

The Days were not church goers. Perhaps that was the only thing against them, but it counted for little alongside all there was to be said in their favour.

The Glenisters were different. They were just as local, their roots if anything buried deeper in indigenous soils even than ours, but what wealth they ever had was inherited rather than earned. They lived in their eponymously named stately home, Glenister Hall, which was surrounded by a substantial stone wall. They had historically held themselves aloof, owning a good deal of the land hereabouts, accepting rents from tenants and giving employment to local men and women, but they did so more as a right than as a bargain in which both sides were equal gainers. They expected to get out what they had not put in, an attitude calculated to rile the sensibilities of local people who were much more accustomed to putting in a great deal more than they ever got out. From time immemorial it had been an unequal exchange—

poor men contributing their labour on the fields and their lives in far distant wars for the benefit of men who were already rich and who would, by the sacrifice of others, grow richer still. The Glenisters were members of the squirearchy who sowed nothing but reaped it all. For generations they had looked on like the Israelites at the first Passover. Drought, deluge, pestilence and plague might decimate the lives of their tenants, but they would be passed by—passed over—protected by their blue blood.

Following a succession of family deaths that incurred crippling death taxes, the Glenisters sold off large swathes of their land, including the parcel bought by the Days—but by no means did they accept that this decrease in their property should reduce their standing or influence. In their eyes they were still "lords of the manor." So it still was in the mid-twentieth century. They would not attend the fête unless invited to perform the opening ceremony or to judge the exhibits. Their children were sent away to school. They bought goods and services from as far afield as London and did not seem to see the frowns of the local butcher, baker, cabinetmaker and upholsterer when delivery vehicles bearing the names of Harrods and Selfridges made their way through the narrow village street.

Of course, you *know* this history, Arthur—who better? But I wonder if you know how your family was perceived by the rest of us?

There was a local legend that women who married into the Glenister family ran mad in one way or another—and your grandmother certainly gave grist to that mill. Word was that she was *very* odd. Gossip said several Mrs Glenisters had been locked away in institutions and some had gruesomely done away with themselves. Hundreds of years ago, one had been burned as a witch.

My sisters enjoyed frightening me with stories of Glenister ghosts and witches, describing crones in rags immured within the attics of Glenister Hall or wraithlike young girls weeping inconsolably in the woods. Grandad said the tales were the result of local spite and envy and I should take no notice of them, but he hinted that if the Glenisters were to integrate with the village community instead of holding themselves aloof, it would be a very good thing. 'People fear what they don't understand,' he had said. Not many people would contradict my grandad to his face, but mention of your Glenister grandmother caused people to twirl their fingers next to their temples when he wasn't looking. At the very kindest, she was described as 'not very well.'

But Granny's daily help, Mrs Gibbs, was much more enlightening on the topic. She was a mine of local information, both current and historical, and I often trailed around after her as she dusted the window ledges and cleaned the windows, collecting whatever gems I could from her abundant store.

'The Glenisters and their ilk, they marry too close,' she told me. 'Their blood is too pure. It's no wonder they go wrong in the head. Look at the royal family!'

I thought about Princess Anne, constantly held up to us Day girls as the exemplar of poise, politeness and perfection. Would she go "wrong in the head" when she married "too close?"

I opened my mouth to enquire further but Mrs Gibbs, warming to her theme, said, 'It doesn't do for cousins to marry each other. Things go all queer. The babies come out wrong, if they come out at all.'

'So,' I clarified, perching on the little stool Mrs Gibbs used to reach into the high corners, 'the Glenisters marry their cousins.' Jack was my only male cousin. He was bony and boastful. Nothing on earth would make me marry him.

'Oh yes!' she said, bending to scrub at a stubborn fly spot on the window frame, 'all the time. It isn't right. It isn't right at all, if you ask me.'

Forgive me Arthur, if this sounds rude—this is your family I'm describing. Perhaps it isn't very respectful, but what can I say? Sometimes, the truth hurts. So. Their consanguinity notwithstanding, the Glenisters clearly thought themselves a cut above the Days and your father personified this notion from the first, setting himself apart from the rest of us as much by his own demeanour—he was distant, taciturn, superior—as by anything else. No one wished to deny their long lineage, or that they had at one time been wealthy, but by this time they were poor, their mansion crumbling. I heard 'delusions of grandeur' muttered by Aunt Hester, and a withering 'poor as church mice' from my mother. Notwithstanding his reputed poverty, it was generally known that your grandfather spent a great deal of time on the continent playing golf.

I didn't wonder your parents preferred the easy-going hospitality and relaxed atmosphere of Granny's house to what I imagined was the loony bin at Glenister Hall, but it made for awkwardness when your father behaved as though he conferred a great favour upon us by his condescension. Even being such regular fixtures as they became, the Glenisters retained the status of "guests" and many was the time I heard Mum mutter, 'FHB' when the buffet was served. 'Family Hold Back,' she meant, indicating that *real* family should allow *you* guests to take first pick.

Although of course we all had our separate homes we ate together at Granny's house several times a week and always at the weekends. We had the business in common and so there were always things to be discussed about that, but there was also a kind of camaraderie … we enjoyed each other's company. We were a self-sufficient, cohesive unit financially, commercially and socially. Why, I wondered, did we need *you?* What did you bring? Not fun, certainly. Your father hid behind the pages of newspapers or periodicals, too busy with those highly intellectual articles to join in the family games; and in any case, he considered himself far too superior. He never unbent himself sufficiently to join in at cricket or take his turn with the washing up. Some might accuse the Days of relishing the éclat that association with the Glenisters brought, but not those who knew anything about it. Granny and Grandad were the last people anyone could accuse of toadying and anyway, look at the strife their connection with the Glenisters produced. Specifically, Arthur, look at your mother.

She was a fragile—not to say flaky—woman, nothing like Uncle Victor. The Bracewells had been dairy farmers for generations until the foot and mouth outbreak in 1953 had decided them to sell up. They were hearty, wholesome folks with calloused hands and generous hearts. Uncle Victor was the first Bracewell son destined not to take over the herd. For some young men, who had believed their life already mapped out, this might have been a blow from which they would not easily recover, but not for Uncle Victor. Undaunted, with that jaunty optimism habitual with him, he looked about him for some alternative profession that remained true to his agricultural heritage and established a moderately successful business crafting dairy products— cheese, yoghurt and ice cream—until his absorption into Salad Days. He was always cheery, practical and enthusiastic. He was irrepressible, until tragedy came.

His sister Blanche—your mother—though never showing any interest in the dairy farm, seemed to have no other plan for her future once it was sold. She accompanied her parents to their retirement property on the south coast and ironically it was there that she met and married Henry Glenister. Who knows what drew them together? Their county of birth seems to be the only thing they shared. He was all haughtiness and pride, she all meekness and cringing, and the age disparity between them—he was fifteen years her senior—can't have helped. I'm sure the marriage was a disaster from the start and not least because of the elder Mr Glenister's antipathy to it. Who can blame him? When you bring your son up with a consciousness of his own superiority, educate him privately and at great expense, protect him from the "pollution" of "ordinary" people and prepare him in every way to take his place amongst the gentry—however faded and outdated such an idea might be—only to have him marry the daughter of a local dairy farmer ... how he must have shrunk from the whiff of sour milk. No, I am sure your mother felt—and was *made* to feel—ill-suited to the role of lady of the manor from the start.

Even the production of a son and heir—you, Arthur—did not mean her acceptance, which perhaps explains why motherhood was not the comfort and validation to her that it is to most women. She just seemed to have no idea what to *do*. She looked on in a sort of bewilderment as the other women rolled their sleeves up and got on with things. She was never ready with the right word of encouragement or guidance, never equipped with enough nappies, bibs, tissues and the like. Surely you were aware of my mother and aunts exchanging irritated looks as they stepped in to praise your—frankly, ham-fisted—efforts in drawing, cheer you in rounders, serve you with food, put you in the bath and tuck you into bed, all the things that *she* should have done but was at first too inept and later too preoccupied with her own self-pity to bother with.

Between your father's standoffishness and your mother's incompetence you *must* have felt your difference, Arthur. Did you? Did you notice that, in the gaggle of grownups dishing up food, getting out and putting away lawn toys, supervising rounders on the beach or bicycle rides along the disused railway line, at bath time and bedtime and even once on Christmas morning, your mother was never in the vanguard and your father was reserved, occupying some rarefied space of his own? *My* family had to take the lead.

Oh! It infuriated me that my parents—already dividing their time and attention between the three of us girls—had to spread themselves even thinner to accommodate you, too. My mother had always been a smiling woman, but I noticed increasingly that her lips had a pursed, sewn-shut look about them as she held back her resentment at getting up—*again*—from the family dinner table to cut up your meat or to mop up your spilled water. I remember looking glumly round the table. At Granny, hot and flustered from cooking and dishing up the meal, her apron still tied round her waist. Did she really need three more mouths to feed? At my father, tired from doing more than his share of the work while Granny had entertained the Glenisters. At Uncle Victor, his usual good humour tempered by a sense of awkwardness. At your mother, shrinking into her chair, her hand darting out repeatedly for her glass of wine. At your father, lofty, holding court from the carver at the head of the table that had been Grandad's until he came, and some excuse about his extra-long legs not being quite comfortable in any other chair. And meanwhile the rest of them—the other children, Aunts Isobel and Hester, Uncle Eric and Grandad himself resolutely carrying the conversation forward, glossing over the unease that hovered like a pall in the room. I'd look down at my plate of stew or pie and find I could not swallow a mouthful for the lump of dismay in my throat.

Once your father left your mother she got even worse, barely able to cope. I'm sorry if that sounds harsh, but it's true. She became an awkward addendum to my family because they felt sorry for her and were too well-mannered to explain that, really, she had to stand on her own two feet. How different our story would have been if they had been cold and unaccommodating, just that once! By then Mr and Mrs Bracewell had died. Uncle Victor was her only living relative, apart from you. Who else did she have? the family asked itself, trying to excuse the fact that she had arrived for some family gathering or other empty handed and dishevelled, sometimes unable to pay for the taxi that had brought her. Frequently she drank too much wine and ended up snivelling into a borrowed handkerchief. She was needy … and we both know what the outcome was.

Speaking like this is mortifying. Why did I blame you for your parents' failures? Looking back, and seeing myself as you must have seen me … I can hardly bear it. I was a horrible child. But the uncomfortable truth is that I did my best to make life very unpleasant for you, Arthur, in those early years. I was sulky and uncooperative. I wouldn't play with you—in fact, I used to hide from you, and watch in a nasty kind of glee as you wandered the gardens calling my name. I never cried, but you wept an ocean of tears as you trailed around the place looking for me, calling for your mother, running from the disapproval of your father, feeling—as you must have done—lost and confused and afraid. But I was unmoved. In the few years that you attended the village school I abandoned you to merciless teasing in the playground—ginger, carrot-top, freckle-face—and although we were supposed to walk home together, I ran ahead and left you to find the way alone.

In truth, life wasn't very pleasant for me either. My antipathy towards you and your family ate me up. I was angry, Arthur. Angry and jealous. I raged and sulked but when, in sheer frustration, my parents smacked me, I blamed you, and my resentment against you only increased.

Just one thing saved me; I learned to read, and reading opened up to me a new world that I could escape into, a world of adventure and mystery, of magic and wonder. In books I could be other people: princesses, pirates, explorers and heroes. I walked in their shoes, stepping away from my sulks and tantrums, my frustrations and disappointments just as Mary, Colin and Dickon escaped into the secret garden. I didn't have 'imaginary friends' but the characters in the books I read were the next best thing—vividly real in my make-believe games. I conjured their voices, fancied I saw a flash of movement between the trees, felt them on the periphery, and so it didn't surprise me as much as perhaps it should have done when I caught glimpses also of other individuals—the back of what looked like an old man shambling away through the trees of the plantation, for instance; a girl with long, white-blonde hair sitting alone on the rocks by the sea. They didn't hail from any book that I could recall reading or having had read to me, but they didn't trouble me. I simply included them into the troupe of players that peopled my daydreams. Once or twice, I mentioned them to my parents, but they dismissed my claims as fancies, product of an over-active imagination.

Oh! Listen to that. A blackbird, the first to stir. It's dawn, and my time is up. I wonder what good all this exhumation of memory can do? Are we just picking scabs off old injuries that should be allowed to heal over and disappear? Is there still time for us to understand each other at last? Or is it just too late?

Chapter Four

I've brought you some wood anemones Arthur. They're still wet—it's been raining all day. They don't smell of much … of the damp earth and of the woods, and of me, I suppose. They're a bit squashed. But I thought you'd like them. I could have brought bluebells, they're nearly out. But there are trillions of those whereas these … I had to search for quite a while before I found them.

I've been thinking more about the sixties. Six decades ago, and yet still as fresh in my memory as … well, as these anemones. I went into town a few days ago. Just quickly, early, before anyone much was about. But I needn't have worried. I didn't see a single familiar face. And the place is almost unrecognisable, but then, so am I.

The high street is full of charity shops and estate agents and hairdressers these days. I had to walk the full length of the street to find a shop that sells *real* things like string and candles and paraffin. Do you remember that in our day the high streets of most towns were populated by specialist stores: the ironmonger and the bakery; the butcher and the cobbler; the chemist, the fishmonger, the barber and the bank? They're all gone now. Ordinary housewives—not *your* mother, I'm sure, but mine and women like her— trudged up and down the street stopping off at each shop and then often walked home or caught the bus with bags that were bulging. Women rarely drove, although Granny did—an Austin 1100, pea green—because she'd been an ambulance driver in the First World War. Aunt Hester drove too—a red Triumph Herald—but that wasn't normal for the times. Women shopped three or four times a week. They simply couldn't carry enough food to last longer than a couple of days, and in any case many of them had only a larder and a small refrigerator to keep food fresh. It was hard work, no doubt, but also quite sociable. They met their neighbours and gossiped in the shops while they waited their turn to be served, and they found out if people were in need and then discreetly did what they could to help. No need for charity shops and food banks *then*. A tragedy, isn't it? But I mustn't get sidetracked. Supermarkets, with their enormous buying power, didn't reach us in our remote corner of the country until the seventies; until then local shopkeepers served their communities, relying on local suppliers. It was rare for the meat in the butchers to have travelled more than ten miles. Bread was baked right there behind the baker's shop. Our fish was landed just down the coast, fresh every day. Nowadays, it's the model people are trying to get back to, I hear. Food is counted in miles … imagine that! But in those days it was the way we always did things. Salad Days—my grandparents' business—was the market garden that supplied fruit and vegetables to local greengrocers' shops. Uncle Eric drove the van around the lanes and byways of the county dropping off crates of tomatoes, sacks of onions, punnets of strawberries—whatever was in season. That's another thing people hark on about these days—seasonal food—but back then, all our food was seasonal unless we pickled or preserved it, as Aunt Isobel and Uncle Victor did. Granny didn't have a deep freeze until the mid-seventies.

So that's how the business was run in the early days of my remembering. Granny and Grandad and my father worked the land. My mother did the accounts and telephoned around the customers every few days to take their orders. Uncle Eric loaded the van and did the rounds. Aunt Isobel and Uncle Victor ran the village shop where they sold all our surplus produce as well as the cheese and other dairy commodities Uncle Victor still produced in a specially adapted kitchen behind the shop, where they also pickled and preserved fruit and vegetables they could not sell. They marketed their jams and chutneys to local tea shops, pubs and guest houses as well as in the shop under the "Salad Days" label.

In the early days, Aunt Hester played less of a role in the business than anyone else, but she had Katherine and Karen to look after, and twins can be a handful. Once they began school she seemed to want to make up for any deficit and took herself off to college to learn about horticulture. Grandad grumbled about it. He said he could have taught her everything she would need to know. After all, he had taught all the others. My father, for example, had initially trained as a lawyer before he discovered that working and living away from the land did not suit him. He had no formal training in cultivation at all and yet it was understood that in time he would take over the business. But that was Aunt Hester for you. She was what we call "an in-comer," not local to the area. She liked to do things differently and—as she thought— better, and although having someone who could see what today would be called "the bigger picture" was sometimes helpful, more often her continual drive to experiment and expand caused tension. Granny and Grandad quite saw the need to adapt the business as times moved on, but they had no desire to be trailblazers.

Not to imply that they could not spot business opportunities. We had a Christmas tree plantation that did very well; Grandad had begun that in the early fifties, clearing some acres of scrub beyond the market garden area. In those days, artificial Christmas trees were a rarity, and I can remember years when there was a queue of cars throughout December as people came to choose and collect their tree. In summer we made up tubs, planters and hanging baskets with annuals that Grandad grew just for fun. Granny kept bees and sold any honey she did not need herself as well as beeswax for furniture polish.

That honey saved you, Arthur. I don't know if you'll even remember, but in the early years you were plagued by hay fever. Spring came and your eyes went red and began to water. Your nose was a spigot of mucus. Your fair skin was so susceptible to the sun and in those days sunscreen was unheard of. People had no notion of the damage the sun could do. Oh! You were miserable in the summer months, just when life at Granny's was at its most wonderful. I took a cruel pleasure in it, of course. But Granny religiously fed you her own honey, on bread and in your porridge, stirred into drinks, and gradually you built up an immunity so that by the time you were seven or eight hay fever hardly troubled you at all.

Granny and Grandad lived on what they always referred to as "the property," the thirty-acre tract comprising the house and its grounds, the market garden—with its poly tunnels and glasshouses, its fruit cages and orchard and long rows of raised beds. Behind this was the Christmas tree plantation and beyond that, on the more exposed promontory where the soil was thin, the wildflower meadow where Granny kept the hives. The house was called Broadacres but was known locally as the Day place. It had been built in the early 1930s in what is now called the Arts and Crafts style—a large house, probably quite impressive when it was built, but comfortably shabby by the sixties. It had twisting stairways and deep window ledges, cosy alcoves with bookcases and an enormous grandfather clock from which I liked to believe Borrowers would emerge at night to navigate the threadbare old carpets and carry away cotton reels, paperclips, matchsticks and crumbs.

Beyond the house the land dipped towards the sea. There was a belt of mixed woodland where the bluebells grew and then the cove, with a jagged cliff of rock to the north and a jumble of fallen boulders to the south. I didn't know if we actually owned the woodland but no one else went there. The paths through it were all made by us, anyway, as far as I knew at the time. To me, it was magical, mystical, a place of adventure where anything could happen. I adored the way the trees leaned together to whisper secrets, the bright runnels of water all a-chatter with excitement as they leapt and burbled towards the sea, the way the forest floor erupted with primroses, wild garlic, and bluebells. The woods agitated an imaginative gland in me and I peopled them with dryads and fauns, elves and ents, informed by my voracious consumption of fiction. Really, the whole property was a paradise for children. Even the work we children were expected to do in the market garden didn't feel like work. Granny made it fun, with games and competitions, singing and stories. There were no strangers, no dangers apart from the obvious hazards posed by sharp tools, the cliff, the rocks, the gloopy and unreliable sands of the beach when the tide was very low, and the swampy pond in the hollow whose depth none could guess at.

Do you remember the little cottage on the edge of the property where my family lived? Now I think about it, I don't recall that you ever set foot inside it. I didn't realise for years that my parents did not actually own the cottage. It was let to them for a peppercorn rent in return for all the repairs and maintenance—which were many, it being a cottage dating back to the eighteenth century, somewhat damp and dark and very draughty in the winter. I have happy but rather vague memories of it and if I'm being truthful Granny's house felt more like "home" to me.

The shop in the village, and the living quarters above where Aunt Isobel and Uncle Victor lived, were also leased—not owned—which was to cause trouble in time. Victor didn't mind the place, but I know Isobel felt the lack of a garden for the children, Erin and Jack. She complained about a lack of privacy as well. Apparently, people felt no compunction about knocking on the shop door even when the shop was closed, demanding some commodity they had run out of. Like us, the Bracewells spent more time at Granny's than they did at their own place.

Aunt Hester and Uncle Eric were the only ones apart from Granny and Grandad who owned their own home. They lived on the outskirts of the local market town in a modern semidetached house that Hester had bought with an inheritance from her parents. My mother envied its smooth plaster and its modern central heating, its fitted kitchen and tiled bathroom. Isobel went into raptures over the square of functional lawn where Hester could dry her washing and where the girls could play in safety. I think I only went there a couple of times. It was only a ten-minute drive but, apart from visits to the dentist or if I went to help my mother with the shopping, I rarely went to town until I started at secondary school. To my pre-teen self—as to my aged one— town felt strange and foreign.

Like the others, Hester and Eric spent the majority of their time at Broadacres. I think that, in the sixties, drink-driving wasn't an issue. I don't know which of them drove home from Granny's house most evenings, but I am sure that neither of them can have been quite sober. Grandad had a liberal hand with the gin-and-tonics and Uncle Victor made wine of varying palatability but of consistent potency. He made cider and beer as well, and all these were a regular feature of evenings at Granny's house. It was their way of relaxing after a hard day at work. After the Glenisters' advent, alcohol became not just nice but a necessity. Your father was so stiff and pompous, there had to be *some* way to unbend him. But in all the years I knew him I never once saw him drunk. Your mother was different, but perhaps we don't need to go into that.

What I remember most vividly about Granny's house was the fun we had there, all of us together, especially in summer. Oh! The games of sardines! Do you remember that time we all crouched in the big closet in the hallway, stifling our laughter, trying to accommodate ourselves amongst the coats and boots, and it was ages before we realised that we were *all* in there and that nobody was looking for us? Hide and seek in the garden was brilliant, wasn't it? I loved that the grownups all joined in—even your father would, sometimes.

My whole family—and yours—were drawn to Granny's house like bees to the hive. Grandad, Granny and my parents trooped wearily back from the market garden at day's end. Eric finished his delivery rounds in the van, washed and changed at home and then brought Hester along. Aunt Isobel and Uncle Victor closed the little village shop and sauntered the half mile up the lane. The kids materialised from shady sun-loungers, trees, the meadow or their chores. The Glenisters, inevitably, would be present.

It might be my rose-tinted memory of those halcyon days but looking back on them now it seems to me that all the family gatherings were like parties. Grandad would emerge from the bath pink and refreshed and come out onto the terrace smelling of Old Spice, carrying the ice bucket and a clutch of highball glasses on a tray. Granny and the other women put the final additions to an enormous spread of delicious things while the men pretended to be useful by rearranging the chairs around the outdoor table on the terrace or choosing records for the stereogram. From a subdued but comfortable exchange of news—sales in the shop, new customers, a worrying aphid infestation in one of the glasshouses—the conversation would gradually energise as Grandad's generous gin-and-tonics did their work. The heat of the day relaxed and so did the adults as they swigged their cocktails. Music laced the rose-scented air from the records on the turntable and people were in festive mood even when there was nothing particular to celebrate. We kids listened to the adults as they laughed and chattered and, later in the evening, warbled out songs like "Barefoot Days" and "Swing on a Star" to the accompaniment of Uncle Eric's guitar. There was something *magical* about it, wasn't there? Even my hostility towards your family did not spoil it for me entirely. The power of the Day family connection—our unity, our affection, our traditions and our genetic bond—was so strong. I felt that nothing could ever break it.

How wrong I was!

I went back there yesterday—to Granny's house, I mean. It was dusk and rain was coming, turning the blue of evening to dark, menacing grey. I stood beneath that horse chestnut tree on the corner—weren't the conkers from that tree just the best! No one could have seen me—these days, I tend to blend into the landscape—but I crouched in the shadow beneath the spreading branches and tried to meld myself with the pool of gloom. There are new security gates across the drive now, and all Granny's lovely herbaceous borders at the front have been ripped up and replaced by block-paving to accommodate the ... oh, I don't know ... there must have been four or five cars. In Granny's day there would have been lights blazing from every window but now they are all shuttered and no glimmer of light shines forth. It had always seemed so *alive* with adult banter and children's laughter and the sounds of saucepans and stirring and ice plinking into glasses, with the lugubrious tones of Roy Orbison and Elvis and Jerry and the Pacemakers, with the buzz of chat and friendly repartee. The other day it looked ... not deserted, but shrouded. Honest to God, Arthur, I was so deluged with grief that it was as though all that death was a thing of only yesterday, and the anguish of it almost killed me.

Chapter Five

And now I've got to a part of our story that is difficult to tell, but I'm *going* to tell it, Arthur, because it was the beginning—and the end—of so much.

The summer of 1966 was poor. It rained more or less constantly from the moment we broke up from school, throughout the remainder of July and for the first two weeks of August. The air was notably cool, and I remember having to wear cardigans and waterproofs over my shorts and tee shirts, something I had never had to do in summertime before. Grandad despaired of the crops, which turned rotten in the waterlogged ground. Onions in particular proved tricky to ripen, and he had to lift the entirety of the potato crop for fear it would all spoil. Blight afflicted the tomatoes in the glasshouses and much of the fruit went to waste.

The work in the market garden—usually made to be enjoyable for the children, with games and competitions, prizes and forfeits and lots of merry chatter, singing and silly rhymes amongst the raised beds—was instead a miserable slog, in sucking mud that caked our wellingtons, with rain dripping down our collars and plastering our hair to our heads. My oldest sister Verity, then fourteen and increasingly conscious of her appearance, sulked and complained that the work was ruining her nails. She shrank from getting mud in her hair or on her face. Granny, impatient with Verity's wincing and mincing, often sent her indoors to warm up soup or make sandwiches. Grace, my middle sister, had just turned twelve. Ironically—given her name—she was a clumsy girl, always slipping over and crushing the delicate salad crops, pulling over the pea and bean wigwams, hoeing up seedlings along with the weeds. Quite often she was sent to help our mother in the office where I suppose she could do less damage. Neither was Erin any help and, looking back, I wonder if it riled Granny and Grandad that just when they needed the extra help the older girls could have provided, for one reason or another it wasn't available.

That summer was when I began to understand that something was seriously wrong with Erin. She was painfully thin and preternaturally pale. Her hair, which had been a lovely, fine but lustrous shade of honey-gold, had become dull and thin. She lacked energy, sometimes languishing for hours on the sofa. She rarely helped in the market garden, even in the glasshouses or poly tunnels where at least it was dry and the temperature less chill. Instead, she stayed in the apartment above the shop. Goodness knows how she occupied her time. There wasn't any television during the day, she wasn't interested in sewing or drawing and Erin was never a reader. Some evenings she would be driven from the village to join us for family dinner, but there were occasions when even that was thought to be too much for her and either Uncle Victor or Aunt Isobel would remain behind with her.

How we could have done with a little help, but we knew that it was no good asking your parents. There was something about Henry—something too posh, too precious—to imagine him rolling up his sleeves and skidding about with the rest of us in the mud. Your mother, Blanche, as a farmer's daughter, should have been habituated to it, but she took her cue from Henry and never offered. I suppose it would have wounded your father's pride to labour alongside the likes of Mick and Bradley, however honest and respectable they were. Grandad tentatively introduced your father to the lawn mower as one might affect an introduction between two chaps at a golf club. He explained its settings and functions in a mild, deferential manner, I suppose thinking mowing to be an aristocratic, refined activity that would suit Henry's hauteur. But to no avail. If he recognised the hint, Henry failed to take it, simply nodding in a distant and noncommittal way, as though being given a tour of a shoe factory, something that was objectively quite interesting but could be of no future usefulness. Granny offered to remind your mother how to make bread, cakes and pastry—tasks that she had surely been well acquainted with in the past—but found her to be woefully cackhanded. Likewise mending, laundry … there didn't seem to be a niche where Blanche could be comfortably shoehorned into the daily routine of the family. The Glenisters simply hung around, idling in some kind of neutral gear that was completely foreign to the Days, who were *always* busy, driven, active, with a task in hand and an end in view. Your parents seemed perfectly content to observe, to be on the periphery, feeling no discomfort in looking on while everyone else was industrious, and no sense of guilt when Granny would abandon her weeding or hoeing or harvesting to offer hospitality, which she invariably would.

So it was in the summer of 1966, the Glenisters turned up, as was their wont, your mother tiptoeing gingerly along the paths between the raised beds holding an umbrella aloft to protect her freshly set hair. She would make sympathetic but wholly ineffectual mewing noises at the mud, the ragged crops, our red-raw hands and soil-spattered clothing but offered nothing in the way of aid, not even so much as to make everyone a mug of tea. Your father stood like a heron, grey and implacable, the collar of his expensive coat turned up against the rain, his beady eye observing the rest of us as we slipped about in the quag until eventually he retreated to the house. *You,* though—I must admit—were willing enough to join in with the chores. As little as you were, you managed to make some contribution to the work in hand however useless your parents might be.

By that time I had ceased to question their appearance almost every day and you were a cross I was learning to bear. My scalding resentment of you had cooled to a viscous pool of chilly antagonism. I suppose that I had become habituated to you, your almost-daily appearance working in the same way as Granny's honey for your hay fever, although nowhere near as sweet and palatable. I would glance up at you from wherever I was busy with my allotted task for the morning: collecting tomatoes, cleaning out the hens, weeding the vegetable beds. I would see the light in your eye which I now recognise as the desire to join in, to be absorbed, to be one of us instead of the "other" that the Glenisters characteristically were, but I would ignore it. If Granny did not give you a job to do you would sidle nearer and nearer to me, and eventually pick up a trowel or begin loading tomatoes into my tray, insinuating yourself into the activity, and as your contribution meant I would win the weigh-in at the end of the morning, I wasn't about to object.

After lunch, one of the adults would be deputed to entertain the children whilst the rest of the grownups continued the wet and unpleasant work on the property. We might cycle along the disused railway line if it looked as though the rain might lessen, or set up a beetle-drive or a game of snakes-and-ladders indoors if not. Sometimes we were taken to the picture house or the local swimming pool but all of these were sad and sorry substitutions for the adventures we had around the garden and the wider acres during summers that were warm and dry.

That summer—the summer of 1966—our family dinners, which were usually such fun with the whole family gathered round the big table on Granny's terrace surrounded by lots of delicious food and the adults made mellow by Grandad's generous gin-and-tonics—were much more sombre affairs. The outdoor table was abandoned in favour of the dining room, a spacious room made cosy in winter by a blazing fire, but in those dreary summer months felt damp and fetid. The grownups wore worried expressions as they held anxious conferences about how they might protect the crops—and the business—from the worst of the weather. We children drifted away from the subdued atmosphere to amuse ourselves. I recall that Kath and Karen built a magnificent Bedouin tent in the attic with quilts they found in a trunk. You and Jack were allowed to join in the game, but I turned my nose up at it. My sisters were too engrossed in *Jackie* and mooning over the Beatles to play a board game, so I tended to settle myself into the alcove under the stairs to read instead. That year I read my way through the whole *Narnia* series. Subliminally—behind the gruffly tones of Mr Beaver and the whingeing of Cousin Eustace—I was conscious of the men, still in the dining room, discussing the possibility of installing additional poly tunnels in order to protect the crops from excess rain, or of introducing more rain-tolerant crops—celery, asparagus—in future years. In the kitchen the women had similar discussions as they washed and dried the dishes. Naturally, your parents played no part in these exchanges and I wondered *again* how they could justify their continued and continual presence in our midst.

We never went away for holidays in the summer. It was the busiest time for the business and no one could be spared. I never felt the lack of the week or two at the seaside that my school friends boasted of. In normal years spending the summer at Granny's was, to me, as good as any holiday and the highlight of it was always the picnic in the cove. We could go to the cove at almost any time in any season. It was a fifteen-minute walk through the woods and so long as we stayed together we children were allowed to go there whenever we liked. The adults rarely accompanied us. But the summer picnic was different. No one worked that day. The shop in the village was left to the care of trusted part-timers. Even Grandad was prised away from the raised beds and glasshouses to take a day's holiday. The whole family spent the entire day and into the evening at the cove. Granny and the other women packed up enough food to feed an army and my father supervised the logistics of transporting toys, games and equipment in barrows and little carts. There was usually a bonfire in the evening and Uncle Eric would play his guitar for a sing-song. We would come home salty from the sea, with sand in our shoes and hair, our skin sun-reddened and tight, weary but happy. The adults were often more than a little inebriated and in thoroughly good humour. In previous years even your father had unbuttoned himself sufficiently to remove his shoes and socks and paddle in the surf.

But that year was different. Week after week went by and our annual summer picnic was postponed, pending an improvement in the weather. At last, towards the end of August, a day dawned that was blue and cloudless, and we threw ourselves into preparations for the day. Grandad went off to do the only work that was permitted on the property that day: watering in the glasshouses and feeding the hens. My father brought out his 'picnic logistic' list with a flourish and sent the children scurrying here and there gathering all the paraphernalia for our traditional beach activities: the cricket bat and stumps, fishing nets, buckets, crab lines and kites. Granny and the other women made stacks of sandwiches, Granny buttering the top of the loaf and then sawing off thin slices with the bread knife as she held it against her bosom. How she did so without slicing her breast was a mystery to me, but it was a skill I longed to learn. My mother filled the sandwiches with cheese, tomato, ham and egg and Grace wrapped the parcels in greaseproof paper, surreptitiously "testing" every fourth or fifth batch as we went. Aunt Hester filled bottles with orange squash and made flasks of tea, cut squares of flapjack and packed up sausage rolls. Aunt Isobel assembled a first-aid kit with cream for nettle stings, sticking plasters, iodine, cotton wool and lint. Uncle Eric was sent off to the bakery for pork pie. Uncle Victor found towels, rugs and blankets, a rickety old folding gazebo, several windbreaks, deckchairs and a rusting brazier. Grandad and my father brought two four-wheeled wagons out of one of the sheds and began to load them with the equipment now piled on the terrace as well as with a crate of Uncle Victor's homebrew and Uncle Eric's guitar.

Verity arrived from home with a bag bulging with suntan oil and magazines, a voluminous towelling cover-all and a pair of outsized sunglasses that I had never seen before. She wore a flowing kaftan type of garment, strappy sandals utterly unsuitable for the walk through the woods and down to the cove and makeup applied inexpertly—heavy black eyeliner, mascara, caked powder, pink lipstick. My mother gave her an appraising look but was sidetracked in whatever critical remark she was preparing when she saw Grace sneaking yet another sandwich.

'Oh no you don't,' she said, slapping Grace's hand away, and when she turned back Verity had disappeared.

You Glenisters arrived on cue, your father in a beige safari suit, your mother in a halter neck dress and large sunglasses very like the ones Verity wore. How on earth had they known, I wondered? But then, I was seven-years-old. Lots of things happened whose provenance and accomplishment were mysteries to me. They just *were*.

You already wore your blow-up arm bands, ready for the sea. They were so fully inflated your arms stuck out awkwardly from your body but then your whole self was stiff with excitement, clumsy and bumping into things and getting in the way. I could see a little damp patch on your shorts where you had leaked. I looked at it pointedly. Your mother, following my gaze, said, 'Oh *do* go to the lavatory, Arthur. I haven't brought you any spare shorts.'

Isobel said, 'I've got spares, for Jack, if you need to borrow some.'

'But you've brought trunks?' I enquired, speciously concerned. 'I mean …' I nodded at the arm bands, 'if you're going swimming …'

You turned agonised eyes up at your mother. 'Have you?' you mouthed.

She began to rummage in a rattan bag she carried over her arm. 'I'm not sure,' she said in a sort of whimper.

'We aren't going back,' Henry Glenister declared. 'If he's forgotten them, he'll have to do without.'

'He can't go in the sea … naked,' Blanche squeaked.

'We often do … *did*,' Grace put in, popping another square of sandwich in her mouth, 'when we were little.'

'What will it matter?' my mother said. 'Who's to *see*? Oh Grace, *really!* There'll be no sandwiches left if you carry on eating them.'

Henry stiffened. 'It's out of the question,' he said.

Your eyes were swimming with tears. You edged round the table until you were pressed up against Granny's side. If you'd had the freedom of movement of your arms, you would have put them around her body. She sawed on mechanically, dispensing slices of buttered bread like a machine, but I saw her move fractionally in response to your pressure.

Aunt Isobel sighed. 'I expect I can find an old pair of Jack's.'

Your mother still rummaged in her bag. At last she held up your trunks. 'Here they are!' she whinnied, her own eyes wet with tears of relief.

Your father barked, 'Arthur! Didn't your mother tell you to visit the lavatory?' and you went scurrying down the passageway. I'd learned to swim the year before so I managed to sneer some derogatory remark about your armbands as you passed. I wondered how you'd manage with the zip of your flies, with your arms akimbo, and enjoyed the mental image of your struggle for a few moments before hurrying outside to see how preparations were progressing.

Apart from his cine camera the Glenisters brought nothing with them—nothing useful, anyway. No contribution to the food or drink, no toys, not even towels. Aunt Hester had to go upstairs and find three old ones from the back of Granny's airing cupboard. Aside from your trunks, Blanche's bag turned out to contain only a cardigan for herself, a novel, a makeup bag and a hairbrush. It was my Aunt Isobel who found you an old sunhat of Jack's to shade your face from the sun and a cast-off jumper for later, in case the evening was cool. My mother rummaged an extra bucket and spade from somewhere and stowed it into the barrow. As soon as your parents had wandered away Granny deflated your armbands and removed them.

'I promise you can have them back when we get to the beach,' she said, 'but they're sure to puncture in the woods, and that won't do, will it?'

At last we were ready, assembled on the terrace in an excited medley of children and adults, bags and boxes, the two carts and a wheelbarrow loaded with supernumerary equipment brought out at the last moment: tennis racquets; a football; an *I-Spy At The Seaside* book; a bowsaw; Granny's beekeeping hat. Granny's Jack Russell dog—Podge, was it? Or Piglet? No. Piglet came later—strained at her leash and barked hysterically. You were allowed to hold her lead. I smirked because I knew that she would probably pull you over before we were out of the garden.

Erin looked whiter than usual, weak, wrapped up in twill trousers and a thick Aran cardigan even though the day was already warm. She stayed close to her father, Uncle Victor, and before we had walked even halfway across the lawn he had hoisted her up, piggy-back style.

The way to the cove took us through a wicket gate at the rear of the market garden and along a path that skirted the Christmas tree plantation. Some stands had been labelled with the name of one of the children, signifying it had been planted in the year of our birth. My trees, planted in 1959, were now much taller than I was. It would be another three or four years before their time to shine would come. I noted sourly that you had been allocated a stand two years behind mine. Your mother pointed it out as we passed.

'Oh, that's *nice,*' she said, turning to address your father. 'Isn't it, Henry? A lovely gesture.'

Henry Glenister was almost at the rear of our procession. Only Verity was behind him, encumbered by her awkward bundle and her ridiculous shoes.

'Oh,' he said, swivelling his head to look. 'Yes. Very nice.'

You were at the very front, dragged along by Podge, tripping and stumbling over the rough terrain. She pulled you past the gate that was set into the stone wall, which was the way into the woodland. From being white with suppressed excitement you were now flushed, your hair tacky and sticking to your forehead. It was all you could do to haul her back to where we all gathered at the gate. It had a fiendish catch and was impeded by grasses and weeds that had grown up through its lower bars. My father wrestled with it and eventually we all filed through. He pulled one of the carts, Grandad the other. Uncle Eric pushed the barrow. The women carried the picnic baskets and the children gathered up the things that fell off the little vehicles: the odd towel, the football, one of the windbreaks.

It had been such a wet and miserable summer that no one had ventured that way for weeks. The path through the mixed woodland was overgrown, hardly visible in places. Grandad went in front, pulling his cart, bending to snip off brambles with his secateurs. A storm earlier in the summer had brought a rotten alder down right across the path, and we had to pause while Grandad and my father moved it to one side. As they did so they pointed out other trees that had toppled or were likely to do so, and Grandad said he would have to come into the woods to make things safe.

The canopy of the trees was thick, casting us in a greenish gloom. It was hard to believe that the sun still shone overhead but for the shafts of bright light that broke through the treetops. Hardly any birds sang in the wood, but insects hung in thick swarms. Grace screamed and swatted crazily as something brushed against her face. My mother said, 'It was a ladybird, Grace. Don't be so silly.'

I fidgeted, leaning one way and then the other to see past the queue of people. I adored the woods, but I was itching to get down to the cove. Kath and Kaz began to weary of their rendition of "A Hundred Green Bottles" having only got as far as sixty-four. Erin was slipping down Uncle Victor's back. He boosted her up and she tightened the grip of her thin little hands around his neck. Podge, yanking at her lead, eventually succeeded in pulling it from your fist. She dashed off into the undergrowth. You gave a wail of dismay and turned distraught eyes to Granny.

Granny sighed and muttered, 'Due on heat,' under her breath, a remark that meant nothing to me, but she didn't chastise you and when, later, I saw the red weal on your hand that clinging on to the lead had caused, I understood why.

'I wondered why you had her on the lead at all,' my mother remarked. 'You don't usually bother.'

'The last thing I need is another litter of puppies,' was Granny's cryptic reply.

At last the obstruction was cleared and we continued to zigzag our way across the forest floor. A stream—turbulent and quite deep after all the rain— crossed the path and required a military operation to get the carts and the barrow across. My father deployed his troops, balancing Jack and the twins on some slippery stones in the brook so that they could pass the wagons across, but in fact I could see that between them, Grandad, Dad and Uncle Eric could manage things pretty well. It was like them though, to include the children, to make us feel that we were important.

'Offer the ladies a hand,' Uncle Victor said, as he crossed with Erin on his back, but Kath, Karen and Jack had already scrambled up the far bank and were hurtling away through the woods. You, solemn with the responsibility of it, and I suppose wishing to make up for having lost Podge, stood solidly on a green-slimed boulder and handed your mother and Grace over the stream. You held your hand out to me but I pushed it aside and made my own way. I was surprised to see that your father, at the back of the platoon again, did take Verity's bag off her, adding it to the bag on his shoulder that held his camera, and helped her across the stream. I think it was the first thing I had ever seen him do for someone else. Verity's face, even in the dimness of the wood, was as red as beetroot.

The path began to descend quite steeply, soil giving way to sand and gravel, then to quite large slabs of rock that formed steps. I could glimpse the blue of the sea through the trees, the sickle of golden sand, the bank of shingle and the steep, deeply scored black rocks at the far side, where I knew the best rock pools were to be found. The tide was coming in. Jack and the twins were already on the sand, throwing off their sandals and racing to the water's edge. My mother was there too, setting up camp in the sandy area at the back of the cove where the overhanging trees gave shade throughout the day and where there were convenient flat rocks so packets of food could be kept free of grit. I had been caught behind the carts. Manoeuvring them down the steep and craggy path was quite tricky, and Uncle Victor had put Erin down so that he could help. She stood near me, her face empty of any expression.

'Are you going to swim?' I asked. Erin was a good swimmer—probably the best of us—and had helped to teach me the year before. Really, I preferred Erin to either of my sisters. I had always been a bit cross that I had been born me, and not Jack. I'd have liked to be a boy and to have Erin as a sister instead of greedy Grace or sly Verity.

She shook her head. 'I don't think so.'

'What will you do then?'

She pondered. 'I might make patterns with shells and stones and things.'

'We did that last year,' I recalled, 'and we balanced stones. I wonder if they'll still be there.'

'I shouldn't think so. The winter storms will have washed them all away.'

'We can make new ones,' I said.

For a thirteen-year-old she had a wisdom that was beyond her years. Later I was to identify this trait as an ability to see things in perspective. She could certainly see two sides of most arguments and, more than once, had settled disputes between the rest of us children. She had a habit of fixing her eyes on some far distant point in the future that only she could see, and I sometimes got the fleeting impression that what she saw there, in the vastness of time, did not always reassure her. She did it then, staring away into the gloom beneath the trees, not looking *at* it but rather in some odd way *through* or *past* it. My understanding then couldn't stretch to it—what or how she might see so far, or why she might look.

I said, 'Can you see Podge?' squinting my eyes in the same direction but making out nothing but trees, shadow, undergrowth and rocks.

Erin said, 'Podge will probably have gone home.'

What I did see, emerging from the dim, was my sister Verity and Henry Glenister. I hadn't known they had fallen so far behind us, but they came up to us now.

At last the wagons were down the rocks and on the beach. Henry pushed past us and strode with ease down the rough steps, half-colliding with Uncle Victor, who was on his way up again to help Erin.

'Come along my princess,' he said, holding out his arms and scooping her up under her knees.

Verity and I had to scramble down after them as best we could.

Chapter Six

We spread out around the cove. Verity stalked off by herself, wobbling and slipping in her sandals, bringing the tiny battery-powered transistor radio she had been given for her birthday a few weeks before from her bag. She had it tuned to Radio Caroline, a pirate station that played pop music the BBC had not yet adopted. The signal was poor, crackly and disjointed, but she extended the aerial as far as it would go and quartered the beach until she found a place where there was a ghost of reception. It was a little enclave towards the southern side of the cove, close to the dangerous jumble of huge rocks that was piled up against the slope of forest. It was half surrounded by other, smaller, smoother rocks that formed a sort of buttress between her and the rest of the cove, but sandy within, sheltered and, I should think, very pleasant. She placed the radio down on a rock and set up her own little camp, laying down her towel and arranging the other things she had brought with her. She slipped off her kaftan—self-consciously, glancing around as she did so. She already wore her swimsuit, a two-piece bikini, very brief, but revealing the swell of her nascent breasts and the slight curve of her widening hips. Unfortunately, it also showed the livid rash of acne across her shoulders. She began to lard herself with suntan oil. When she was done—glistening like a sardine fresh from the tin—she pulled her hair into a ponytail, affixed her sunglasses and lay down in the sun to fry.

I saw all of this from the top of the rocks, where I scrambled immediately on grabbing my fishing net and a bucket from one of the wagons. The rocks were sharp in places and I was glad I'd worn my jelly shoes rather than sandals. I scraped a knee as I climbed, but you know me, I didn't make a fuss. I felt triumphant to be the first to make the ascent, but the conquest was oddly hollow, as no one else had made the bee-line I expected. Jack, Kath and Kaz thrashed about in the surf, not quite ready to take the final plunge. For a moment I wondered if I'd made the wrong choice—if *that* wouldn't have been more fun, if I shouldn't have saved the rock pools until later—but then I saw my father striding across the beach towards the outcrop and I was glad that I would have him to myself, even if just for half an hour. He climbed up easily and we made our way out onto the spur that juts into the sea and forms the northernmost arm of the cove. Even so far out there was hardly a breeze, and the waters around the point were smooth and glassy with barely a spume of foam. He helped me poke about between the rocks and stir the waters to see what we could find. The rock pools were disappointing, to tell the truth—they are better at a retreating tide than an encroaching one—but we still found several crabs and shrimps, sea anemones and a starfish. I shouted each find across the cove, dangling the crabs from ginger fingers before dropping them into my bucket, and my mother made congratulatory cooing noises and waved enthusiastically at each one.

Dad took his shoes and socks off and rolled up his trousers and we both sat on a ledge and put our feet into one of the pools. It was nice, the water surprisingly warm, the soft brush of the various plants feathery against our legs, having dad pressed beside me, his arm around my shoulders and the sun on our faces, all tempered by the little thrill of dread that some creature might come out and nibble at our toes. He brought two apples out of his pocket, and we sat and munched in perfect contentment.

It was from here that we looked down and watched Verity below, and the women as they sorted and organised the food, placing the bottles of beer and squash in the little rill that tumbled down the rocks while Grandad and Uncle Victor erected the chairs and deployed the windbreaks. There was scarcely a breath of wind but that was not the purpose of the windbreaks. Grandad brought out the mallet and began to hammer the poles to make a U-shaped enclosure to provide the grownups some privacy for undressing. Aunt Isobel had settled Erin in one of the chairs and swathed her in a blanket although the day was increasingly warm and humid. Uncle Eric emerged from the woods with an armful of branches and deadwood, ready for the brazier, later. Aunt Hester stood in the shallows watching Jack and the twins, who were fully submerged now, gasping and swimming doggy-style. After a while she stepped out of her sundress to reveal that she already wore her swimming costume. She walked without flinching into the waves and launched herself into a smooth and competent breaststroke, out into the bay.

Your mother had perched at first on a convenient boulder, absorbed and seemingly caught up in the scene while the rest of the adults got on with the organisation of the equipment or supervising the children. But once the deckchairs were ready, she selected one and sank down into it, sweeping her hair back from her face and using her sunglasses as a hairband before reaching into her bag for her Harold Robbins paperback. Your father had walked to the other side of the cove, closer to where Verity lay, and unpacked his camera equipment with the fussy diligence habitual with him, wiping the lens, checking the settings, consulting his light meter. Now he had the thing to his eye and was sweeping the bay in what I supposed would be a panoramic shot that would encompass the whole scene: the cove, the bay, the backdrop of woods, the dark bluff where Dad and I were sitting and the rest of the Day family.

All the while, Arthur, you hopped and fidgeted, now up by the camp as the wagons were unloaded, now down on the shoreline where the surf encroached further and further inland with every wave, but not quite daring to step into the water. Your armbands were back in place and your shorts replaced by trunks although I hadn't seen you change. I supposed Granny had helped you, true to her promise, as she always was. Aunt Hester was far out by then, and the other children out of their depths and beyond your joining. Only Grace, picking through the shingle above the tideline, took any notice of you. I think you must have asked her a question—was she going to swim? You held out your hand: an invitation? A request? She shook her head and continued her search for pebbles. Your shoulders slumped.

My father said, 'Poor little tyke,' and levered himself from our perch, gathering his socks and shoes in an easy sweep. 'You'll be alright up here, Prue, won't you?' he asked me. 'Or, are you ready to come down?' He held his hand out to me, but I knew what his intention was, and I shook my head quickly and would not meet his eye. He said, 'Alright then. See you in a little while.' Then he was gone, back along the spur and down the cliff in a few easy leaps— bare feet notwithstanding—and walking across the beach to where you dithered.

I pulled my feet from the water. Somehow it was not so much fun without Dad, and my courage against the squirmy, squiggly or biting things had shrivelled. I tucked my feet up against my thighs and hugged my knees, continuing to look down on you all from my high eyrie, keeping very still and nursing my resentment at you—at all of them really—feeling forgotten and sorry for myself. Beside me, my crabs climbed frantically over each other in the bucket and the starfish began to inch its way up the side in a bid for freedom.

I saw Granny open the first flask and begin to pour tea for the grownups into the enamel cups she kept for outdoor use. My father, up to his rolled-up trouser legs in the surf by now, holding both your hands in his as you leapt delightedly over the waves, shook his head at the offer. Your mother accepted a cup with barely a murmur, engrossed in *The Carpetbaggers*. Aunt Isobel handed her cup to Erin. My mother took a cup to your father, picking her way with difficulty across the shingle, being careful not to spill. He remained fixed, his back pressed against a slab of rock, his cine camera to his eye. She held out the cup to him and I distinctly heard him say, 'Oh, tea? No thank you, Lucille. Coffee perhaps, if you have any.' I knew that she'd be fuming at his rudeness and wondered if she would fling the tea at him in spite. I know I would have done. But she marched back to the camp in high dudgeon and drank the tea herself. Grandad and my uncles had already broached the first bottle of beer.

I sat and felt very sorry for myself for about half an hour, wallowing and morose. My jealous resentment was sharp and cutting—a whetted knife. I can feel it still, dividing memory.

In one version of that day, I sniffed back my sulks and climbed back down to the beach. By then Granny and my mother had emerged from behind the windbreaks wearing their ancient costumes and made their way to the water. I joined them, leaving my clothes in a tangle and struggling into my bathing suit while they were still shrieking and splashing their arms and legs with water. I was in the water before either of them, reminding myself of the frog-like motions that Erin had taught me, spitting out the salty water and laughing at the chill and the thrill. Aunt Hester returned from her long swim and the other swimmers—blue now, with chattering teeth, yet unwilling to leave the sea—thrashed their way to join us. Grace changed her mind and crept behind the windbreak to put on her costume. She had grown since the previous summer—in every direction—and when she did eventually emerge her costume was stretched so thin I was sure it would tear. Her flesh bulged from the elastic, white and blubbery. She rushed into the sea and submerged herself immediately, hiding beneath the surface. Granny had you in hand while my dad got changed. She had got you waist-deep in the water. You gasped and held your arms above your head, denying yourself the buoyancy your armbands would have given, but you must somehow have got your hair wet. It stuck up in red spikes, much like the sea anemone I had spied earlier. My uncles and Grandad joined us and for a glorious half hour we were all in the sea, laughing and splashing each other, playing volleyball with the football. Only your parents, Aunt Isobel and Erin remained on the beach although they all made their way to the edge of the water to cheer us on. And Verity. She remained on her towel as though glued in place, the music from her transistor making a shrill, tinny squeal like a wasp trapped beneath a glass.

Then we were out and hurrying for our towels, pulling shorts and tee shirts back over damp, sandy flesh. Granny began to dispense the sandwiches and my mother cut the pork pie. We sat around the camp, perched on rocks or cross-legged on our damp towels, eating the warm, slightly squashed food and slurping orange squash and it all tasted delicious—better than food usually did or ever could, the flavour of it enhanced by the fun and family, the love and loveliness of the day.

But in the other version of that day my sulks got the better of me and I tipped the crabs and starfish out onto the hot, abrasive rocks and watched them squirm and struggle for a while. The arms of the starfish curled and arched in distress as it reached blindly for any kind of shade or moisture. The crabs scuttled this way and that, falling into crevices and getting stuck, and I watched them dispassionately as the sound of your glee rose up, and the salt of the waves that were now only feet from where I sat—the tide rising almost to its zenith—made my eyes water. When I felt the sprinkle of it on my tee shirt and its damp seep into my shorts, I strapped my jelly shoes back in place and walked away before I could see if the ocean would save the dying creatures.

Now with the rock pools filling, it was harder to navigate back along the spur and to the place where I could climb back down the rocks and regain the beach. I had to use my hands as I inched along sharp edges and once slipped and sank into a pool up to my thigh. The graze I'd sustained earlier stung. I righted myself and looked over the cove. No one was paying any attention to me. Everyone was busy, happily occupied. Your father had sunk down onto his haunches and was absorbed in a little booklet I presumed was the instruction manual for his camera. He was close to Verity and it's possible they exchanged a few words. Perhaps he was explaining the technicalities to her. She had propped herself up on her elbow and, like Blanche, had pushed her sunglasses onto her head. She was very pink from the sun, and I was surprised my mother hadn't told her to cover herself as it must have been almost midday by then and the sun was getting fierce.

Aunt Hester had returned from her swim and now encouraged you so far into the water that you were out of your depths. Your face was a smudge— white, but extraordinarily pleased with yourself—as your arms and legs windmilled beneath the water. Kath, Kaz and Jack squatted in the shallows examining something—seaweed, a fossil. Grace and Erin sat close together in the shade. It looked as though they were playing a game of cards. Granny and the other women were—for once—at rest, seated in deck chairs, their eyes closed and their faces tipped up to the sun. The men were busy gathering driftwood for the fire.

Instead of making my way back down the rocks to the beach I turned and looked in the other direction. The cliff leaned slightly backwards away from me at a steep but not perpendicular angle. It was severely fractured with gouges from top to bottom from which little tufts of plants grew. I could see several places that would make excellent hand- and foot-holds and I speculated that the plants would be deeply rooted in the crevices. I had no concept then of distance, but I know now that the height of the thing is no more than ten or fifteen feet. At the top of the shale—so I now believe it to be—the surface turned to stony soil punctured by roots from the trees and shrubs above. These too, I thought, would be easy to grasp and could be trusted to take my weight. If I'm honest, I'm not sure if I really wanted someone below to spot me, to race up and prevent me from embarking on my risky adventure, or if I wanted to gain the top and hail them all from the very summit of the cliff. Either way, I thought that it would teach them to forget about me, which patently they all had done.

I lifted my foot and placed it in the first crevice, reaching up for handholds. I vaguely remembered some detail from a book about climbing, exhorting the mountaineer to maintain three points of contact. I followed this advice, not moving a hand or foot until I had a firm grip for the three others. The plants proved to be poor support, coming away as soon as I grasped them. Little stones came with them, and I looked over my shoulder to see if anyone had noticed me halfway up the cliff. But no one had. The scene was as tranquil as before, the women asleep, the men intent on the construction of a bonfire, the children variously occupied around the cove. You were digging a hole in the sand—a pointless exercise, I told myself, although in the past I had passed many a happy hour in the same activity. I thought the tide must have turned. A rim of rubbery seaweed, glinting in the sun, marked its highest point.

I was alarmed to see how far I had already climbed. The people on the beach were shrunk down versions of themselves, and if I'm to be truthful my heart did skip a beat or two and my eyes began to sting from a sudden ooze of perspiration from my forehead. But more pressing than my fear was a sense of mounting outrage that they really did not care where I was or what I was doing.

I climbed on, my nose about four inches from the cliff face, my arms and legs feeling blindly—as the starfish had earlier—for refuge. My feet were small and it wasn't too difficult to wedge them sideways into the grooves of the rock, but my hands lacked the strength they needed to support me or to haul me that few inches higher. My fingers were sore, abraded by the rough surface, my palms burning. Then, reaching up, I felt the firm, woody loop of a tree root. I tested it. It was strong. I was a good tree-climber and now I felt on more familiar territory. I held onto the root with one hand, then the other, as though it were a branch of one of the orchard trees I had climbed so many times. I scrabbled with my feet, hoisting myself up until my hips were between my hands and also supported by the root. My eyes opened to see the summit was at eye-level: light brown soil topped with short, tufty grass. I threw an arm forward and grabbed the trunk of some bush, scratching my arm in the process on its thorny leaves. I pulled myself over the edge, my stomach half on and half off the grass. My feet windmilled, finding no purchase, then also landing on the tree root. I was up.

I lay for a while panting on the very edge of the cliff, my body pressed into the lumps and bumps of the thin soil and the rib-like roots, my heart thumping fast. The cove below me was a still life, the bright colours of tee shirts and summer dresses, the stripey windbreaks and deck chairs garish splatters against the dun of the shingle, the beige sand, the dimpled surface of the sea. Now was my moment, I thought. I would stand up and shout my triumph, wave my arms, have them all look up at me and be amazed. Of course, they'd also be a little angry. I knew I'd taken quite a risk. But the punishment—if punishment were to be applied—would be worth the scare I'd give them.

But then I thought again. Wouldn't it be better to keep this whole feat to myself? To make my way back through the woods to the cove and saunter out of the trees as though I had been in there to spend a penny, or to explore or—even better—to carry out an armful of kindling for the fire. Punishment would turn to praise then. 'What a helpful girl,' they'd say, and my achievement could be saved for a time when it would give the greatest kudos. I could leave something of mine, or some sign, to prove that I'd made the climb. I could boast of it at a later date. 'Go and see for yourselves,' I'd say. 'There's a prickly bush at the top of the cliff and on its trunk you'll see the letter P carved into it.' And the grownups would still be startled and somewhat ashamed that I'd got up the cliff, down again and back through the woods without them even noticing, so I'd gain that point even if I lost out on the shock and awe of showing myself straightaway.

So I inched away from the edge and found a piece of flint amongst the leaf litter and gouged a shaky "P" into the grey trunk of the holly bush. While I went about my task I waited for some cry of alarm from below, for the urgent calling of my name, but none came; and in fact I heard the guffaws of the men and the glassy tinkle of an empty beer bottle being dropped into the crate.

My dudgeon stoked, I crawled under the bush, putting my back to the cove, and made my way on all fours through thick undergrowth. It was hard going, the ground stony as well as thick with desiccated holly and other prickly leaves, the shrubs just there all bristling with spiteful thorns. I tried to tell myself that I was an explorer, forging a route through virgin territory, but in truth I was hot and cross, scratched, stung and, by now, rather hungry as well as very thirsty. At last the bushes thinned and I came out hard against a rabbit wire fence that turned about twenty yards beyond my position to run along the cliff edge. Within the fence was a meadow I didn't recognise. Beyond the meadow was a high wall over which I could just see the grey roof and steepling chimneys of a large house.

My sense of direction told me that if I could get through the fence and follow it to the right I'd come to a gate or some other way back into the woods. It wouldn't be far from there to the cove. But there were cows with calves in the field, a combination that anyone brought up in the country knows has the potential for danger. Cows are very protective, much more aggressive than bulls when they have calves to guard. They might be placid now, lying in the lush grass and chewing their cud, but if I were to be on the other side of the fence I'd pose a threat they would not tolerate. A safer plan would be to remain on my side of the fence and push myself through the unkempt bushes until I found a path. My desire to rejoin my family—however neglectful they had been—was by this time very strong. I'd had my adventure and I'd made my point. I didn't relish the prospect of more cuts and scratches, but I couldn't see an alternative.

I'd just about decided to pursue this course when two other matters brought themselves to my attention. The first was the distant sound of a dog yelping. I was sure it was Podge, and it occurred to me that if I could restore Granny's dog to her it might mitigate any ill consequences of my derring-do. I couldn't see Podge, but the noise was coming from the bottom of the meadow to the right, where it sloped so steeply down that I couldn't see the fence line. I wondered if she was hurt, or had got her lead caught. Perhaps she had seen me and was appealing for help. I might have to make my way round half of the meadow, which would take longer and could put me in further danger, but I was in it up to my neck and to an extent I decided I may as well be hanged for a sheep as for a lamb.

The other thing that struck me as odd and rather sinister was the sky over the sea, which was boiling with an eruption of enormous purple, grey and brilliant white clouds. They were dense and towering like giants' galleons, darkly ominous underneath and luminous above, roiling and growing with every moment and moving inexorably towards the cliffs. Whereas down in the cove there had been no breeze at all, here on the clifftop the air was very turbulent, warm but gusty. No one down in the cove would be able to see the clouds or know that some dramatic weather event was on its way. I didn't quite know then that the clouds augured a thunderstorm, but a crackle in the air and the sheer menacing aura of them made me feel suddenly very small and vulnerable. I wanted to rescue Podge if I could, but my overriding urge was to return to the safety of my family before whatever the boiling clouds and angry sky presaged, arrived.

I began to shoulder my way quickly along between the hedge and the fence, turning my face from the worst of the thorny branches. The cows didn't move but they stopped their chewing and watched me with wary eyes. The meadow itself was benign grass and softly waving cow parsley but its periphery was a tangle of nettle and thistle and my legs were scratched and stung before I had gone even a few yards. Podge's cries grew more pitiful but also louder.

I wanted to cry myself, but what would have been the point? And, in any case, crying is not something I do.

After a while the wire fence was replaced by a lichen-encrusted drystone wall. The vindictive bushes gave way to saplings and trees that were kinder if they were not less dense. I pushed my way past them, almost panicked, gasping and half-sobbing in my alarm, careless of the whip of withies as they sprang back to slap me, the greenish stains from the bark on one side and the lichen on the other, the spider webs and crawling things that got caught in my hair and on my clothes. Above me the clouds had risen so high into the sky that they threatened to overwhelm the sun. If I'd known anything about Armageddon or the End of Days I'd have believed the day of judgement had come. As it was, I only had a deep and terrifying sense of impending doom. A dark shadow loomed onto the meadow at its far side and began to rush across the grass, like dark ink across a green tablecloth, absorbing the cows and their calves, sucking the brightness from the day. I watched its advance in horror. The wind in the trees at my back made them thrash and shiver frantically, as though they too feared annihilation. And suddenly the gloom overtook me, the sun blotted from the sky by enormous peaks of apocalyptic cloud, the heat drenched by an inpouring of chill, everywhere plunged into preternatural darkness as though the sun had been totally eclipsed.

I burst out of the trees and found myself on a rough track. There was Podge, leaping and barking hysterically, her lead tied to the rung of a metal gate that separated the woods from the meadow. When I knelt beside her I could see that, like me, she was scratched and dishevelled, one ear torn, one eye swollen and half closed. I released her lead and stood up. Podge was beside herself with joy, jumping up, the sharp scratch of her claws only adding to the numerous abrasions on my legs. The air in the woods was thick and gloomy, a greenish night, stirred into a frenzy by the wind that now coursed like a wild thing through the canopy and between the trunks. Distantly, I could hear branches snap and fall. I peered into the dimness. The track disappeared into a throat of darkness.

Close by, a tree moved, separated itself from the shadows of the surrounding undergrowth and stepped towards me. I gasped and started backwards. I was not afraid because I'd been conjuring fantastical entities for as long as I could remember, but I was very startled—none of my imaginary figments had ever been as close as this. The figure was cloaked from head to foot in green—a Macintosh, a cape, a tarpaulin, I couldn't tell. It was tall, towering over me, but also thickset and sturdy, very like the tree I had believed it to be. I couldn't tell anything about it, its face shaded and shielded by its covering and the light in the woods so poor. It could have been a dryad like the ones in the *Narnia* books and I swear to God, Arthur, at that point I was so hopelessly disoriented that if Aslan himself had leapt over the gate I would not have been surprised.

The thing bent down and spoke to me, but its voice was low and cracked as though unused for eons. The noise in the woods was so loud, the storm shaking the canopy. Podge kept up her incessant barking. In spite of myself I yelled, 'What?'

And then the storm broke right overhead. A rending of skies in a thunder crack that made my teeth rattle, and a simultaneous streak of lightning, as though heaven shone through the gap the thunder had opened. For that instant, the light was blinding—the interior of the forest lit up in silver and white—before the darkness returned, blacker and more otherworldly than before. The rain came, as though a bladder in the sky had been burst open, and the sound of that added to the cacophony, pebbles of water pounding onto leaves and slapping onto the ground forming instant rivulets and runnels that ran crazily across the woodland floor. Rain plastered my hair to my head. My clothes were instantly soaked. Water coursed off whatever covering the figure wore and Podge cowered against my legs, her tail under her belly and her ears flat.

The figure croaked again, but it was just impossible to make out anything it said to me. It shook its head—irritated or resigned—and a gnarled old hand reached out from its coverings and took hold of my shoulder. I found myself turned from the gate and faced down the track, into the deep dimness of the woods where there was no light and where I did not recognise a single stick or stone or tree.

It propelled me forward, guiding me left or right as the way zigzagged through the trees. The faint track petered away almost at once. I couldn't see any path but my guide was unwavering. We seemed to descend for a hundred yards or so and then to climb again. We passed a narrow opening of some kind—not much more than a space between two trees—and the figure pointed vaguely up it before moving me forward. My eyes were full of hair and rain and I kept tripping over Podge, who wove herself between my legs, tangling her lead.

We walked for about five minutes, but it felt much longer, as the rain continued to pour relentlessly down and as the thunder and lightning ricocheted overhead. At last we pushed through a thicket of saplings and rounded a huge boulder and suddenly I could see a flash of colour down below us, in the cove. I shook off my chaperone's hand and ran forward, finding the steep boulder steps that would reunite me with my family. I didn't look back. I didn't make so much as a gesture of thanks.

I've felt bad about that, since.

The scene on the beach was dismal, full of panic and dismay. Aunt Isobel crouched beneath the rickety old gazebo. She shielded Erin and the other children as a hen might shield her chicks from a buzzard. Erin—shivering and wan—was swathed in blankets in the very centre of the huddle, but the rain poured off the inadequate shelter and they were all soaked to some degree or another. Grandad was trying to get the windbreaks situated around the gazebo in a fruitless attempt to improve the shelter it afforded. He was as wet as possible, his shirt transparent and adhering to his bony back, water literally pouring from his trouser hems. My mother had taken some kind of shelter beneath an overhanging rock and I could see her struggling to protect Grace in the dank cave behind her. Grace was crying, her flesh blubbery and very white against the drenched rocks—she must have decided to swim after all. She was half-naked, wet, larded with sand, and by no amount of struggling in that confined space could she get herself dressed. Granny strode around the cove careless of the onslaught of the storm, gathering together the strewn-about belongings—buckets, nets, the ruined picnic—and flinging them anyhow into the carts. Your mother cowered beneath a tree, pressed up against the trunk, shrieking with every successive crash of thunder. Under a different tree I could see your father and Verity. Her kaftan adhered to her oily skin like a limp rag and her makeup ran blackly down her face. Your father's safari suit was a ragged, ruined thing. They were pressed together, seeming to be shielding something between them, wrapping it in the folds of Verity's peculiar towelling thing. I thought it was you, but it turned out to be the camera bag.

The sea had turned turgid and brown, whipped into foam that adhered to the rocks where I had earlier scrambled. Grey-black clouds pressed down like a lid and rain fell relentlessly. Though not so dark as in the wood, it looked like dusk even though it could not have been later than one o'clock. The wind coursed around the cove like a trapped animal, making towels flap, sending tumbleweeds of seaweed across the shingle, which shifted and clicked in an eerie, unsettling concerto.

Podge yanked her lead from my hand and ran howling to Granny. At this new addition to the ruckus every eye turned to where I stood, a lone and bedraggled figure at the top of the steps. My mother made a strangled cry and launched herself from her bolthole, leaving Grace exposed and half-dressed behind her. Mum ran across the shingle with long-legged strides and took the steps two at a time. She grappled me into her arms and I sank into her, only to be wrenched away again for two resounding slaps, then pulled close again.

'Where's your father?' she yelled into the teeth of the storm. 'And where's Arthur?'

Chapter Seven

It wasn't until much later that I pieced together what had happened on the beach once I'd ascended the cliff. I was soon missed. That, at least, is a comfort. My abandoned bucket bobbed on the surface of the sea over the rocks where I had been sitting and it was at first assumed I'd been swept off the rocks and into the sea on their other side. Aunt Hester plunged back into the water and swam round the outcrop while my mother suppressed hysterics. This I gleaned almost immediately from Kath and Kaz, who were eager to tell me of their mother's heroic role in my rescue.

My father attempted to climb out along the rocks but was turned back by the strong swell of the high tide and the jagged perils of the submerged terrain, which did in fact damage his big-toe nail so badly that in time it fell off. This I know because I was made to look at it—as black and hard as a mussel shell—and in fact, I found it when I was clearing Mum's things after she'd passed away. It was in a small tin, along with our baby teeth and the wizened remnant of cowl that was all that remained of a baby that had been stillborn.

Presently Aunt Hester returned, having got herself badly beaten against the sharp rocks on their far side, where there was less shelter than there was within the cove. She had a deep gash on her thigh that nothing in Aunt Isobel's first aid kit could staunch and it was soon agreed that she had better go back to the house and then drive to the cottage hospital for stitches and a tetanus injection. Of course, Uncle Eric wanted to go with her, but Uncle Victor said that he had to return to the village in any case, to check on the two part-timers who had been left in charge of the shop. He'd drive Hester in the van, because she would not wish to get blood on the seats of her Triumph. Victor promised to look out for me on the route home and, if he found me, to bring me back.

And all the time—while they ran frantically about to see if I was hiding, and asked each other who had seen me last and where did they think I could have gone, and as their mood turned from annoyance to real anxiety—the air was becoming thicker and more charged with static, the wind warmer and more portentous, sucking oxygen from the cove so that no one could think clearly about anything but were oblivious to the reason why. Hester had made no mention—perhaps she had not seen—the approaching storm, and Granny decided that it would distract the children from the crisis—and lure me back, if I was lurking nearby—if she were to begin dishing out the sandwiches.

My father got his shoes and socks back on and declared his intention of searching the woods in the direction opposite to the path that would take Victor and Hester back to Broadacres. My mother wanted to go with him, but

Grace clung to her and refused comfort from any other source—this I got, witheringly, from Verity. Uncle Eric said he would search the woods and the big rocks to the south but when he asked your father to go with him Henry declined, saying he wasn't familiar with the terrain and would likely get lost himself. He would stay behind to look after the women. I know this because I heard Aunt Isobel recount the conversation—in a tone of appalled astonishment—later on that day. By that time, we were home and dry, but that was about the best that could be said for us.

So, my father and Eric set off in different directions, into the woods. Of course, Henry was no practical use in the cove. He strode around wringing his hands and muttering, 'Dear, dear,' while Granny and Grandad and Aunt Isobel did their best to comfort the children and to stop them devouring *all* the food, for at that point it was assumed I'd be found safe and well and that the day in the cove would continue as planned, into the evening.

It wasn't until the first tranche of sandwiches had been eaten and the flapjack unpacked that your mother looked around her in a mildly curious way to wonder where *you* were.

Everyone looked to the place on the sand where you had been digging. Your spade was abandoned, the hole nowhere near deep enough to conceal you. Erin murmured that she felt sure you had been there only a few moments before. Hadn't you requested a ham sandwich rather than an egg one? But no, that might have been one of the twins.

I can imagine my mother opening her mouth to deliver a homily: how *could* your parents have been irresponsible enough to lose track of their own child? But under the circumstances this would have been somewhat hypocritical. No doubt she decided to hold her tongue.

Unbelievably, your father did not go off into the woods in search of you.

The conclusion that we had absconded together had just been reached when the cloud closed in like a cap across the cove and that first, sky-rending explosion of thunder and lightning detonated over their heads. Jack told me it was hard to say whose hysterics were better, your mother's or Verity's. Both screamed as though confronted by a gorgon and were hustled to the shelter of trees by Henry, although anyone with any sense knows this is the worst possible place to shelter in a thunderstorm. Grace only cried and clung onto our mother. Jack claimed to have *loved* the storm and to have retreated to the flimsy shelter of the gazebo under protest, although I must say he looked as miserable as the rest when I did eventually make my reappearance.

Even under the shelter of the forest canopy the onslaught of the rain had been biblical. What it must have been like in the exposed cove I can hardly imagine. The hard pellets of rain on skin reddened and tightened by sun and salt must have been very painful.

Moments ticked by and there was no sign of you, me, my father or Uncle Eric. Henry asserted that the two runaways—you and me, Arthur—were no doubt sheltering somewhere together and would emerge before long. Then he retreated with bedraggled dignity to the comparative shelter of the tree where Verity cowered.

And that's how I found them, a sorry, sodden little party indeed.

I was roundly chastised and squashed in with the other children beneath the dripping gazebo, and given food and orange squash while Aunt Isobel did her best with her saturated and ravaged first aid kit to tend the multiplicity of scrapes, stings and cuts on my arms and legs. No one actually asked me where I'd been, and given the furore I decided that if asked I'd stick with the explanation that I'd wandered into the woods to find kindling, got lost and then been frightened by the storm. But an account was not demanded of me; everyone's principal concern at that point was *you*.

Time went by. The storm continued but I thought that it was weakening slightly, or maybe passing over us. Or—more likely—my fear of it was less once I had been restored to the bosom of my family. The rain seemed less torrential, and the thunder and lightning were now several hippopotami apart. All the children were woebegone by this point, even Jack and the twins who were probably the most resilient of all the children under normal circumstances. Even Granny—whose spirit of positivity was usually unshakable in even the most appalling of situations—allowed Grandad to place an arm around her shoulders briefly and to wipe the water from her face before placing a chaste kiss on her cheek. Grace shivered and whimpered in her little cave shelter.

Your parents shrieked accusations at each other from beneath their respective trees, your mother—to do her credit—imploring your father to go off and find you, your father arguing the utter pointlessness of such an escapade.

At one point she wailed, 'But he's all alone, Henry, in the storm. He'll be so frightened.'

'Serve him right,' your father roared. 'It will be better for the little shit if Trevor or Eric find him before I do. I don't know what I'll do with him, when I get my hands on him.' But I must say in his defence that his habitual poise had utterly forsaken him. I think he really was very worried; but like many men who project an aura of assurance, when it came to a crisis he was clueless.

Then we heard a small voice shouting from the woods, the still, small voice that makes itself heard in earthquake, wind and fire. We hushed each other and Grandad climbed the steps, followed by Aunt Isobel and Granny. Then you appeared, and I wondered if the green dryad had found and rescued you, as it had me. You were drenched of course, your copper hair darkened and stuck to your head, your shorts and tee shirt sagging, but you stood staunchly enough on the top boulder, the place where earlier Erin and I had paused while the carts were carried down, when we'd had the whole glorious day ahead of us with no notion that it would come to such ruin and disaster. Your face was white and solemn but not panicked, and I found I quite admired that, and wondered if I had looked as calmly controlled as you did when I emerged from my ordeal. I doubted it, and the thread of admiration, however reluctantly pulled from me, tugged at my conscience.

You projected your voice into the storm as though speaking lines in a school play. 'You had better come. He's hurt. He's stuck, and we can't move the tree.'

My mother gave a sort of screech. 'Who? *Who?* Oh God! Is it Trevor?'

But you shook your head. 'No,' you said, and this time your voice did warble a little, but you took a deep breath and spoke out. 'No, it's Uncle Eric.'

Chapter Eight

Naturally, the children were not allowed to go. A very quick confab decided that Grandad, my mother and Isobel should follow you to the spot where Eric was trapped. Your father could hardly refuse to accompany them, and in fact was the one to remember the bowsaw, which was retrieved from the barrow where it had been flung earlier along with all the other paraphernalia. So we were left with Granny and your mother and Verity who, once Henry had quit the cove, seemed in some way to awaken from whatever enchantment had rendered her so distant and sullen that day. She emerged from the shelter of the tree and came to join us, resettling towels and rugs around our shoulders and reassuring us that everything was sure to be all right. She was especially kind to Kath and Kaz, who clung to each other while tears poured from their eyes like fountains. Her own eyes were smudged with eye-stuff above and beneath, and yet also white around their periphery, and oddly staring. It took me a while to realise that it was the outline of the large sunglasses she had worn all day. The rest of her face was very sunburned.

Granny must have been beside herself with anxiety to think of her youngest in some way injured, but she squared her shoulders and took charge, announcing that we had spent *quite* enough time here in the cove and that we must be brave like the knights of old and make our way home. What was a drop or two of rain, she asked us, and she stood out in the teeth of the squall that still tumbled around the sky, shaking her fist at the weather and shouting, 'We are not afraid of you!' Then she gathered us up one by one, hugging us and whispering a word of comfort, making sure we had our shoes on and properly fastened, and getting us into twos, like the animals who were about to escape the flood by entering the ark. Kath and Kaz could not be separated. Grace took Jack's hand and I took Verity's. It was cold and bony, and it reminded me of the dryad's hand, earlier. Granny made a nest in the wheelbarrow from towels and rugs and settled Erin into it. She couldn't possibly have walked, poor thing. She was so pale as to be ghostly, with a bluish tinge about her lips. Raindrops adhered to her skin like beads of sweat and her eyes were glazed, looking at that faraway place that no one else could see. She allowed Granny to tuck her in and then we made our way to the steps. Your mother and Verity helped get the barrow up the boulders and then it was actually not too hard to push Erin up the path; she was so light, and the barrow had a well-inflated tyre that bounced over roots and stones while we slipped around in the soft mush of the forest floor. I think I was as much help to Verity as she was to me, and I know she threw the ridiculous sandals in the bin the next day.

Granny took us a different route through the woods so we didn't have to cross the stream—which would surely have been a swollen torrent by then—and we were all quiet in the sudden and relative calm beneath the trees, away from the thrashing waves and the hiss of shingle and the devastation of our toys and the picnic and all the other equipment we had left behind us, the most poignant of which was Uncle Eric's guitar, which lay against a rock, ruined.

I suppose the grownups questioned you about your time in the woods: how you had found Eric, how long it was before my father came across you straining and fighting with all your might to get the fallen branch off Eric's shattered body. It must have been a long time before the ambulance and coast guard people arrived and, in any case, by then it was too late. But you'd been brought away by that time, carried up through the woods by my father and bundled past the drawing room where the rest of us kids—bathed and changed into pyjamas and cocooned in nests of blankets—drank hot chocolate by an unseasonal fire while Granny read *Stig of the Dump* aloud. She must have known that my father brought some news, but she went on in a voice that never wavered or faltered, until we were all asleep.

Whatever you told them, we kids didn't get to find out. Why you'd even gone into the woods remained a matter too tender to probe, although I had my uncomfortable suspicions. The Days—as they always did—avoided unpleasantness. They didn't name-and-shame. What would have been the point? Knowing who was at fault could not undo the outcome. It could only undermine still further the suddenly fragile fabric of our family. We only knew that Uncle Eric had been crushed beyond saving by a branch dislodged in the storm. It was a terrible accident, a tragedy, unbearably sad.

I comforted myself by thinking that he had been looking for us *both*, allowing the timeline of events that day to become muddled in my mind. I chose to believe that we—you and me, Arthur—were equally to blame. But that isn't true, is it?

Be that as it may, I felt then and I still feel now that the person who should carry the heaviest burden of guilt was your father, because he refused to go with Eric when asked, at whatever point in the episode that occurred. And that's one of the things I mean when I say that the Glenisters brought disaster on the Day family.

PART TWO
1969 - 1972
Chapter Nine

Hello Arthur. It's me again.

The place is very quiet and no one saw me enter. I don't mean to disturb your peace—really, I don't. But now I've started on this memoir I find it's got hold of me. There'll be no rest for either of us until we've told the whole story.

In 1969, when you were barely eight, you were sent off to boarding school. We were told that it was a Glenister tradition; your name had been put down before you were a month old and your years at Holmewood School would be 'the happiest of your life.'

Things in the interim had been just as fraught between us, but the quality of our antagonism—of mine, anyway—had changed. From being chilly but crystalline it had become cloudy with things that could not be spoken of. Before the day Eric was killed I had been a self-righteously spiteful little girl. Afterwards, my piety was undermined by a deeply buried but nevertheless uncomfortable suspicion that I might not *always* be right. You provided a mirror, and I didn't like what I saw in it.

If I analyse it now, I can see that I was envious of you. Why you had gone into the woods was a question I chose not to ask, but the fact I couldn't get away from was that while there you had found and attempted a heroic if doomed rescue of my uncle. *You* were not chastised for disappearing, because without that Eric might never have been found at all, and certainly not alive. He would not have had the small crumb of comfort that Grandad and his sister and even my mother offered as his life ebbed away.

You were lauded and thanked. I was shunned for quite a long time. This comparison stung me almost as much as my father's inability to give me a kind look or a friendly word as he mourned his brother and picked up the slack in the business. His brow was shadowed by a bleak disappointment that was worse than yelling, slaps or the withdrawal of every treat and privilege would have been. My mother constantly lectured me about "consequences," exhorting me to "think" and "consider" the future outcome of any word or deed.

Setting our actions that day side by side, I asked myself what *I* had done that *you* had not? How could I possibly have known that the "consequence" of my action—if it *was* the consequence of it—would be so awful, while the consequence of yours would be commendable? Why was I more blameworthy than you? Except that in truth there *was* no blame. Not one accusing finger was ever pointed, even by the twins, who were utterly broken hearted. And not by Granny, either. If anything, she was even kinder and softer towards me than she had been before, plucking a troubling string of guilt.

I stopped being maliciously mean, but our physical rivalry escalated. Whatever game we played—cricket, tag, tree-climbing—it felt imperative that I beat you. And in the market garden, I set myself to pick or plant more than you did. I was two years older than you, but you were strong and sturdy, tall for your age. It wasn't always easy to come out on top.

Life went on, and I learned that the passing of time can assuage most emotions: grief and guilt, resentment and remorse. The Days recovered, both from the loss of Uncle Eric and from the damage that the summer of 1966 wrought on the business. The hard look in my father's eye softened and then disappeared altogether. I worked hard at school and I know he was proud of me. We had happy times again. We ate out on the terrace in summer, we had our traditional Christmases and Easter egg hunts even though we were all much too old to believe in Santa or the Easter bunny. My mother brushed up her piano playing so we could have sing-songs and not miss too abjectly the accompaniment of Uncle Eric's guitar. She also learnt to drive, taking over some of the delivery duties that had previously fallen to Eric's lot. Widowed Hester continued her horticulture course and she and the girls were as integral a part of the Day clan as before, even if the twins drew more closely together than previously. In fact, they were so upset by being placed in different classes when they began secondary school that one of them had to be moved so that they could be together.

But we did not go down to the cove as a family again.

The years between '66 and '69 are a bit blurry to me. I suppose they were a time of readjustment. I did well at school, took up and then abandoned the flute and broke my wrist in a fall from my bike. These are the only events I can recall with any clarity. At some point Erin ceased to attend school and had a home tutor. She was weak and unwell, laid low by some malaise that was never named—to me, anyway. Grace had a growth spurt, losing her puppy-fat and metamorphosing into a tall, shapely and unexpectedly beautiful girl. She became graceful, as her name foretold, the only one of the three of us ever destined to fulfil the prophecy of their name. She started going out with the star of the school rugby team, Gary Bell, whose parents ran the village pub. The liaison was cautiously approved by my parents, but the couple's dates were closely supervised, curfew rigidly imposed, and the pair was never allowed to be alone behind a closed door. Grace would not turn sixteen until the following year.

Grandad did proceed with the plan of planting more rain-tolerant crops, but no subsequent summer was as wet as '66. In fact the summer of '69 was a scorcher, breaking all records.

The next event I recall with clarity was your departure for boarding school and the seismic shift that occurred afterwards.

We Days hardly ever went away for so much as a weekend, let alone for weeks, so your departure for Holmewood was a huge event. New uniform appeared and there were labels to be sewn on and trousers to be turned up. You were taken for a savage military-style haircut. Your usual rumbustious, easy-going demeanour evaporated as the new term drew nearer. I knew you were anxious about the change but couldn't bring myself to offer a kind word. At last the time came for your departure. The evening before, the Glenisters had dinner with the Days. Granny cooked your favourite dish and made a cake, trying to make the occasion a festive, celebratory one. But anyone could see that she and Grandad disapproved of your parents' decision. I noticed that you ate little but sat, pale and blinking back tears, while your father regaled us with his school memories—tales of mischief in the dormitories and valour on the sports field—making the whole affair sound like an episode from an Enid Blyton book.

Cynically, I looked forward to your going away; I thought the relief of not having to maintain our rivalry would be immense, and I believed that your absence would remove the unfavourable reflection that always confronted me when I looked at you. Out of sight, I told myself, out of mind. I thought—in my naivety—that you going away would mean the Glenisters would have less reason to hang around Granny's house. As it turned out I was right—about *one* of them, anyway—but not at all for the reason I had supposed.

It came as an unexpected shock to me that the space you left behind felt raw and hollow and full of aching. I liken it to someone who has an amputation. The removal of a diseased limb must be a relief, and yet it's so permanent and so radical, and I'm told the ghost of the limb remains, tender or itchy. So it was with you, Arthur, when you went away to school. Your empty chair at the dinner table and the place absent-mindedly set for you by Granny was a reproach. If we divided into teams for a game, there was always someone without a partner. We were all off kilter without you. I found myself wandering around the playground at school looking for the red-headed boy who had been transported to some other playground far away. It felt all wrong, and I was preoccupied with wondering what that other playground was like. Had you made friends? Or were you teased there, as you had been here? I pondered the oddness of sleeping in a room full of strangers, of finding your way around a building that I imagined was old and draughty and full of looming statues and grim old portraits. I tried to see myself in that foreign and frightening situation. How would I have coped? It didn't take me long to realise that I'd be utterly miserable and homesick, and with that revelation any remnant of bitterness I might have harboured against you was washed away. I was deluged by a sweet inpouring of compassion. I don't know if it is a normal stage of development for a ten-year-old—the sudden ability to look at a thing from another point of view, through someone else's eyes—but it happened to me that autumn of 1969.

It took me a while, but I realised that I missed you. I was lonely. And in a strange and contrary way I think I was happier once I'd realised that, during all the years that had passed by, it was my war of attrition with you that had so thoroughly sabotaged my own contentment. I was eager for your return at Christmas, to begin again on a better, kinder footing, but as it turned out your return at the end of term was under circumstances I could never had anticipated, because by then your parents had separated.

The term "separation" seems such a clinical, cold description of an event that was cataclysmic and fraught. The glassware in Granny's cabinet rattled and chimed at the row that preceded the severance of one Glenister from the other, and the shrieks and lamentations of your mother sounded as though she was being literally torn limb from limb. Your father's voice was dark and thunderous, a raging tornado that pulled the Days into its maelstrom.

I had no idea what precipitated it; not anything sudden, surely? It must have been fermenting for weeks or even months—perhaps longer. It may even have been your departure for Holmewood. If it had upset *me*, how much more must it have disturbed *them*? Whatever it was, it erupted one Saturday afternoon in November of 1969. A wet afternoon, and dark before four, labour on the property had been terminated for the day and Grandad was looking forward to an hour's work on the accounts followed by his favourite seat by the fire for a rugby match on the television. Isobel and Victor were at the shop—closing up for the day, perhaps. Jack and Erin must have been with them; I don't remember them being there, anyway. Granny and my mother were in the kitchen clearing away the tea things. Grace was out somewhere with Gary. Kath and Kaz were staying at Granny's for a few weeks while Aunt Hester was on a work placement at a National Trust garden in Northumberland. I have an idea they were on their way back upstairs to finish their homework when the drama began.

Verity—just seventeen—and my father arrived at Broadacres in our family car after a driving lesson as the last teacup was dried and put away. The

Glenisters, naturally, had withdrawn from the kitchen at any suggestion of domestic drudgery. I know that Henry had gone into the sitting room and for a long time I assumed Verity must have found him in there when she went to warm herself at the fire, or possibly had found both Glenisters, already simmering their way up to a boiling point. My father had hardly begun his report on Verity's progress with clutch-control and mirror-signal-manoeuvre when there was a scream from the sitting room and the sudden clatter of the standard lamp being knocked over. Its shade—a pleated silk and chiffon affair with little tassels all around its circumference—fell into the hearth. There was a shout of alarm and the sudden acrid smell of burning. My father launched himself from his chair and hurtled through to the sitting room, closely followed by Granny who clutched a tea towel she had hastily plunged into the washing-up water. She met Grandad on his way back downstairs from the little box room he used as his office. He squeezed narrowly past Kath and Kaz who had been arrested in their ascent by the furore in the sitting room. They all crowded into the sitting room and all I could see through the narrow aperture of the doorway was jostling shoulders and a forest of legs and Verity, backed into the corner behind Grandad's chair, her hand clamped to her mouth, her face very white and her eyes a-swim with tears. Blanche's initial screech—which I presumed at the time to be a shout of warning at the falling lamp—clarified into a tirade of accusation and abuse directed at Henry. Had *he* knocked over the lamp, I wondered? I craned, but couldn't see him. He must have been on the other side of the room, by the window. Blanche's rant was hardly articulate, and before we could begin to make any sense of it the twins and I were urgently hurried from the scene, sent off to collect logs that were not needed, to lock away hens that had already been shut up and to gather leeks for a soup that never got made. Only Verity was allowed to remain.

When we got back to the kitchen twenty minutes later the argument in the sitting room had not abated and, if anything, had escalated, my mother's and father's voices added to the others in vehement denial and affronted dignity. In between their exclamations I could hear Verity sobbing, 'No. No, of course not,' and Henry's barked-out defiance, until the crescendo of Blanche's hysteria reached a peak that ended with the unmistakable sound of flesh on flesh. Grandad—it can only have been him—must have raised his hand and slapped her across the face. The effect was immediate, as curdling and shocking as the needle being knocked from a record: a sudden cessation, the storm instantly stilled, but replaced by an awed, stupefied silence that was almost as dreadful as the row that had preceded it.

From the kitchen, where the twins and I sat before the trug of dirty leeks, we could make nothing of it. 'All this fuss over a lamp?' we asked each other.

The silence from the next-door room was replaced by a low, sober mumble.

Granny said, 'Yes, I think that will be best.' Her voice had a brittle quality I had never heard in it before.

The sitting room door opened and softly closed again, then the front door, likewise. Then there was a brief scrunch of gravel and the sound of Henry's car driving away.

Granny and Grandad were terribly upset. They re-entered the kitchen and Grandad made for the cupboard where the spirits were kept, pouring them each a large brandy although it was barely five o'clock. Scenes like the one they had just endured—the raw emotion and hysterics—were anathema to the Days. Verity followed closely behind them. The effect of the episode on her was easy to see; she was red-eyed with weeping and of a pallor that was almost green; she was sick with distress. My mother announced that we were going home. I was to fetch my coat and outdoor shoes immediately; she and Verity would wait on the drive—Verity needed some fresh air. As I laced up my shoes in the hall I could hear Blanche's soft sniffling in the sitting room and the low, reassuring tones of my father soothing her. He, clearly, was to remain behind.

By the time I had found my things only mum waited for me in the unlit driveway. Verity had gone ahead alone, though the way was dark.

Chapter Ten

It became obvious very soon that the breach between your parents was serious and permanent. Your mother never went back to Glenister Hall at all. My father and Grandad collected her things and she moved into one of the spare rooms of Broadacres. Henry came a few times to see her, bringing a bouquet of flowers on one occasion, clearly intent on reconciliation but also maintaining a stiff, offended manner that suggested strongly he believed himself wronged. Although Blanche was generally a flaky and ineffectual woman, she must have found some grit from somewhere because she was absolutely determined that no reconciliation was possible. In vain did my uncle Victor try to convince her that she should try to save her marriage, arguing *your* best interests, Arthur, as well as her own. Where would she live, he asked her. There was no room above the shop, and they had not another relative in all the world. How could she provide a home for you if she did not go back to Glenister Hall? Didn't she realise she risked losing you altogether? Of course, in those days, marriage was much less easily put aside than it is now, and women who chose to do so had a tough time of it financially and socially. So few of them then had a career to fall back on, or independent finances. It can't have been an attractive prospect for Blanche, but she only sobbed and said she knew she was a terrible nuisance, wrung her hands in despair but remained unshakable in her determination. The doctor gave her some tablets that made her listless but not more pliable. She sat for hours on a chair by the range in the kitchen, or lay on the bed in her room, but when the subject of Henry was introduced, she set her face in defiance.

My grandparents hadn't the heart to send her away. And of course there was *you*. By that time, you had been grafted so effectively onto the family rootstock that they could no more consign you to some seedy bedsit with Blanche for your school holidays than they would have consigned me. The Days were kind and compassionate, but I got the distinct sense that there was more to it than that. They seemed to feel in some way to blame for Blanche's situation, although for the life of me I couldn't see how. Verity, having been so intimately caught up in the fracas, also behaved as though she felt culpable, avoiding Blanche altogether if she could. She must have felt terribly awkward about the whole thing.

You returned in the third week of December, and you had Christmas at Broadacres before decamping to Glenister Hall for the New Year. In the Day family, Christmas was for kids, but New Year was for grownups, so you had the best of it as far as that was concerned. Maybe the Glenisters threw an extravagant New Year party? I don't know. You and I never discussed the new arrangements between your mother and father. I assume you'd been apprised of them either at school or on the journey home. You showed no surprise, anyway, and no particular emotion either. You were quiet and polite, said little about Holmewood, your new classes or any friends you might have made. You were painfully thin—I recall that particularly—and Granny spent the brief time you were with us plying you with mince pies, cake and chocolates.

I'd wanted to make peace with you, but under the new arrangements I didn't know how to begin. I didn't want you to think I felt sorry for you. My newly discovered empathy had nothing to do with the situation between your parents. I tried to be kind and considerate. I'm not sure you even noticed.

We didn't see you at all for the Easter holiday. Henry took you away to a ski resort. Your mother took the announcement in her stride. She was a fixture at Broadacres by that time, like an aged, incapacitated aunt, or perhaps more like Mr Rochester's mad wife. She spent a large part of each day in her room, rarely went outdoors, contributed nothing at all towards the household or business and participated in only a very perfunctory way at family gatherings. At the same time, she managed to make herself felt in ways that were subtle but potent. She had a way of leaving a room with a handkerchief pressed to her mouth just at the point when things had become relaxed and almost normal. We might all be laughing at some joke only to find that her laughter had turned to tears. She was abjectly grateful for everything but could be sulky at any perceived lapse of hospitality. She never failed to materialise for grandad's pre-dinner gin-and-tonic.

So it was the following summer before we saw you again and, without speaking a word, you and I made our peace. Your year at boarding school had changed you. You'd lost your childish puppy-fat and grown several inches so that you were half a head taller than me. Your hair was still shorn, a crop of coppery bristles. You were lean to the point of emaciation—Granny took one look at you and headed to the kitchen to bake—and your new, adult teeth seemed too large for your mouth. The sturdy little boy who had gone away came back stretched out and squashed flat.

Your father had been to the school to collect you and he dropped you off outside Granny's house which, because your mother was now resident there, was also your home when you were not at Glenister Hall. He decanted your trunk on the gravel and sped off before your mother or Granny—or I— could get to the door to greet you. You stood alone on the shallow step looking lost and rather afraid. You hardly spoke a word as the family bustled round, as Grandad hefted your trunk upstairs, as your mother dabbed at her teary eyes with a damp handkerchief and as my mother and Aunt Isobel made all the effusive gestures of welcome that Blanche was unable to muster.

That night, as we got undressed in the attic, I glimpsed bruises on your white, fleshless buttocks because your pyjama trousers were so loose they kept falling down. You had to tighten the drawstring, which you did with a frantic fumble, your back turned to me, the narrow slice of your cheek that was visible to me suffused by a furious blush.

There were only two beds left in the attic. The others had been dismantled and taken away, their occupants either too big or considered old enough to stay up until the grownups were ready to depart, or even to stay at their own homes without adult supervision. Verity, then eighteen, had passed her driving test and had a battered Mini to travel to the local college, where she was doing a secretarial course. Erin now spent prolonged periods in hospital undergoing treatment that was as debilitating as whatever ailed her. Grace was almost always to be found at the Bells' with Gary; with Mr and Mrs Bell serving drinks and food in the pub, Gary and Grace had the run of the upstairs accommodation there. Kath and Kaz, fourteen, had outgrown the little beds in Granny's attic the previous year and had been allocated a room at the back of the house. Jack, then thirteen, was very athletic and represented the school in several sports. He was often at far-flung locations in the county for matches at weekends, getting back late and tending to sleep at his own house rather than at Granny's. His bed had been the last to go, leaving just yours and mine, and yours had been left unoccupied since the previous Christmas. Without the beds—or the other children—the attic had lost its homely, communal atmosphere and for a number of months I had felt very lonely up there. I noticed that the floor was rather dusty and that there were cobwebs looped amongst the eaves. One of the panes in the little round window had cracked and there was a chill draught. It occurred to me that Granny had given up on our childhoods, not bothering now to come up and clean, to place the occasional new book or game on the shelves. The others had moved on. Only you and I were left, marooned in the last dwindling years of our infanthoods to garner the last drops of innocent pleasure from them if we could. And, looking at you—so changed—I felt suddenly as though you had moved a step or so ahead of me. That you had crossed the invisible threshold into adulthood already.

Noticing these things, and seeing the great alteration in you, Arthur, I suddenly felt deluged with emotions I couldn't identify—compassion, nostalgia, loss, guilt—and on impulse I said, 'Would you like the bed by the window Arthur?' I didn't ask selfishly, because of the draught, but because in all our early years we had fought over that bed and—whether by superior strength or sheer stubbornness I don't know—I had usually prevailed. For the first time I wanted *you* to win. I wanted to give you something. Call it an olive branch, a peace offering … I couldn't say, but we were both so surprised by the gesture that we stared at each other speechlessly for a few seconds, your hands snared by the cord of your pyjamas. Your blush deepened but there was a whiteness around your lips I'd never seen before. Your eyes—as blue as ever but unreadable in the gloom of the ill-lit room—were wide and strangely luminous. I took half a pace away from the bed and reached a tentative hand to the neatly folded-back top sheet of the one adjacent, as though to get in.

But you said, 'No. It's okay,' and your gaze slid away to where Grandad had left your trunk against the far wall. Holmewood, the name of the school, was stencilled on its lid. The whiteness of the lettering glowed in the dim, like your eyes.

You mumbled, 'I ought to … I'll probably … I've got a …' but you got no further with the sentence before Granny came bustling in with some clean towels.

She too cast a furrowed glance at the trunk and then back at you and there seemed to be a little dialogue between the two of you that had no words. A raised eyebrow, the merest possible shake of the head seemed sufficient for you both to reach an understanding and Granny said, 'Go and clean your teeth please, Prudence,' and stood aside, pressing herself into the slope of the eaves to let me get past. When I came back from the bathroom your school trunk was open, displaying neatly folded shorts and shirts and rolled up socks. There was the echo of bustle and busyness in the room, motes floating in the air around the feebly glowing light bulb and scuffs in the dust around the other bed. Granny twitched the crocheted blanket into place and you all but dived between the sheets even though, to my knowledge, *you* had not cleaned your teeth.

Granny paused by the door as I slid in between the cool, crisp sheets and then she switched out the light. 'No talking, darlings,' she said. 'Arthur is very tired after his journey.'

I lay on my back with my hands behind my head. Even with the light off, the room was not dark. The summer nights were short even though the longest day had passed, and the curtainless round window glowed with the remains of the day.

'Are you?' I asked into the silence.

Your answer took a while to come. 'Am I what?'

'Are you tired?' I turned and propped myself on an elbow.

I saw the sheets rise and fall. A shrug. 'At school,' you said at last, 'we're not allowed to speak after lights out.'

I considered this. 'We're not *at* school,' I offered.

You seemed to process this. Presently I heard you sigh, and it was as though some rope of tension had relaxed. Your breathing became deeper, more regular, and I knew you were asleep.

When I woke up in the morning you were up and dressed, your bed stripped down to a rubber sheet I had never seen before, and all at once I knew what that peculiar business with Granny the night before had been about. A year earlier I would have been filled with scorn, scheming about the best way to humiliate you. But I felt no desire to do so now. Instead, I got up and fetched clean sheets from the airing cupboard and made your bed up fresh and new.

Chapter Eleven

For the rest of that summer of 1970, I felt we were as close and conspiratorial in our way as the twins were in theirs, until your time with us was up and you had to decamp to Glenister Hall. Three short weeks, but they stand out in my memory as a golden time.

By some unspoken agreement I ate and slept at Granny's for the three weeks of your stay. The weather was nowhere near as good as the previous year. Temperatures were cool but we had little rain, so Grandad was up early to do the watering. We got into the habit of rising early too, up as the purple-blue dawn warmed to rose-pink, dressing in shorts and cotton sweaters and ready to do our stint on the allotment before we were free to pursue our own adventures in the woods and further afield. You stripped your bed and I brought clean sheets. We made it part of our routine—like cleaning our teeth and eating breakfast—just a task to be done before we could go out.

We were not allowed to play in the polytunnels and glasshouses, nor to run along the long rows of marrows, onions and beets. It was understood that these were sacrosanct places, where the family's sweat and toil brought forth crops that were our lifeblood. But the Christmas tree plantation, the orchard and the hen run, the lawns and shrubberies of the formal gardens and the wild, wooded areas were all available for us to play in and we took full advantage of them. And, that year, we wandered further afield: along the disused railway line on our bikes, and into the village where we bought ice creams and sweets with our pocket money. We even ventured back to the cove. And do you remember the day we found the old graveyard? We had followed a path that led us south through the woods towards the rockfall. We'd been warned about the dangers of going that way: the likelihood of falling and smashing our skulls to smithereens on the rocks, of getting our legs wedged between the boulders and being drowned by the incoming tide. In former years, my sisters had tried to scare me witless with stories of tramps and hoboes and the ghosts of lunatic Glenister wives rumoured to inhabit the place, but their imaginations had fallen far short of my own. Since our reconciliation—yours and mine—I'd had less occasion to resort to those make-believe worlds and, in any case, I believed that in the storm of the summer picnic I'd faced the worst those woods could throw at me. I knew—as Verity and Grace did not—the truth about the phantom in the forest. I'd never told a soul about the peculiar being who guided me back to the cove that day. Sometimes I only half believed it had happened at all. The whole episode was a jumble in my mind. But if I *had* been guided, there was nothing malevolent about my rescuer; that much I *did* know.

You walked ahead of me that summer day, and swished at the encroaching nettles and brambles with a stick. It amazed me that the bluebells, which carpeted the whole forest floor back in May, had now utterly disappeared. It was cool beneath the trees and clouds of midges swarmed, sheltered from the sun above the canopy. You swatted them away from time to time, but they never bothered me. We followed a rough low drystone wall that divided the woods from the fields above, and then struck out along a faint path that might have been only an animal track through a wild tangle of undergrowth. You wore blue jeans, but I wore only shorts and before long my legs were scratched and stung, but I forged on. The way took us down a steepish scree of loose stones and then we saw a rusted gate set into another wall, higher, and of dressed stone. The gate was padlocked and swathed in ivy, so you boosted me up to see over the wall. I scrambled up and then held out my hand to help you climb up beside me. A square plot about the size of two tennis courts was entirely surrounded by the wall. Within, the undergrowth was surprisingly tame. The wild roses, nettles, thistles and snaking bramble vines that grew everywhere outside the wall had been held back. The grass was long and studded with wildflowers. Amongst the greenery were tumbled gravestones, leaning obelisks, lichen-encrusted statues and the pillars of a mausoleum whose roof had long-since collapsed and been lost amongst the undergrowth. We scrambled down and roamed amongst the stones. Frustratingly, we couldn't read any of the inscriptions. Most of them were worn away by weather.

Out of the blue, you said, 'I'll be buried here.'

I said, 'That's maudlin talk.' But then, 'Why?'

You threw me a questioning look that said, 'Isn't it obvious?'

I cast about me. 'It's peaceful, I suppose. And close to …' I nodded over my shoulder, indicating the rise in the ground behind us, beyond which was Granny's house. 'But it's probably a private plot,' I said. 'In the olden days, the landowners must have brought their dead here. Maybe there was a chapel?'

If there ever was a chapel, it had long-since crumbled to rubble. I squinted, summoning a cavalcade of mourners behind a coffin borne on the shoulders of frock-coated funeral men, watching the awkward passage of it through the trees and down the slope, observed weeping women in crinoline dresses … but no. I had an idea that women had not attended funerals in days of yore. My daydream evaporated.

'I wonder who they were?' I mused, 'the landowners hereabouts. We could go to the library and find out.'

You screwed up your face in an expression of astonished disbelief. 'You're kidding,' you said. 'You must know.'

'Know what?'

You blew out between flaccid lips. 'Who the landowners were … *are*. The Glenisters, of course. My grandfather, then my father, and then … it'll be me.' You had the grace to look embarrassed by this awkward truth. You threw out a hand to encompass the entire plot. 'All these dead people were Glenisters, and the people who worked for them.'

'You can't know that,' I objected. 'We couldn't read any of the inscriptions.' Even so, I followed the trajectory of your gesture with new appreciation and a sense that perhaps I hadn't shown sufficient respect when I'd trampled over the graves earlier. We watched a robin hopping along the stone wall for a while. Then you said, 'I *do* know. There are maps in the library … not the town library, the one at Glenister Hall.' You seemed to consider something for a while. I could see your mind working, and every so often you threw me a covert look as though trying to decide if I was … trustworthy. Then you made up your mind. 'There are all kinds of interesting things there. Would you like to see?'

I shrugged. 'One day, I suppose.'

'Let's go *now*,' you said, getting up and brushing grass seeds from your jeans. 'Come on.'

I'd had no inkling that Glenister Hall was so close to Broadacres. Through the woods and across a meadow it was no more than a twenty-minute walk, although I suppose by the road it would have been longer.

It wasn't until we were halfway across the meadow that I recognised it as the one the cows and calves had been in the day I'd climbed the cliff; the day Uncle Eric had died.

I pointed to the grey wall and towering chimneys of the grand house beyond, clearly visible to me now although, with the drama of the oncoming storm, I had only glimpsed them then. 'That's Glenister Hall?'

You nodded, half ashamed of its splendour. 'It looks okay from here,' you said, 'but wait until you see inside. The place is a wreck.' You strode across the field with the confidence of someone who knows he isn't trespassing. I had to half-run to keep up with you.

'Won't there be someone home?' I panted. 'I mean, are you allowed …?' I didn't know what the rules of the custodial arrangements were between Blanche and Henry. These three weeks of the summer holidays were allotted to Blanche. Did that mean you were not permitted to see your father at all?

But you said, 'It'll be fine. Come on. The garden door is always unlocked, so that Grandma can come and go.'

We came to a five-barred gate and climbed over it onto a grassy track that followed the line of the boundary wall. About twenty yards along, a small, studded door was set into the wall. You grasped its handle and it swung open. Your confidence of a moment before seemed to evaporate suddenly. You hesitated and narrowed one eye in a querying look, and I had the distinct impression again that you were weighing up if I could be trusted. My throat was thick, and I swallowed with difficulty. All at once I realised that mum was right about 'consequences.' My cruel behaviour towards you for the first years of our relationship had a consequence and it was this: you did not know if you could trust me. I felt myself blush with shame. I wanted to say something, but the words wouldn't come. We stood for about a minute on this important threshold, just outside the wall of Glenister Hall, just outside the boundary between your life at Salad Days and your life here. For that moment it felt like an unbroachable chasm. I grasped that while you knew virtually everything about my life, there were whole tracts of yours—school, Glenister Hall, the separation of your parents, your peculiar grandparents—that were a foreign country to me.

Were you going to let me in?

At last you said, 'Do you know much about the Glenisters?'

I shook my head, suddenly in awe of the great privilege you were offering me. In my head I heard echoes of comments I had overheard at home. 'Poor as church mice,' 'peculiar' and 'out of touch,' but I was determined not to spoil this moment by repeating them.

'Not much,' I said, not meeting your eyes.

You sighed. 'They're not like the Days,' you said heavily, and ushered me through the door.

Chapter Twelve

We walked through what had plainly been, at one time, formal gardens—squares of lawn bisected by flower beds, a sunken garden, a huge rockery—but these were now sadly overgrown, the lawns rank with couch grass and moss, the beds infested with weeds, the rockery swathed in thick moss. Lines of hedges were wild, long-untrimmed. The gravel of the paths was full of pernicious creeping plants that had no business being there. I was surprised to find I had a strong urge to bend down and pull them out. The windows of the house were all shuttered and blind, one or two boarded over. Here and there streaks of green slime oozed down the dressed stone of the walls from gutters that sagged and sprouted with buddleias and ferns. Nevertheless, I could see that the house was—or had been—very grand indeed, a real stately home. It was enormous, built to face west and look out over the sea. You led me round what I suppose I must call the south wing to the gravel sweep, past the impressive door with overhanging portico, round the north wing to an area at the rear where what looked to be stables, garages and storerooms clustered round a utilitarian yard. Henry Glenister's car was parked in one of the garages.

'Your father's home,' I observed.

You nodded. 'Where else would he be?'

We made our way to an ordinary-looking door that yielded to your push.

'You don't use the front door?'

You shook your head. 'Tradesmen's entrance for me.'

Inside, the place was gloomy and, in spite of the warmth of the day, rather chilly. You kicked off your trainers and I followed suit. We padded down a long corridor with doors on either side of it. I wanted to know what was behind them all, but you walked quickly and it was all I could do to keep up.

There was neither sight nor sound of any person: cook, housekeeper, maid. I could smell no aromas of cooking although by that time the afternoon was well advanced and it seemed reasonable to suppose that some preparations for supper should be underway.

We climbed a stone staircase and you pushed open a heavy door. 'This is the grand hall,' you announced, gesturing expansively to a large, empty, echoing space. Your voice was shockingly loud and bell-like in the silence. High above our heads I could see some kind of glass roof—very grimy, letting in only a green, subterranean light. Dimly, I made out galleried landings on the upper levels, all presumably reached by the sweeping stairs that rose from the centre of the room. The floor—a chequerboard of marble slabs—was littered with a dozen buckets and other receptacles, all filled to some degree or another with water.

'The roof leaks,' I said, unnecessarily.

'No kidding,' you said. 'We all have to help empty the buckets when it rains. Not just here. In every room, just about. Come on. The library is this way.'

We skidded across the hall floor in our stockinged feet, skirted the stairs and headed down an unlit corridor. I was completely disorientated by then. There were no windows to let me see which part of the house we were in.

You motioned towards a sequence of large and heavily ornamented doors as we passed them. 'These are called the state rooms. We never use them. Everything is covered in sheets, but Dad says all the valuable stuff was sold years ago.'

I longed to peep inside, but hurried in your wake.

Presently you stopped at one of the doors, turned the handle and ushered me through. The room was impenetrably dark and smelled musty. It might have been my imagination, but I thought I heard a sudden scurry and snuffle of rodents. Then you found the light switch.

Even with the many-branched chandelier that flickered into life at your touch, the room was only partially illuminated. Some of the lightbulbs weren't working and the rest were swathed with dusty cobwebs. Even so, I couldn't help gasping aloud. I'd never seen so many books, rank upon rank, shelf upon shelf of them, the shelves lining three walls of the room from the floor to the lofty ceiling. Here and there sliding ladders allowed access to the higher levels. The books were beautiful, mostly bound in leather with gold tooled detailing. The floor was covered in a threadbare carpet, at the centre of which stood a large, sturdy table. There were two windows, both tightly shuttered, either side of a massive marble fireplace. Beneath one of the windows was a large bureau with many shallow drawers. You strode across the carpet, yanked open a drawer and pulled out a leather folder that you carried across to the table.

'These are the maps I was telling you about,' you said, untying the binding and shaking loose a number of yellowed, leathery leaves. I joined you at the table and squinted at them. Maps and plans, carefully annotated in copperplate handwriting, much faded but still legible.

You pointed. 'Here's the house, look. This is where we came in. These are the domestic rooms we passed.' You pulled out another sheet. 'This is the ground floor. We're *here,*' you stabbed the place with your finger. I made out the word "library." Other rooms were labelled "salon" and "billiard room" and "ballroom."

'It's like a game of Cluedo,' I breathed. 'Where's the corpse?' But you didn't seem to like the joke.

You brought forward another drawing. 'This is the one I wanted to show you. This is the whole property, see? The house and gardens, the woods, the cove—it looks as though there was a boat house and a little jetty there at one time, doesn't it? And look there … can you see?'

I leaned down to make out the tiny legend, "Glenister Cemetery."

I said, 'Yes,' but my voice was half-strangled. The malign demon of my resentment had me by the throat. So the Glenisters owned the woods and the cove, all the special places I had believed to be *ours*—the Days'. I stepped coolly away from the table while you shuffled the papers together and restored them to their place. I feigned interest in the books but in fact was locked in mortal combat with my jealousy. Why must the Glenisters always take away from the Days? Why must they impose upon and despoil what had been whole and pure before they came? I glanced around the room with a sneering eye, encompassing in my disdain the whole house. How dirty, dilapidated and shabby it was! How austere and comfortless! How cold it must be in the winter, and damp, with the rain pouring in. It wouldn't be long, I speculated, until the whole edifice came crashing down, or mouldered away. I pictured rotten, worm-infested joists and crumbling masonry … But then I saw you, Arthur, standing by the bureau, your hands in your jeans pockets. You were dwarfed by the room—by the whole house—so small and vulnerable and—crucially—*innocent,* and my compassion soared into the ascendant. What did it matter who owned the woods? No one else used them but us. No one had ever tried to stop us and surely no one ever would. If Henry Glenister had objected to our trespass he would have said so, wouldn't he? And *you* would never debar the Days from anything, I was sure of that. I was filled again with gratitude for your gesture, for letting me into this part of your life that had been a closed book.

You stood patiently while the death throes of the battle played themselves out in my mind, my fondness for you and a sense of humility at your trust in me completely vanquishing the jealous resentment that had briefly burned. You couldn't possibly have known what I was thinking but it was clear to me that you were *waiting.* I even saw you glance down at your watch.

You pointed at the open drawer, almost—but not quite—an invitation. 'There are other things in here. The Glenisters … there are legends and … there's supposed to be a curse.'

Then we heard the scrunch of tyres on gravel. It seemed to galvanise you. You slammed the drawer of the bureau shut and leapt across the room to hit the lights, plunging us into cave-like darkness. A slice of greyish dimness showed me your silhouette against the door you had partly opened, and I made my way towards it. We regained the passageway and you closed the library door with infinite care so as not to make a noise. My eyes must have been like saucers. What on earth was going on? You held your finger to your lips and I nodded to show that I understood, although of course I didn't at all comprehend this sudden need for silence and secrecy. What had changed?

We crept along the corridor, back towards the hall but keeping to one side, pressing ourselves into the deeper gloom. From up ahead I heard the swift tread of footsteps descending the stairway and crossing the hall. There was the clang of a bucket inadvertently kicked, and a muttered expletive. Then the metallic grind and grate of a large key in an outsized lock and a flood of golden, late-afternoon light cascaded in as the weighty door of Glenister Hall creaked open.

You urged me forward, but cautiously, keeping us both shrouded in the gloomy periphery of the passageway where the light had not penetrated.

A man's voice—Henry Glenister's voice—said, 'Here you are at last! You're very late.'

'Not *very* late,' objected the newcomer.

I stiffened, might have gasped, except you grabbed my hand and squeezed it hard. Verity! What was *she* doing there?

She must have stepped into the hall. Her voice was shrill, amplified by the enormous scale of the room.

'We'll hardly have an hour before you have to leave,' Henry said mulishly. 'Come on. Hurry up.'

He closed and relocked the door, plunging us all back into preternatural darkness. I heard them progress across the hall and ascend the stair, their muttered conversation seeming to be sucked up into the impossible height of the atrium. Then, somewhere at a distance, I heard the thud of a closing door.

I turned to look at you and immediately knew that *this*—and not the library with its maps and plans—had been your primary object. Your face, even in the dimness, was white, your eyes huge and anxious. Your lips were pressed together as though restraining torrents of words. My own mind was a whirl of questions, of outrage and confusion. What did this mean? What should be done about it? And all my bewilderment was mirrored in you.

We made our way in silence back down the stairs to the servants' area, collected our shoes and stepped out into the sunshine. I hadn't realised how cold it had been in the house. The warmth of the late afternoon was wonderful, taking the edge off the chill and shock. We walked swiftly away from the house, through the tatty gardens to the door in the wall. Only then did I glance back with a kind of awful fatalism to see my sister Verity's battered little Mini parked brazenly on the grand sweep before the house.

We didn't speak of it, not then, anyway. I suppose that neither of us really understood it. You were only nine and although I was almost eleven, in those days children kept their innocence for much longer. I understood why you'd gone to such elaborate lengths to show me what you must have known for some time. You had an instinctive sense that these clandestine visits were wrong without being able to say exactly why. The sneaking secrecy of it troubled you to the extent that you'd found it too heavy a burden to bear alone. After the initial shock had subsided my dominant emotion was *gratitude*, Arthur, that you'd chosen *me* to confide in, to share the conundrum with. It brought us even closer together, I think.

In all the fiction I devoured that summer—*Swallows and Amazons* and the *Lone Pine* series—kids explored and had adventures in the countryside with no grownups to hinder them. They followed clues and uncovered crimes and for those three weeks with you at Granny's I looked up from the pages and believed myself still inside the book. You and me, Arthur, freed of our old animosity, had become the kind of chums who solved mysteries. The puzzle of Verity's liaison with Henry remained and we mused about it as we roamed the woods and splashed about in the rock pools on the beach, made dens in the compost area and lay reading in the little meadow where Granny kept the bees. Why did she go back there day after day? Of course we were not absolutely naïve; we considered the possibility of a romance between them. But we dismissed the idea as ludicrous as well as revolting; Henry was old enough to be Verity's father, older even than my father, who was the eldest of Granny and Grandad's brood. Our imaginations simply could not encompass it. It was too outlandish—and too horrible—an idea to entertain. I think we both felt that although the Days and the Glenisters weren't related in the ordinary sense, our daily proximity over the years meant that we *felt* related, and I recalled Mrs Gibbs' dark prognosis that the Glenisters were in the habit of marrying "too close" although naturally I didn't repeat it to you.

We speculated that Verity was doing some secretarial work for Henry. Or maybe he'd asked her to keep him discreetly informed about Blanche's state of health. Both of those—to our pre-pubescent minds—seemed much more plausible explanations than the other. We watched Verity very closely, like undercover detectives or spies in a James Bond film, but she never gave away by a word or a gesture where she went on her way home from secretarial college. This—her secrecy—was the most powerful proof we had that, whatever she was up to with Henry it was—in some way we couldn't fathom—wrong. There must be something shameful about it.

We rather enjoyed our involvement in the subterfuge, holing up in the gardens of Glenister Hall to monitor Verity's visits there, crawling commando-style through the long grass to eavesdrop on her conversations with Henry on arrival and departure.

Your three weeks were ever shrinking, and even though I then knew that your removal to Glenister Hall would only take you a walk through the woods away, there was no knowing what plans Henry might have for the remainder of your summer vacation. In the meantime, it didn't suit our purposes to bring the thing to a head. I didn't want to waste the time we had on the interrogations and recriminations I instinctively felt would be the fallout of revealing Verity's strange little secret.

That summer was happy. Even our curiosity over Verity added zest to it. You, Arthur, filled the aching hollow of my loneliness. But oddly, now, my recollection of it is like an old photograph. The colours are muted—as old photographs often are—the bright paisley of the women's dresses and the men's shirts faded to pinkish grey, their faces shadowed by the brims of straw hats so that they are indistinguishable one from another. My sisters and cousins are blurry, caught in motion, outlines that should have been in sharp relief instead shadowed, as though each one is followed by their own ghost. Only you remain, a clear focal point in time-defying, eye-searing technicolour; wiry but strong, your eyes large and penetrating in your still-thin face. You alone are sharply defined amid the smudge of movement generated by the rest of us, your hair always a fiery beacon in the faded image.

Chapter Thirteen

I never felt especially close to either of my sisters but, of the two of them, it was Verity with whom I had the most acrimonious relationship. The nine-year age gap between us always seemed unbridgeable, and then Verity was always such a scheming, sneaking person, a morass of hidden agendas and dark-doings. Her name might mean "truth," but honesty was a quality she lacked. And so was kindness. She had frequently been mean to me, and so now I had some information about her—even though I didn't quite understand it—I liked the idea of getting my own back.

So, for the time being, I didn't reveal Verity's secret but invested it like money in a bank, putting it away in the hope that one day I could withdraw it to find it bigger, more useful and hopefully more comprehensible to me.

You went off to Glenister Hall at the end of your three weeks with us and almost immediately were taken abroad for the remainder of the vacation. Our plans to meet up in the woods between our two houses all came to nothing. I didn't see you at all in the autumn half-term. I'd started at secondary school and was burdened down with homework, the task of navigating my way round both the bewildering corridors of my new school and the complex and surprisingly bitchy minefield of teenage girls' relationships, plus the onset of my periods. The whole of the new intake was taken away for the autumn half-term break for a week of rock-climbing, orienteering, hiking and canoeing. "Team-building" they called it. I called it sheer hell. I didn't make friends with any of my classmates and apart from a nasty, sloppy snog inexpertly foisted on me in the bushes by some chancer probably dared to kiss the grumpy girl in tooth-braces, I managed to keep myself to myself. By the time I returned home—full of a cold no doubt courtesy of the snogger—you'd gone back to school.

For many reasons, that Christmas of 1970 wasn't a happy one. You spent it at Glenister Hall; on its own, that was enough to spoil the festivities, as far as I was concerned. It was a white Christmas—but not a pretty one—with gale-force arctic winds that banked the snow up against hedgerows and froze the ground underfoot. Even so, what fun we could have had!

Erin's hospital treatment in the summer had been deemed "a success" and yet had taken so much out of her that it hardly appeared to be an improvement. By December she was thinner and paler than ever, and her hair had all fallen out; she looked more like an old lady than the beautiful, golden seventeen-year-old she ought to have been. Her habit of staring into some far distance only she could see was more noticeable. She spent many hours on

Granny's sofa, swathed in blankets although the fire was always alight, her pale eyes fixed on the flames in the grate, her empty hands small and vulnerable on her lap.

Hester and the girls did not join us at all. Hester had met a man at the National Trust garden where she had done her placement and the two had been corresponding. She and the twins were to spend Christmas with him in Northumberland.

I watched Verity closely for signs of restlessness. With *you* at Glenister Hall I assumed she would be forced to stay away from Henry. She had completed her shorthand and typing course and was now employed at an accountant's office in town. She went out a couple of nights a week "with friends" but never mentioned a boyfriend.

We spent Christmas Eve at Granny's. It was cosy, being indoors while the blizzard howled around the house like a banshee. Granny worried that the electricity might go out. I was lonely in my attic room but also oddly excited. I could hear the trees in the forest creaking in the wind.

On Christmas morning Verity annoyed me by snatching up my new Rubik's cube and mixing up the squares—I never did solve it—then went off to help prepare the vegetables before I could remonstrate with her. Grace couldn't wait to get out of the house and to the pub, where she was to work the lunchtime shift. She was sixteen by then, and unofficially engaged to Gary Bell. She had given up ideas of sixth form and university and taken employment in the pub instead, collecting glasses and helping in the kitchen. I know my mother was bitterly disappointed. Not that she disliked Gary—he was personable enough—but Mum had wanted more for Grace than the life of a publican's wife.

Jack was absorbed in his *Dandy* annual, Verity busy trying on the new makeup she'd received, the women were cooking and the men out doing various chores on the property. By half past nine I was bored out of my mind.

Possibly as a consequence of Eric's demise in that *other* storm, we were debarred from entering the woods to find our traditional Yule log—a long-established Day Christmas morning activity—but I donned boots and a thick coat and stumped off into the woods without giving any explanation as to where I was going. In the summer, you and I had made a tentative arrangement to *rendezvous* at a certain location in the woods, and I headed there in defiance of my personal safety, just in case you'd been able to get away too.

The slog up the Christmas tree plantation was hard, into the teeth of the wind—I fell into the drift at the side of the hedge more than once. But once I got into the woods things were calmer. The bare canopy high above me crashed and slashed but between the trunks the air was eerily still. Snowflakes fell, but not many. They hissed as they hit the tilth of the forest floor and it sounded as though the forest was whispering. Snow crystals lay atop the wilted undergrowth like tiny premature snowdrops. Dimly, I could hear the smash of waves on the shore and half of me wanted to head that way to watch the spume of water on the rocks, but the relative stillness beneath the trees was too awesome and somehow portentous, so I made my slow way along the pathways, narrowing my eyes to peer into the shadowy depths of the woods.

I saw the white, bobbing rear of a roe deer, heard the delicate snap of twigs as she bounded away. A badger had made a new set in the sandy bank beneath an ancient beech tree. I wondered if that other posse of woodland inhabitants would materialise—the fictional and fantastical characters who had been the companions of my early years—but my pleasurable anticipation of seeing *you* made them paltry and irrelevant. I didn't need them anymore. I had a real friend. I had you.

I arrived at our *rendezvous* but there was no sign of you. I cast around to see if you'd left me any kind of message, and berated myself for not bringing anything I could leave for you. My pockets contained only a manky tissue and a rock-hard stick of chewing gum. I kicked around in the undergrowth for a while, my hands thrust into my pockets, wondering if I should continue towards Glenister Hall. It was possible that I might meet you on your way from there. I squinted up at what I could see of the sky through the network of branches above me. It seemed to me that the sky was darkening, its bruised purple deepening to an angrier violet. I sighed and turned for home.

And that's when I saw it again—the queer, tree-spirit I'd encountered on the day that Eric died. It was swathed in green again but now—against the grey-brown and silver trunks of the trees and the peppered white forest floor—the colour was less effective a camouflage than it had been in the summer. I could see that the covering was a cape or coat—long and oversized, furred with moss or possibly mould. The hem of the garment touched the ground as the figure stood—perfectly still—about thirty yards away from me. The apparel had a capacious hood that completely swallowed the head of its wearer so that I could make out nothing at all of its sex, age, or appearance. I can hardly describe my feelings as we stood there and looked at one another across the dim, hissing, whispering woodland. I wasn't afraid, I don't think. The thing posed no threat and in fact had helped me a great deal at our last encounter. But I was surprised. Hadn't I just come to the conclusion that these manifestations were a thing of the past? I was startled and almost mesmerised by its motionless, watchful demeanour. It had a human form—no doubt of that—but it seemed so completely indigenous to the woods, as though it had grown there like the trees themselves, the rocks, the undergrowth and sky.

Then it turned and walked away and was soon lost amongst the brush.

When I got back to Broadacres I met Verity on her way out, swathed—like me—in sensible outdoor gear. She had Podge on a lead—clearly very reluctant to go for a walk—but the snow did seem to be abating somewhat and I supposed that it was as good an opportunity as any to give the dog some exercise. We didn't speak as we passed each other.

I collected an armful of logs from the woodpile and dumped them in the basket in the back porch before divesting myself of my outdoor clothing. No one seemed to have missed me, particularly. Mum asked me to lend a hand setting the table.

Verity was gone for quite a long while but returned in good time for the meal, bright-eyed, with a face that was flushed with cold and exercise. She exuded suspiciously good humour, which alerted me to mischief, and I hadn't forgotten about the Rubik's cube. I was determined to get my own back if I could.

Granny delayed Christmas lunch so that Grace could come home and eat with us between her shifts but we all got the strong impression that Grace would rather have stayed with the Bells, and she had clearly had a falling-out with Verity. The two looked daggers at each other but didn't exchange a single word over lunch. This intrigued me and I remained vigilant, keen to get to the bottom of whatever was going on.

Your mother's alcoholism had been getting more pronounced since the summer and there had been talk of treatment at a residential centre somewhere down country. She had promised—and succeeded to a degree—to curb her consumption, and as a gesture of good faith had shown Granny the loose floorboard in her room where she kept her stash of vodka. In response, my grandparents had redoubled their efforts to find some occupation for her on the property that would take her out of the house and into the fresh air, away from the temptation of the drinks cupboard, which was not locked, Blanche's weakness notwithstanding. My father was teaching Blanche to drive with the idea that she could take over some of the delivery rounds. My mother had initiated her into the complexities of bookkeeping. Neither of these schemes had borne much fruit in any practical way, but the kindly attention and patient goodwill, especially of my father, did seem to have mitigated Blanche's introspection somewhat. Even so, I noticed that Grandad's hand with the gin was markedly less liberal that year and Granny put so little brandy round the pudding it hardly flamed at all. We were all on tenterhooks, eager to avoid the situation that would see Blanche rise on a brief tide of giggling good-humour before plunging into an abyss of inebriated despair.

The smaller gathering around the table, Erin's inability to eat more than a mouthful or two of turkey, Grace's keenness to get the whole deal over with so she could get back to Gary and the crackle of animosity amongst we three sisters all cast a pall that even the most determined efforts of the others with crackers, paper hats and mottos could not dispel.

And I'll be honest with you, Arthur, I was worried about you. Now that I'd seen Glenister Hall with my own eyes—its inhospitable rooms and cold, neglected atmosphere—I couldn't imagine what kind of Christmas you might have there. I hadn't seen sight or sound of your grandparents but their "eccentricity" was well-known. How might that manifest itself? And Henry was no one's idea of fun company. The best I could come up with was a plentiful—if mass-produced—Christmas dinner eaten before a warm— perhaps electric—fire in a snug and comfortable little room with a television. After the Queen's speech there would be *Billy Smart's Christmas Spectacular*, *Disney Time* and then a pantomime of *Robinson Crusoe*. Even that scenario felt lacklustre, to say the least.

Perhaps Blanche was worried about you too. Towards the end of the meal she excused herself, her eyes swollen with tears we all knew she would barely contain before gaining the privacy of her room. Grandad took the opportunity to replenish the adults' wine glasses while they girded themselves for the task of soothing and encouragement that we knew would be required. The grownups looked at each other. Which one of them would go up to Blanche, was the unspoken question.

'At least there's no alcohol in her room these days,' Granny murmured. 'I can't think how she used to get hold of it. She never leaves the house.'

Grace and Verity exchanged a venomous look that further piqued my interest.

At last Uncle Victor heaved himself to his feet but my father said, 'That's all right, Victor. I'll go. I'll tell her I've booked her in for her driving test. It might cheer her up.'

Grace rose abruptly and began to gather up our used dishes. 'I'll put these in the kitchen Granny,' she said, clashing the lid of a tureen down. 'I'm sorry I can't stay and help with the dishes. I'm due back on shift.'

'I'll help,' said Verity with nauseating sweetness.

The two exited the room and I heard a fierce but whispered conference in the kitchen as they stacked the dishes by the sink.

'What's got into those two?' Isobel asked, but then, not waiting for an answer said, 'Erin darling, you look exhausted. Let's go through to the other room and get you comfortable.'

Jack said, 'Can we watch *Billy Smart's Circus?* With any luck the lion might eat the circus master.' He followed his mother and sister from the room.

The prospect of the television was tempting but I was too intrigued by whatever was going on in the kitchen. I picked up the sauce boat and was in the kitchen just in time to hear Grace hiss, 'What were you *thinking?*'

Verity, in a pleading and conciliatory tone I had never heard her use before wailed, 'I don't know. She asked me and I didn't know how to say no.'

'Who did?' I asked, 'and what did she want?'

'None of your business Prue,' Verity snapped, giving me a little shove as she bustled past me to get a clean tea towel from a drawer.

'And who dropped you off?' Grace went on. 'It was madness to take a car out with the roads as they are. Mum will be furious if she finds out you were stupid enough to get into one.'

Verity snapped, 'You'd better not *tell* her then, had you? In the same way she won't find out from *me* what you and Gary get up to.'

I decided to stir the pot. 'I expect it was Henry Glenister,' I said, and then to Grace, 'What *do* you and Gary get up to?'

From the doorway, my mother said, 'Yes indeed. That's what I'd like to know. Or perhaps I wouldn't. And what's this about Henry?'

We all turned to look at her aghast; none of us had realised she was within earshot.

Grace stammered, 'I saw a car in the village—in this blizzard! Prue thought it might have been his.'

Mum arched an eyebrow at me. 'Of all the cars it *might* have been, you guessed it was Henry's. How come?' Then she turned to Verity. 'And you got out of it?'

Verity might have extricated herself even then by denying the car had been Henry Glenister's, but she didn't think quickly enough. 'He picked me up along the lane,' she mumbled. 'Podge was struggling with the snow drifts.'

It was plausible, but Mum didn't buy it. 'But he didn't bring you all the way home? How odd.'

'No, he dropped me outside the pub.' Verity turned and busied herself with the dishes, running water noisily into the sink, clashing the plates against one another, playing for time.

'Why?'

'I wanted to see if Grace was ready to walk home,' Verity threw out, but this idea hadn't the least glint of credibility. In those days Grace and Verity did not seek out one another's company. Grace's mouth flapped in astonishment, perhaps at Verity's lameness in coming up with this far-fetched explanation or—more likely—at being drawn into Verity's web of untruths.

Mum turned to Grace. 'Is that right Grace?'

I could see Grace struggling with her dilemma. Should she reveal whatever it was she knew? If she did, would Verity spill all the beans she held about Gary? It was an unenviable quandary, and my sympathies were with Grace. I could probably save her if I told what I knew about Verity.

For the time being I was saved from having to make my choice by the arrival of our father from upstairs. He held out a bottle of vodka, more than half empty. 'Does anyone know how Blanche got hold of this?' he demanded fiercely. 'She's being violently sick up there. She must have drunk it straight off. I know she didn't have it yesterday.' He eyed Verity and Grace. 'You two are the only ones who have been out of the house aren't you? And only the pub is open. One way or another this *must* have come from there.'

Ah, I thought. So that's it.

'Oh Grace,' Mum wailed. 'How could you?'

That was too much for Grace. '*I* didn't buy it for her,' she shouted. 'How could you even think such a thing?' She threw a fiery look at Verity's back. She spoke no word of accusation, but she didn't need to.

'Verity!' my father thundered, holding the bottle aloft like an awful exhibit. 'Did you buy this for Blanche?'

They must have forgotten about me. Ordinarily I'd have been sent from the room, but by some miracle I was permitted to remain. I stood very still and tried not to breathe.

Slowly, Verity turned from the sink. Her face was a picture of remorse—abject and appalled—but her eyes were steely. She threw out a look loaded with dire warning that encompassed both Grace and me even as she wrung her sudsy hands, entering into role. 'She begged me,' she burst out. 'Oh Daddy, she gave me the money and then wouldn't take it back. What was I to do? Refuse? What excuse could I have made? I *am* old enough to buy alcohol. And she said …' but here she faltered, fearing that she had gone too far. The gimlet light in her eye went out to be replaced by blind panic. Now she looked to Grace and me for aid, but what could we do, even if we wanted to? We exchanged helpless looks.

'What else did she say?' Dad's voice was low but insistent.

'Oh no. Well, nothing really—'

'Verity!'

My sister, backed into a corner, mumbled, 'About … that time … you know, when she said … she thought she saw … Henry and me … kissing.'

Kissing? I had believed the whole episode to be about a burnt lampshade! I almost willed myself to become invisible. To be expelled from the room *now* would be a disaster.

'What about it?' Dad said, ominously grave.

Suddenly the words were spewing out of Verity, much like the Christmas dinner must have spewed from Blanche. Tears erupted from Verity's eyes and began to pour down her cheeks. 'She said I *owed* her. She's held that over me ever since,' she blubbed, 'always accusing me when there's no one else there, and looking daggers the rest of the time!'

'Oh Verity,' Mum cried, lifting a sympathetic hand.

My mind worked furiously. Accusing her? What of? *Oh* ... of kissing Henry!

So many pennies were dropping it was a surprise not to see them glinting and winking across Granny's kitchen floor. The furore over the broken lamp appeared in an entirely new light. Doubtless Blanche, on her return to the sitting room from the lavatory, had surprised Henry and Verity in a clinch. No wonder Blanche had screamed, sending Verity to a place of refuge behind Grandad's chair and Henry cannoning into the standard lamp, knocking it into the fireplace. Blanche's hysterical tirade had been an accusation, but no one had taken her seriously and eventually Grandad had slapped her into silence.

Finally I understood the mysterious connection between Verity and Henry; after all, and as impossible as the notion seemed, it *was* simply a hole-in-corner affair. For Verity, I supposed that was absolutely true to type. But why had she chosen Henry Glenister for her grubby liaison? He'd always been so stiff and stuffy. He wasn't remotely handsome. What on earth did she see in him? I hadn't time then to pursue these thoughts to any logical conclusion as the horrible family drama continued to play itself out amongst the dirty dishes.

'She's been *blackmailing* you?' Dad roared. 'All this time?'

'Y ... yes.' Verity agreed, but very hesitantly, unsure of her ground. What was she admitting to? Once more she attempted to inveigle Grace into her plot, to shore it up. 'And always trying to wheedle other people's secrets out of me. Not that I know any, of course.' She turned an innocently enquiring face towards Grace. 'Has she ever asked *you* to buy vodka for her, Grace?'

Grace shook her head, but now it was her turn to look embattled. 'What secrets could *I* have?' she croaked, answering a question that had not been asked.

'I think that's where I came in,' said Mum faintly, looking reproachfully at Grace.

I think now that Mum saw the whole truth, as I did. Verity's denials in the face of Blanche's allegations had been lies. For two years Verity had maintained her innocence when in fact ... and worse, to keep Blanche quiet she'd been abetting her alcoholism. That must have been a bitter blow. And as for Grace and Gary, you only needed to look at Grace's beetroot face to see that their relationship had gone far beyond kissing and holding hands. Poor Mum. How disillusioned she must have felt.

But Dad, for the moment, was blind to the deeper layers of deceit, to his daughters' mendacity. His anger was focused on Blanche, the poor, hapless victim of Verity's subterfuge. 'Good God,' he erupted. He swivelled to confront my mother. 'In our own house! After all we've done for her! This is how she repays us, is it?' He still held the bottle and for an awful moment I thought he was going to hit Mum with it, but instead he motioned with it towards the ceiling to where Blanche was presumably crouched over the toilet bowl or lying semi-comatose on the floor of her room.

The atmosphere in the room was so terrible I thought I was going to choke. The smell of congealing scraps and the greasy turkey carcass was nauseating. I'd never heard Dad address Mum with such spleen and although she held her ground, her face was white. Her bloodless lips formed words but I couldn't make them out.

'I can't believe it of her,' Dad spat out. He turned and slammed the bottle down on the kitchen table. Then I saw his eyes, swimming with tears—of disappointment, I identified. Hadn't they been just the same after Eric's death? But that time *I* had been the cause. Now his disappointment was directed at Blanche. As easy as it would have been to restoke the flames of my resentment against the Glenisters by allowing my parents to believe the dreadful calumny that Verity had conjured to protect herself, I could see that this was simply unfair. Blanche was a troublesome burden and no doubt she harboured a bitter resentment against Verity, but she had her reasons. My mother's words after Eric's death came powerfully back to me: "actions have consequences." It wasn't right for Verity—or Henry—to walk away from theirs.

So I opened my mouth. 'I expect Verity *was* kissing Henry,' I declared. 'She has been visiting him in secret for months. I saw her at Glenister Hall in the summer, lots of times. He must have ...' I fumbled for the word, '... *seduced* her.'

Somewhere in the distance I could hear the tinny noise of laughter and applause from the television. It seemed such an odd response to what I'd said. The rest of the house was absolutely quiet with an intense, listening silence. The air in the kitchen had all been sucked away. I felt the weight of snow on the roof pressing down.

Then Verity broke the spell. She screamed, 'You little bitch,' and crossed the kitchen, slapping me so hard across the face that I was sent cannoning into the stove. Fortunately, it was cooling now, otherwise I might have been seriously burnt. Grace and my mother both cried out and Grace hurled herself into Mum's arms.

My father, whose disenchantment with Blanche can have been *nothing* in comparison to *this* revelation, lunged forward and grabbed hold of Verity before she could attack me again. 'Is this true?' he yelled, shaking her hard.

That's when Grandad appeared at the kitchen door. His face was a funny colour, and all out of shape. He muttered something. He had saliva dribbling down his chin. He reached out for the door jamb, missed, and fell to the floor like an empty sack.

The family argument was instantly forgotten. Mum pushed Grace from her embrace and ran from the kitchen to where the telephone was located in the hallway. Dad knelt at Grandad's side and tried to raise him up. Verity called for Granny in a shriek like a banshee, bringing all the rest of the family crowding into the hall.

My feeling of self-righteous pleasure in having exposed Verity's secret so effectively completely vanished, leaving me with a sick, hollow sense of having released a cat that would have been much better left in its bag.

Chapter Fourteen

There's a storm, Arthur. Such a pity—the apple blossoms have just set. It will all be spoiled and the apple harvest will … but what does it matter now? Those trees in the old orchard haven't been pruned for years. Such fruit as they produce is left on the ground to rot. What a waste. I dread to think what Grandad would say.

I still visit him in the church cemetery. I visit them *all,* one way or another. The churchyard is quiet and peaceful at night, which is the time I am generally abroad. I get no sense of unfinished business, of remorse or lingering accusation. That comforts me because I harbour none myself. I've faced my mistakes—and they are legion—and made peace with them. The Verity-Henry thing, for example. I saw *that* in entirely the wrong way.

It all went back to that doomed picnic; an episode I was reluctant—for obvious reasons—to revisit. But once the scales fell from my eyes, things that seemed merely curious to me at the time took on a new and more sinister significance. Didn't the two of them lag behind on the way to the cove? What occurred in that quarter of an hour they were out of view while the other adults manhandled the barrows down the boulder steps? Wasn't it strange that Henry loitered near Verity's little encampment for so long? What had they been speaking of as I looked down upon them from my rock-pool eyrie? Why didn't it strike any of the adults as odd when Henry chose to shelter beneath Verity's tree and not Blanche's when the storm struck?

I'm not saying Verity wasn't willing, caught up in the thrill and apparent romance of it—her first crush. She was only fourteen! She can't have known what she was getting herself into! Look how she literally stripped off and laid herself on a plate on the beach that day! But isn't that how abusers work, exploiting weakness and gradually sucking their victims into compliance? Verity must have believed that driving to Glenister Hall every afternoon on her way home from college was her choice when, of course, it wasn't.

However we might see it with hindsight, at the time it was taken at face value. My mother said Verity had made her bed and must be made to lie in it. She and Dad drove over to Glenister Hall the day after Boxing Day, when the snow had abated enough to make driving safe. What occurred there I can't say. You probably know better than I do. The upshot was that Henry and Verity were to be married.

It seems very old-fashioned now. It might have been old-fashioned *then.* We were children of the sixties—the age of the permissive society, counterculture and the generation gap—but to all intents and purposes the

Days existed outside of all that. My grandparents and even my parents remained firmly entrenched in the first half of the century. They'd lived through wars—Granny and Grandad through two of them—and seen peace and prosperity replace the carnage of the trenches and the blitz. They were content to have survived, to be well-fed and housed, to have family around them. These were the important things. Ideologies and progress meant nothing to them. The wider world was a frightening place where they had no desire to go and from which they sought to protect their offspring. They believed in tradition, in old-fashioned values, in moral rectitude and personal responsibility. At the time it seemed nice to me—loving and safeguarding—that Granny and Grandad kept all the children around them, provided work and homes and maintained an iron-clad family unity. But later I came to wonder if it wasn't a bit … controlling. Mum, Isobel and Hester—did they resent Granny's matriarchal dominance? Those two- or three-times weekly meals at Granny's—were we invited? Or summoned? I wonder how much pressure had been put on Dad to give up the London law practice and come back to Salad Days. As far as I knew his siblings had never even attempted to leave the area. Was that because they knew Granny and Grandad would somehow prevent it? Dad and Isobel had married into respectable, local families and although Hester had been born a southerner she had migrated north of her own volition and there was no question of her going back and taking Eric away with her.

It wasn't until I began at secondary school that I realised how behind the times I was in so many ways. I'd never used makeup. I was ignorant of current fashion and teen culture. I was sexually innocent and morally hidebound—just like my parents and grandparents. I had no idea of it, but by the 1970s pre-marital sex was common, girls were on the pill and condoms were to be bought easily across the counter of any high street pharmacy. The idea of a girl being "ruined" at the precipitate loss of her virginity was ridiculous and I realise now that in many families Verity would not have been compelled to marry. But to my parents there was no alternative, and I must say that, at the time, Verity seemed deliriously happy about it. Henry agreed to "do the honourable thing" and "make a decent woman" of my sister—these are the terms I can imagine my parents using. He was then forty-two years old. She had just turned nineteen.

Surprisingly, it was only my grandparents who were unhappy, but they did not interfere. They *could* not interfere. Grandad's stroke was serious and had a lasting impact. Granny was traumatised by the long wait for the ambulance as it made its tortured way through the blizzard, the hours sitting in chilly hospital corridors and the days of waiting to see what the outcome would be. She aged a decade in just a fortnight. When he finally came home Grandad couldn't speak, a disability that annoyed him intensely. He would thrash about in his chair making incoherent roaring noises but no one—not even Granny—could make anything of them. His left side was paralysed and he needed twenty-four-hour personal care that took all Granny's strength and forbearance to supply. Grandad was not a good patient, the stroke seeming to have swept from him all his former good humour and quiet serenity. From that time on he was sour and curmudgeonly, his brow etched by a permanent scowl. He could take no more active role in Salad Days. As spring of 1971 came on—a late spring that year, delaying sowing of the salad crops—he was strong enough to be brought out and wheeled about the property as Granny and Dad went through the motions of consulting him about planting and crop rotation, interpreting his sullen silences or inarticulate grunts as agreement to whatever they suggested.

Mick Pullman did his best to plug the gap that Grandad had left, and Bradley Fox, who had retired the year before, agreed to come back to work a few hours notwithstanding his rheumatism. Even with their help, Dad and Granny could hardly keep up with the physical work required and we kids were drafted in to take on more. Jack had two more years of school until he could leave, but declared his intention of coming to work full time at Salad Days the moment his last exam was done. In the meantime, he worked on the property every afternoon. Grace relinquished her daytime shifts at the pub so that she could put in more hours, and even brought Gary with her sometimes. Erin did her best to free Mum up for deliveries by helping in the office, although she frequently got tired and had to be taken home. Victor and Isobel were too tied up with the shop and the dairy to do much on the land but tried to take the weight off Granny by cooking up the family's meals.

What amazed us all was how much Grandad had done, on his own, that now required the input of almost the entire family to make good.

Hester proved a godsend. Her course completed and her liaison with the man in Northumberland declared "a mistake," she threw herself into the business, bringing all her horticultural knowledge to bear. She and Dad clashed quite often as she insisted on new techniques, different seed stock and, in particular, a "no-dig" approach that she said would save hours of heavy labour and enrich the soil. Dad and Hester had quite a few battles over the way the business was run, but in the end he had to let her have her own way because of course a corollary to Verity's engagement to Henry was that he and Blanche would have to be divorced.

Dad's law qualification meant that he became her chief advisor as they negotiated the complexities of the Glenister estate, plumbed Henry's finances and tried to arrange who should have the management of you. It was to become fairly nasty, as Henry at first argued that Blanche was an unfit mother and sued for full custody. Where nothing else had persuaded Blanche into sobriety, this did. I think that will please you, won't it Arthur? She began to attend sessions of Alcoholics Anonymous and gradually weaned herself off the sedatives the doctor had been prescribing to her since the split. She emerged from her battle with depression and addiction as a butterfly emerges from its chrysalis—a transformed creature. She was helpful about the house, sitting with Grandad on wet or windy days when he could not go outside, painstakingly reading seed catalogues and articles from *Farmers' Weekly* aloud. Some afternoons Isobel would arrive with a vat of casserole to find that Blanche had made a start on the vegetables. She washed her hair and took pride in her appearance, something that had gone by the wayside in her doldrum days. She passed her driving test. From being an unkempt, overly emotional drunk, old before her time, she regenerated, becoming girlish and giggly, charmingly forgetful, as adorably timid as a kitten. She came across as much younger than her twenty-seven years.

When you came home for the summer holidays that year, I think you hardly recognised her. In her newfound confidence she took you away to London for a few days to visit museums and see *Show Boat*. I was jealous—I'd so looked forward to your coming back to Broadacres and I had a hundred plans for our time together—but I couldn't begrudge you time with your mother. In truth I felt that Blanche had coped so well with the whole situation—accepting not only Verity's apology but the whole family's acknowledgement that she had been right all along about what she had seen in the sitting room that November afternoon in 1969. She'd come to terms with the need to divorce Henry and she'd tackled her demons. I couldn't deny either of you the chance to begin afresh.

You and I had a good time that summer I think, although the details are hazy. Grandad's illness threw a pall over us all. I think we felt that the foundations of an edifice we'd believed would last for ever were beginning to crumble. We didn't wander as far from home as we had the previous year, fearing, I think, that something catastrophic might happen while we were away. We were permitted to occupy our old beds in the attic although, to be truthful, we were both getting too big for them. *You* were, especially, Arthur. How tall and rangy you were, even for a ten-year-old! I'd feared that the onset of my periods would signal my removal from the attic. I'd worked out that this had been the catalyst for the other girls being found sleeping accommodations elsewhere in the house. I'd considered the possibility ahead of time and decided that if Granny insisted I sleep in a different room to you,

I'd creep up in the night and join you, even if I had to sleep on the floor. The idea of you spending the nights alone in the attic was too sad to contemplate, and I was determined to save you from the prospect. However, we were put up there together. Your rubber sheet remained in place although in point of fact you didn't seem to need it anymore. I was happy about that, figuring that whatever trauma had necessitated it—the shock of your new school, the split up of your parents—had subsided.

I don't know if you recall it, Arthur, but I do, all too vividly: the sound of Grandad in the room below us; the continuous, low moan of his distress—heartbreakingly sad and also terribly unnerving—and Granny's sobbing attempts to soothe and reassure him. The sounds rose up to us there in the attic and melded with the lament of the wind in the eaves, the lonely call of a barn owl in the woods. I think we both lay there, not sleeping, not knowing what to say.

In the autumn of 1971 Grandad caught a chill that turned into a chest infection, and by Christmas he was dead. He was seventy-five years old when he died. He had been hale and healthy and a dynamo of energy, easily equal to twelve-hour days on the property, still full of vitality when the younger men began to flag. He was the cornerstone of the Day family and his death left a vacuum that the next generation vied to fill.

His funeral was a sombre affair, the chill, gloomy January day doing nothing to alleviate the shock and grief that overlaid the entire family like a damp blanket. The whole village turned out to pay their respects as we Days walked behind the hearse the short distance between Broadacres and the church. Friends and neighbours lined the way, the men removing their hats, the women dipping their heads. Granny walked directly behind the sleek black car, flanked by her two remaining children, my father and Isobel. Victor came next, between my mother and Aunt Hester. We children followed. I walked between my sisters. Kath and Kaz helped Erin and then last of all came Jack, acting as a rear guard, perhaps sensible for the first time of the weight of Day family expectations upon his shoulders.

When we got to the church its pews were packed with mourners and many more stood outside. I saw you, brought back from school for the occasion, sandwiched between your parents on the second row from the front. You wore your school uniform. I'd never seen you in it before. It made you seem much older—crisp white shirt, neat black tie, flannel trousers and a smart grey blazer. You rose as the coffin passed and I saw that you were half a head taller than your mother. She sat closest to the aisle and snuffled into a handkerchief, but she reached out a hand and touched my father's arm as he passed by. Your father, on your other side, stared rigidly at the altar. Beside me, I could see Verity trying to catch his eye, to receive some sign of sympathy or concern, but she received none.

We filed into the front pew, just in front of you. I felt your hand on my shoulder, Arthur, a brief squeeze, but it meant a lot. I recall looking around to smile in response, and that's when I saw the two other people on your row.

I'd never seen your Glenister grandparents before, or I didn't think I had. I couldn't help staring. Seeing them here, in the village, was so very unusual and I was aware that others, like me, were craning to get a view of the elusive squire and his reclusive wife. Your grandfather was a diminutive but dapper fellow wearing a beautifully tailored greatcoat, smart leather gloves and a soft, expensive-looking black scarf that together formed the sartorial epitome of funereal decorum. He was almost entirely bald but for a scraping of thin grey hair over the dome of his head. His eyes were steely beneath wiry eyebrows. His skin was very tanned and I remembered that he often played golf abroad. Had he flown home especially for Grandad's funeral? From the Glenisters, that was quite a gesture. He sat very still and composed, his face neutral but also somehow lordly. In this respect alone did he bear any resemblance to his son Henry.

Your grandmother was as different to her husband as possible, portly where he was thin, and clothed in a curious and not entirely appropriate ensemble—a shabby brown tweed coat buttoned up wrong so that the collar stood out awkwardly, a rather gay silk scarf knotted clumsily at her neck, a balding velvet hat squashed onto her halo of grey, unkempt hair. Her face, despite its round fleshiness, was much lined and weathered, like the bark of a tree. She looked—to me—so old as to be almost beyond time, ancient as standing stones. Her hands were large, unadorned by jewellery of any kind and not very clean. They clasped a grubby handkerchief to her mouth but it did not quite muffle the little mews and groans of distress that issued from it in cracked, hoarse tones. Her eyes poured tears she made no attempt to staunch. Her shoulders shook with grief. She was as discomposed as her husband was poised, but he made no gesture and spoke no word of comfort or reassurance.

Suddenly she met my eye and something—some connection or bolt of sympathy—crossed the little space between us before a loud chord from the organ announced the first hymn.

Afterwards, I looked for you. Both outside the church where the congregation milled about and examined the floral tributes, and in the function room of the pub, where Granny had provided sandwiches and cake, huge pots of boiling tea and glasses of whisky and sherry. But none of the Glenisters showed their faces after the service. After all Grandad had done for them, I thought your parents slipping away like that was outrageously rude, and added their lack of respect to my stockpile of resentment against them.

We will never know what caused Grandad's stroke I suppose, but I can't help feeling that *again* Henry Glenister and his malign interference in our family was at the root of it. How much of the argument in the kitchen had Grandad overheard? How much of its subtler nuances had he understood? Was it Blanche's relapse that tipped him over? Or Verity's fall from grace? Either way, if you trace it back, Henry was the fundamental cause.

Chapter Fifteen

It proved quite simple for Henry and Blanche to divorce one another. The Act of 1969 allowed for the irretrievable breakdown of a marriage without either partner having to prove the other was at fault. What took far longer to negotiate was the financial settlement that had to be agreed upon in tandem with the divorce. Glenister Hall was in a parlous state, but the family still had money and were obliged to provide for Blanche, who had none. Interestingly, your father's most lucrative source of income was his mother, who came from old aristocratic stock bringing a considerable dowry. It was only the terms cunningly devised by her family lawyer that had prevented her whole fortune from being sunk into the house. Theoretically, Henry—her only child—was her sole beneficiary, but his legal team argued that as she was still alive, any potential inheritance from her could not form part of a divorce settlement. Who could say how her will might dispose of her money? Certainly not old Mrs Glenister herself, who by that time, was hardly competent to dispose of a paper handkerchief, let alone her fortune.

Nevertheless, Henry did receive a generous income from her financial holdings, and he had monetary dealings of his own that he revealed very reluctantly to the scrutiny of my father, acting on Blanche's behalf. You might argue that Dad was the last person to act for Blanche. Wasn't it in his interest to make sure that Henry got the best of the bargain, since Dad's own daughter was to be the replacement Mrs Glenister? Dad did attempt most earnestly to persuade your mother to consult another lawyer, but she would have none of it, becoming tearful at the very suggestion and tugging pitifully at the lapel of his jacket. The most she would agree to was the involvement of a third party— her brother, Uncle Victor. He looked over the various draft agreements, but it was Dad and Blanche who spent many hours closeted together countering the bullish letters that came from Henry's solicitor. All of 1971 and most of 1972 went by before the parties arrived at any kind of agreement.

In the meantime, work on Salad Days went on, the whole family pitching in to make good for Grandad's loss. Dad's preoccupation with Blanche's affairs meant that Hester took over the management of the business. In some ways this proved to be a very good thing. She foresaw that the rise of the supermarket would mean the commensurate demise of the small, local greengrocers who were our bread-and-butter customers. What's more, the seventies saw the increasing importation of fruit and vegetables from abroad. People began to expect to eat tomatoes at Christmas and asparagus in November as well as exotic produce that we couldn't grow in the UK at all.

Domestic freezers and a general move towards prepared convenience foods further undermined our business. Hester proposed we broaden our scope from just fruit and vegetables to include shrubs, perennials and annuals. Salad Days would become a garden centre. These were on the rise. A big upsurge in house building—specifically new homes with gardens—and in home ownership, plus horticultural improvements, meant that gardening became a popular national pastime, widespread amongst the rising middle classes. We would still produce seasonal fruit and vegetables and continue to supply those of our customers who remained in business, but we wouldn't be solely dependent on them.

Hester began to buy in a selection of perennials and shrubs for propagation even while the family discussed the proposed changes. Additionally, she mooted the building of a farm shop at the entrance to the property, where we could sell our own produce and that of other local artisan makers direct to the public, plus the shrubs, perennials and annuals we were already beginning to raise ourselves. It was a huge change of direction, hotly debated for months. Granny was reluctant to adopt the proposal and argued for the status quo but in truth, losing Grandad had eroded her strength and confidence and she eventually gave way to the urging of Isobel and Victor, who were very keen on the idea, taking Hester's side in the argument and leaving my father's lone voice in support of Granny. The new premises would be an outlet for the Bracewells' dairy produce, jams and pickles and would also provide a new production facility. The lease on the village shop was due for renewal and new food hygiene laws might require a huge investment in their current kitchen arrangements to bring them up to scratch.

Mum supported my father's opposition to Hester's scheme even though it placed her in conflict with Isobel, her closest friend up to this point. Mum quailed at the increase in administration that would inevitably fall to her lot. Bookkeeping already threatened to become more complicated by the introduction of VAT scheduled for 1973. Hester's new farm shop and the complete amalgamation of Victor and Isobel's business into Salad Days would take months of work. Mum was already stretched very thinly between the accounts, some deliveries and the extra physical labour in the polytunnels and glasshouses. Plus, she was still a "housewife" in the traditional sense; she did our laundry, cleaned our house and prepared some of our meals. She would collect me from school if I had to stay late for choir practice or a hockey match. She was the repository for my various teenage woes.

She had grasped the nettle and taken both Verity and Grace to the doctors so that they could be put on the pill, something that went against the grain of her conservative morals. I suppose she decided that a pregnancy out of wedlock would be worse. It is my belief that she kept this course of action from my father. It was impossible not to see the strain that the discovery of her two eldest daughters' secret sex lives imposed on Mum, not to mention the decision to go behind Dad's back in managing their contraceptive health.

Since that awful scene in the kitchen on Christmas Day of 1971, there had been a strange reserve between my parents, a loss of confidence. Perhaps Dad blamed Mum for Verity and Grace's sexual lassitude. Both girls had dissimulated, sneaked and lied, gone ahead and entered into sexual liaisons *knowing* he would disapprove. Maybe he was simply ashamed to have been so thoroughly hoodwinked by his oldest daughters—he had always prided himself on being so close to us all, so approachable, to know us so well. Then, after Grandad died, I suppose Dad felt undermined by Hester's competent and assured assumption of the reins of Salad Days. That can't have been pleasant, but Mum had her own burdens to carry and her alliance with Dad against the new business proposals, though staunch, might not have been as wholehearted as it could have been because it set her at odds with Isobel. Whatever it was, there was an estrangement between my parents, and Isobel— who would previously have been Mum's confidante and ally—was no help. Isobel had lost her father—of course she was grieving his loss—and Erin's health was poor. The proposed development of the business would impact Isabel and Victor hugely. No doubt both women had a lot on their minds, but rather than sympathising and supporting one another they became petty and acrimonious. I overheard the two of them having fractious exchanges over stupid little things, like whether carrots should be cut in rounds or batons, and how much butter should be added to the mashed potatoes, a situation that would have been impossible to imagine before this.

Mum was only forty-one but looked ten years older; her face was haggard, her hair often unkempt, her hands calloused, and she drooped with fatigue at the end of each day. Her habitual good humour became soured; she was often snappy and sometimes disproportionately emotional over what appeared to be quite trivial things. She complained bitterly at the difficulties of keeping our small and ancient house clean and well-maintained. Except in the height of summer it was always dark and damp, with frequent outbreaks of mould. It needed decorating. Why couldn't Dad see how dingy it looked, and do something about it, she wanted to know. But he was much too busy with Blanche to notice, she grouched. The cottage had only three bedrooms. Grace and I shared but were increasingly in each other's way. Verity might marry and move out as soon as Henry's divorce was finalised, allowing Grace to move into the vacated room, but that would not make the house any easier to clean or any less seedy.

At last Mum told Dad straight that she wanted us all to move into Broadacres. What was more natural, she argued. There was that big house with only Granny and Blanche rattling around in it. It would be Dad's one day, why not take possession now? I could see Mum's point. At Broadacres there was plenty of room for us girls with all our paraphernalia, which was spilling out of our rooms at the rented place. Blanche's room would make a decent-sized office for Mum. Surely when the divorce settlement came through Blanche would move out. The little potting shed where Mum had managed things for years would be bulldozed to make room for the new shop, so she'd need somewhere new for the filing cabinets and so on. I liked the notion that life would be easier for Mum. The modern electric oven and fire that she had insisted on at the cottage would be a liability if the coal miners' strike continued. Broadacres had an oil-fired Aga and open fires. Even without coal there was enough wood in the forest to keep us amply supplied. Last of all, I loved the idea of living permanently at Broadacres. After all, it had always felt like my *real* home.

Of course I gave a thought to you, Arthur—more than one. But I didn't think Blanche would move far away—perhaps just into the village. She might even take on the lease of our little cottage! So you wouldn't be far away from Broadacres when those precious school holidays came around.

Dad couldn't fault Mum's logic, but when he suggested the idea to Granny it turned out that Isobel had got there before him, countering all his arguments with others more persuasive still. Giving up the lease of the shop would leave the Bracewells homeless. Their current flat wasn't suitable for Erin anyway—she could barely manage the stairs some days. There was a little-used parlour at Broadacres that would make an ideal ground floor bed-sitting room for Erin. Simply knocking a door through one wall would give access to the old scullery, easily converted into a little bathroom. Mum and Dad listened aghast as Granny repeated all the contentions put forward a day or so beforehand by Isobel and Victor. Granny was sympathetic to Mum's frustrations and even offered to pay to have our rented place entirely redecorated. She said it seemed likely that Grace would marry Gary and decamp to the pub as soon as she turned eighteen, and Verity would be moving into Glenister Hall in the next few months. That would ease the overcrowding in the little house. In the meantime, Granny couldn't possibly deny Isobel and Victor a home; *they* had no alternative. And as for Blanche moving out, certainly not. They'd never get to see you, Arthur, if that happened and Granny wouldn't tolerate *that*. She claimed Blanche made herself useful in a dozen different ways these days—she was part of the family now. The only concession she was prepared to make was in the matter of

Mum's workplace. Grandad's old office in the box room would do, wouldn't it? But surely dedicated office accommodations could be included in the new premises. They'd have to ask Hester.

Mum was furious, and also terribly upset. She railed on and on about it while we walked home, and as she began to prepare supper.

'I've always been so close to Isobel,' she moaned as she fried liver and onions in a pan, 'and counted her as a friend, even a *sister*. This is a terrible betrayal, as far as I'm concerned.'

I agreed. How could Isobel have gone behind Mum's back like this? Didn't she see that she was usurping Dad's birthright? He was the oldest son, and it had always been understood that Broadacres would be ours one day. I felt sure that Granny would make things right with the other children, but the house was *always* to have been Dad's. I busied myself with setting the table while Mum violently mashed the swede-and-carrots. Dad leaned against the kitchen counter with his arms folded across his chest.

Mum said, 'It was implicit right from the start, Trevor. You know it was. Our tenancy here would be temporary; Broadacres would be our home in the end. I might not have married you otherwise,' she spat out, flinging the masher into the sink. 'I had other offers you know, *better* offers, some might say. Gary's father, for instance. He would never have *looked* at Maureen if I'd been free.'

'I know. I know,' Dad murmured. 'I promised you Broadacres would be ours and so it will be.' He reached out a placatory arm, but Mum knocked it aside. 'Just not yet,' he forged on. 'Isobel's need *is* greater than ours just now. And think of Erin. Who knows …' but he left the end of his sentence unspoken. It was unspeakable, that prospect, and even Mum, in her disappointment, could not dismiss Erin's claim.

'We'll never be able to ask them to leave,' Mum said bitterly. 'Once they're ensconced and they've got everything just as they like it—new wallpaper, new carpets—you just see if I'm not right, Trevor. We won't be consulted. Even if we can get them out, we'll have to live with whatever *she* chooses.' She slammed the plates onto the table but made no move to sit in her usual place. She stood with her hands on the back of her chair, her face a picture of woe, tears of anger and disappointment brimming. She had a smear of gravy on her cheek. Dad reached out again, to wipe away the tears or the smut, but she dodged away. 'I'm not hungry,' she threw out. 'I'm going out for a walk.'

Later that evening, when I was in bed with my light out, I heard Grace come home from the pub. She brought Mum with her. 'I had to wash *all* the glasses *and* clean the urinals,' Grace complained. 'Gary's dad couldn't be prised away from the end of the bar. Mum kept him talking the whole time.'

There was the sound of stumbling on the stairs, Mum's voice, lugubrious, '*So* many cocktails, Trevor … I didn't know the names of half of them! Oh, with *cherries* and *olives* and little *umbrellas* …'

'Lovely,' said Dad distractedly. 'Only I wish you'd told me where you were going, Lucille. I was worried. Now let's get you into bed …'

In the morning, I expected a rapprochement between my parents. Mum had a stinking hangover and asked Verity to drop me at school on her way to her office. Dad had already left for work. That evening they barely spoke a word over their smoked haddock.

Mum's coolness towards Dad extended to Isobel and Victor. We dined less often at Granny's, where Aunt Isobel now presided in the kitchen. I gathered Mum preferred to prepare our meals in her own kitchen—dingy though it might be—than to go through a charade of *bonhomie* at Broadacres while Isobel discussed alterations to the place and browsed through books of wallpaper samples. Dad would eat with us and then walk up to Granny's to discuss business, the plans for the new building or to go through paperwork with Blanche. Mum remained at home even though I was quite old enough by then to be left at home on my own. Very often I would find her in the sitting room staring into the artificial flames of the electric fire, her hands empty of the usual knitting or sewing that filled her few spare evenings.

1972 was a year of walking on eggshells, not just for us but for the whole country. A wave of sit-ins and factory occupations threatened to bring the country to its knees. People even spoke of a general strike. Violence abounded, with a proliferation of terror attacks in Northern Ireland and talk of the spreading out of the IRA's campaign to include targets on the mainland. Eleven people were killed by Arab terrorists at the Olympic games in Munich. I was thirteen years old, and my world was expanding, but the more I knew of it the more frightened I was. My instinct was to hunker down in the safety of Broadacres and Salad Days, but even there I found the shifting sands of change made life feel very uncertain.

Planning permission and various legalities delayed the breaking of ground for the new premises. Isobel and Victor extended the lease on the shop for just one additional year, not so much for the sake of the shop itself but in order to maintain the production of their various dairy lines and preserves, which had become their main source of revenue—all local village shops were finding it hard to compete with the spread of supermarkets. Even with a start-date early in 1973 the new state-of-the-art dairy and kitchen could not be ready to use before autumn. So they continued to work at the place in the village but moved themselves into Broadacres. With no one living above the premises the shop was burgled twice in quick succession. The second time the thieves attempted to cover their tracks by setting a small fire in one of the stock rooms after getting away with a large quantity of cigarettes and several cases of spirits. You could see that Isobel and Victor were torn between establishing their new ménage at Broadacres and maintaining vigil on the shop in the village. They were both tetchy and defensive, as taut as wires.

Nevertheless, they effected the alterations to the ground floor that would accommodate Erin. I noticed various changes—small, gradual, but significant—as the Bracewells took possession. The lovely, dusty book alcove beneath the stairs was removed, replaced by a telephone table with a plush seat attached to it. If you used the telephone you had to be aware that the entire house could overhear your conversation. The ancient, patterned hearthrug on which we had all lain and played in our infancy disappeared, a hideous and brightly coloured shag-pile monstrosity taking its place. The kitchen cupboards were rearranged and on the few occasions that Mum attended family dinners and assisted with the washing up, she couldn't find where anything belonged.

The lovely Mrs Gibbs, who had helped Granny for years, handed in her notice. 'Too many changes for me,' she said regretfully, folding up her apron and tucking it into her wicker basket.

Isobel declaimed airily on the new arrangements, 'So much more practical,' and 'Crying out for reorganisation for *years*.' Granny's menu of homely stews, grilled chops and roasts appeared less often. Isobel cooked exotic dishes like spaghetti Bolognese and *chilli con carne*. It wasn't as comfortable at Granny's. We all felt that there was a new regime, but we didn't know the rules. I got told off by Aunt Isobel for helping myself from the biscuit tin. Victor shouted if anyone changed the channel of the television without asking him first. We were all on tenterhooks, guests in a house that had always been home, but now wasn't.

Equally uncomfortable was the awkward triangle connecting your two parents and Verity. Henry remained obdurate about the financial settlement between himself and your mother even though it postponed his marriage to Verity. This made Verity querulous and moody whenever Henry was not around. She took it personally, blaming both sides for raining on her parade. Even my father came in for her caustic complaint. Why was he on Blanche's side? Didn't he want *his own daughter* to be happy and decently married?

Henry was now admitted back at Broadacres as Verity's fiancé but his visits there were excruciating. None of us could forget the period of his former visits, when Verity had been little more than a child. Had he set his sights on her even then? It was impossible to generate much warmth or welcome towards him even though he would soon become—as he had never been in the past—a real member of the family. He had not changed. He was still stiff and formal, very superior in his manner. I noticed that Verity abetted this attitude by fawning over him. Was he comfortable? Quite warm enough? Should she get him another cushion? She insisted he had first choice from whatever food was on offer—the largest portion, the tenderest slice, the first cup from the pot. To be honest, it nauseated me, the way she fussed around him, and it was all I could do to keep my mouth shut. At the same time, I was brought powerfully to mind of Blanche, who had been just the same, once upon a time. Now Blanche maintained what I considered an admirable restraint and composure. Usually she contrived to be busy elsewhere when Henry was in the house—just ironing those few shirts, on her way to post a letter—but there were times when she could not avoid sitting round the table *en famille*. Henry, inevitably, would take the chair that used to be Grandad's and make the authoritative pronouncements that passed for conversation with him. Sometimes he would go as far as to take up the carving knife or to pour the wine, hovering the bottle more than once over Blanche's glass, speciously forgetful. There was an air of artificial politeness amongst the rest of us and almost forced jocularity as we tried to divert attention away from Blanche's stricken face and the hands that trembled as she clutched her glass of water.

Those were strained occasions, and I think we all breathed a sigh of relief when the gravel spurted beneath the tyres of his departing car.

And then there was the standoff between Mum and Isobel that endured throughout 1972. How Dad and Victor worked out the situation I don't know. They had been friends from boyhood, and to find their wives at loggerheads can't have been easy. But I suppose, like many men, their way of dealing with the impasse was to avoid speaking of it. Mum and Isobel were brisk, ineffably polite, speaking only of practicalities like whether the washing ought to be brought in off the line—did it look like rain?—and whether Jack would be home from cricket practice in time for supper or would need a plate put to one side. Many times, Mum did not attend the family gatherings at all. Dad would make an excuse—a WI meeting, or the last-minute recollection of an overdue library book that must be returned. No one was fooled, I don't think, certainly not Isobel, who would sniff in an offended manner and remove Mum's place-setting with a martyrish air. Quite often I found the ordeal to be more than I could stomach, my old dyspepsia returning, emotional turmoil churning my innards and making a lump in my throat that I couldn't swallow down. I began to plead an overload of homework and stayed at the cottage with Mum.

It might have been my adolescent hormones, but I felt blighted, weighed down by some invisible but oppressive cloud. Many nights I knelt at my bedroom window looking despondently out at the trees, my whole self a maelstrom of emotions I could neither understand nor control. Tears pressed behind my eyes although I didn't allow them to fall. Grace slept on, oblivious to my turmoil. I mourned Grandad, of course, but also the loss of something else: my childhood; those happy years of perfect family accord that now seemed only a vague memory; and innocence.

Chapter Sixteen

Your coming for the summer holidays was the bright spot in an otherwise dark and disturbing year, Arthur, although it highlighted for me yet another change to the situation at Broadacres.

I finished my school year halfway through July and went home to pack my things—you were due back from Holmewood the following day. I assumed that, as in former years, I'd be welcomed at Broadacres for the duration of your holiday. I ran past Mum, dropped my school bag in the hall and raced upstairs to shed my hated uniform in favour of cut-off jeans and a tee shirt. I hastily packed a holdall with a selection of clothes, my toothbrush and the latest *Earthsea* novel and set off, shouting, 'Off to Granny's for the holidays,' to Mum. I pushed through the gate and passed the building site where the old potting shed, various ancillary storerooms and the compost area had been cleared away, ready for the new premises.

In those times Hester and the girls were almost always at Broadacres. She needed to be on site for consultations with the architect and the summer was our busiest time with demand for salad crops and soft fruit at its peak. She'd taken on several seasonal workers, mainly foreign students, who were housed in an old caravan and some tents in the meadow. They needed constant supervision to prevent them gathering in chattering knots or drifting off task. The twins, now sixteen, had finished school earlier that summer having taken their GCEs; they were now working full time under their mother's tutelage, learning to take root and leaf cuttings, to divide perennials and to cultivate annuals, to plant up hanging baskets and planters. They took naturally to the work, habituated—as we all were—from their earliest years. They worked hard, I'll give them that, and exceptionally long hours, often out amongst the raised beds before seven in the morning and not finishing the watering until after eight in the evening. Many times they would migrate up to the camp in the meadow, where there was guitar music and a campfire and the herby aroma of exotic cigarettes. The twins had grown into lithe and attractive young women. Rather than seeking some individuality by adopting different hairstyles or clothing, they perpetuated their identical looks. They liked the same foods, the same music, the same books and films. They continued to be the other's best friend and soulmate. To be honest, I envied them their closeness.

That day, as I walked to Broadacres, I waved to them both as they stretched their backs from harvesting lettuces.

The inside of the house was cool, with all the windows open to the breeze. I could hear the drone of a play on Granny's wireless in the kitchen, the soft scrape of her wooden spoon in a bowl. The door of Erin's room was ajar. A record played on her portable turntable but when I peeped inside she lay on her bed asleep. I mounted the stairs. I hadn't been upstairs at Granny's house for quite a while—the upsetting sense that this was no longer Granny's house, the standoff between Mum and Isobel and all the other uneasiness prevailing had made me feel uncomfortable about doing so. Now I noticed that some things were different. There was a new runner along the landing. The old brass chandelier had disappeared. The doors of the various bedrooms— in former days always left open, welcoming, inviting; there had been no secrets and no one had felt the need for privacy—were now firmly shut. I turned at the end of the landing and mounted the attic stairs. I planned to make up our beds, open the little round window to freshen the air, place my shorts and tee shirts into the little chest of drawers. Imagine my surprise to find the attic utterly altered. The dark, well-loved old beams had been painted white. The sloping ceiling panels in between were festooned with diaphanous fabrics of various psychedelic hues that draped down to the floor in a manner that reminded me of the Bedouin tent the twins had made some years before. An enormous bed with an ornate iron headboard stood in the centre of the room. Various technicolour rugs were spread across the bare boards along with a number of squashy beanbags. An ashtray overflowed with cigarette ends. Of all the family, Hester was the only one who smoked, and I recognised some of her clothes hanging from a rail.

I retreated down the stairs and reviewed the various bedroom doors that gave off the landing. Granny had one front room and I knew that Isobel and Victor had fixed on the second. Blanche's room was at the back of the house, down a little passageway; it had been the nursery wing back in olden days, when my father and his siblings had been small. The box room—Grandad's former office—was down that way too, along with a tiny bathroom. The house's main bathroom was opposite to me now, its door, like the others, firmly closed. There were two other bedrooms, both twin-bedded rooms. One would be Jack's. The other—theoretically—would be spare. But which? I pushed open a door at random, half expecting to find Jack's cricket gear, his posters of Raquel Welsh and his Leeds United supporters' magazines. But there instead were the twins' matching pyjamas, their favourite LPs, their washed and neatly folded jeans.

So Hester and the twins had moved in to Broadacres.

I moved down the passageway towards the box room. Perhaps it had been turned back into a bedroom and prepared for you. But no. Grandad's scarred old desk was just where he had left it, the carpet beneath bald with the shuffle of his feet over decades. His shelves of ledgers were undisturbed, piles of seed catalogues teetered on the windowsill, all very dusty. It looked like no one had been in there since he had died. I lowered myself into his chair and willed him to speak to me from wherever he was, to reassure me that life would go on as it always had; that change, the future—everything I feared—could be kept at bay. But my only reply was the bat and buzz of a bluebottle as it threw itself again and again against the window.

When I returned home, Mum was unpegging washing from the line.

'Hello Prue,' she said. 'Have you changed your mind about staying at Granny's?'

I shook my head miserably. 'There isn't room for me,' I wailed. 'Hester's taken over the attic and the twins are in the other room. I don't know where they plan to put Arthur. There isn't room for him, either.' I dropped my holdall and collapsed onto the lawn. I expected this further proof of the family's collusion would inflict another wound on Mum, but curiously my deflation seemed to cause a commensurate expansion in her.

She dropped the laundry basket and took a deep breath. 'We'll see about *that*,' she said.

I followed her to Broadacres at a half run, eager and at the same time anxious about the irate genie I saw shimmering in Mum's set shoulders and pursed lips.

Granny, Isobel and Hester were seated at the kitchen table with cups of tea before them. Both Isobel and Granny rose as we entered, but it was Isobel—now clearly the dominant female of the house—who said, 'How lovely to see you, Lucille. Will you have a cup of tea?'

Ignoring the offer, Mum turned on Hester. 'I hear you've moved in,' she barked. 'When was *that* decided?'

Hester lit a cigarette. 'I haven't moved in, exactly' she said, blowing a stream of smoke at the ceiling. 'But the number of hours we're spending here, it seemed sensible to bring a few things over *pro tem.*'

'You've redecorated the attic,' I burst out from where I stood half a pace behind Mum.

'That doesn't seem very temporary,' Mum threw out. 'Does Trevor know?'

'Of course he does,' Isobel said, pouring Mum a cup of tea and placing it on the table, but with the air of Brutus sticking a knife into Caesar's back. I could feel Mum rock with the impact of the blow. 'It took our combined efforts to get Hester's bed up the attic stairs. Why?' Her mouth creased in a simpering smile I recognised for the first time as downright bitchy. 'Didn't he mention it?'

Of course he hadn't. But then Mum and Dad had barely exchanged more than ordinary daily politeness for weeks. It was a stumbling block, but Mum gathered herself and stepped over it. 'I thought we were a family,' she said in a voice that was low but as sharp as a whetted blade. 'I thought we were *friends*. You must see how this feels to those of us who have been shut out in the cold.'

'Trevor hasn't been shut out of anything,' said Granny, who prided herself on scrupulous fairness. She beckoned to me and held out the biscuit tin. I was not to be placated with a custard cream but even so I couldn't help but glance across at Isobel. Everything at Broadacres belonged to her now, didn't it? I was surprised Granny had the temerity to offer the tin. I shook my head but then remembered my manners. 'No thank you, Granny.' I stepped closer to Mum and took hold of the hem of her dress.

'Trevor's been rather distracted of late,' Hester said with specious mildness. 'I expect it slipped his mind. Blanche has occupied *so* much of his time.' She looked around the room as though only now aware that he was absent from it. 'He must be with her now,' she concluded with a shrug. 'Perhaps I ought to take them their tea.' She stubbed out her cigarette and reached for the teapot. 'Oh dear,' she observed. 'I'm not sure there'll be enough. I'd better make a fresh pot.'

'He can have mine,' said Mum, gesturing to the cup that was cooling on the table, 'I don't want it.' But Hester ignored her and placed the kettle back onto the hotplate.

'Oh Lucille,' said Granny, rising to her feet. 'Don't alienate yourself even *more*. We *are* a family and you *do* have friends here. I know you were disappointed not to be able to move in, but you *must* see why Isobel's need was greater. And as for Hester … she's here from morning till night just at present, and so are the twins. I can hardly expect them to travel backwards and forwards, or to get home after a long day and begin cooking. Where would we be without them? Where would we be without any of you?' She held out her hands in appeal, and I thought Mum would succumb.

Perhaps Hester saw it too. She said, 'Nothing here has changed, Lucille. Only *you* have. That's why they call it "the change." It's hormonal. We understand.' With a sigh. 'It will come to us all, I suppose.'

I looked sideways at Mum. The change?

'That's nothing to do with it,' Mum snapped. I could hear a quiver in her voice but she carried bravely on. 'You don't understand how it feels to be left out. I feel betrayed. I feel that *you* have betrayed me.'

How much clearer could she be? Even if it wasn't true, I wanted just one of them to say they were sorry that she felt that way. I think that's all it would have taken to placate Mum, an acknowledgement of her feelings.

But I was to be disappointed.

'You're being melodramatic, if you don't mind me saying so,' observed Isobel. 'You have chosen to alienate yourself. That's not our fault. If you'd been here, you would have been party to all the conversations we've had, and your point of view would have been heard. But you stayed at home and sulked. Well, that's your prerogative I suppose. But life goes on, Lucille. Life has *had* to go on. All our livelihoods depend on Salad Days.'

I was angry that my aunts had allowed the opportunity for reconciliation to slip by. I piped up, 'Mum works as hard as anyone. Some evenings she is up past midnight doing the accounts.'

'It isn't a competition,' Granny urged. 'We're a team. We are all on the same side here.'

There was a moment, a tableau, while everyone in the room considered this assertion. Perhaps Granny really believed it, but I didn't think anyone else did. The women eyed each other doubtfully. Hester lit another cigarette. The kettle on the hob came to the boil and began to scream, its familiar note suddenly infused with a hysterical edge I'd never been conscious of before.

Isobel yanked it from the stove, breaking the spell.

From the hallway, I heard the rumbling note of my father's laughter and Blanche's fluting reply as they descended from her room in search of tea. I looked up at Mum, but her face was turned away from me. I scanned the room and caught the lift of Hester's ironical eyebrow, Isobel's answering frown. Granny stared at the floral pattern of the tablecloth, awkward as I have never observed her before.

Then Dad and Blanche were in the room. Dad's laughter died in his throat. Blanche blushed guiltily. 'Oh, Lucille,' she trilled at last. 'How lovely to see you. And Prudence. You will have broken up from school I suppose.'

Dad crushed me into an embrace, but I remained stiff within it. Then he turned to kiss Mum, but she turned her cheek from him.

I addressed Blanche. 'Arthur is coming home tomorrow. Where is he going to sleep?'

'With Jack, of course,' Isobel said, pouring water into the teapot. 'Blanche and I made up his bed this morning.'

'And what about me?' I asked in a small, quavering voice.

'What about you, dear?' Blanche enquired blithely, fetching milk from the fridge. But in the scraping of chairs and the bustle of finding more cups, the question went unanswered.

Chapter Seventeen

In point of fact that summer of 1972 turned out to be brilliant, didn't it? Until it wasn't.

Mum came to our rescue by finding an old tent in one of the sheds and helping us to set it up in the meadow. The weather was perfect—warm, with bright sunshine every day, but refreshingly breezy. The ground was dry, the meadow a sea of dancing wildflowers and whispering grasses. We pitched our tent at a little distance from the students but still within the curtilage of their encampment.

Bjorn, deemed the most mature and sensible of the students, was asked to keep his eye on us. We were given a curfew of nine o'clock and one of our parents walked up to the meadow most evenings about that time to make sure we were somewhere about the camp, but essentially we ran wild for the three weeks of your stay at Broadacres. Oh! It was glorious. Do you remember scavenging food from the kitchen at Broadacres? What mischievous pleasure I took in *that,* creeping in to raid Aunt Isobel's stores of cake and biscuits, bananas and oranges from her fruit bowl, ham and cheese from her fridge. Sometimes we ate the doubtful vegetarian concoctions brewed up in a huge cauldron over the fire by the students. Some of their stews were really horrible—heavily spiced, or thick with lentils and pulses that gave us dreadful flatulence—but we were so hungry that we scoffed it down. We bathed mainly in the cove and drank water from one of the little streams that ran through the woods—we never thought of boiling it. I drew the line at using the stinking and often blocked toilet in the caravan that served the students though! Every few days we would go to the cottage or to Broadacres for a proper bath, but my abiding memory of that summer is of my skin and hair—stiff with sea salt—and the strange sense that my body was a chrysalis from which I would soon burst, new-made, grownup and suddenly wise. For the time being though I was still a child, and I revelled in the freedom and irresponsibility that was still mine, however briefly.

Ironically, our defection to the meadow gave Jack and the twins the same idea, and soon we were all encamped amongst the students. Jack, fifteen by then, had a dreadful crush on one of the Polish girls. Do you remember? And the twins seemed to take turns with Bjorn—so much for his being mature and sensible! I have no idea if he knew that the twin he kissed one night was not the twin he had kissed the night before, or if he was quite aware that they were playing him. Either way, there was an unspoken code amongst us all that what happened in the meadow stayed in the meadow.

So, as it turned out, we could easily have been accommodated in the main house if we'd wanted, but the camping was better even than that. And anyway, I didn't *want* to sleep at Granny's house. My happy memories of it had soured in the clannish behaviour of my aunts and a vague but uncomfortable feeling I had that Dad was being disloyal to Mum. I wanted him to take her side, but he didn't. Mum spent most of that summer almost entirely alone, as Verity and Grace dropped all pretence of virginal purity and regularly stayed over with their respective boyfriends. Mum did her share of the picking and packing, made her deliveries and kept the accounts. She cooked meals for Dad but they often went untasted as he stayed at Granny's for the traditional summer suppers round the big table on the terrace. Mum was always invited, of course, even urged to join in, but she pleaded some excuse and walked home on her own once the day's work was done.

I'm sorry to say that although I knew in an absent-minded way that she was lonely and very unhappy, I was too caught up in our adventures to pay her much heed.

That was the year that, in defiance of all the rules, we began to visit the pond. It was situated at the far southern end of the woods, past the peaceful little cemetery and the rockfall, in a curious, bowl-shaped depression amongst the trees. A small rivulet fed into it at one end, but we could find no drain and it intrigued us that the water level remained more or less the same. We speculated about an underground sump leading to a system of caverns and water-hewn passageways. They might connect up to the caves in the rocky cliffs we had glimpsed in days gone by from Grandad's boat. We lamented the loss of that boat. What fun we could have had with it! Sadly, it had been torn from its moorings and lost in a winter storm some years before.

The pond was overhung all around with deciduous trees. In the autumn, when the sun could penetrate the canopy, it would be a shining mosaic of gold and russet and bronze leaves but then, in the height of summer, the light scarcely pierced the gloom beneath the trees. The pond was a fathomless emerald, skinned at its edges by vibrant green weed. Its waters were strangely opaque, its murkiness suggesting gargantuan pike or fantastical, reptilian monsters. We thrashed through the undergrowth around its whole perimeter, chucking in sticks and stones to hear the satisfying gulp of the viscous waters as they swallowed our missiles whole, laughing at the sulphurous stench that rose up from the disturbed depths.

One day we took fishing rods but caught nothing but rotten branches and skeins of slimy weed. We were desperate to know how deep the pond was. Ten feet, we guessed. Twenty? Or perhaps it had no bottom at all. We dared each other to wade in and both succeeded in getting thigh-deep before the squelch and suck of the mud and decomposed leaves beneath our feet—and the dreadful bad-egg smell—caused us both to retreat, honour intact.

We pondered the conundrum for a while before you came up with the idea of building a raft. You said you'd done it at school a couple of times—you knew what sort of equipment we'd need. I'd seen it done on an episode of *It's a Knockout*. We spent a few days filching materials from Salad Days: rope, planks and four empty kerosene barrels—rather rusty, but good enough, we thought. We collected long, straight branches and lashed them together end-to-end to make the all-important probe. I measured it with Grandad's big tape measure. Eighteen feet. Not nearly long enough. We tried to make it longer but it became too unwieldy, likely to overbalance the raft and maybe even tip us into the water. Although we were terribly excited by the whole project, we weren't stupid. We knew that to fall into the pond would be a serious error. At last I suggested a plumbline with a large stone tied to the end. We could mark the line off in one-foot sections and count how many of them disappeared beneath the surface of the water before the stone hit the bottom—if it ever did. You said that we couldn't know if the stone was at the bottom or resting on a submerged log. I saw the sense in that, and so we agreed to take several soundings at different points around the pond. Our plan required more rope, and we struggled to think where we might find more than we had already pinched from various outhouses. Eventually you said there might be some in the garages behind Glenister Hall, so off we went.

We took a circuitous route through the woods, stopping at the cove for a quick dip in the sea to wash the stinking green slime from our legs, before continuing on up the zigzag slope towards the gate into the meadow where a tractor was cutting the grass for hay. You climbed over the gate without a pause and raised your hand to the driver of the tractor, who nodded as he passed by. It was the briefest possible exchange—nothing at all, really—but it impressed upon me again that you had a life that was separate from mine, a life I knew little of, peopled by strangers, lived in the shadowy and damp interior of Glenister Hall whose privations I could hardly guess.

We crossed the field, the swish of the dry grass making our ankles tickle. I glanced sideways at you to see if it would set your hay fever off, but that seemed to be a thing of the past—like so many other things, I thought gloomily.

As before, the side gate through the garden wall was unlocked. The gardens were in an even worse state than I remembered, rank with weeds.

I said, 'Doesn't anyone care about the garden?'

You shook your head. 'No one has time. No one ever even comes out here apart from me and Grandma, but she only passes through.'

Your remark brought me to mind of the odd, emotional woman I'd seen at Grandad's funeral. I was curious about her. There had been—in that swift moment between the pews—some sense of connection, but I didn't know how to describe it. The subject of your family was barely explored territory between us, fraught with bogs I was afraid to fall into lest I betray the trust you had placed in me.

The question I came up with was lame, a poor attempt to broach the terrain.

'Where does she go to, your grandma?'

You gave me one of those looks that told me I'd asked a stupid question and so I didn't pursue it.

On the gravel sweep—matted with moss and a small-leaved weed I didn't recognise—we came across your father. He was just climbing into his car. Even though the day was warm he wore a shirt and tie, pressed trousers and a linen jacket. His hair, as always, was carefully groomed. Even so, he paused before inserting his long legs into the footwell of the car to extract a comb and pull it through his already neat coiffure. My first instinct was to laugh—he really was such a ponce; my second was to dash back round the corner so that he wouldn't see us. But you strolled across the drive with your hands in your pockets kicking up sprays of loose gravel with your trainers, and I could only follow in your wake.

'Hello Henry,' you said. 'Where are you off to?'

Henry? Not "Dad?"

'Just into town. I'm picking Verity up after work.' He ignored me utterly, and showed no pleasure at all in seeing you, but bent down to check his teeth in the wing mirror. 'Polly's in the kitchen if you want something to eat,' he said through a rictus snarl of slightly yellow incisors.

I gazed up at the sky. I wore no watch, and I had no idea what time it was. Ought we to be getting back to the camp?

But you said, 'Sure. Thanks,' and continued round to the far side of the house.

I hurried after you. 'Who's Polly?'

'A sort of cook and maid. She's supposed to keep on top of the washing and cleaning, but she spends most of her time with her feet up in the kitchen reading magazines.'

I was avidly interested in Glenister Hall. Was that because it was a part of your life of which you'd allowed me only a glimpse? Or because it was to become so integrally connected to mine, through Verity? Or had it to do with your grandma?

'Shall we?' I said. 'I'm quite hungry.'

You shrugged. 'Okay.'

The lower passageways and kitchen areas of Glenister Hall were deserted, as before, but this time with the ghostly echo of a radio playing somewhere in their depths. We padded on stockinged feet down the cold, tiled corridors. My eyes struggled to adjust to the dimness after the brightness of the day outside.

At last you pushed open a swing door and we were in the kitchen, a cavern of a room fitted with oversized shelves and cupboards, with a huge table in the middle and an enormous, deep stainless steel sink at one end. Some light came through a window very high up—too high to see through unless you climbed onto the countertop—but it was laced with dusty cobwebs, very grimy. In the main the space was illuminated by a rank of florescent strip lights that cast a flat, arctic glare over every hard and ugly surface. The tinny blare of the radio set my teeth on edge.

I'd imagined Polly to be young and energetic but in fact she was quite elderly, perhaps even as old as Granny. She wore a shapeless dun-coloured dress with a stained apron over the top of it, legs showing a map of varicose veins even through thick tights, and feet thrust into sturdy but hideously ugly sandals. As you had predicted, she sat on a kitchen chair with her feet resting on another, deeply absorbed by *Woman's Own*.

'Hello Polly,' you said brightly. 'Anything to eat?'

She motioned with her head towards a pantry door but did not look up from her reading.

Inside the pantry we found a jostle of tins and jars—all looking rather ancient to me—a slab of cheese under a cloche and half a loaf of stale bread in an enamel bread-bin.

'Still hungry?' you asked.

I shrugged. 'We could make cheese sandwiches. Is there any butter? And …' I rose on tiptoes so I could survey the row of jars, '…isn't that one of Victor's chutneys? That might be okay.'

You reached some butter and the chutney down from the upper shelf and found a breadknife in a drawer. We began to make sandwiches right there in the cramped confines of the pantry. It seemed ridiculous to me, when there was the huge kitchen with acres of workspace only a step or two away. But there also was Polly, and I guessed you didn't want to disturb her. 'Isn't she supposed to do this for you?' I murmured. We were making a terrible hash of the loaf, sawing it into uneven slabs. 'I mean, what do you normally do for meals, when you're here? Do you eat at the big table through there? Or on a tray in your room?'

'I do *this,* mainly,' you said, paring cheese off the slab. 'If I'm lucky Polly will boil me some eggs for breakfast. Come to that, I'm pretty good at boiling my own eggs now. I can grill bacon too, if there is any.'

'But your … Henry and your grandparents. What do they eat? Do you *all* scavenge about in the larder when you're hungry?'

'Grandfather eats at the golf club every day that he's in the country. But he's away a lot. Henry eats out, or at Broadacres if he's invited.'

'No wonder he and Blanche used to turn up so often,' I mused.

You said, 'The penny drops at last.'

I was astonished. In all the rationales I had ever come up with to explain the Glenisters' constant presence at Granny's house, simple hunger had never been one of them.

'And your grandmother?'

You made a fuss about opening the pickle jar. At last it yielded with a pop. 'She gets by,' you mumbled. 'She finds things … out and about.'

'Do you mean …' I struggled to make sense of it, '… in shops?'

You laughed, and began to smear the chutney on our sandwiches. 'No! In the countryside. She forages. Nuts and berries. Birds' eggs. Fish. Rabbits, sometimes.'

The picture your revelation conjured was shocking but vivid. *Eye of newt and toe of frog* leapt into my mind. We'd been reading *Macbeth* in English classes. My mouth flapped. 'You mean … you mean like a …' A witch, I had been going to say, but I stopped myself. 'And she cooks them *here?* Or does she eat them *raw?*'

'She isn't a savage,' you scoffed. 'She just loves the countryside and the outdoors and nature. She cooks them, mostly, but not here.'

We cleared up the crumbs by sweeping them onto the floor and replaced what was left of the cheese and the loaf where we had found them. We carried our doorstep sandwiches back into the kitchen, but Polly was nowhere to be seen. The radio was off and the lights likewise.

'She's gone home,' you said.

'Shall we eat these in your room?' I ventured, keen to see more of the bizarre Glenister lifestyle.

But you ignored the suggestion. 'Oh! I know.' You laid your sandwich gingerly on the table and pulled the chair over to a tall dresser. Climbing up, you reached deep into a high shelf and pulled out two chocolate bars. 'This is Polly's secret stash,' you said. 'She doesn't know I've found it.'

'How did *you* find it?' I had a sudden image of you here, alone in this cavernous house, left to your own devices, wandering from room to room, opening drawers and rifling through cupboards. My thoughts must have showed on my face. You blushed a little and took a big bite of your sandwich.

When you'd chewed and swallowed you said, 'I nose about. What else is there for me to do?' You looked me in the eye then, challenging me to criticise.

'I would too, if I were you,' I said loyally. 'Have you found anything interesting?'

You narrowed one eye, considering.

'I'm good at keeping secrets,' I offered.

'Not very,' you mocked. 'You spilled the beans about Verity, didn't you? See where *that's* got us!'

I realised that the prospect of your father remarrying—and such a young woman, someone closer to your age than his—must be cripplingly awkward for you.

'I'm sorry about that,' I said. 'I was between a rock and hard place.'

You'd finished your sandwich and were tearing the paper from your chocolate bar. 'It would have come out eventually I suppose,' you said with a shrug. And then, 'I've found loads of stuff, in the library mainly. Books of accounts, letters, legal documents. None of it makes much sense to me. But did you know your grandad used to work here?'

I shook my head.

You chomped on your chocolate for a moment. 'He did. I've seen his name in a book of wages for the staff. He was a sort of woodsman I think, back in the late twenties.'

'His parents bought the smallholding in 1925,' I said. I knew that because there was a framed copy of the deed in Grandad's office. 'I thought he worked there. They'd lived on the property for years before, but only as tenants. They knocked down the old house and built Broadacres in 1935. There's a date on the lintel over the front door.' I'm ashamed to say this was the sum total of my knowledge of Day family history.

'Yes. I've seen it. But he didn't live at Broadacres when he was a woodsman,' you said, licking your fingers and then wiping them on your tee shirt. 'There's a woodsman's house in the woods.'

'*Is* there?'

'Yep. It's on that map I showed you. Didn't you see it?'

'No.' I'd been too surprised and disappointed to discover that the Days didn't own the woods to look at the thing in detail. 'Can we go and look at it again?'

You shook your head. 'We've the rope to find, remember?'

We began to retrace our steps along the tiled corridor. I thought the subject of Grandad's historical connection with Glenister Hall was closed but as you tied your laces you said, 'I do wonder how your grandad afforded to build the new house, on only a woodsman's wages, don't you? According to the wages book he only got seventy pounds a year.'

'I don't think Broadacres was his until much later.' I was guessing, ignorant of the exact timeline. When *had* Granny and Grandad taken over the property? 'He probably didn't pay anything at all towards it. But yes, it does seem odd that his people could afford to build such a nice house. They weren't well-to-do.'

'Not *then,*' you put in, and there was a terse note in your voice I hadn't heard before. 'My family got poorer and yours got richer.'

'Now we're all going to be one family,' I suggested, but my voice sounded false and sort of strangled. I'd resented your family's intrusion at Broadacres, considering them rude and entitled, but it had never occurred to me to wonder *why* they had been permitted to inveigle themselves amongst us. Could there be a connection between the Days and the Glenisters other than the tenuous one afforded by Blanche's relationship to Victor?

Were you wondering the same, Arthur?

Chapter Eighteen

We found a good coil of rope in one of the old stables, but by the time we'd carried it to the pond and marked off the one-foot lengths it was too late to embark on our enterprise so we walked back through the woods to the camp.

It must have been past six o'clock by then. The sun had dropped below the trees and a creeping shadow encroached across the meadow. Our tent was hot, though now in shade, and we threw open the flaps to let it air as we set off in search of food. We passed Bjorn and two other students gathering wood for the fire, and the queue of girls outside the caravan, waiting to use the shower. One of the boys, Andrzej, was setting off on his motorbike to collect beer and fish and chips. He stopped to ask us if we'd like any, but we hadn't any money and it didn't feel right to let them subsidise us from their meagre wages.

Jack, Kath and Karen were still hard at work amongst the raised beds—they would not stop work for at least another hour. Through the opaque skin of one of the poly tunnels I could see my father's outline as he harvested tomatoes for the following day's deliveries. I would have gone in, but a sudden shriek from Blanche, 'Oh! Trevor! There's a toad under the bench!' stayed my steps. I looked at you. Would *you* go in? You gave a little shake of your head. No. Perhaps we both knew that we'd be asked how we'd spent our afternoon, and feared our scheme would be winkled out of us and kiboshed before we'd had the chance to put it into action.

My mother was alone, as she so often was in those days, watering the plants in one of the far greenhouses. She raised a weary hand in greeting before running it through her tangled hair. I was stabbed with remorse. Had she spent the entire day alone? But then we met Hester coming from the house at a half run, calling out to Mum about a last-minute order for emergency courgettes from a seafood restaurant down the coast.

'Hello, you two,' she panted as she hurried by. 'Looking for something to eat? Granny's in the kitchen. She's making an omelette for Erin. She'll make you one, if you can't wait until later. But hurry.'

Granny came into the kitchen from the hallway at the same moment that we entered via the back porch, kicking off our shoes and leaving them amongst the heap of other boots and shoes, vegetable crates, egg boxes and empty bottles waiting to be returned to the shop for the repayment of a deposit.

The kitchen was cool, in its usual homely, muddled state. Someone's cardigan had been abandoned on the back of a chair. A recipe book was propped against the teapot. There were eggshells strewn across the work surface and the cups from afternoon tea remained unwashed in the sink. Podge's bed lay in the alcove beside the Aga, covered in her short white hairs and smelling powerfully of old dog. I couldn't help but compare it to the pristine but clinical kitchen at Glenister Hall. Did the same notion cross your mind?

'Hello, dears,' Granny said brightly. 'Fancy an omelette?'

We nodded enthusiastically. 'Yes please, Granny. And is there any pop? We're so thirsty.'

At that time, our fizzy drinks were delivered weekly by the Corona man. Granny had always kept in a goodly supply of lemonade, cream soda and dandelion and burdock, but since Isobel's advent I'd noticed the children had been relegated to ordinary cordial.

But Granny gave us a mischievous wink and nodded in the direction of the larder. 'Look under the shelf, behind the spuds,' she said. 'Right at the back.'

I poured our drinks—cherryade, what a treat!—while Granny got to work whisking eggs and putting a pan with a good knob of butter onto the stove. 'What have you been up to today?' she asked over her shoulder.

We looked at each other, an unvoiced reminder that we mustn't breathe a word about our activities at the pond.

I said, 'Arthur took me to Glenister Hall. I met a lady called Polly. Do you know her?'

You stiffened; your glass arrested halfway to your mouth. You had a cherryade smile but the shape of your mouth was more shock than smile. I made a 'well what else was I supposed to say?' expression.

Granny said, 'Polly Tindall? Is she *still* working there? I thought she'd retired years ago. Her husband was head gardener, wasn't he? Back before the war? I think they had a cottage somewhere about the estate.'

You stammered, 'Yes, I think so.'

'Is that when Grandad was the woodsman?' I asked with specious innocence. You almost choked on your cherryade.

But Granny just said, 'I suppose it must have been. Gosh! That's years ago.'

'Why didn't he work *here*?' I asked, since Granny seemed unfazed by the subject.

'I suppose there wasn't enough work, or—more likely—not enough money. Grandad was the youngest of three boys, you know. His parents couldn't keep all three of them on what they made out of the smallholding. Not to start with. We moved in when we were married. It was a squash, in the old place! That's why we built Broadacres.'

'I didn't know Grandad had brothers,' I said. 'What happened to them?'

'Killed in the second war,' she said matter-of-factly. 'Such a waste. Farming was a reserved occupation, and in any case they were too old, so they didn't go as soldiers. But there was such a labour shortage in the munitions factories and the money was good, so they went down to Manchester and were killed in an air raid in 1940.'

'Grandad didn't go?'

'No. We had this place and the children to think of. Grandad and his brothers took over the smallholding when his parents died in 1935—they both died of smallpox. Such a pity. The house was barely finished. Your aunt Isobel had only just been born. Gosh! That was a busy time! I had three children and the three men to cook and clean for! And some of the rooms hardly fit for use! But the other two were unmarried and when the war started they wanted to do their bit. They'd stayed behind in the first war, you see. Unlike your grandad.'

'Grandad fought in the First World War?'

Granny slid yellow pillows of omelette studded with ham and mushrooms onto our plates. They smelled delicious. 'He certainly did. Just eighteen he was when it broke out. He fought under the command of Arthur's grandfather, Colonel Glenister, along with Mick and Bradley and the man who married Polly. Arnold, his name was. I drove an ambulance, amongst other things, so I'd done my bit too.' She began to butter slices of bread to go with our omelette. It was sliced bread, shop-bought—another of Isobel's innovations. 'This stuff is horrible,' Granny muttered under her breath, 'there can't be any goodness in it.'

You and I exchanged looks. Mine had an air of triumph about it. What a lot of information we'd gleaned from one simple question!

'Is that how you met?' you asked, your mouth full of omelette. 'In the war?'

Granny said, 'Oh no. That was much later.'

She tidied up while we ate our food. You ate more quickly than I did and excused yourself to go to the bathroom before I'd finished. While you were gone, I decided to risk one more question. 'Is that why Mr … Colonel Glenister and Mrs Glenister came to Grandad's funeral? Because they were in the war together? They'd stayed friends?'

Granny's garrulous demeanour suddenly disappeared. She winced and I realised that I'd hit a nerve. 'N … no,' she said, her eyes suddenly shifty as I'd never seen them before. She glanced at the doorway and lowered her voice. 'There was a falling out between the Days and the Glenisters,' she said, stacking our crockery with exaggerated busyness. 'Or perhaps a parting of the ways would be a better way of describing it. The two hadn't spoken to one another in years. I was flabbergasted that they turned up at the funeral … but don't mention anything to Arthur, will you, Prue? The poor boy's torn enough as it is between the two families. It's all old history. No point in digging it up.'

I murmured, 'Of course not,' but I wasn't sure I'd be able to keep my promise. I'd need to talk to someone about it. The clear line of sight I thought I'd found connecting my family and yours—the enduring camaraderie of wartime, your grandfather and mine as longstanding brothers-in-arms—which would explain your father feeling able to make himself at home at Broadacres—had suddenly been obscured.

If the Glenisters and the Days were at loggerheads, why had Henry Glenister wheedled himself into Broadacres, and why had Grandad permitted it?

Chapter Nineteen

The next morning we got up and did our chores as usual. I was tasked with cleaning out the hens, a job I didn't mind. The flock was friendly, clucking round me. They raked through the soiled straw I pulled from their sleeping quarters, looking for bugs. I replenished their nest boxes with sawdust and clean straw, scrubbed and refilled the drinkers and topped up the feeders. Then I checked the fences of their enclosure for rat holes. Rats pose no threat to hens—they're only interested in the corn and pellets—but our flock had been decimated twice by mink that had been released by so-called animal rights warriors from fur farms in the nineteen fifties, and were now breeding in the wild. Mink used rat holes to gain entry to the run, so it was important to monitor the periphery. I found no sign of ingress, however, and moved on to my next job, which was helping Mum pack lettuces. Several people were busy in the packing shed so it wasn't possible to have a proper conversation with her. She asked me if I'd had breakfast, where and what I'd eaten, if I'd washed my hair recently. I trimmed the stalks of the lettuces and pulled off their dirty outer leaves before handing them to her to be packed, and racked my brain for something to say that would show I was concerned for her welfare but that could be spoken within earshot of others. I viewed her from the corner of my eye. Her own hair was unwashed, and her skin was dull. She wore sunglasses—a sure sign that she had been crying. When I pressed close to her she emanated a strange, sour smell I recognised but couldn't identify at first.

'We're loving the tent,' I said at last. 'Thanks for finding it for us. It's *much* better than being at Granny's.'

'Or at home,' she said under her breath.

'Well,' I hesitated, feeling guilty, 'there wouldn't be room for Arthur at home, would there?'

'And you two are joined at the hip? But I don't see why not,' she said grimly. 'Neither of your sisters use their rooms very often.'

'Poor Verity,' I said. 'I don't envy her staying at Glenister Hall. It's all shut up and the roof leaks.'

'Does it?' She turned, interested.

I glanced around the shed to make sure you weren't there. I wouldn't for the world be caught gossiping behind your back. 'I haven't seen much of it,' I admitted. 'Just the library and the kitchen. But yes, it's pretty grim.' I suddenly saw a way to scratch an itch that had been bugging me. 'Surely it won't be long before the wedding. Why don't we suggest to Verity that we go over and see what needs to be done to make the place more homely for her? I mean, I suppose Blanche had things quite nice, but Verity will want to make the place her own, won't she? Curtains and so on?'

I assumed—but didn't absolutely know—that Henry had his own set of rooms somewhere within the house. I didn't for a moment expect Verity's *trousseau* to incorporate a complete refurbishment of Glenister Hall. But my mention of Blanche conjured her in my mind, and I suddenly recognised the odd smell that hung around my mother. Stale alcohol.

On impulse I said, 'Shall I come home for dinner tonight? I can wash my hair and we can … spend some proper time.'

The prospect seemed to appeal. She said, 'Oh *yes*, Prue, that would be lovely.'

Thoughtlessly, I said, 'It's days since I saw Dad.' The image of his silhouette through the greyish polythene came back to me, along with Blanche's silly, girlish squeal. The two of them had been together in there while my mother had been alone. Why could Blanche not have watered the things in the greenhouse?

'Oh! *He* won't be there,' Mum threw off. 'It's days since *I* saw him, either.'

Our boxes of lettuce were done. Andrzej began to carry them out to the van.

'Just us then,' I said, dusting the soil from my hands, trying to sound as though this was entirely satisfactory.

'What about Arthur?' Mum wanted to know. 'Won't you bring him?'

I wanted to, of course I did, but it felt important just then to show Mum that she was someone's priority.

'Oh no,' I said, planting a quick kiss on her cheek. 'Arthur can fend for himself for one evening.'

Just then a bell rang, and people began to wander out to where Hester and the girls were distributing cups of coffee from an urn. The days were long gone when Granny could supply the workers with refreshments from the kitchen—with the addition of the students there were far too many—although she did usually appear with packets of biscuits to hand around. This in itself was quite shocking. In days gone by Granny wouldn't have permitted any shop-bought confectionery to pollute her biscuit barrel and certainly no cake or cookie would have been served other than on a china plate with a doily. I sighed inwardly as I accepted a mug of weak instant coffee and two custard creams. How times had changed!

The mid-morning coffee break signalled the end of the period during which you and I were expected to give our time to the business, but our departure for the woods was delayed by talk around the coffee urn of a party to be held that evening. Apparently it was Bjorn's birthday. And in addition, the Polish girl with whom Jack was besotted—I can't recall her name—had just heard that she'd been accepted at medical school, commencing in autumn. The students rummaged in their pockets and brought out money to buy beer that Andrzej would get while he was out on his delivery rounds. Hester said she felt sure Victor would contribute some of his home-brew and Dad suggested a cookout on the field—he'd get some meat from the local butcher and look out the old barbecue, if the women would throw together some salads. Granny suggested that if everyone got on quickly with their work the students could clock off early to help prepare for the celebration. Hester looked askance at this—she didn't want the workers to fall behind—but everyone seemed so excited as they discussed the event, I suppose she didn't like to pour cold water on it.

I looked past the huddle of students to where Mum perched on an upturned crate at a little distance from the hubbub, sipping at her coffee. The impromptu party might change our plans for the evening, but I didn't want to be the one to back out of our arrangements.

It almost seemed as though she hadn't heard the plans being made though. As we passed by her on our way to the woods she said, 'See you tonight then, Prue. I'll cook sausages and jacket potatoes. Your favourite.'

I'd had a tight, pent-up feeling about our prospective adventure at the pond since I'd woken that morning, and my concerns about Mum only added to it. Plus, I had to let you know that I'd be leaving you to your own devices for the evening meal. I felt mean and disloyal. I flattered myself that the party on the field—without *me*—would hold little appeal to you. For the moment, my interest in the historic connection and subsequent rift between your family and mine was forgotten.

I got the impression that the enormity of what we were about to do hung heavily on you too, Arthur. You stalked ahead of me and didn't speak as we made our way along the narrow, overgrown trails towards the pond and our stash of equipment. It was quiet in the woods. Hardly a bird could be heard in the canopy, and the sea in the cove—usually audible as the rhythmic hush and rush of water on shingle—today was muted to no more than a whisper.

At one point I said, 'Did you remember to bring a knife to cut the rope?' and you simply patted the back pocket of your shorts to tell me that yes, you'd remembered it.

We arrived at the pond. It undulated slightly beneath a thick mat of duckweed—luminously green even in the subdued, filtered light—as though it too felt anxious about the ordeal to come. We walked all the way around its perimeter once more. The grasses were trodden down and flattened where we'd explored on previous days. We pretended to be discussing the best place to launch our raft from, agreeing a point that was roughly the centre of the pond where it was likely to be the deepest, but in fact I think we were both having second thoughts about the whole scheme. We'd been warned repeatedly how dangerous it was. Hadn't a dog drowned in it once? What kinds of germs and diseases might we catch from ingesting its viscous, oddly tepid waters?

We came back to where our equipment was stashed, and as neither of us had the courage—or the cowardice—to suggest giving the whole thing up, we pulled out the planks and barrels and got to work.

It took much longer than we'd anticipated. The barrels were heavy and unwieldy and took a good deal of manoeuvring into position. Looked at critically they really were very corroded. It was hardly to be trusted that they would float. The planks wouldn't sit level no matter how often we altered their position and retied them. The rope burnt our hands, and the knife was nowhere near sharp enough to cut through its coarse, gnarly fibres. Our combined strength just couldn't seem to lash the ropes securely enough so that the raft was sturdy. The moment we began to inch it towards the water something would shift and come loose. Finally, we were unhappy with every stone we found to make the weight for our plumb line. They were too heavy, too round, too tricky to tie, or else too light—we didn't trust them to sink through the gelatinous waters to the bottom, if there was one. In the end we'd amassed quite a little cairn before we found something we thought would do the trick.

The day was well-advanced before we were finally happy—or at least reasonably confident—that the raft would float and bear our weight. At a distance, through the trees, I heard the whoops and yells of the students making their way down to the cove to swim. Hester must have told them they could put down their tools for the day. From the loud, wild sound of them they'd already broached the beer. We both froze mid-launch. If they came this way our conspiracy would be over. I wonder if we both half-hoped for such a reprieve. But their exuberant voices died away as they descended to the cove and the silence of the woods swallowed us up again into its murky, secretive hush.

We shuffled towards the edge of the pond, the awkward raft between us, lifted and then with a mighty heave launched it out onto the milky green surface of the water. It landed with an odd, gloopy splash, wobbled, righted itself and then settled in rather than on the water, like a crouton on a thick pea soup. Inexorably, pulled by enigmatic currents, it began to move across the pond. You only just managed to grab a trailing rope, or it would have sailed out of reach. You hauled and brought the thing with difficulty back to the shore.

We gave each other a long look. I think if either one of us, even then, had expressed doubts in the enterprise the other would have been only too glad to give it up. But neither of us spoke the word and so the thing pursued its course.

You said, 'Grab the plumb line, Prue,' and I ran to where it was coiled in the grass like an enormous brown snake. The stone we'd picked to weigh down the end wasn't inconsiderable and the rope itself was long and so quite weighty. It was a struggle to pick it up and bring it to the brink.

'You hold the raft steady while I get on,' I said, stepping into the sucking mud of the shallows. You braced yourself and I scrambled aboard, throwing the coiled rope and its stone ahead of me onto the precarious planks. The raft dipped wildly and also moved away from me. I lost my footing. My trainers and legs were drenched. I found myself lying prone on the rough-hewn planks clinging to the rim of one of the barrels with one hand, the other on the rope, which had overshot when I'd thrown it and threatened to slither off the raft and disappear into the depths. I kicked my legs a couple of times, conscious of whatever malign entities might lie below the surface of the water, but managed to get myself onto the raft and into a kneeling position. When I looked back at you your face was white with tension, your whole body braced against the rope, the only thing holding the raft to the shore.

'It's quite tricky,' I called out. My heart was pounding in my chest.

You said, 'You've really done it, Prue!' And I couldn't tell if you were amazed or appalled.

'Didn't you think I would?' I called back, buoyed up by my achievement. 'Come on. Your turn.'

You waded into the shallows of the pond, making odd whorls and eddies in the duck weed. Slimy little waves slapped onto the shore. You grasped the end of the planks. 'Hold on tight,' you croaked, and with a great leap, launched yourself onto the raft.

Again, it tilted and teetered crazily in the water. Green ooze splashed up between the two planks. I'd transferred my handhold to one of the rope lashings, but it felt slack and unreliable to me, and my stomach lurched. There wasn't much room on the raft for the two of us and the huge coil of rope. We were pressed together. I could smell the sweat on you and feel your heat. Involuntarily, I groped with my spare hand and found yours. It was hot and wet. The raft began to move across the surface of the water.

'We didn't think about how we might steer,' I observed through tense lips.

At the same time, you said, 'We should have talked about emergency evacuation procedures.'

That made us both laugh. We were probably experiencing some kind of hysterical outburst. The raft quivered and bucked like a live thing as we laughed helplessly, tears rolling down our faces. I wished I'd found a bush to squat behind before we'd embarked, because I felt a little leak in my knickers which I was powerless to control.

The raft sailed seemingly of its own volition right out into the centre of the pond. Here and there an ancient tree bough stuck up out of the water and we fended our craft away from these as best we could with hands and feet, although to be truthful I think we were both clinging so tightly to the planks and to each other that we were pretty ineffectual navigators. We were both breathless and almost stupefied that the raft had not sunk, but yet not so amazed that either of us felt it could be trusted not to do so in the next five minutes. Indeed, I could hear the hollow seep and trickle of water somewhere below me as one of the barrels began to take in water.

'Let's do the measuring,' I said, suddenly sober. I rummaged amongst the coils of rope to find the end and then pushed the stone over the end of the board. It disappeared with a gloopy plop and the rope slithered through my hands as the weight descended.

We both held our breath, but we didn't have to do so for long because the stone came to a rest hardly two feet below us.

'There must be something submerged,' I said, hauling the plumb line back on board.

We allowed the raft to drift a little before we tried it again. This attempt was better. Fully four feet of rope disappeared into the green water before the stone came to rest.

'Maybe it's just not very deep,' you mused.

I think we were both feeling a bit more relaxed, our concentration on the task in hand taking our minds off the extremely hazardous nature of our situation.

'It *must* be,' I countered, pulling the rope back in. 'We've always been told so.'

'Probably to keep us away from it,' you said. 'Here. Let me try.'

We transferred the rope. When I rested my hands on my lap I was surprised to see they were trembling.

The raft neared another partly-submerged log and you began to feed out the rope. This time we counted six knots before the stone came to rest.

I said, 'Six feet,' and had the sudden image of your father—who never tired of boasting of his six feet six height—up to his neck in this foul, stinking water.

'Quite deep,' you said, and began to reel in the rope.

Then there was a sudden sense of tension in the raft. One of the barrels, weighed down with water, had begun to sink, tautening the rope restraints to the degree that they began to exude brownish water from their sodden fibres. That corner of the raft dipped alarmingly. Then there was a jolt as the rope gave way and the barrel came free. The raft, critically unbalanced, catapulted upwards to an alarming angle and then dipped perilously back down at that corner. We had to cling to each other to stop from sliding in. We watched in horror as the barrel wallowed, rolled over and disappeared from view. One of the planks was drifting, secured only at one end and not very securely at that. Water lapped around our thighs.

'Time to get off this thing,' you cried, paddling with your hands notwithstanding the nasty smell and clinging green slime of the water. I tried to help. At first we splashed uselessly, the raft swaying first one way and then the other.

'Do it together,' you shouted, and I tried to match my flailing arm with yours, but the raft was so unbalanced, so cumbersome, that I thought we were done for. Eventually, with the loose plank shifting beneath our knees and skeins of rope steadily detaching themselves, we seemed to get into some kind of rhythm that would take us to safety. I allowed myself a little breath.

But too soon. Our progress—wavering and untidy—came to an abrupt halt. I risked a glance behind us, imagining some antediluvian serpent or ghostly, weedy hand drawing us back into the centre of the pond.

'The rope!' I shouted. You must have dropped the plumb line the moment the crisis had occurred, but it had wound itself around the end of the one secure remaining plank and now anchored us to the partly-submerged log. I leaned as far out as I dared to try to free us, but the raft was too unstable, the rope too tightly bound. The alteration in ballast must have further undermined the stability of the raft as another barrel broke loose and began to drift away.

We were waist-deep in water now, clinging to the one plank that seemed secure between the two remaining barrels but unfortunately the one to which the plumb line was irrevocably attached. We kicked our legs—an instinctive action—but the plumb line remained taut, snared both to the raft at one end and to the log at the other. We weren't more than twenty yards from the shore, but it seemed like an uncrossable expanse, and I couldn't shift the notion of something sinister beneath the surface. I hated the feel of the water on my face. It was warm and tasted bitter. The idea of swimming in it was revolting.

Your thoughts must have coincided with mine. 'We'll have to swim for it Prue,' you gasped out. 'It really isn't very far. Keep yourself on the surface as much as possible. There may be sharp things we can't see below us.'

'I can't! *I can't!*' I panted. I nearly said, 'I'm afraid,' but you filled the space of my hesitation.

'I'm scared too,' you said, sliding your hand across the plank and covering mine. 'But you're a much stronger swimmer than I am. You can do it. Go on. I'll be right behind you.'

You yanked me from the plank and launched me forward in the water. I struck out for the shore, a messy hybrid of breast-stroke and doggy-paddle I'd have been ashamed of in ordinary circumstances. I could hear you behind me, breathing heavily. I closed my eyes and tried not to take in any water. Then my hands met the soft leaf-mould of the shoreline and I crawled from the pond.

But when I looked back, the raft had sunk without trace and you were nowhere to be seen.

I screamed.

Suddenly the surface broke about ten yards from the edge. Your hand and then your head emerged, your red hair dark with water, plastered to your head and also larded with green weed. You thrashed, threw me a terrified look and then disappeared again. I hurled myself back into the dreadful water, churned up and silty by then and emitting the most awful smell of dead, decaying things. I reached you in just a few strokes, groping beneath the surface until my hand found your tee shirt. I reached down with my feet to see if there was something I could brace against and there was. The water was barely two and half feet deep. I hauled you to the surface. You were heavy. I could hardly hold you as I dragged you to land, your stumbling efforts to support yourself more of a hindrance than a help; we fell over each other countless times. You coughed, retched and spewed up a spume of greenish, watery sick. Then we both collapsed on the dry soil of the forest floor.

Chapter Twenty

It may be that we lay unconscious for a while. It seems impossible that we could have slept—the adrenalin, the relief, the knowledge of the near-escape we'd had—you wouldn't think we could *sleep* in the aftermath of all we'd been through. Whatever the explanation, when I came back to my senses, I could tell the afternoon had waned and evening was coming on fast. The air was cooler, the light beneath the trees greenly-golden and almost magical. It would have been easy to believe I'd crossed some mysterious veil and arrived in a land of unicorns and sprites.

A figure loomed above me, blocking out the eerie light. My eyes were heavy, crusted with silt, and I couldn't make anything of it. I felt a rough hand shaking me and heard a voice speaking your name.

It was your father.

'Arthur! Arthur!' he barked. 'What are you doing? Get up at once! What on earth have you been up to?'

I sat up and rubbed my hands over my face, but to no avail. My hands, face, my whole body was covered in dried weed and the crustiness left behind after the pond water had evaporated. My shorts and tee shirt were still damp but not sopping wet, which is what made me realise that I'd been out for the count for quite a while.

I felt you rouse beside me and sit up.

'Henry?' you croaked out. 'Dad?'

'Yes,' he said crossly, not an iota of kindness or concern in his tone. 'Come on, you'd better come with me.'

We scrambled to our feet and meekly followed him away from the scene of our crime. I cast a quick glance around but all evidence of our endeavour—rope, planks, barrels—had sunk without trace in the speciously benign tranquillity of the pond, and the only thing that remained—a sort of testament to our derring-do—was the little cairn of stones we'd rejected for our plumb line.

'We're for it now,' you muttered, and I nodded grimly, expecting to be marched home where we'd face an inquisition. But to our surprise—and relief—Henry strode past the route that would take us back to Broadacres and led us instead to the cove.

'You'd better get in the sea and wash yourselves off,' he growled. 'You both stink to high heaven.'

We stepped sheepishly into the sea and tried to scrub the worst of the dried slime and crispy duck weed from our skin and clothes. The sea was beautiful, golden as a burnished copper dish, the sun just dipping its toes. In other circumstances it would have been enchanting but, situated as we were, I hardly had leisure to enjoy it. What was going to happen to us?

We were salty and sandy when we came out but I suppose we must have smelt fresher because Henry gave a satisfied nod before taking the boulder steps from the cove two at a time.

'Come on,' he said, 'or you'll catch your deaths.'

We made our dripping way in his wake. I wondered if we were being taken to Glenister Hall. It seemed an odd choice. You might have had clean dry clothes there, but I didn't. Would Verity lend me something? I doubted it. Was there even hot water for a bath? My idea of the privations of Glenister Hall hardly ran to such luxuries. Perhaps Henry thought we needed taking to hospital. You had certainly ingested quite a lot of pond water. But if that was the case, why bother delaying for a dip in the sea?

It was a conundrum, and while I pondered it I followed tamely behind your father as he wove through the pathways between the trees. Dusk was fully present now, and the gloaming light made the familiar topography seem weird. I was cold, hugging my arms around my sodden body. My feet squelched in my trainers. I hadn't bothered to take them off to go in the sea. You trudged behind me. I could hear your teeth chattering.

Abruptly, Henry veered off the path and plunged into the undergrowth. There was a path, but it was narrow, through a variety of saplings, switch backing right and left, round a large boulder and then steeply upwards. The dusk was such that our surroundings were more shadow than anything else, insubstantial shapes in a deeper dim. I dug in and followed as closely as I could, although my whole body was shaking with cold now and I had a blister developing on one heel.

I smelt woodsmoke, and … fried fish. My stomach roiled with hunger pangs. I was starving. It was hours since breakfast and lunch had passed us by. I remembered the cookout for the students. Would we somehow emerge at the meadow? My heart leapt in relief, even though I knew I'd be in trouble. But to be home, and safe, and to see Mum … I stopped so suddenly that you cannoned into me.

'Oh no,' I said, clapping my hand to my mouth. 'What time is it?'

You squinted at your watch, but it was too gloomy to make out the dial and, as we soon found out, its dunking in the pond had ruined it. 'I don't know. Come on Prue, follow Henry. I'm frozen.'

'Me too,' I said, 'but I'm supposed to be having supper with Mum. She'll be worried about me.'

'I suppose we'll have to explain it all,' you said. 'But just now we need to get warm and dry. Henry's right about that.'

I gestured up the slope. 'But this way isn't …' I began.

But you pushed roughly past me. 'It *is*,' you said. 'Don't you remember about the woodsman's house? It's up here.'

I could only follow as you hurried up the slope between the indistinguishable trees. The path levelled out and then we were in a clearing. At the back there was a low-roofed building, stone-built, a single door separating two small square windows. The door was open wide and a flickering light within gave a glimpse of low beams and a rough flagstone floor. In front of the dwelling was an area cluttered with paraphernalia—I made out a lobster pot, some wooden barrels and a stack of firewood. There also was a blackened circle on which a bright fire now burned. A tripod over the fire supported a skillet and here were the deliciously cooking fish. Two roughly-hewn log benches flanked the fire and Henry gestured to one of them.

'Sit down. I'll find some blankets.'

We did as we were told, gaping at each other in amazement.

'Have you been here before?' I whispered, gazing around at the shambolic but actually quite comprehensively equipped encampment. I could see a lean-to with a variety of tools and fishing tackle; a large water bowser fed from some water-collection apparatus at the side of the house; a row of stoneware jars on a plank shelf. What might *they* contain? Sweets? Biscuits? My mouth watered.

'A few times,' you whispered back. 'But I've never seen Henry here.'

I turned to look at you. 'Who *was* here then?'

Your gaze travelled over my shoulder towards the cottage. 'Grandma.'

Your grandma bustled out of the building with two large grey blankets over her arm. 'Here, dears,' she said kindly. 'Put these round yourselves. The kettle's on and you shall have some hot tea in a jiffy.' Her voice was cracked and scratchy, as though she didn't use it very often, but unmistakably "posh," like Henry's. Her appearance was extraordinary. She wore a shapeless dress that seemed to be made out of sacking, tied at the waist with a piece of string. Beneath the dress she wore what looked to be a man's flannel trousers and what I would describe as workmen's boots, very scuffed at the toe and laced up with more string. Over the dress she had thrown a woolly cardigan of indeterminate colour which she had buttoned up wrong, and I was reminded of the coat she had worn to Grandad's funeral, also buttoned up awry. I recognised the untidy mop of grey curly hair but I couldn't see her face properly. The light of the day had gone now and the fire didn't throw enough brightness to make out her features.

You said, 'Thank you, Grandma,' and I echoed your thanks, grateful for the dryness and warmth of the blanket, although it was rather rough and prickly.

Then she moved to the other side of the fire and I could see her properly—her round but deeply lined face and penetratingly blue eyes that fixed on me, seeming to speak words her broken old voice could not articulate. An astonishing thought came to me, and I looked again around the clearing. I saw tarpaulins—heaped up anyhow, some fishing net, lengths of rope coiled up and hanging from nails and … yes … there amongst a variety of other unidentifiable bits of cloth I could see a peculiar but instantly recognisable waxed greenish cape or coat.

Your grandmother stood across the fire and watched the slow click and whir of my brain as I made sense of things, her own expression patient, but anticipating the inevitable. Then she smiled and gave me a little nod, and shuffled off in the direction of the house.

I turned towards you. 'Your grandma,' I said. 'I think I've met her before. I don't mean at Grandad's funeral, I mean *before*.'

'You *have*,' you replied. 'I wondered when the penny would finally drop.'

Then Henry emerged from the house with two thick clay mugs of steaming tea. 'No milk,' he stated, handing them to us.

The tea tasted funny—herbal and green—but it was sweet and hot and we gulped it down as fast as we could without scalding ourselves. Meanwhile your grandma brought out some earthenware plates and began to rake about in the ashes of the fire with a stick, pulling out charred potatoes. They brought Mum powerfully back to my mind. *She* had promised me jacket potatoes. I pushed away the blanket and stood up.

'You're very kind,' I said, 'but I must get home. Mum's expecting me.'

'Sit down!' Henry barked, and in spite of myself I did exactly that. 'You'll stay here and have some hot food,' he added. 'I can't send you home starved. And I want to know what the devil you've been up to.'

Mrs Glenister used an old brass fire shovel—not at all clean—to transfer the fish onto the plates. 'You'll have to use your fingers,' she said cheerfully. 'I haven't enough cutlery. Not used to having visitors.' A gleam of firelight caught her eyes and found its match in the shine of glee I saw there. 'Such a treat for me,' she beamed.

We began to pick flakes of fish from our plates. It was delicious. The outsides of the potatoes were charred but inside they were buttery and soft. We scoffed them down. Henry and Mrs Glenister ate too, and yet there was still more fish on the skillet, and you and I both had second helpings. I remember thinking it was a sort of miracle that a meal Mrs Glenister had prepared for just the two of them could stretch to two more with lots to spare, and the story of the loaves and fishes came to mind. Was there something magical about the place? Was there something magical about *her?* I was intrigued, excited—this woman, so important a figure in my recollection of that fateful day, and also inextricably linked to *you,* Arthur—and I felt that it was yet another hawser of convoluted connection that bound us together. I'd have been completely absorbed in the oddness and thrill of it if not for my nagging anxiety about Mum. What must she think of me? Perhaps even now there was a hue and cry as our absence was discovered.

When we'd finished, your grandma took the plates away and again I made to leave. 'I really should get home,' I said. 'There'll be an awful fuss if we're not at the camp by nightfall.'

'It's a bit late for that,' Henry sneered, wiping his fingers fastidiously on his pocket handkerchief. 'It's long past nine.'

'On no!' I squeaked. 'My parents will be frantic!'

'I shouldn't think so,' he opined. 'There seems to be quite a shindig going on over there. Can't you hear the music?' I tuned my ears, but could hear nothing. 'Quite a return to the old days,' Henry went on. 'Before Eric croaked.'

Croaked? How disrespectful. Henry's tone was so withering it shocked me. Clearly he looked back on those Day family gatherings in which he had been graciously included with utter contempt. To have our kindest and most cordial hospitality sneered at was galling.

'Even so,' I said stiffly, 'I must go home.'

'Not yet, young lady. Sit down and tell me what kind of scrape you've got Arthur involved in. I gather you'd been swimming in the pond. Have you any idea how dangerous that was? Arthur isn't a strong swimmer. You put him at terrible risk.' Henry was so domineering I found I couldn't stand up to him, but I'd have taken the blame, Arthur. I would. After all, an ill-advised dip in the pond was far less serious than what we'd actually attempted. Although why he thought we would swim *there,* rather than in the sea I couldn't imagine. I opened my mouth but before I could say a word you put in, 'It wasn't like that, Henry. We were fighting and we fell in.'

'Fighting?' Henry sounded incredulous and it was all I could do not to turn and stare at you in astonishment. What would we have been fighting about? That, to me, was the obvious question, but Henry said, 'That wasn't very chivalrous of you Arthur. We don't fight girls.'

You laughed. 'Prue isn't a girl!' And I felt partly proud—I despised girlishness—but also oddly wounded, although I didn't know why.

'I assure you she *is*,' Henry said, 'though I grant you she doesn't behave like a lady, and just now she doesn't look like one. She's always been the ugly duckling of the family.'

'That's what I told her. And so we had a fight about it,' you said coolly.

I was astonished and speechless, deeply offended. But then I felt the press of your hand against my thigh beneath the folds of the blanket, and I cottoned on.

'I'm more than a match for Arthur,' I declared, entering into the fabrication. 'So, now we've explained ourselves, perhaps you'll let me go home.'

'You should have more tea,' Henry said. Mother is just making it. And I'm not sure I feel comfortable with your returning to the company of those foreigners. They're all drunk, from what I can tell. They were when I went to collect Verity earlier. They weren't the only ones. And it wasn't even dark, then. The sun not even approaching the yardarm.'

'Where's Verity now?' I wanted to know.

'At Glenister Hall, of course,' Henry said. And I thought, what? All alone in that empty, leaky house? 'But don't try and change the subject,' Henry went on. 'We're discussing those disreputable hobbledehoys.'

'They're harmless,' you said. 'And Prue's right. We ought to let people know we're okay.'

Henry growled. 'I think you might do your grandmother the courtesy of spending some time with her, as she's has been so hospitable. I'll go and let the Days know you're with me.'

He rose from his seat and disappeared into the darkness of the woods.

Mrs Glenister emerged from the house with more tea and a bowl of something that looked like batter. She began to pour it onto the skillet with a rusty ladle even though some remains of the fish still stuck to the surface.

'Drop scones,' she announced.

When the little pancakes were done, we drizzled them in honey. They were light and golden and crispy at the edges, the slight flavour of fish not at all unpleasant, the sweetness of honey almost intoxicating. I remained anxious about Mum—she'd be worried sick, or possibly very angry—but Henry would put her mind at rest, and his last remark had struck a chord with me. The Days were nothing if not polite. As bizarre at the evening had been, it *would* be rude to up and leave so abruptly.

It occurred to me that I'd been presented with a unique opportunity, so when the three of us were settled round the crackling fire I said, 'You spend a lot of time in the woods, don't you Mrs Glenister?'

She nodded. 'I like it.'

I said, 'I do, too.'

She said, 'That's as well.'

I didn't really understand that remark, so I moved the subject along. 'So this is the former woodsman's house? I understand my grandfather lived here for a time.'

Mrs Glenister stared into the fire. 'Yes,' she said simply. Deep in the forest, an owl called its mate, but there was no reply.

'I don't suppose you knew him very well,' I ventured. 'He was just a woodsman, after all, and you were ... you *are* the lady of the house. And so my granny was very touched that you attended his funeral.'

Mrs Glenister sighed and pulled the folds of her cardigan more tightly around her, although the evening was not cold and the fire provided extra warmth. I thought my remark would go unanswered but at last she said, 'I knew him. I knew him very well.'

Her face was fully illuminated by the fire and I could clearly see the features that had so intrigued me in the church—aged and timeless, both. Her eyes shone brilliantly, abrim with tears.

'You were very fond of him,' I murmured, and she nodded ever so slightly.

I risked a glance at you, Arthur, but your chin had sunk onto your chest, your eyes were closed and your shoulders rose and fell as you breathed, deeply asleep.

'Granny said Grandad had been in the first war with Mr ... with Colonel Glenister,' I said quietly, 'and I suppose ... I guess that when they came back afterwards the Colonel offered Grandad this house and work as a woodsman. His parents had two other lads and there wasn't enough work on the smallholding ...' I trailed off, waiting to see if my words would penetrate her reverie.

I thought not. She seemed lost in her own thoughts. But then she said, 'There were so few men, after the war. And those who did return ...' she shook her head. 'They were hardly fit to hold down employment. And then, they didn't want to go back to the old ways. Being a "servant" was considered demeaning. But he ...' she seemed to stumble, and a tear rolled down her cheek. '... he wasn't too proud to do it. And he was glad to be so close to ...' again, she seemed to struggle to get her words to come.

'To home?' I suggested. 'He *would* be glad. Grandad *loved* Broadacres. It was everything to him.'

'Yes,' she nodded, but sadly. 'To home. But also ... also ...' She lifted one of her gnarly hands and pressed it to her bosom. She opened her mouth to complete her sentence but before she could do so there was a thrash and crash of undergrowth and Henry was back in the clearing.

'Just as I said,' he announced loudly, breathing fast. 'You hadn't even been missed. It's an orgy up there. Half-naked bodies round the campfire and the reek of marijuana. I've half a mind to let you sleep here, or to take you back to Glenister Hall. I shall have words with your parents, that's for sure. Broadacres isn't a suitable environment for children. Arthur, I shall insist that you remove to Glenister Hall immediately. I don't care what the courts decreed.'

His arrival and his declaration roused you from sleep and you stood up stiffly. 'Oh *no!*' you objected, your eyes wide with shock and glittering in the firelight. 'No, *please* Henry! Don't take me away yet! I've another week with Mum and … and I don't want to!'

I thought you were going to cry. I wanted to cry too. The idea of cutting short our precious time together was too dreadful. I rose and we stood shoulder to shoulder. 'They've never had a party before,' I pleaded. 'And I'm sure they won't be allowed another, if they've misbehaved. Really, they are very nice young people. One of them is going to train as a doctor.'

Our combined protestations seemed to make things worse. Henry's expression was one of appalled disgust as he looked down on us, side by side, in the flickering firelight. 'You two are getting too close,' he said. 'It isn't healthy. Neither of you are children anymore and … it isn't decent.'

I think we both blushed at his implication. Anything … like *that* … was unthinkable.

Your grandmother said, 'They can't sleep *here,* Henry. This is *my* place. Mine and …'

'I know, Mother,' Henry snapped.

'And we can't take Prue to Glenister Hall,' you argued. 'There isn't room.'

I wanted to laugh at that. No room? In that enormous pile? But I kept my face straight.

At last Henry said, 'Very well. You can return tonight. And tomorrow I shall speak to your parents. Off you go.'

He turned on his heel and disappeared again, swallowed by the dark wood. You disappeared into the shadows—I presume to pee. I wanted to, badly, but girls always have to wait. I started to fold the blankets but was interrupted by the fierce grip of a bony, urgent hand on my arm.

Your grandmother pointed to a hollow in the bole of a nearby tree. She said, 'The key is in there, when you're ready.'

I stammered, 'R… right. I see,' although I didn't see at all.

'You're the one,' she urged. 'I'm sorry, but there it is.'

I turned as I heard you returning from the bushes. 'Arthur,' I began. I hoped you'd be able to make sense of your grandmother's curious declaration. But when I swivelled back to where your grandmother had stood the place was empty. The door of the woodsman's house was closed.

'Oh well,' I said. 'I suppose we'll have to find our own way. It can't be far.'

But in fact it took us quite a while to find our way back to Broadacres. Although our eyes had adjusted to the dark and a pale moon threw a weak silvery light, everything looked different, and we took several wrong turns before finding ourselves—more by luck than judgement—at the gate through to the Christmas tree plantation. I could hear the faint strains of music but the untrammelled bacchanalia implied by Henry seemed to be over, if it had ever taken place at all.

We trudged along the edge of the cultivated area, but when we got to the turn that would take us up to the meadow I said, 'I'm not sleeping in the tent tonight, Arthur. I promised Mum I'd have supper with her and I ought to go and apologise for letting her down. I suppose I'll tell her the same story we told Henry. But since I have to go home, I might as well sleep in my own bed. Grace's will probably be empty. You can use it if you like.'

But you shook your head. 'That's all right. I'll go to the big house and sleep in Jack's room. I need a proper wash. See you in the morning?'

I nodded, but we both lingered.

'Quite an adventure we had there,' you said, grinning. I could see the whiteness of your teeth in the darkness.

I said, 'If you ever call me an ugly duckling, I *will* fight you.'

And you said, 'I know.'

When I got home the door wasn't locked—it rarely was—and there were no lights on. I groped my way to the kitchen and flicked on the light. The clock told me it was a quarter to eleven. The kitchen was clean and tidy, all the pots washed and put away. The only anomaly was a covered plate on the worktop. I peeped beneath the tinfoil. Four cold sausages, a pool of baked beans and a jacket potato. I was seized with remorse. How could I have let Mum down so badly? I knew she was sad and lonely and yet I'd allowed my own pleasure to take precedence.

I crept up the stairs and knocked timidly on my parents' bedroom door. When there was no answer I wondered about opening the door but decided against it. They'd be fast asleep at this late hour. Let them rest.

For myself, I slept like the dead and woke in the morning feeling bleary and disorientated—it was so long since I'd slept in my own bed.

Grace's bed was empty. Had she come home at all? What time was it? But the bedside clock told me it was only just after seven.

I got up and took a long shower before going downstairs.

Dad was in the kitchen, waiting for the kettle to boil.

'Hello, you,' he said, folding me into a hug. 'Fed up with the tent?'

'Oh no,' I said, reaching for a cereal bowl. 'But I promised Mum I'd have supper with her and then I was late, and so I thought I'd better come and apologise, but when I got home you were both asleep. But since I was here, I thought I'd stay.'

'In point of fact,' Dad said with a little cough, pouring water into the teapot, 'I didn't sleep here last night. I fell asleep on the sofa at the big house. I've only just walked across.'

'Oh.' I poured milk over my cornflakes. 'I feel worse now. Mum spent the whole evening alone.' I wanted to add, 'again,' but thought better of it. 'I'm a bit worried about her. Aren't you?'

'Yes, I am,' Dad said, but his voice was stiff and hard. 'But it's her own choice. Your aunts would be delighted if she'd join them. They want things to be as they were.'

'Before Isobel and Hester moved into Broadacres? Mum wanted to live there, so badly. I don't think she can forgive them,' I said.

'That's very silly,' my father said. 'Have you heard the expression, "cutting your nose off to spite your face"?' He'd poured three cups of tea from the pot. He picked one up. 'I'm due in the greenhouse,' he said. 'I'll have to take this with me. Will you take your mother her tea, when you've finished your cereal?'

I nodded, munching, and he left the room.

But when I carried Mum's tea upstairs and opened the bedroom door, the room was empty and her bed had not been slept in.

Chapter Twenty-One

No one knew where Mum had gone. We thought for a while that she had simply left, but her clothes were in her wardrobe, her handbag in its accustomed place with her purse inside. The family car was parked on the drive. And I couldn't believe she would do such a thing without saying goodbye.

The family searched the entire property—the woods, the plantation, the cove, all the outbuildings, poly tunnels and greenhouses. We even searched the hen run. It was like one of the scavenger hunts we used to have of old, but with a sinister twist. It was possible, we thought—but didn't say—that Mum's drinking had caused her to pass out, go astray. We searched the makeshift office Mum had been using to do the accounts—a shabby old shed that stank of mice—but there was no note or anything to suggest she had planned her departure.

It was a frantic day, the family's panic and hysteria rising higher and higher as we considered every likely and unlikely possibility. When every other potential had been exhausted, you and I went to Glenister Hall. It was a long shot. As far as I knew Mum had never been there or had any connection with the place. But I had suggested a visit to see Verity's prospective living quarters and so we wondered … but the place was shuttered and empty, the furniture shrouded, and our shouts only echoed through the vast, untenanted rooms. Although I'd long desired to explore the place my only focus then was on finding my mother, and I barely took in the grand salons, the enormous fireplaces, the mouldering panelling.

On our way back to Broadacres we located the woodsman's house. It was tricky and we made several wrong turns before we stumbled on the right pathway. But the house was locked up, the fire cold. There was no evidence that you and I had been there, or that anyone had.

I felt dreadful, of course, absolutely eaten up with guilt. If only I'd got home for my promised supper with Mum. Had my absence been the catalyst, the last in a whole bunch of straws that had broken the camel's back? I unburdened myself to you Arthur, didn't I, as we walked together into the village to see if anyone had seen Mum that day. Specifically, we were to enquire at the pub. Apparently Mum had been spending quite a bit of time there. I'd no notion of that. But you said that I shouldn't blame myself too much. Neither Grace nor Verity had been home either, had they? Why was Mum more my responsibility than theirs?

'But I *promised*,' I wailed. 'And she would have been upset about Dad. He fell asleep on Granny's sofa and didn't come home either.'

You stopped and looked at me. 'What?'

I repeated to you what Dad had said.

You chewed your lip but then said, 'No, Prue. I'm sorry, but that isn't true. When I got back to the big house the sitting room was empty. Your dad wasn't there. I know because ... because I went in and raided Granny's sweetie box. You know the one she keeps on the dresser in there?'

We stared at each other, trying to unravel the mystery of it.

'Where *was* he, then?'

'Up at the field with the students, perhaps,' you suggested. He may have come in later and fallen asleep.'

'I suppose,' I said. But I wasn't convinced.

That was the last real conversation you and I had for so many months that they amounted to years. Henry turned up at Broadacres later in the day and took you away. In the circumstances, your mother couldn't object because by then we had called the police. In point of fact he took you *and* Verity away for the rest of the summer, and when they came back the two announced that they'd married. Granny was terribly angry. Maybe she'd been looking forward to a big flashy affair with a marquee on the lawn, and felt cheated of her new hat. Or maybe she just disapproved of the whole thing. Henry was twice Verity's age and their relationship had begun when he was married. She condemned that; but knowing Granny, it wasn't just the couple's clandestine sneaking and dishonesty she decried, it was the terrible betrayal of Day hospitality on Henry's part, and its dereliction on Verity's. The Glenisters had been guests. They were due—and owed—more.

Once Verity was married we saw next to nothing of her, or of Henry either. We heard she'd given up her job and now helped Henry with his "business affairs," whatever they were. I can't say I missed my older sister much and I certainly didn't miss Henry at all.

But all that came later. In the aftermath of Mum's disappearance the Days did what the Days always do. They gathered, clannish and exclusive, as a police detective came to question us all, and a forensic team came to search the property and the woods, and press reporters gathered outside the gates of Broadacres, accosting anyone who went in or out with a barrage of questions.

I must say the students were marvellous, in the main, taking on all the deliveries, keeping up the schedule of picking and packing and also bringing in groceries to keep us going, saving us the ordeal of running the gauntlet of newspaper photographers and even a television crew. But one of them must have yielded to the pecuniary inducements offered by the tabloid press.

Suddenly the papers were full of talk of mum's "depression" and "alcoholism." There were stories of her stumbling about the property, drunk, of uncontrollable weeping and of vitriolic rows between her and my father, her and my aunts, even her and Granny, which was utterly ridiculous.

Days passed. My father sat at the hideous little telephone table in the hallway of Broadacres waiting for Mum to call, his head in his hands, his pallor and stricken expression increasing with every hour, with every day that went by. In vain did Granny and my aunts tempt him to eat or drink. He would do neither, just waved them away with an impatient hand. He was no comfort to me or Grace. We were both utterly distraught, imagining nightmarish scenarios—Mum was lost; Mum had been kidnapped; Mum had checked herself into some mental asylum; Mum had been murdered. Mum was dead. Mum was dead. Mum was dead. We both wept ourselves to sleep at nights—yes, even I cried. But no one—not Dad, not Grace, not even Verity—can have felt more abjectly culpable than I.

And how much more, then, when Mum was eventually found.

The forensic team brought in dogs and used them to quarter the wider environs of the property. Mum was traced to the pond. Frogmen came, and brought Mum's body from the thick, slimy depths. She had weighted her pockets with stones from our cairn, but they really were not sufficient to hold her below the surface, and the police detective said that even a suicide's natural instinct was to fight for life at the end. In this case, we were told, the pond wasn't more than four or five feet deep—how *that* detail stung!—and, having second thoughts, she could easily have got out. The principal cause of her death was a snarl of rope beneath the surface, in which she had become hopelessly entangled as she fought for life even though she had sought death. No one knew how it had come to be there or how long it had lain in wait—a fatal trap, ready to ensnare the unwary.

No one asked any questions about that rope and I certainly offered no explanation, but I felt as guilty as though I had tied Mum up and drowned her myself. All the neuroses of my earlier days came crashing back down on me and I could barely choke down a mouthful of food. I didn't sleep. Many times I went out of the house in the middle of the night and made my way to the pond. Its fringe of grasses whispered reproaches at me, but I didn't have the courage to follow Mum's example.

There had to be a post mortem of course, and then an inquest. It all took many weeks and delayed the funeral until mid-September.

I couldn't go back to school; I was listless and depressed, lost in a labyrinth of guilt and recrimination. I spent my days at Broadacres with the only person who had the time or patience to listen to my litany of self-blame—

Erin. We would sit in her room—a lovely room, with a large window that let in the afternoon sunshine—but our eyes hardly saw it, both concentrating on the place in the distance that absorbed so much of Erin's time and attention. It was a bleak, grey, formless expanse.

It was Erin who gave me a new perspective on the tragedy, quite unintentionally I'm sure, scratching the scab off an old wound I was only too ready to reopen.

I'd been bewailing—again—my failure to return home to supper with Mum when Erin said, 'You know, Prue, you really mustn't blame yourself so much. You're only thirteen—still a child, really. It's the grownups' job to look after each other, not yours.'

I thought of Dad—certainly, he'd been neglecting Mum. And my aunts—hadn't they wilfully excluded Mum from their nasty little coven?

Erin said, 'I know your mum confided in one grownup the day she died. He should have done something, but he didn't.'

I turned my head to ask, 'Who?'

She sighed. Erin wasn't one for long speeches or explanations and I could see she was gathering her energies. 'I felt quite strong that day so I went out to see if I could write up any invoices. Your mum was in her temporary office. I heard her talking to someone so I waited. I thought she was on the telephone at first, but it was Henry. He was in there with her.'

'Yes,' I murmured. 'He told me he'd dropped by for Verity to get some things.'

'I didn't mean to eavesdrop,' Erin said. 'But my heart went out to her. Poor Aunt Lucille. She sounded so unhappy.'

'Did she?'

'She'd been drinking. I'm sorry to tell you that, but you must know …'

I nodded.

'… so she wasn't quite coherent. But she was telling him that her girls were growing up and moving on. She wondered what she'd do when you were grown … who she'd *be* if she wasn't your mother.'

'Oh,' I sniffed. 'Did she? That's … so *sad*.'

'And she mentioned that Uncle Trevor seemed keener on Blanche than on her.'

'Well that's just silly. He's helped with the divorce, that's all. Mum must have been imagining things. What did Henry say? I hope he put her right.'

'I'm afraid not. He said that for what it was worth, Trevor was welcome to her—to Blanche, he meant.'

'That was unkind. And cruel.'

'Yes. It was, but then we all know Henry can be a cold fish. And then he suggested that Aunt Lucille should look for a way out. At the time I thought he meant a divorce … pastures new, a fresh start. But now … I wonder if she didn't mistake his meaning … or …'

'If he was *goading* her?'

All my old hatred of Henry boiled back up like magma from a volcano. I leapt off the bed and began to pace the room. If he'd been there right then I think I might have strangled him. How *could* he have been so callous? Why hadn't he told Mum she was being ridiculous? Why hadn't he informed someone about Mum's state of mind, like Dad. Or perhaps Granny? And why—that night round the fire at the woodsman's house—hadn't he told *me* any of this? Surely any reasonable person would have said, yes, hurry home Prudence. Your mother needs you. But no. Rather than that, he'd *prevented* me from going home. I'd felt bullied, more or less, into staying away, into eating, into drinking more of that peculiar tea. He'd even told me that we hadn't been missed, which I *knew* could not be true. He'd gone off to let people know we were okay. Or *had* he? Had he actually told *anyone* that we were safe with him?

Further questions piled into my shattered mind. What had he been doing, patrolling the woods? What had brought him to the pond to find us there, you and me, Arthur, passed out in the grass? Had he been waiting for Mum? Doing the rounds of all the places where she might … take her own life? To what end? To stop her? So that he'd be the hero of the hour? Or so that he'd have some hold over her? Or—and this was the most sickening explanation of all— to *watch?*

My imagination began to conjure macabre scenarios. Rather than going to Broadacres to set my parents' minds at rest, what if Henry had gone back to the pond. What if he'd been there, hiding in the shadow of the woods when poor Mum came that way, drunk, miserable beyond endurance. Had he watched her fill her pockets with stones? Stood by as she'd stepped into the milky jade waters of the pond, heard her cries of desolation and despair? And when her natural instinct to survive kicked in, and she began to slip and slide in the mud, become entangled … had he looked on still, some sadistic gland engorged? And finally, when she'd become exhausted and slipped below the surface, what had he thought? What had he felt?

Nothing. He had simply returned to the woodsman's house, cool as ever, to announce that no, no one had missed us at all.

It was speculation of course, but it grew until it was a monster, and it devoured me.

Oh Arthur! I can't talk about this anymore. I can't! And you! You don't say anything! You don't even seem to hear me. Why don't you speak? Oh Arthur! Arthur! Why won't you speak to me?

PART THREE
1978 – 1980
Chapter Twenty-Two

It's June now, a beautiful time of year. The sky is full of swifts by day, collecting insects to feed their young, and when the sun goes down the bats come out. I see them flit and swoop beneath the trees, blue-black darts against the inky sky.

I need to skim over a few years, Arthur. I don't remember much about the rest of 1972 or 1973. I spent some time in a psychiatric ward, diagnosed with General Anxiety Disorder, a condition that seemed to cover my dysphagia as well as the terrible trauma of losing Mum. When I was discharged I asked Dad to send me to boarding school. The prospect of being at Broadacres—of life going on without Mum—was too terrible. I'd missed a year of school and had to go back a class, but the new school was nice, the girls friendly and the teachers all kind. One of them—the English teacher, Miss Taylor—took me under her wing. She encouraged me to read the English classics and also to begin writing. I regularly had short stories published in the school magazine and a few of them were entered into national competitions, which they won. Finding a creative outlet did me the power of good. I'd always been a keen reader, but discovering that I could create my own fiction was a kind of therapy.

It so happened that my first year at Casterley school—1974—was the year of widespread strikes and power outages. The lights and heating all went off at seven in the evening and we were sent to our dormitories with extra blankets and a hot water bottle. Sometimes matron would come round with hot chocolate that she'd made on an old camping stove. The kitchens had to be rather inventive as there was a shortage of all sorts of things including bread, yeast and flour. They made what they described as "scone bread," which was glutinous and almost impossible to choke down. Interestingly, the result of these privations was a real sense of camaraderie amongst the girls that extended to the staff. There was a siege spirit of cooperation and I was absorbed into it. I felt part of something bigger than I was, part of a community. It reminded me of those early years at Salad Days. It was the best thing that could have happened to me.

The school welcomed girls from all kinds of backgrounds. There were students there whose parents worked abroad in the diplomatic service or in the military. Others had been sent to England from India, Pakistan and Hong Kong to gain a solid English education that would stand them in good stead later on. I think most of them went on to Oxford or Cambridge. For many reasons, some of the girls weren't able to be reunited with their parents in the vacations and so the school laid on various educational and sporting activities and expeditions between terms. I chose to take part in these as often as possible. I spent several Christmases skiing and my summers at Camp America. I helped build a clinic in Mexico and cruised the Mediterranean visiting places of historical and cultural interest.

I had to go back to Broadacres sometimes, but there had been changes I didn't like.

My Dad had moved back into the big house, swapping with the twins, who now lived at our old cottage. It felt wrong to me, that Dad had essentially returned to his boyhood days, looked after by Granny, as though he had never been married at all. As though Mum had never existed.

Granny must have liked having her remaining children and at least some of her grandchildren back beneath her roof. It wasn't the same, of course. Those halcyon days of our childhood were never to come again. Perhaps there had been too much tragedy, or everyone was just too tired. There were no parties on balmy summer evenings. The Easter egg hunt was discontinued and Christmas lunch was just a family meal like any other. But Granny remained spry, took part in business decisions and enjoyed pottering amongst the flower beds of her garden as she always had. She attended various village groups and did her stint at the annual summer fête. She rarely worked on the property though—happy to leave that to Hester and the others.

Grace married Gary and began popping out babies almost immediately. They lived above the pub, Gary's parents having retired and moved away. The accommodations were cramped and shambolic, pervaded by the smell of laundry drying over the radiators, stale beer and cigarette smoke. I did enjoy spending time with my niece and nephews, especially Pansy, who was a timid child, but seemed to take a liking to me. Grace's brief spell of elegance and beauty was over. She was overweight, always either pregnant or breastfeeding, wore shapeless, inelegant clothes and tied her unwashed hair back in unbecoming ponytails. She drank too much, and smoked, and had developed a coarse way of speaking that I suppose reflected the clientele of the pub. She'd taken over the catering and always smelled of chip fat. But she seemed happy, so that was something.

You will know more about Verity than I do. She rarely came to Broadacres even on the few occasions I was home. She and Henry had no children and from the way I saw her eying Grace's brood, I think this was a disappointment to her. I did ask Verity why she remained childless but she shrugged and said that Henry didn't want kids. Verity was as thin as Grace was fat, as stylish as Grace was slovenly. From what I could gather they travelled abroad a great deal, but whether this was business or pleasure I could not divine. On balance I don't think Verity was happy with her lot. She had a pinched, sour expression and had begun to bite her nails—a habit she'd never had as a child. The Days were never invited to Glenister Hall so I had no clue as to Verity's living situation. I never heard of any improvements or renovations so I can only assume that the place continued to deteriorate.

The same cannot be said for Salad Days. Hester pursued her programme of improvements. The new premises were constructed and open to the public by the end of 1973. Mercifully, the focus of the business shifted from fruit and vegetables to plants and flowers as Britain's entry to the Common Market opened our borders to floods of cheap salad crops. Increasingly, local greengrocers were closing their doors, unable to cope with the competition from supermarkets or frozen foods produced in factories. But as a farm shop and garden centre, we survived. Salad Days became a destination as people came to peruse the plants and shrubs, drink tea in the café and buy the cheeses and other dairy products that Victor made in a state-of-the-art facility. Jack and the twins worked full time alongside my father and Hester. Victor and Isobel supervised the shop, café and of course the dairy. Blanche did the accounts, assisted by Erin when she was able. One good thing the Common Market brought was the free movement of labour. Salad Days employed foreign pickers to do the majority of work on the land. I presume they rented accommodation in the surrounding villages. One or two brought camper vans, but the caravan on the meadow was towed away and, as far as I know even in summer, no one ever camped up there again. It was returned to the bees.

And what about you, Arthur? You didn't write, but then neither did I.

What could we have said?

I had news of you from Erin, who was a regular correspondent. You were doing well at school but—like me—found ways of avoiding going home for the holidays. I heard you'd made friends with a boy whose parents had an estate on the Isle of Mull and spent your summers up there fishing for salmon and your Christmases listening to bagpipes and doing the highland fling. The idea of that made me smile! At Easter you skied in the Alps or in Liechtenstein, often with Henry, but I never heard that Verity joined you on these occasions and I worried that she'd go a bit crazy, being left alone at Glenister Hall, like your grandmother did. It seemed that fate was determined to keep us apart. I'd get home for a brief stay to be told you'd been there the week before, or were expected the week after. I missed you, but I'd made the decision to allow my life to move forward. Looking back was too painful—and too dangerous.

And so, my tale brings me to 1978. I was nearly nineteen. I finished my A levels, a year late because of the terms I'd missed earlier on. Interestingly, that time-out meant that you and I were at the same point in our education—looking forward, applying to university, ready for our real lives to begin. I planned to take a year travelling, heading to Australia and New Zealand via Hong Kong, where I had an invitation to visit Zhi, a girl I'd made friends with at school. I'd renewed my passport and begun to plan my itinerary. I had an offer of a deferred place at Birmingham University, where I would study English literature; but before that I had the idea that I'd give myself the time and space to try my hand at a novel. I'd even bought a second-hand portable typewriter in a junk shop.

The only fly in the ointment of my ambition was money—I had none. My school had not permitted boarders to take part-time jobs in shops, bars or restaurants. To be honest, most of the girls didn't need to work—they had allowances or trust funds—but Dad had always made it clear to me that my school fees were as far as he could stretch. He refused to buy my open flight ticket or to subsidise my travels in any way. It was Granny who'd paid for my various trips between terms.

'You'll have to earn it, Prue,' he said. 'Like everyone else.'

Reluctantly, then, I'd agreed to return to Salad Days for the summer of '78 and work *for wages*—I'd made that clear—before setting off on my adventure. The twins invited me to share the cottage with them but nothing on earth would have persuaded me to go back *there,* and when I said so I was told that room would be found for me at the big house—"somehow." I hoped to ask Grace if she could give me some shifts at the pub and intended to ask around at other restaurants to see if there was any evening waitressing or cleaning work. I reasoned I'd be fed and housed and able to save virtually everything I earned for my trip.

How could I have known that you'd have the same idea?

My last exam completed, I arrived home in early June of 1978. Isobel was waiting for me at the station. She leaned over and opened the car door for me. School had organised to send most of my belongings by carrier, so I only had a small bag with me.

'Fling that in the back,' she said, 'if you can find room.' The back seat of the car was stacked with what looked like catering supplies. 'You're lucky I was going to the cash and carry today,' she said. 'Otherwise, you would have had to wait for the bus.' She didn't attempt to kiss me or show any other sign of affection or pleasure that I was home. I suppose she recalled that I'd taken Mum's side at the time of their falling-out. It may be that my resentment—hard though I'd tried to bury it—still showed.

'Thanks,' I said. 'I hope you haven't had to wait long.'

'I was worried I'd be late,' she said, pulling out into the traffic. 'Things always take longer than you think, these days.'

I glanced across at her. She hadn't changed much. There were grey steaks in her hair, perhaps a little suggestion of belly where her body was folded into the seat. She wore spectacles—that was new.

She said, 'Can you drive?'

I shook my head.

'You'll have to learn. Arthur's already booked his test. He's had lessons at school, apparently.'

I swivelled in my seat to look at her. 'Arthur's at Broadacres?'

She nodded. 'He's been home a week.'

Home? How could Broadacres be *your* home? 'You mean at Glenister Hall?'

'No. He's come home to work, like you.'

I pretended to watch the scenery—the low roofs of the town giving way to housing estates I didn't remember, a retail park, a cinema complex—but my mind was struggling to adjust to this surprising turn of events. I'd missed you, Arthur, and thought about you sometimes, but in the past tense. In my head you were still eleven, still gangly, still wide-eyed with wonder at the world. We were still kids in our tent on the meadow sharing contraband crisps and sweets after we were supposed to be asleep, in some rose-tinted remembering that was more of a dream than reality.

In an attempt to fit you into the picture of Broadacres I'd drawn—a pre-handling of my expectations on my return to the scene of the crime—I asked, 'How are we all to be accommodated? I don't mind sharing with Erin.'

Isobel sucked her teeth. 'That's out of the question. Erin needs her rest. You'll have the girls' old room.'

'But I thought Dad must …'

'He's made other arrangements.'

'Oh? What?' I conjugated the rooms at Broadacres in my mind but couldn't produce any formula that would accommodate *two* extras.

Isobel concentrated on emerging from a tricky junction and did not reply.

Everything at Broadacres was just the same. And yet so very different. The house was as magnificent as ever, its weathered old brick swathed in roses and wisteria—classically, timelessly beautiful. In contrast the new farm shop was modern—square and squat, faced in plate glass, the forecourt cluttered with ugly statuary, pots and urns, painted gnomes, artificial ploughs and decorative wheelbarrows—garden ornaments, I suppose they must be called, but to my mind not the least ornamental. A huge patch of what had been shrubbery had been cleared to accommodate car parking. There were strangers wandering about wheeling trolleys. There were even litter bins, and a plethora of signs: "the café"; "cottage garden plants"; "hedging plants"; "climbers" and so on. It was all so sickeningly commercial and intrusive, trampling on the wonder of my childhood.

'Do people ever wander into the garden of Broadacres?' I asked, as Isobel pulled up in a "reserved" space outside the café. 'I mean, how do they know what's private and what's public?'

'Sometimes,' she said, quite brightly, as though this would not be an appalling trespass, 'but we soon put them right. Come on. Help me unload this stuff and then we can go to the house. Granny's laying on a celebratory tea for you.'

'The return of the prodigal?' I muttered, but not quietly enough.

Isobel said, 'Something like that.'

Tea was set out on the terrace, as it always had been in former days. Plates of sandwiches, scones, a Victoria sponge cake oozing with jam and cream. Granny stepped out of the shadows through the French windows carrying a huge teapot. Except the teapot was the same one she'd always used. It was Granny, I saw, who was smaller. When I hugged her I was a full head taller than her. She felt frail in my arms.

'Look at you! Look at you!' she repeated, holding me at arm's length. She reached a thin hand up and combed through my long, Farah Fawcett hair. Zhi had died it platinum blonde for me, *à la* Debbie Harry. Oh! I'd quite thrown off the tomboy by then!

My dad arrived, presumably from work on the property. His usual tatty boilersuit had been replaced by a pair of blue twill dungarees with a Salad Days logo embroidered on the bib.

'What's that!' I jeered, pointing. He looked like something out of *The Hollywood Hillbillies*. But then I looked around and saw that they were all wearing the same uniform. 'Oh,' I said. 'I see, it's the new corporate look.'

Hester stepped forward. She was thinner than I recalled, with marked lines round her eyes and mouth. She was still smoking. She had a cigarette in one hand and another behind her ear. She stroked the bib of her dungarees proudly. 'Kath designed the logo,' she said. 'What do you think?'

It was embroidered, a traditional Suffolk trug overflowing with Disney fruit and vegetables. We couldn't have been further away from Suffolk, and I knew that produce was the least of our business nowadays, but I said, 'Very nice,' and turned to greet the girls.

Kath and Karen were the same, their strawberry-blonde hair tied in simple ponytails, their faces without makeup of any kind, but still very pretty. They were both tanned, looked slim and athletic. I supposed their hard physical work on the property kept them trim. I wasn't in bad shape myself, but I had three years on them. They were twenty-two years old at that point. As far as I knew they'd had several boyfriends but none of them serious, and it would be quite a man who would be able to separate them from each other. They both greeted me with hugs and told me they were glad to have me home.

I continued to greet my relatives as I moved round the terrace, and all the time I had you in the periphery of my vision, standing just outside the circle of Days. I wanted to turn and look at you properly but your hovering there—on the edge of things—gave me the impression that you were as nervous of the encounter as I was.

Erin reached out a pale hand from where she sat on a lounger beneath a light blanket. 'Hello, you,' she said with a wan smile. I squatted down and enfolded her in a hug.

Uncle Victor had gained a lot of weight. His Salad Days workwear strained at the sides. He enfolded me in a big bear hug though, genial and good humoured as always, then helped himself to a large slice of cake.

Jack came next. We both hesitated, blushing, trying to decide whether a hug or a hearty clap on the shoulder would be acceptable. He was twenty-one, but thin and rangy, with stooped shoulders and a wary expression. I'd expected him to be more confident of himself—more of a man—but his swift, limp little hug made me realise he still hadn't "found" himself.

Isobel rescued him from his embarrassment by asking him to take his sister a cup of tea.

Blanche was the only one not wearing the ridiculous dungarees. She wore a pretty summer frock that showed off tanned arms and legs. Her hair was glossy, becomingly arranged around her elfin face. She gave me a wide smile but avoided the need for any more demonstrative greeting by handing me a cup and saucer.

'You must be famished,' she said. 'Let me get you some cake. Or a scone?'

'A sandwich first,' I replied, 'please.'

'Oh yes!' She let out a peal of laughter. 'How silly of me. Of course, a sandwich first. At least one!' and bustled off in search of a plate and napkin.

So that left you.

Mercifully, everyone's attention had turned to the food and drink. I stood on the edge of the terrace and swept my hair back with my hand, pretending to survey the garden. I felt you beside me, quite a bit taller, my shoulder just reaching your bicep. I glanced sideways. It was a substantial bicep, I noted, as it stretched the sleeve of your tee shirt. I turned slowly and took the rest of you in. Unlike Jack, you'd filled right out. You were tall—but not as ridiculously tall as Henry—and broad-chested. Your jaw was square and furred with red bristles, your skin still peppered with freckles. Your blue eyes met mine.

'You got through that okay,' you said. 'Mine was last week. Much the same, except there was chocolate cake.'

Your voice was low. I hadn't expected that. And, in spite of your reticence on the terrace, I discerned no diffidence. *You* weren't nervous.

I was—unnerved by your manliness. By how good-looking you were. I repeated the line I'd used earlier with Isobel to cover my confusion. 'The prodigals' return?' I murmured.

You smiled. Ah! *There* was the Arthur I remembered. I was filled with nostalgia and made a show of looking down at your hands. They were large and capable—a man's hands. 'No ring?' I joked. 'No fatted calf?'

You turned and, like me, surveyed the garden. 'About a ring …' you began, but then from the corner of the house we heard the approach of Grace and the children, and no further conversation was possible. Grace wore a shapeless and not very clean dress. Her hair was straggly and greasy. She hugged me and said, 'Gary says … oh no! What *now?*' and had to waddle off after one of the children, who had fallen into a rose bed. Pansy, with uncharacteristic effusion, hugged my knees, until tempted away by Granny with cake. Next came Verity and Henry, bringing with them—to my great surprise—Colonel Glenister. Henry and his father were immaculately dressed as always, in three-piece suits, with well-polished brogues. Their get-up was as artificial and pretentious in their own way as the dungarees were, and I had to smother a smile. Instinctively I looked to where you now stood in conversation with Jack, but you didn't meet my eye. The colonel—whose hair was thinning—wore a straw fedora which he lifted, gentlemanlike, to all the ladies. It seemed he was no stranger to Broadacres, greeting everyone cordially before turning to me and extending a hand.

'Miss Day,' he said. 'An immense pleasure to meet you. How was your journey?'

I muttered some reply, racking my brain to think why his appearance here should be so odd. I watched him bend to say a word to Erin, shake my father's hand and raise Granny's hand to his lips before taking a seat in the shade and accepting a cup of tea. I scanned the family, but no one seemed the least surprised at his presence here with us.

Henry fixed his eyes at some far point above our heads. Verity said, 'So, you're back. Everyone comes back in the end,' in a drawling, bored tone that suggested she thought Broadacres, Glenister Hall, Salad Days, the family, *everything* was a depressing sump of bleak, tiresome *ennui*.

I said, 'Just for the summer,' but a general hushing and a clearing of throats made me realise that someone was going to make a speech.

We turned. Nearly everyone was seated now, apart from Verity and me, Henry—who had retreated to the far end of the terrace—my father and Blanche. Those two stood close together, he looking sheepish, she unable to suppress a beaming smile.

Dad said, 'Now that the whole family is gathered, Blanche and I have something to announce.' He groped for Blanche's hand.

I felt a stab of horror. The sandwich I'd eaten turned to bile in my throat. You turned your head just a fraction and threw me an apologetic look that said, 'I tried to warn you.'

'It is six years since our dear Lucille left us,' Dad said. 'They have been unhappy years for me. For *all* of us,' he qualified, looking my way but not meeting my eyes. 'However, I have come to accept that life must go on. My beautiful girls have all done so, and I've realised that I have as much right as they do. And so …' he paused, lifting Blanche's hand to his lips and kissing it, and now I saw the icy sparkle of the diamond ring on her finger. '.. and so I'm delighted to tell you that this lovely lady has consented to be my wife.'

There was a ripple of applause. I scanned the faces round the table—so familiar in memory but now subtly altered—and saw pleasure and approbation, but no great surprise.

They all knew.

Seeing that something more than applause was required, a few people got up and hugged the couple. Grace did so, as did Granny and Isobel. My aunt Isobel looked particularly gratified. I wondered if this had been a scheme of hers. She had grown close to Blanche over the years. And that made me think of my mother, who had been Isobel's particular friend until suddenly, she wasn't. Poor Mum. She'd been utterly and thoroughly supplanted. Blanche had taken everything that had been my mother's.

In the hubbub I lost sight of you. You'd been forewarned, that was obvious. Why had I not been given the same consideration?

'Aren't you pleased?' The voice from behind me made me jump, and I swivelled to see Henry looming over me. 'Everyone else seems delighted,' he observed. 'You ought to go and offer your congratulations. Oh! But I suppose you're thinking of your poor mother. I wouldn't worry. She'd want Trevor to be happy.'

'What do *you* know of what my mother would want?' I croaked out.

He moved fractionally to one side so the sun suddenly shone into my eyes so I had to squint and use my hand as a visor. Even so, I couldn't make out his expression, but he seemed to think the question a serious one. He considered for a moment. 'Well,' he said at last, 'I want Blanche to be happy.'

'Oh?' I snorted. 'I thought "anyone was welcome to her." *That* doesn't sound like much concern for her happiness!'

Henry waved my words away. 'Our positions—your mother's and mine—aren't so very dissimilar.'

'How can you even *compare* them?' I spat, astonished. 'You're alive. And you're nothing like my mother.'

'We both chose something *else,*' he murmured, 'that's all. The only difference is …' He moved again, plunging me into his shadow, and I felt the soft brush of his finger on my cheek. I recoiled and he gave a little chuckle. 'The only difference is,' he repeated, '*I* can do it again. *She* can't. 'My, my,' he hurried on before I could object, his voice crooning, his mouth so close to my ear I could feel his breath lift my hair. 'Not such an ugly duckling after all, are you?'

I lurched away from him, turning instinctively to Dad, but then realised I couldn't approach him without some appropriate words on my lips. I stammered through my congratulations and then moved away.

Five minutes later, as though programmed, the whole family rose from the table and went back to work. The easy informality of the early days was replaced by an almost military punctuality. Everyone had a job to do, had somewhere to be. You, Jack and the twins all returned to work on the property. Isobel and Victor went back to the shop. Hester and my father climbed into two new-looking vans emblazoned with the Salad Days logo and set off to complete the day's deliveries to nearby pubs and restaurants and the few remaining greengrocers that stocked our produce. Grace took the children home, stopping only to parcel up the leftover cake in some spare napkins. Henry and Verity claimed an appointment in town but left the colonel behind them. He and Granny commenced a tour of the garden. Blanche began to clear away the tea things. What could I do but help? She talked inconsequentially about my journey, having made up my bed for me and the menu that was planned for supper as she stacked the dishes in a dishwasher.

'This is new,' I exclaimed, looking at it. 'I'm amazed Granny has permitted it.'

'Oh well,' Blanche prevaricated. 'Your granny, you know … and Isobel is much more … and so we all agreed. We have a freezer, too! It's in the scullery. Ice cream whenever we want!'

'Nice,' I said, but faintly. Ice cream had been a staple at school. I surveyed the kitchen. Just the same apart from the dishwasher, and the absence of Podge's smelly little bed by the range. She had died the previous year.

I grasped the nettle. 'Naturally, you and Dad will take over here at Broadacres,' I said. 'You'll know that it was always promised to him. You mustn't let Isobel usurp you. Maybe now the new premises are up and running Hester will go back to her own house, and Victor and Isobel will find somewhere else. They *ought* to. They should all understand that Dad will want to be master in his own home. And you'll want to look after him.' I thought—but didn't say aloud—that it's what Mum had wanted, what Mum had been promised. And if Blanche was going to step into Mum's shoes she ought to get the whole package.

But Blanche looked at me blankly. 'Oh no,' she said. 'I'm not much good at that sort of thing. I expect things will remain as they are. Now, dear,' she wiped her hands on the tea towel, 'your things all came yesterday and Trevor put them in your room.'

She seized a cloth and began wiping the work surfaces although they looked perfectly clean to me. I had the powerful sense that she wished our *tête à tête* to be over.

'And where is Dad …?' I began, but I left my question hanging. Of course, Dad slept in Blanche's room. He probably had been doing so for months, even years.

Blanche didn't seem to have heard. She kept her back to me as she said, 'You'll want to unpack and change. Leave this with me. I can finish up.'

But I lingered in the doorway, perhaps stubbornly, not wishing to be dismissed until I was ready. 'You'd already told Arthur,' I said.

'Yes. I wanted to tell him privately.'

'What did he say?'

'Oh well,' she turned to face me, her eyes wet with tears, exuding happiness, 'of course, he was *very* pleased.'

'He would be,' I thought, as I turned and left the room.

Chapter Twenty-Three

It was quite late when I got to bed and had the leisure to think things over. Once the farm shop had closed, I'd been taken over it and shown what I'd be doing for the holidays. Not working amongst the plants, as I'd hoped, but serving teas, clearing tables, selling produce and operating the till.

'I'd rather work outdoors,' I said, remembering the happy hours of my childhood. 'Like in the old days. Granny and Grandad had made it all such fun.'

But Isobel said, 'It isn't like the old days. Everything we do nowadays is witnessed by the customers. We have to show professionalism and discipline. We can't be seen to be having *fun*. Customers expect detailed horticultural knowledge—what soils plants like, how much they need to be watered. Hester has the twins pretty well trained up and Jack is catching on fast. Arthur and the students do the heavy lifting. So you're not needed out there. We're short-handed indoors. It seems impossible to get people who understand hospitality, who can turn themselves out neatly and engage in polite conversation. My God, Prue! If you could *see* some of the local girls we've tried out in here! They can't string a coherent sentence together between them! And we never trust anyone but family with the till. So you should feel rather privileged.'

She'd taken me along the shelves, stocked with speciality produce—jams, chutneys, honey, artisan baking—as well as decorative household items, gifts, local handicrafts. A refrigerated cabinet held cheeses and yoghurts. 'Most of this we produce ourselves,' she explained, 'but we do support some other local makers. As far as fruit and vegetables are concerned, Jack or Arthur will bring those in daily. People help themselves and then you weigh their purchases at the till. We never mix old and new stock—otherwise people will just take the fresh stuff and leave us with the rest. But the boys will monitor that. Really, Prue, we just need you to smile and take the money.'

I made a last attempt. 'I really want to work with Arthur,' I said. 'I've missed him and him being here just seems like too good an opportunity to pass up.'

Isobel sniffed and curled her lip. 'Don't go there, Prudence,' she said. 'Trust me on this. No good can come of it.'

I'd been issued with my own pair of dungarees and a couple of tee shirts along with a zip-up hooded sweatshirt to put on if the weather was poor. I regarded them dismally as I washed and got into bed. What *would* I look like?

I switched off the light. It was a long time since I'd slept alone in a room—even as a privileged senior student I'd shared a twin room with Zhi. I could hear low voices through the wall—you and Jack getting ready for bed. The rest of the house was quiet, everyone already gone to their rest.

I lay with my arms behind my head, thinking over the events of the day.

I should have seen the writing on the wall regarding my dad and Blanche. I thought back to the months he'd spent helping her get her divorce settlement sorted out. Was that when their romance started? Certainly, it was the time when Mum began her decline. I'd put that down to her finding out about Verity's affair with Henry, but maybe I was wrong about that.

I knew from Erin that Mum was jealous of Blanche but dismissed the idea as a fantasy. I couldn't believe that Dad would ever betray Mum in that way. And yet, now I thought about it, a burgeoning affair with Blanche would explain why Dad took so much care over the divorce settlement. Hadn't Blanche received a substantial sum? Now Dad would have access to it. Could he *really* have planned it all along? I felt no pleasure in my thoughts. I didn't want to believe that Dad could act in such a calculating and self-serving way, but having suggested itself to me I found I couldn't get the possibility out of my head.

I speculated that Isobel had orchestrated a liaison between Dad and Blanche from the moment the Glenisters had split. Was that why she'd shut Mum out?

Then I had another notion. As much as Dad could lay claim to Blanche's Glenister settlement, as his wife she would be entitled to a share of the Day property too. You, specifically, Arthur, could end up owning at least a part of Salad Days, or Broadacres, or both. For surely, you'd be the sole beneficiary of her estate.

I didn't like thinking that way. We'd had more than our fair share of death in the family and thinking about estates and wills seemed macabre. Deliberately, I moved my thoughts on to other matters.

How surprising it had been to see the arrival of the colonel that afternoon. He'd seemed right at home, and behaved very chivalrously towards Granny. It didn't sit comfortably for some reason, and it took me a while to identify why. Then it came to me. Granny had told me there had been a falling out between the colonel and Grandad. Was that all resolved?

And where, I wondered, was Mrs Glenister? What a curious woman she was! I hadn't given her a thought in years but now I wondered if she was still living in the woods, foraging for food. As a child it had seemed magical to me as well as thrillingly Gothic—the stuff of fiction—but now it occurred to me that perhaps she was ill, mentally unbalanced in some way. She was certainly eccentric. Or it might be—and the thought made me unaccountably sad—

she'd died. *That* would explain the colonel's sudden emergence into local society.

A quiet tap on my door arrested my thoughts. I said, 'Come in,' and the door opened enough to admit a slice of moonlight from the landing, and you.

'You aren't asleep, are you?' you whispered, crossing the room and perching on my bed. You formed a greyish shape, slightly darker than the surrounding dim.

I sat up. 'No. Just thinking about Dad and Blanche. You already knew?'

I saw you nod. 'I tried to let you know.'

'I know. It's okay. What do you think about it?'

You shrugged. 'I'm pleased, I suppose. You Days have made Mum—both of us—part of the family. This will just be an extension of that.'

It wouldn't be, I thought. It would be much more.

But I pushed my cynicism away. 'Tell me everything,' I said.

We talked a lot that summer, Arthur. Do you remember? As kids we'd talked, but of random things. 'Imagine this,' and 'what if that,' we'd say, sharing arbitrary imaginings and haphazard impressions we plucked from our juvenile, unformed brains, melding them with snippets of books we'd read, TV programs we'd seen, and all jumbled together in a *smorgasbord* of inconsequential chatter.

But that summer of 1978 we talked about important things—our hopes and plans, our experiences of school, our friends—everything except our feelings. I suppose these were just too shapeless and unwieldy, or too half-baked, defying description. We were poised between childhood and adulthood. The familiar setting of Broadacres was all of the past—those family parties, our games in the grounds and the wider environs, the Day traditions that had been the building bricks of our lives. But now we'd come to the very edge of it—the border between the familiar and the strange—and stood with our toes on the cusp. We were just forming our ideas about things both plebian and sublime: politics; our taste in music—I liked disco, you liked rock; philosophy; religion; whether we preferred McDonalds or Burger King. The sense of potential was palpable and yet I felt we were both conflicted about grasping it; we were eager *and* terrified.

Like me, you planned a year out, but your travels would take you to the historically and culturally important centres of Europe. Then you had a place at Portsmouth to study architecture. Your choice of Portsmouth dismayed me—it was so far away—but I didn't say so. You were projected good grades for your A levels—but not as good as mine—especially in history, but we'd studied different curricula and so it was difficult to compare. You told me about your friends in Mull. I had been right about the traditional Hogmanay celebrations but I'd never suspected a romance with your friend's sister, Amy. You spoke of her with great gentleness and sensitivity. Clearly, it had been much more than just a hotly hormonal teenage fling. Sadly, once her parents had discovered the attachment, they had discreetly put an end to it by ceasing to invite you to their castle.

I was untouched by love. That isn't to say I hadn't been round the block once or twice, but in comparison to your true romance with Amy, my fumblings felt sordid and I didn't mention them.

Our work kept us apart—perhaps Hester and Isobel had organised that deliberately—but once work was done and we'd eaten and showered, we'd drift off together. My plans of gaining additional evening work were shelved. We liked to walk down to the pub. Grace knew very well that you hadn't turned eighteen but she didn't refuse to serve you pints of lager. After you'd passed your driving test we'd borrow one of the vans and drive out to a spot on the coast that overlooked the sea to watch the sun go down in a blaze of colour. Many nights you crept into my room and we'd talk in lowered voices by the light of a lamp. And on some of those evenings you'd appear still fully clothed and say, 'Get dressed, Prue, and let's get out of here.'

We'd tread barefoot through the silent house and let ourselves out by the back door before struggling into our shoes and tiptoeing over the gravel to gain the lawn. Then up past the plantation—growing fruit trees now as well as Christmas trees—and into the woods as the moon poured her milky light in a sort of blessing on our ramble. And then it really was as though we'd stepped back into our childhood—or some romanticised, semi-fantastical version of it. You and I were like the first people, filled with wonder at the new-made world.

Sometimes you brought strong, cheap cider that tasted like paint stripper. We'd sit on the rocks of the cove or in the quiet little cemetery and get sozzled, laughing helplessly over nothing at all. Once you brought weed that you rolled up inexpertly. We smoked awkwardly, neither of us used to it. I liked the sensation of euphoria that flooded my limbs. My mind—never wholly at peace—stilled. But I found the weed excited my libido. Or maybe it was you? Either way, I wasn't ready to take any step in that direction and the next time you proffered a joint, I refused.

But those summer nights in the woods, Arthur! Oh! They were happy.

Chapter Twenty-Four

Our days on the property were long—often seven till seven. What with that and the time I spent with you, three or so weeks had gone by before I opened my typewriter and slotted the first sheet of paper into it. It was about nine in the evening. You'd gone to see a film with the twins, but I'd already seen it so stayed behind. I'd had the opening chapter of my book in my head for months, and spent slack times in the shop honing and tweaking it, but getting it onto the page was still much more difficult than I'd imagined. I wasn't a trained typist for a start. As careful as I was, and using two fingers, I still made mistakes and had to start over. Naïvely, I thought I'd be able to produce an error-free manuscript at the first attempt!

Annoyingly, even that tentative start was stymied by a peremptory knock on my door. Isobel didn't wait for my 'Come in,' but stepped briskly over the threshold.

'You'll have to stop that,' she snapped. 'You're right above Erin's room here. She can't stand the noise. I'm surprised you could be so thoughtless.'

Her attention seemed to be caught by the way I'd personalised the rather featureless room—photographs of various schoolfriends and of myself skiing; certificates and school prizes I'd had framed; the shelf crammed with many books; my *Saturday Night Fever* posters and a map of the world with pins and string plotting my prospective journey across it. She spent a moment perusing these things and when she turned back to me her eyes were wet with tears.

'What a life you've had already,' she murmured. 'And what a future you have before you.'

I felt stabbed with remorse. Poor Erin. And poor Isobel, to know that her daughter's future was a story that would remain unwritten.

I knew the nature of Erin's illness by then—she had leukaemia—and also that the treatments she'd had could never cure it. I don't know if the family was in denial, but the terminal nature of Erin's condition had never been discussed. She was cosseted and spoiled, cared for and considered in every way, but as far as I knew no one had ever discussed an approach to her end-of-life care, least of all with her. So it was a complete surprise to witness Isobel's stubborn defiance crumble. She groped her way to my bed and perched on it, bringing a tissue from her pocket.

'You must have noticed how ill she is,' she got out.

I *had* noticed. Erin was pale and thin, with little appetite. She seemed to suffer headaches and pain in the rest of her body. I knew she was particularly prone to infection because the family was especially wary of bringing in coughs and colds. Erin was never allowed to do anything that might result in a cut or scrape that could become infected. Sometimes her breath seemed laboured. Any pretence that Erin assisted with the business accounts had been abandoned. She was listless and inactive, lying outdoors if the weather was fine—but still covered in layers of blankets—or if the days were cooler she remained indoors. What meals she ate were usually taken on a tray in her room, one or other of us sitting nearby to fill the space with inane chat while she moved the food around on her plate.

There was a sense of tiptoeing we had all unconsciously adopted, but it felt futile and perhaps even cruel for us all to behave as though Erin's condition was temporary. In her shoes, I thought, I'd want to *talk* about things.

'Yes,' I said simply. 'I have. Do you mind if I ask, Aunt Isobel, what *is* the prognosis?'

She shook her head and pressed her lips together as though to keep back the words she couldn't bear to utter. But then, 'Not good,' she croaked out. 'We'll be lucky if she sees the year out. That's why we were so glad that you wanted to come home this year. And that Arthur did. Erin needs her whole family around her.'

'Of course,' I said faintly. 'And, when the time comes, will she go into hospital?'

'Oh no. She'll stay here. I'll nurse her.'

'We all will,' I said. 'Have you discussed things with her? Has the doctor? Do you know how much Erin understands? Do you know what Erin wants?'

Isobel blew her nose. My questions seemed to appal her. 'How on earth can I ask?'

I thought, 'How on earth can you *not?*' but didn't speak the words aloud. Instead, I asked, 'When she goes to see her consultant, does she go in by herself?'

Isobel said, 'Oh yes. She's insisted on that since she turned eighteen. I don't know what they discuss and I haven't asked. Oh Prue! I can't bear to know! I'm such a coward, while she's being so very brave.' She dissolved into tears again and I moved across to the bed and put my arm around her.

'I know it's very hard,' I said soothingly. 'But we're all here for you, and for her.'

From then on I made a point of spending more time with Erin. She seemed genuinely interested in my ideas for my novel, and I outlined the story arc and the characters for her, as far as I had conceived them. She'd never been much of a reader so I was quite surprised—also flattered—by her interest, but really the topic was a way of closing the space that had grown between us since I'd gone away to school. From there I told her about some of my other exploits, including the teenage fumbles I hadn't shared with you. I tried to describe how I'd felt after Mum died, and once the subject of death had been broached I found she was quite willing to speak of her own prognosis. We had a lengthy and quite cosy conversation about it one afternoon when a power cut had forced the shop and café to close.

Isobel was quite right in that Erin didn't want to go into hospital or a hospice.

'I shall die quietly here,' she said, 'as I have lived. I don't want a fuss. I hope it doesn't hurt too much.'

'I'm sure they can give you drugs,' I said.

She cast a glance at a cabinet across the room. 'I have plenty of those already. And many times I've thought of just having done with it and taking the lot.'

'Oh Erin,' I breathed, moved beyond speech. 'I'm so sorry.'

She gave a wan little smile. 'It isn't your fault. It isn't anyone's fault. I hope Mum and Dad realise that.'

Presently I said, 'What stopped you from …' I gestured towards the cabinet.

Erin considered. 'I wasn't ready,' she said simply. 'I think—I *hope*—there'll come a moment when I realise I'm done. Or I'll go to sleep and just not wake up. That would be the kindest, don't you think?'

I stared at her. As much death as I had seen in my relatively short life, I had never given serious thought to what it might be like to die, to face death *myself*.

Erin must have read my thoughts. 'I've had plenty of time to mull it over,' she said. And then I realised what she had been looking at, all those times I'd seen her staring into some distance I could not penetrate.

I swallowed a lump of grief. 'And, do you see anything … afterwards?' I asked tentatively. 'Anything, I mean, that gives you hope … or comfort?'

She turned her head on the pillow. 'I have looked,' she said. 'For a few weeks, when I was more able, I walked to the vicarage and talked things over with Reverend Parslow. My parents don't know. He explained things as far as he could but … I don't know. I can't truly say that I feel like a sinner. What chance have I had? So I'm not sure I need "saving." On the other hand, I've had few opportunities to earn my own place in heaven either. So …' She sighed and closed her eyes, folding her hands across herself. I thought she would fall asleep. I got ready to go quietly from the room.

But then she said, in a voice so faint I could barely make out the words, 'I suppose I'll just have to hope for the best.'

I spoke to you about Erin, Arthur. I'm sure you'll remember. We both railed at the unfairness. There we were with our lives in front of us, but she … Ah well. She found peace with it. We all must, in the end.

157

Chapter Twenty-Five

One of the things that came out of the conversation I had with you about Erin was your suggestion that I use the library at Glenister Hall to write my book. I'd complained about the difficulties of getting on with it. There really was nowhere at Broadacres where I would not be in the way, interrupted, or an annoyance to Erin. Every room was occupied. Even Grandad's old office was now used as a storeroom, the desk made inaccessible by stacked suitcases, boxes and spare bedding. Then there was the question of opportunity. I didn't have much time off. On Sundays, the shop and café were closed but we would use the time to clean and restock. Work amongst the plants went on seven days a week. I was allowed two half days plus every other Saturday to myself, and so were you. Our Saturdays coincided and we generally spent them together, but our half days never did, and you said I should use them to begin my novel.

'No one will disturb you,' you said with what I thought at the time was unnecessary emphasis; and, 'Help yourself to anything you need. The place is full of history.' This last remark was accompanied by a significant look, as though you meant something by it.

But I said, 'I already have an idea quite well developed. I just need time and a place to get it down.'

I began to take myself off to Glenister Hall every Tuesday and Thursday afternoon. It was very odd at first, crossing the meadow and going through the little door in the wall without you. I couldn't help scanning the windows of the house to see if anyone was watching, might object. But who would? Colonel Glenister had given his approval. The only other people likely to be in residence were my own sister and her husband. Surely I had nothing to fear from them?

Even so, as I padded along the dim corridors of the below-stairs region, and mounted the steps to the hall, and crossed the marble slabs through the greenish gloom that was the only light that filtered in through the moss-encrusted atrium far above, I felt almost choked with apprehension. I had to try several of those impressive, panelled doors before I found the library. I was afraid to peer into the gloomy interiors of the various rooms. My heart beat quickly and the hand that gripped the handle of the typewriter's carrycase was slick with sweat. I found a music room—a grand piano shrouded in a white sheet, ranks of chairs set ready for a ghostly audience. Another room whose purpose I couldn't divine—enormous, with barely any furniture, blank spaces on its walls where once your oil-painted ancestors had frowned down. There was something so sad about it tears prickled my eyes. But then I recalled that the last time I'd been at Glenister Hall was the day my mother had gone missing. How I had longed to find her then, crouched in a musty corner, distraught but alive.

How I *still* longed to find her.

I finally found the library, carefully noting to myself which door it was amongst the many. As before, the room was dark. I found the light switch but only a scant three or four of the bulbs responded. I crossed the moth-eaten carpet to the large table and placed my typewriter on its surface before going to one of the windows and wrestling with the catch of the shutters. They were stiff, matted with cobwebs, and complained as I forced them open, but the room flooded with light even in spite of the filthy windows. It illuminated the glint of gilding, the rich patina of wood, the figures on the wallpaper that might be watermarked now but whose intricate detail still declared its quality. Emboldened, I undid the catch of the sash and forced the window up a few inches. The inrush of fresh air was intoxicating, dispersing the spectres. I went to the other window and opened that too, then turned to survey the room. It was dusty and crusty with ancient dirt, spiderwebs, mouse droppings and a sticky residue of old, stale air. But it was also excessively grand, its grandeur not snuffed by time and neglect. The books were beautiful. I let my hand skim their leather spines and gold tooled lettering. The fireplace was massive, ornately carved. What a roaring fire there would have been, in days of yore! The table was the largest I'd ever seen. I eyed the shallow-drawered cabinets from which you'd brought the estate maps and other curious folios. I knew you'd spent many hours rifling through the contents and my own inquisitiveness flared.

But I was there to write, and I had only a few precious hours to do it. So I opened my typewriter and got to work.

There can't be many debut novelists who have the privilege of writing in such rarefied surroundings. Generally, I believe they write in bedsits or cafés or public libraries. I count myself fortunate now to have been given the opportunity to write at Glenister Hall, for the peace and space. No one interrupted me. The keys clacked relentlessly as I got my long-hoarded narrative down in black and white. Often it was only the encroaching dusk that told me I must stop. I felt neither hunger nor thirst in the meantime but allowed my story to feed me, nourishing my soul.

It was neither hunger nor thirst that sent me down to the kitchen one day, but a wasp that flew in through the open window and stung me on the wrist. I went in search of vinegar or proprietary sting cream and found Polly

Tindall, exactly as before, seated with her feet up reading a magazine. She showed no surprise on seeing me and once I'd explained the nature of my visit she lumbered to her feet and disappeared into a pantry, emerging with a bottle of cider vinegar and some lint. She gestured that I should sit down while I applied the remedy and went to fill the kettle without asking if I'd like a drink.

She offered no conversation, so I said, 'My granny remembers you. She told me your husband was in the war with my grandad and Mick and Bradley. Then he got the job of head gardener here, and you moved into a cottage on the estate.'

She nodded. 'That's right. I still live in it, though Arnold is dead and gone these many years.'

'That's nice,' I said, 'about the cottage I mean. My grandad lived in the woodsman's cottage. I've been there, but it's hardly habitable these days.'

'No?' she replied cryptically, and I wondered if she knew about Mrs Glenister's predilection for the place. Polly poured boiling water into the teapot and reached down two cups from a shelf.

'I had no idea my grandad was connected with Glenister Hall,' I said, 'until Granny told me.'

'Oh yes, he worked here for quite a few years.' She chewed her cheek while the tea brewed, and she did some mental calculations. 'He came after the first war, same as me and Arnold,' she said slowly, 'and stayed until about '29 or '30. Whenever he was married.'

'My dad was born in 1931,' I said, 'so that sounds about right. It was kind of the colonel to employ members of his old regiment. I think things were very tight financially at my great-grandparents' place.'

'They were *then*,' Polly mumbled, bringing over the tea things. 'On the up, since. Unlike *here*.' She sounded resentful. I wondered why. What was it to do with her? But then I had a vague recollection that you'd mentioned something similar, the seesaw that had improved the Day fortunes as the Glenisters' had declined.

I sipped my tea. It was much stronger than I liked, and I hadn't been offered any sugar. 'I suppose Mrs Glenister must have entertained a great deal,' I said. 'House parties and balls, hunts. Even though her husband was away.'

'Oh no,' Polly sniffed. 'Mrs Glenister was never one for society. She was a queer fish from the beginning, if you get my meaning. Oh! People called, of course. That was the way of things in those days. But she was never 'at home' wasn't Mrs G. A virtual recluse, except … you know … not in the house.'

I mulled this over. Then, 'Such a pity the two families fell out,' I remarked.

Polly clamped her lips shut.

We drank our tea and the throbbing in my wrist eased. I said, 'It's a rather awkward thing to admit to you, Mrs Tindall, but although I know my sister lives somewhere within the house, I haven't a clue where. If I wanted to see her, where would I go?'

'Top of the stairs, on the right. But you won't find her there today.' Polly collected our teacups and carried them to the sink. 'I'd better get along,' she said over the rush of water from the tap. 'I haven't time to natter.'

I glanced at the magazine she'd left on the table, but rose to my feet. 'Me neither,' I said. 'Thank you for the tea. And the vinegar.'

I made my way back to the library, but my intense interest in the peculiar connection between the Days and the Glenisters that had so exercised me in my youth now sparked back into life. I think it had been smothered by Mum's death and all I went through in the aftermath of it. I closed the library door and turned the key before crossing to the cabinet and pulling out the top drawer. All my old questions crowded back, as well as some new ones— specifically, the nature of the schism between your family and mine. It made Henry's entitlement to make himself at home at Broadacres even more extraordinary. Why had Granny and Grandad allowed it? And then there was the question of money. It *did* seem odd that a smallholding that had struggled to support its owner's three sons had suddenly been so prosperous it could afford to build such a large house as Broadacres.

Was the answer somewhere amongst those papers and files? I touched them gingerly and even lifted an inlaid wooden box from where it nestled amongst account books, maps and charts. But it felt wrong—rude and disloyal—to pry. I replaced the box, shut the drawer firmly and got back to work.

Sometimes you would come to meet me as I retraced my steps through the darkening woods to Broadacres. That day—the day I'd been stung—was one of those occasions. My physical self was present there beneath the trees, my feet were on the narrow path that wove through the vegetation. But my mind remained behind in the esoteric air of the library, so intensely conscious of the words I had yet to pluck out and write down that I could sense them still hovering on silvery wings beneath the richly embellished ceilings, waiting for my return. Seeing you emerge from the gloom with a smile of welcome eased me gently from one world to the other.

I raised my hand and hurried towards you. You handed me a cold beer from a rucksack you had slung over your shoulder and said, 'Let's go to the cove, shall we? We could swim.'

'I haven't any kit,' I lamented.

You patted the bag. 'I made so bold. Your swimsuit was in the airing cupboard. I promise I won't look while you get changed.'

'I haven't got anything you haven't seen already,' I laughed, but then clapped my hand over my mouth, appalled at the note of flirtation I'd introduced.

Thankfully, you took it at face value. 'It's been many years since we ran about naked,' you said. 'But I'm willing if you are.'

Even so, I felt awkward, and my awkwardness was compounded by the temptation I'd fought off earlier in the library. There was subtext between us. I was very fond of you, Arthur. I thought of you as my best friend still, even after the years of our separation. But there was no doubt that another layer was adding itself to our relationship. You were undeniably good looking and there was a *frisson* in my feelings for you now that would have been impossible six years earlier. Could it be that you felt the same?

And there was that other snake that had just that day reared its head again. We'd pondered it together in those earlier days and it felt wrong of me to remain silent on the subject now. I'd been tempted, but I hadn't *done* anything to be ashamed of … yet.

We went down to the cove, and I got changed discreetly while you made your way down to the water's edge to strip off your jeans and tee shirt. You already had your swim shorts on and plunged into the water before I'd struggled into my costume, but I soon joined you and we swam for a while, not talking, watching the golden brilliance of the sunset as it touched the sea, the rocks and the woods with burnished gilt. Afterwards we lay on the warm rocks to dry until I felt a little breeze spring up and begin to pucker my skin, bringing my nipples to hard points beneath the thin fabric of my swimsuit. You threw me a towel and wandered away to the shadow that was lengthening beneath the cliff to dress.

The air had cooled but still we lingered, kicking the shingle to find the little nuggets of sea glass that proliferated on that shore, until it was too dark to make them out.

You brought more beers, two slabs of pork pie wrapped in greaseproof paper and a couple of apples from your bag, and we sat and devoured them. The sun slipped beneath the horizon and the air glowed ultraviolet in that mystical interval between day and night.

You said, 'I could light a fire if you like,' but I shook my head. Why? I think I needed the darkness to hide whatever was going to happen next. That way, I thought, if it all went horribly wrong, if I spoiled the precious connection we shared, I could pretend nothing had happened at all.

'I saw Polly today,' I said into the gloaming. 'She made me a cup of tea and we chatted for a while.'

'Oh, yes?'

'She reminded me of something you said, a long time ago, about the way the Days' fortunes seemed to increase as the Glenisters' decreased.'

'Mmm. Well, that's true. But what of it?'

'I began to wonder if the two things were connected.'

'Did you?' I could hear your feet shuffling around in the pebbles. 'That's funny. I wondered that, too, for quite a long time. And in fact, I did find out something quite interesting.'

'Did you? When?'

'Oh! Years ago, when I was staying at Glenister Hall with nothing much to do.'

'You looked in those drawers?'

I saw your outline nod, but it was too dark by then to make out any of your features. 'The top drawer was particularly interesting. There are letters, and account books going back decades. I've no idea who kept the accounts. They're all written in long hand in old fashioned ledgers.'

I'd seen them that very afternoon, but I didn't say so.

'Anyway, from what I could make out, your grandfather received regular payments from mine for years.'

'Those would have been his wages. He worked as woodsman for about ten years. Polly told me so. Until about 1930.'

'That's what I thought at the time. But these payments were more than the wages—considerably more—and they went on beyond the end of his employment. I can't recall now how long. At least ten years, I'd say.'

I began dribbling sand into the neck of my empty beer bottle while I thought about it. 'Maybe your grandfather loaned the money to build Broadacres. Could that explain it?'

'It would do, but the house was finished by 1935. The lintel over the front door tells us that. Why would he continue to loan money beyond that? And how come I saw no sign of any of it being paid back?'

'Maybe that's what they fell out about,' I mused.

You turned sharply. 'They fell out?'

I cursed myself. Granny had asked me not to tell you. 'I believe so. Granny said something about it. Well, she said there had been a parting of the ways. She was surprised your grandparents attended Grandad's funeral. But then she said it was all water under the bridge. And from the way your grandfather is made welcome at Broadacres these days, I'd say she's right. We know that our grandfathers served in the first world war together. Perhaps there was some debt of honour …'

You snorted. 'You read too many books, Prue.'

'No, but really. I mean, your grandfather cared enough about Grandad to give him employment and somewhere to live. There could easily have been some incident, a rescue … I don't know … but something.'

You stirred. 'I suppose so. We could always ask him.'

'Yes.' I upended my bottle and let the sand run out again. 'And that's another thing I'm finding slightly strange. Is there any significance in your grandfather's visits?'

'It's another end of the same stick,' you said. 'Money. His travels have had to be curtailed. They just can't be afforded. Mum had to contribute towards my school fees last term, and it's been made clear to me that I'll have to finance my own year-out.'

I rummaged around in my memory. 'Isn't your grandmother independently wealthy?'

'She was. But no one has a bottomless reserve of cash, do they?'

'Does she still …?' Live wild in the woods, I was going to say, but you got abruptly to your feet and spread your arms out, encompassing the cove, the woods, the whole area. 'She's here somewhere.'

It was properly dark by then. Above us, I head the trees shiver as night descended. I wanted to ask you more about her, to tell you of the impression I'd got that she'd been more than passingly fond of my grandad, but the brisk way you began to collect up our damp towels and empty beer bottles and put them into your bag told me you didn't want to discuss her.

Even so, I risked, 'I think we should see if your grandfather is willing to talk about it,' as I followed you up the steep boulder steps.

I saw your shoulders lift and droop, a shrug. 'Okay,' you said.

Chapter Twenty-Six

The weeks passed and Salad Days was busy. I got to quite enjoy my work in the shop and café. As I proved myself competent, Isobel and Victor initiated me into more of the behind-the-scenes work—food hygiene, calculating profit margins, minimising overheads by playing one supplier off against another. From the conversations I had with you, Arthur, I gathered that Hester was likewise allowing you more responsibility with the plants.

As in years gone by, the Day family worked as a seamless team, everyone having a role to play. We worked cooperatively, with purpose but also with an air of positivity. I don't know if it was our advent, Arthur—yours and mine— but a spark of banter and fun did emerge. We played the occasional practical joke that amused the customers no end even if it did annoy Isobel and Hester. It felt to me that the younger generation was eager to revive the party atmosphere we'd enjoyed in years gone by. We drank wine and played music in the balmy evenings when work was done. Both twins had learned the guitar. They played *Country Roads* and *Streets of London* and hits by the Carpenters and the Beatles. They were rather good! We all sang along, the aunts and uncles and even Granny joining in as they picked up the lyrics. It was like being conveyed back in time. Sometimes, when I'd drunk too much wine I saw, through my alcoholic haze, Mum and Grandad and Uncle Eric sitting in the shadows, singing and smiling. The vision brought tears to my eyes and it was all I could do to stop myself from running over to throw myself into their arms.

Only my worries about money soured those first weeks of the summer. I did my best to save all my wages, but nights at the pub and the occasional trip into town for a burger or pizza ate into my savings. I couldn't see how I was going to save enough for my open plane ticket by September, which is when I'd need to leave if I was to catch Zhi in Hong Kong before she flew back for the beginning of her term at university. At that point I had no hand in the business accounts but from the amount of cash in the till at the end of each day I couldn't doubt that we were making plenty of money. Dad's claims to be unable to fund my travels seemed hard to believe, but then I had no idea how the proceeds of the business were shared out. I made several attempts to broach the topic with Dad, but he was too distracted with plans for his wedding.

The wedding was set for a day in August. The ceremony was to be small, at the registry office, since Blanche was divorced and in those days few churches would agree to sanctify the remarriage of divorcées. Blanche asked me to be a bridesmaid, but I declined as graciously as I could. It wasn't that I didn't like her, but I couldn't quite get out of my head the cynical notion that she had planned to supplant Mum right from the beginning. I could see that Blanche made Dad happy, and that counted for a good deal. She was as entrenched as any of us in the firm and the family; like you, Arthur, she was already so much a Day that a certificate and a ring would make no difference. She took my refusal in a dignified way and asked Grace's little girl, Pansy, instead.

The reception was to be at Broadacres, again a small affair. Even so, catering for it would be well beyond Granny's scope these days and the café cook had agreed to lay on a buffet.

What with my work in the shop and my twice-weekly trips to Glenister Hall to write, I didn't encounter Granny often. Of course, she'd slowed down a good deal—she'd just turned eighty—leaving the lion's share of the household management to Isobel and Blanche. Hester had never been very domesticated. Although she'd help with serving meals and so forth, she was the first to declare that housekeeping wasn't her forte. She occupied herself with the horticultural side of the business and even my dad would accept that Hester had a better handle on it than he did. Nevertheless, they all paid lip service to Granny as the matriarch of the family and the head of Salad Days. No decision was ever made without Granny being at least consulted, but I got the strong impression this was more of a formality than anything else.

I began to notice small peculiarities in her behaviour. I got in extremely late one night—well past three in the morning—to find Granny up, dressed and preparing breakfast. Another time I had quite a lengthy conversation with her throughout which she addressed me as 'Lucille.' I passed my driving test and was told to use Granny's car whenever I liked and in fact to make sure the keys were never left where she could find them—it was no longer considered safe for her to drive, although no one was prepared to tell her so directly. We must all have known that Granny wasn't as sharp in her mind as she had been, but with her family around her at all hours there was no need to worry.

The date of Dad's wedding coincided with the publication of A level results. We'd both done well, and our university places were secure. What a relief! Granny produced a bottle of champagne at breakfast, which we ate at the big table on the terrace as we opened our envelopes and shared our results. There was to be no work that day anyway, because of the wedding. The hairdresser had already arrived to do Blanche's hair. Grace had brought Pansy, who was to have ringlets. I got the impression that shy little Pansy was reluctant to play her part. It took much coaxing to get her to go with the hairdresser to the room where Blanche was being prepared for her marriage.

Grace sat at the breakfast table with us and helped herself to toast and marmalade although it was obvious from the egg smears on her smock that she'd already had breakfast. She drank more than her share of champagne as well.

'What a perfect day,' she said, surveying the garden. Granny had been hard at work all week, deadheading roses and adding fresh annuals to the borders. You and Jack had mown the lawn to a bowling green perfection. The sky was beautifully blue and cloudless, the air warm. 'It's just what I would have liked for my wedding,' she went on. 'But …' she sighed, '… it wasn't to be.'

'You got married in November,' I pointed out. 'Not the ideal month for an outdoor reception.' Privately, I added that she'd also been five months pregnant.

'True.' She reached for the champagne bottle, but it was empty.

'You ought to go and get changed,' I suggested. 'We're to set off for the registry office at quarter to eleven.' It was already nine thirty. I wondered what on earth she would wear—she seemed to have few clothes that were not stained with beer or baby sick—and if she would wash her hair. I really hoped so. The Days would be "on show" and although I deplored "keeping up with the Joneses," I also shrank from letting ourselves down.

Granny had hired limousines for the whole family. I was to travel with Grace and Gary and their three youngest, and Verity. It had been decided that Henry's presence at the ceremony would be a bit awkward, so he was to join us with his father at the reception. No mention was made of your grandmother. I assumed that in those days she was more witch than woman—far beyond any kind of social intercourse. Dad would travel with Victor—his best man—Isobel and Hester, Erin and Jack. You were to escort your mother and be the one to walk her down the aisle. Pansy and Granny would also travel in your car. The twins had volunteered to stay behind and make sure everything at the house was in readiness for our return.

I'd bought a lovely dress for the occasion—eating further into my cash. Off the shoulder, with a flounce over the bosom, cinched at the waist and then falling to the floor with a frilled hem. It was in a gauzy, floaty floral material I'd convinced myself would be forgiving when I packed it into my rucksack for my travels. I had a tepid shower—I suppose others had used up the hot water—and spent more time than usual recreating my Farrah Fawcett look, although my Debbie Harry platinum blonde had long since faded to my natural reddish-gold. I used mascara and discreetly blended my eye shadow, but went easy on the eye liner, aiming for the bare eye look that was so popular just then. Buckling up my sandals, I was done, and hurried downstairs to help Erin with her outfit.

I could see immediately that she wasn't well. She sat by the open window of her room fighting for breath.

'I don't think I'm going to manage it,' she wheezed. 'I'm so sorry. I'll rest and be better when you all get back.'

'Oh no!' I cried, but there was no question she was right. With the bright light of morning falling on her face I could see how thin she was. Her cheekbones made sharp cliffs above her cheeks and her eyes were sunken and dull. She'd washed her hair, but it lay flat and lifeless on her shoulders. 'What can I do?' I wailed, glancing over at the cabinet. 'Isn't there some pill? Some medicine?'

She smiled bravely but shook her head. 'I need to rest,' she said. 'The twins will keep an eye on me. Don't worry. You go and make my excuses, and then, when you get back, I'll be ready to party.'

I helped her back to bed and pulled the curtains across the window to dim the room. As I stepped out into the hallway, I met you.

Oh, Arthur. You looked so handsome! In a light linen suit, a blue shirt that matched your eyes and a bold striped tie, your hair new-washed and flopping over your forehead, its copper burnished like the tongues of flame that touched the disciples' heads on the day of Pentecost.

'Wow!' you said, looking me up and down with approval. 'You've scrubbed up nicely!'

I laughed, ridiculously pleased. 'It's such a relief to be out of those hateful dungarees, isn't it?' I ran my hand through my hair, feeling suddenly shy. You smelled delicious—tangy with citrus and spice. The smell of you made my insides fizz, a bit like drinking alcohol on an empty stomach. I swallowed. My mouth was dry.

'There's champagne on the terrace for those who are ready,' you said. 'Courtesy of my grandfather. Will you partake?' You held out your arm to me, like a gentleman in a Regency romance, and led me out.

It was a wonderful day, although not without a sting in its tail. I floated through the hours in a kind of trance. I felt beautiful for the first time in my life. Was that because of the compliment you'd paid me? Not the words you'd spoken—they were part and parcel of our usual, jocular double-edged wit— but the look in your eyes as you'd said them. They gave me a sort of confidence to push away the sad backstory of the day, to be genuinely pleased for Dad as he took Blanche to be his wife and for her, too. She'd been dealt such a difficult hand and had been through so much. What would it cost *me*, I thought, if *she* found happiness? I must say she did look very lovely, in an eminently suitable dove grey outfit, clutching a bouquet of pure white roses.

I stood with my sisters in the drear little room that was used for marriage ceremonies, and we took each other's hands as Dad spoke his vows. I suppose we all felt the breath of Mum's reproaches on the backs of our necks, but we steeled ourselves not to look over our shoulders. Verity shed a few tears. That surprised me. She'd grown into such a hard-nosed woman. Perhaps she was comparing this affair—the staunch support of the entire Day clan—with her own marriage—witnessed by strangers in a French *hotel de ville*. I made a mental note to ask you about it, later. You were the only family member who had been present.

Then, in what seemed like just a few moments, we were back out in the sunshine on the steps of the town hall, hugging and kissing and throwing confetti. You and I embraced, and I thought it went on for a second or two longer than was really necessary. Was it just me who didn't want to let go? But then you spoiled it by saying, 'Now you really are my sister, Prue.'

We got all jumbled up in the cars on the way back to Broadacre so that the new Mr and Mrs Day could travel in privacy. You and I got separated but it didn't really matter. The journey was short, and we all arrived more or less at the same time. We were greeted by Kath and Karen in identical and very sophisticated tailored white suits. They were heavily made up, forerunners of a style that would not take hold until the early eighties. They looked lithe and tanned, sultry and sexy, and I suddenly felt my dress—and myself—to be gauche and frumpy. They forestalled my attempt to gain your side by each taking one of your arms and leading the way round to the garden where bunting and lights had been hung between the trees and a string quartet played beneath the rose arbour. A long table with a fancy cloth and laden with food had been prepared in the shade of a gazebo. Two of the café's waitresses in smart black dresses stood ready to dispense champagne. The colonel sat in the shade, and I was pleased to see Erin beside him, up and dressed, looking much better. Henry occupied his usual position at the end of the terrace, his beaky nose and beady eye searching eagerly for Verity. She saw him and hurried to his side.

I realised then what an opportunity I'd wasted. We never saw Verity at Broadacres without Henry beside her, and I hadn't used my afternoons at Glenister Hall to seek her out. If I'm honest, it wasn't that I cared about her particularly, although I think by then I had realised the probable manner of her seduction—her grooming —by Henry. It was only my characteristic nosiness—call it my writer's curiosity—that was interested in her marriage, her life as Mrs Glenister, her existence in the dreary, damp confines of that mausoleum of a house.

Dad and Blanche hadn't invited any guests. It was just us, the Days and the Glenisters—the usual suspects I suppose you could say—who celebrated with food and drink, with jokes and laughter. I drifted round the garden, a glass of champagne almost constantly in my hand, participating but also observing as different members of my family gathered and separated, gave speeches and made toasts, took and posed for photographs against the backdrop of the dear old house whose funding was such a conundrum. I kept you in the periphery of my vision, saw you place an affectionate arm around your mother, produce a clean handkerchief when she shed a tear of happiness, fetch a shawl for Granny when the evening grew a little chill. I saw you shake my father's hand a number of times, and noticed the way he looked at you, Arthur—the son he'd always wanted—with pride and fondness. I could quite understand his admiration. You were indeed admirable: tall and handsome, capable, clever. You had a bright future in whatever direction you chose to pursue. I envied you his approbation, Arthur, just a little bit. But I shared every ounce of it myself, too.

I felt eyes on me even as I watched you. It was like we were engaged in a complex dance that day as we moved around each other. We were seated either side of the bride and groom, separated but also now connected by their new relationship, able only to lean back or forward to exchange a smile. I'd be on the terrace while you danced with Kath or Karen. Then you'd assume a watchful stance as the girls and I did a rendition of "Close to You" that we'd been practicing, one of Dad's favourites. We circulated with champagne bottles, topping up glasses, our orbits coming close but never colliding. Even when I couldn't see you, I felt you, felt watched, felt admired. I became conscious of myself, of how I might look. I acted a little part—a woman slowly, inexorably falling in love. Once or twice, I saw an opportunity and began to make my way to where you sat or stood to claim a dance, exchange a word, but when I got to where you'd been the place was empty. Were you playing with me? Paying me back for the times in our childhood that I'd hidden from you while you searched and searched? Or was it part of our choreography, teasing out the moment we were both sure would come?

The day ended in a glorious sunset and when evening arrived it was time for the newlyweds to leave. They were to take a short holiday—none of us knew where—and then come back and take their places within the Day family machine. Shortly after that—although I still had no clue how I was to manage it—I'd set off on my travels. It felt like the end of an era, as well as the beginning of one, reaffirming that sense I'd had the whole summer long of being poised between two things, eager—but not quite ready—to take the first step.

Dad and Blanche's taxi crunched away along the gravel of Broadacres's driveway. We all stood and waved until it was out of sight. Grace and Gary took the children home immediately. Two of them were already asleep in the buggy and the other two had become increasingly querulous over the last hour—it was well past their bedtime. In the garden, the quartet packed away their instruments and the staff from the café cleared the leftover food and abandoned crockery. The lights between the trees emitted a rather feeble glow. My aunts fell into chairs and eased off their shoes, sighing with relief. Perhaps it had just hit Uncle Victor that with my father's departure he was the last man standing. He became brusque and dictatorial—quite out of character—giving orders to the waitresses and clearing away the empty champagne bottles as though suddenly angry that so much had been spent on the day. The party was over.

I went across to where Erin sat, brave but drooping with exhaustion. The colonel had remained by her side for virtually the entire day. I saw now that he was snuffling into a handkerchief. Was he ill? What the hell was he doing here, then, right beside Erin, who was so vulnerable?

'Let me help you to bed, Erin,' I said, holding out my hand. I turned to the colonel. 'You'll excuse us?'

'By all means,' he said, blowing his nose. 'Off home myself before long, I should think. I wouldn't have come—got a bit of a sniffle—but Henry insisted.'

When I came back from Erin's room he remained in place, but you were seated beside him.

You threw me a significant look as I approached. 'Grandfather is just telling me about the old days,' you said, 'in the war, with your grandad.'

'Not the war,' the colonel said lugubriously. 'It doesn't do to speak of that. Only to say that Day was a good man to have beside you.'

He dabbed his eyes. I realised that the colonel was a little tipsy. Probably we all were.

'You were good friends,' I murmured, perching beside you.

'I was his commanding officer. There were boundaries that had to be respected or order would break down. It was the way of things in those days. No matter how good a man was, non-commissioned officer was the best he could aspire to. Others, regulars like me, we were destined to be *real* officers. Different now, of course. And quite rightly. But in any case, he was a volunteer, not a career soldier like me.'

He peered at you. 'You wouldn't fancy a career in the military, Arthur? There's a lot to be said for it.'

You shook your head. 'It's not for me. So, tell me Grandfather, what's the difference between a volunteer and a regular soldier?'

'Well.' He plied his handkerchief again. 'The young men like Day, Tindall and the others signed up when the war began. They volunteered to serve. Bloody brave. I was already commissioned. After the war, the volunteers came home—some more willingly than others! I think Tindall preferred the yelling of the Sergeant Major to the haranguing of his wife. Anyway, the volunteers returned and I stayed on.'

That was interesting. 'So, when Grandad got the job of woodsman, and his cottage, you were still away?'

'That's right. Clearing up the mess, as you might say. We occupied the Rhineland until 1929, and then there was the business in Abyssinia. One thing and another, I didn't get back to Britain until 1937.'

'Do you hear that, Prue?' you said, cutting your eyes at me.

I nodded, but felt I'd missed a step. I said, 'Not at all?' while I tried to catch up.

'Had leave occasionally. But not very often.'

You stretched out a little pause. Then, 'So who ran the estate, Grandfather?'

'Your grandmother, of course.'

You made an expression of astonishment, but I could tell it was manufactured. 'What? All alone?'

'She wasn't alone,' your grandfather blustered. 'Made sure of that. Now where's that boy of mine? It's time we went home. Help me up, Arthur, we must say our farewells to our hostess.'

I went off in search of Henry while I tried to make sense of what Colonel Glenister had told us. If he'd been away such a lot, no wonder your grandmother had become so attached to my grandad. The colonel considered my grandfather's position at Glenister Hall as one of trust. He'd deliberately placed good men there to look after his wife. Had she allowed him to do the estate's accounts? Was it possible that he had diverted Glenister money into his own pocket? Surely, if so, he wouldn't have been so brazen as to show the payments in the accounts? Once his employment ceased, he would hardly have had access to them, would he? And in any case, I couldn't imagine him abusing the colonel's trust.

You must have misunderstood whatever you'd seen in those accounts. In my mind I flew through the woods and into Glenister Hall, desperate to see what you had seen in those ledgers in the library.

While I was distracted, Henry materialised in front of me proffering a fresh glass of champagne.

'For you,' he said genially. 'You've worked so hard all day. You deserve it.'

I took the glass automatically and sipped. It was deliciously cold.

Henry said, 'I opened a fresh bottle for us,' and lifted his own glass to his lips.

I said, 'The colonel is looking for you,' but Henry waved my words away. He gestured behind him to where there was a little seat in the shadows of a rose arbour. 'Why don't you sit down for a few minutes,' he asked, bringing out his pocket handkerchief and dusting away a few fallen rose petals from the bench. I was so astonished that I did as he suggested.

He said, 'May I?' indicating the place at my side.

I nodded, wondering what had come over him, and he lowered himself down beside me.

'Such a pleasant day,' he said. 'You can't know what it means to my father to have been included. My family has all kinds of reasons to be indebted to yours.'

'Well, yes.' I said, wondering, what kinds of reasons? My intrigue warred with my instinct to make a cutting remark about the colonel's state of health— he ought not to have put Erin at risk by attending. I sipped my champagne while the little battle played itself out. The seat was quite small, and I felt Henry's bulk pressing against my side.

He must have been conscious of it too. 'This is cosy,' he said, with what I interpreted as an attempt at flirting. The champagne turned sour in my mouth. I turned astonished eyes on him. The light was poor and I couldn't make out his expression, but any effort at coquetry was suddenly replaced by an air of earnest intensity. He said, 'I know you dislike me, Prudence, but I'm quite a nice chap when you get to know me. Perhaps we ought to try. For Verity's sake. And for Arthur's.'

I floundered, unable to think how a *rapprochement* between Henry and me would benefit you, Arthur. I said, 'What are you suggesting?' as a way of drawing him out. What could he be up to?

He pretended to consider. 'Well,' he said after a few moments, 'You're over at Glenister Hall fairly frequently. You could pop up to my apartment now and again. We could really begin to get to know each other.'

My mind, blunted as it was by the day's alcohol consumption, failed to fathom his intention. I said, 'I've often wondered about your accommodations. Verity doesn't speak of your living arrangements.'

'It wouldn't necessarily have anything to do with Verity,' Henry said smoothly. 'In fact, her being there would prove more of a hindrance, don't you think?'

At last, the penny dropped—as you would have said, Arthur. I stifled the inclination to laugh. Did he really imagine …? That I'd … with my own sister's husband?

I tried to inject my tone with sarcasm but I fear my next remark may have sounded more coy than cynical. 'So you're suggesting that I come and see you in secret?'

He demurred. 'In private, perhaps. What would be the harm? You're not a child anymore, after all.' The word 'unfortunately' hung on the perfumed air of the arbour.

I swallowed down my horror by draining the champagne in one draught—a mistake. I'd already consumed more than was good for me. I gasped, 'Oh! Henry!'

He utterly failed to read my repugnance, meeting my exclamation with a little chortle—a sound I'd never heard from him before. 'Naughty, aren't I?' he said, waggling his eyebrows, and then, with a direct look I couldn't possibly misinterpret, 'Quite exciting though, isn't it?'

'Henry!' You were right there. Like his, your expression was veiled by the night, but I could see your hands bunched into fists by your side. 'Grandfather is ready to leave,' you said sternly. 'And Verity is waiting by the car.'

You led him away.

How much had you heard? I tried to replay the conversation I'd just had from your point of view. Surely, you couldn't think …? The disgust I'd choked down along with the champagne began to rise back up. I knew I was going to be sick. I ran to the far hedge and threw up.

Chapter Twenty-Seven

I woke up the next day feeling jaded, ill and disinclined for work, but pulled on my dungarees and went downstairs in search of tea. I met Isobel in the hall. She looked wan and worried.

'I've been up all night with Erin,' she told me. 'I've called the doctor. Can you cover for us in the shop today, Prue? I can't see either of us being able to get over there.'

Just then Victor emerged from Erin's room with a breakfast tray—untouched. His expression was woebegone.

'Of course,' I said. 'Leave things with me.'

Isobel enumerated a list of things to be done—suppliers to be paid, staff who could be called in at short notice to oversee jam and chutney production. She was distracted, with half an ear for the doctor's arrival.

I burst out, 'It's the colonel's fault. She's caught something from him. He said he wouldn't have come at all yesterday if Henry hadn't insisted. What's wrong with people? Don't they know how vulnerable Erin is?'

Isobel looked as though she would combust. 'What? Really?'

'I'll murder him,' Victor fumed.

It suited me that we'd all conveniently forgotten that Erin had already been unwell before the colonel arrived and that in any case, she would not have displayed symptoms of his virus so soon. I revelled in laying the blame at Henry's door. After my experience of the previous night there was no crime of which I would not have accused him.

I'd hoped to see you before I began work, to see how much you'd seen and understood of what had transpired with your father, but the kitchen was empty when I entered it, the remains of breakfast showing that I was probably the last down. I hastily scraped some butter and jam on a couple of slices of toast and poured myself a cup of tea from a pot that was only lukewarm and carried both across to the shop. I was busy all day, making up for the absence of Isobel and Victor. Although I was worried about Erin I quite enjoyed being in charge. I kept the waitresses on task, signed for a number of deliveries and dealt with an awkward customer who thought the cream in her cake was artificial—as though Victor would ever serve such a thing. Jack brought in the day's vegetables, and we exchanged a brief word about Erin. Had he heard what the doctor's opinion was? He shook his head.

The day passed, heartlessly blue and beautiful, heedless of my hangover, my anxiety about the fallout from my conversation with Henry and my acute consciousness of Erin lying ill in her room. The shop and garden centre were busy even though the summer season was all but done. Customers bought spring bulbs, mulch, winter flowering pansies, primroses and cyclamen—the kinds of plants that would endure the winter in their tubs and baskets. As I put their purchases through the till it occurred to me that by the time they were *in situ*, I'd be in Hong Kong. Who knew when I'd be back? But then, being realistic, I was still hundreds of pounds short of my target, and there was no way I could leave Broadacres until I knew that Erin would be okay.

I had no opportunity to pop back to the house during the day. By the time I'd overseen the closing of the shop and the kitchen clean-down, cashed up, entered the day's takings in the ledger and placed the takings in the safe it was well past seven. I locked up and went in search of you. You were watering the plants in the poly tunnel. You lifted your chin in greeting but left me to speak the first words.

'Are you nearly done? I don't want to go back to the house on my own.'

There was a long pause. 'Because of Erin?'

I nodded. 'I haven't heard anything, have you?'

'No.' You played a fine spray from the hose over leek seedlings. 'Any other reason?'

I picked up a trowel from a bench and turned it in my hands. 'Maybe we should talk about last night?'

You made a show of shutting off the hose and coiling it. It was still extremely hot in the poly tunnel, but I didn't think your red face had anything to do with that.

'You can't think …' I began.

'I'm disgusted,' you burst out, flinging the rest of the hose down. We faced each other across the bench. I don't think I'd ever noticed before how extraordinarily long and pale your eyelashes were but now they made a bristling frame for your eyes, which were wet with angry tears.

'So, you heard—'

'I heard everything,' you spat out, turning away so I would not see the swift movement of your hand as you dashed the tears away.

You'd heard. But what had you understood?

I waited, affront hammering at the door of my feelings, waiting to be let in. What did you believe me capable of?

'I want to smash his face in,' you snarled.

I'd never seen you so riled, Arthur, and although it shocked me, I can't tell you how it reassured me too—you wouldn't be so angry if you didn't care. But then, what was the use? We were both to go away, to pursue our different dreams. Our paths lay in opposite directions.

You turned and we looked each other in the eye. Were you thinking the same thing? Even if we had feelings for each other, was *now* the moment to admit to them? Wasn't it just too late? Or too soon?

I opened my mouth. It was parched and I licked my lips. But before I could say anything one of the twins put her head in through the door.

'You're to come to the house,' she said.

Everything after that is a blur. The entire family was overcome with woe at the doctor's prognosis: Erin had just weeks to live. The alteration in the family's mood from the previous day was so precipitous I thought we would all be sick. Our pallor ranged from chalk white to virescent green to deathly grey as we sat around the kitchen table nursing cups of tea that no one drank. Nobody knew what to say. At last Hester began to make tentative suggestions as to a way forward in the short term. We agreed that there was no point in spoiling Dad and Blanche's honeymoon. They would know the awful truth all too soon. In the meantime, Isobel and Victor would take turns to nurse Erin and the rest of us would keep the house and business going.

Summer ended. Not just the weather, which turned to autumn overnight, but the re-enactment of happier times that being back at Broadacres had briefly revived: the inebriated evenings; the singing; the carefully curated reminiscing; the ever-decreasing circles of my feelings for you. Clouds gathered, veiling in impenetrable fog the wistful and wishful past I'd tried to recreate during my weeks at home. The coming storm brought back more powerfully the troubled times we'd gone through at Broadacres, and I realised that the Shangri-la of my childhood was a fantasy. I'd never been happy there and I never could be. At the same time, the book of my future had been slammed shut. How could I leave *now?*

At work, I served teas, made the staff rota, wiped tables, paid suppliers and balanced the shop accounts. Each day was just like the one that preceded it except Erin was a little paler, a little weaker. On my afternoons off I abandoned my writing at Glenister Hall and sat beside her to read aloud from the books that Granny had read to us as children. I don't think Erin enjoyed or even heard much but it helped me to fill the room with words rather than to listen to the laboured rasp of her breathing.

The house did not feel like our own, but rather occupied by strangers: doctors; specialist nurses; well-meaning neighbours who brought casseroles and cakes; the vicar. One afternoon a smartly suited man with a briefcase arrived—a funeral director, perhaps?—and was closeted with Isobel and Granny for the whole afternoon. When he left it looked like both women had been in tears. Most intrusive of all was the spectre of death, which hovered in the hallway outside Erin's room. It was quite tangible to me, reeking of mouldy earth, a chill, shadowy pall. Was I the only one who felt it? I know I entered and exited the room by opening the door as little as possible, in the stupid belief that death could not creep in through a barely-open door.

A week passed and my father and Blanche returned, tanned and relaxed, but their smiles slid from their faces the moment they stepped into the house. Their cases were abandoned in the hall and they were ushered into the kitchen to receive the news they'd probably already guessed. More tears, especially from Blanche, but short-lived ones, as she dried her eyes and appointed herself Isobel's deputy in all household affairs. 'The cooking, the laundry … leave it all to me.'

'I've been seeing to the accounts,' I said, wishing to be helpful. 'I can continue, if that helps you Blanche.'

I thought her tan faded by a shade or two. She said, 'Have you? Oh! I hadn't thought … I mean, I left everything in order. There shouldn't have been any need …'

'We've been tremendously busy,' I said. 'There was too much cash. I had to bank it. And then, it's getting close to the end of the month. Some suppliers were getting a bit restive for payment. But it's quite okay, Blanche. Mum talked me through a lot of what *she* did …' I trailed off. Was it indelicate to mention Mum? Were we to pretend that she had never existed?

'Well, *thank you*, Prudence,' Blanche said. 'That's very kind.'

The matter was dropped. Next time I looked for the accounts books in their usual drawer it was locked, and I couldn't find the key.

August ended and the children went back to school. From ice cream sundaes and milkshakes, the café's menu shifted to warming soup and hot chocolate. The canopy in the woods turned from green to gold and the departure date for my trip abroad came and went. I removed the map with its pins and string from my wall.

I was restless, with no reassurance from the past and no sense of the future. I found my mind drawn to the dark and dangerous things and, as if in pursuit, my fidgety feet trod a pathway to the tragic places. I sat for hours on the hard rocks of the cove and watched the autumn tides bash the cliff and throw spumy foam onto the shingle. One wind-tossed evening I went to the pond—a sort of pilgrimage—and stood looking at the tapestry of fallen leaves that tessellated the untroubled surface of the water. I didn't hear your approach and it wasn't until your hand touched mine that I knew you were there at all.

We'd barely spoken, you and I, since the wedding. The thing with Henry was unfinished, just another jagged edge to add to the pile of broken things of which our lives were made.

I couldn't lay hold of that, but reached out instead and seized another. I said, 'You know, they said … it was the rope … she got tangled in the rope and that's what killed her.'

You took me in your arms and held me like a brother. I gulped and swallowed the tears that threatened to overwhelm me—and failed. My tears soaked the front of your jacket, and I wondered if you'd make a remark—I'd always made such a fuss about not being a cry-baby—but you wisely kept your counsel.

'I know,' you said. I could feel the vibration of your words in your chest. 'It haunts me. And I wanted to tell. Truly I did, but how would it have helped?'

'It wouldn't,' I sobbed. 'No. It would have done no good. It wouldn't have made any difference.'

There was a pause. I wondered if I had a tissue anywhere about me.

You released me while I searched fruitlessly through my pockets. 'I wondered if maybe you'd blamed me?' Your voice was very low, your words tentative.

I looked up at you. In the filtered evening light your skin, although tanned, seemed wraithlike. 'Oh no,' I assured you. 'Never for a moment. I blamed myself. But more than myself I blamed …' I stopped.

But you picked up my train. 'You blamed Henry,' you said with a sigh.

I nodded. 'I blame Henry for everything.'

You stepped away and put your hands in your pockets. 'I can understand that,' you said. 'And you're right. Oh, he's …' You stammered to a halt, perhaps prevented by some sense of loyalty from saying more.

A little silence stretched out. Only the trees, above our heads, whispered into it.

'I don't think Verity is very happy in her marriage,' I said.

'Verity isn't married,' you said flatly. 'She can leave Henry any time she wants.'

'What?' I turned to look at you in disbelief. 'They were married in France.'

You shook your head. 'No. They *said* they were married in France, but Henry convinced her it wasn't necessary. They would live as husband and wife. How things *looked*, that's all that mattered. Whoever asks to see someone's marriage certificate? He bought her a ring. That's all people look for.'

I let it sink in. 'Bastard,' I muttered, and then surprised myself with 'Poor Verity.'

You half-turned and rummaged through the tilth with the toe of your boot. 'You could argue that it was Henry's way of protecting Verity,' you said with an air of testing the water. 'Glenister wives, you know …'

'Oh,' I caught on. 'The old legend? But surely that's just humbug.'

You wrinkled an ironical eyebrow, and I had the strong impression I often got with you that I'd said something dumb. I wasn't going to let Henry get off that easily though. I dismissed your suggestion with an impatient hand. I said, 'There's nothing in the Day family he won't interfere with and spoil, if he gets the chance.'

'Such as?' you said, but I could see that you already knew very well.

I began to rummage through the shattered pile of grudges, picking them up, but gingerly, knowing that really, I could not make them fit. 'Eric,' I began. 'If Henry had gone with him! And then Mum … you know Erin told me Henry had …'

'His behaviour that night was … unaccountable,' you interrupted. 'Even him being here in the woods … that was unheard of. He hates all of this.' You held out your arms to indicate the still, quiet pond, the regiments of faintly swaying trees, the labyrinthine pathways, the distant cove—the whole magical, tainted extent of our childhood playground.

'Does he? Why?'

You didn't answer me, and we added the question to the heap, too sharp to handle.

September passed, a month of maddening calm and waiting, the slow decline of the year, the fading and falling of nature's bloom. Erin continued to deteriorate. It was terrible to see her, such a small and pathetic mound in the too-big bed, her frail little face on the pillow. She was disappearing before my eyes. Suffering, I had no doubt—her face was sometimes etched with pain—but she never complained.

One day, when the house was quiet, her parents taking a brief nap, everyone else about their business, it was my turn to sit beside her. The curtains were closed but the room was filled with a pale roseate light from the Virginia creeper that grew up the walls on that side of the house and framed the window. The specialist nurse had been and gone. Erin was washed, her sparse hair combed, the bed changed and smoothed, and Erin laid into it like a baby into a cot. She was passive. Barely there at all. A tiny remnant of her body remained behind but for the most part her essence had passed on. I thought she would go to sleep, but her eyes remained open, focused and intent on the place in the distance that I couldn't see. I suggested playing some music, but she shook her head. Did she want anything to eat or drink? Again, no. Should I read? The briefest movement of her head on the pillow. My questions were wearying her. I asked her if I could get her *anything*, and with an infinite effort her head turned to allow her gaze to cross the room to the cabinet where the pain-relieving drugs were kept. She extracted a bony hand from the covers and took hold of mine.

'You understand,' she whispered. 'You remember …'

'Our talk?' I ended the sentence for her. I was so breathlessly appalled I thought I might faint, and sank to my knees beside the bed so that our faces were on a level. I gripped her hand and her fingers responded with a strength that astonished me. I made my eyes meet hers. They were clear, quite unclouded by doubt or fear, and they were dry.

'Are you ready now?' My mouth formed the words, but no sound came. I had a stone in my throat. Even so, she heard me and nodded.

I crossed to the cabinet and extracted the bottle of liquid morphine I'd seen both Isobel and the nurse dispense to Erin in carefully measured spoonfuls. I picked up the spoon as well but when I approached the bed Erin shook her head.

'Put the spoon back,' she said, her voice little more than the passage of air between her dry lips. 'Leave me the bottle and in a little while, before Mum and Dad wake up, be sure to wipe it with a cloth and put it back.'

I was astounded at her calmness; the way she'd thought about how it would have to be.

I placed the bottle in her hand.

She said, 'I'd like to be alone now.'

I leaned down and kissed her forehead. 'I always wished you were my sister,' I said. 'Goodbye, Erin.'

I stepped out onto the terrace. The summer furniture had been put away and the old slabs were scattered with leaves. Geraniums and petunias drooped in the summer tubs; no one had watered them for weeks, and the first frost would see them off. Across the garden I could see Granny kneeling beside one of the flower beds cutting back the perennials. She was so large in my memory, the driving force of everything, the provider of food and the giver of cuddles. She made everything exciting and fun. But now I saw she was tiny, a shrunken, reduced figure, a little old lady. She raised her head and saw me. 'Hello!' she cried, raising a gloved hand. But then she frowned, and I could see she'd forgotten my name, was rummaging in a jumbled box of forgotten things to find it.

'Erin is sleeping,' I said.

Beyond Granny was a low fence that divided the garden from the woods. I could see the slender trunks of ash and elder and a greyish green shadow beyond. And then a figure separated itself from the umbra, a little more stooped, slower of gait, but more indigenous to the surrounding woodland than ever before. She seemed imbued—permeated as though dyed—with all the woodland colours: green; grey, brown, ochre, chestnut. Or perhaps she had a cloaking aura. It was hard to differentiate her from the landscape of which she was so entirely a part. I squinted my eyes but they were tired from sitting up with Erin, and in any case my head was so absolutely gripped by the enormity of what I'd done that I couldn't trust myself to see or think clearly. The woman stood and regarded me for a while. I looked across at her in anguished despair and somehow felt that she understood. Then she nodded her grizzled head, and I knew it was all over.

Every time I encountered your grandmother, a member of my family died.

When I went back into the room Erin had gone. Her body was at rest, and I could see that the last vestige of her spirit had departed. Her face was smooth, the etchings of pain quite disappeared. She was at peace.

I found the little bottle amongst the bedclothes and put it back into the cupboard. Even there she had been clever—I suppose she'd had weeks to think through all the ramifications—not drinking the whole amount but leaving some to bamboozle the memory. Who could remember how much had been in there the last time they looked? Not Isobel, who was so felled by grief that she had to be given tranquillisers; not the nurses, who had many patients on their books and did not wish to be caught up in any inquisition.

And so, we laid another Day in the graveyard as October winds swept the leaves from the trees.

Chapter Twenty-Eight

You departed soon after Erin's funeral, although how you'd amassed enough money for your trip when I'd so signally failed, I couldn't fathom. I suppose your mother paid. How you could *bear* to go was another mystery. I couldn't have deserted the family even if I'd been able to afford it; they needed me. I'd abandoned them on the occasion of our last grieving, disappearing into a bottomless hole of depression, the psychiatric ward and then to the brisk, impersonal routines at Casterley School. I couldn't do it again; it wasn't my turn.

Isobel grieved. I think she'd been in denial about Erin's illness and so she was unprepared when the end came. Isobel's grief came not in the form of weeping and woe, sleeplessness and sorrow, but in a tornado of work. She threw herself into the dairy and the shop, increasing production, introducing new lines, reorganising the shelves and subjecting the staff to rigorous training programmes. Often, I'd begin my shift at eight thirty to find she had already swept the forecourt and tidied the displays—tasks that should have been mine. Our cook took me aside and complained to me that she hadn't enough to do. Isobel had done the day's baking, made the soup of the day before the cook's shift began. The waiting staff scurried away if they saw Isobel approaching, sure to be ticked off for some small lapse.

Isobel was tetchy, both at home and at work, finding fault in the smallest thing. She cleaned the house with almost manic energy, decrying the efforts of the rest of us with vacuum cleaner and duster. She couldn't sit still at mealtimes, constantly getting to her feet to fetch condiments or wipe up spills, sometimes filling the sink with hot water for washing up—the dishwasher notwithstanding—before everyone had finished eating. All Erin's things were unceremoniously bundled together and sent to a shelter for homeless people. I managed to save her quite impressive record collection only because I happened to come round the corner of the house as Isobel was loading it into the back of a van. Isobel slapped my face, but then dissolved into tears and said she was sorry. I gently suggested that Jack and the cousins might like to have something of Erin's as a keepsake. Later, Isobel laid out some of Erin's possessions on the dining room table and invited people to take what they wanted, as though it had been her own idea.

They say that in times of personal anguish we turn on those we love, and this was true for Isobel. She turned on Victor with absolute vengeance; he could do nothing right. Victor was seriously overweight by then, slow and ponderous in his movements. He couldn't keep up with Isobel in any way and she complained cruelly that he was lazy. Perhaps in response to this, but also as a way of dealing with his own grief, Victor withdrew himself from the field, finding excuses to be out of the house and away from work.

He was aided and abetted in this by Henry Glenister. It was strange to me, but in spite of the breakup between Henry and Blanche, Victor had maintained a cordial relationship with your father, his former brother-in-law. It may have been because Victor resolutely kept out of the—sometimes acrimonious—negotiations that went on over Blanche's financial settlement, or simply that Victor was by nature affable and big-hearted.

Since Henry's reintroduction to the family as Verity's husband, Victor had again taken him under his accommodating wing. The two had nothing whatsoever in common, but rather like Morecambe and Wise, a comedy duo just then enormously popular, their differences seemed more of a bond than a bar. It was actually rather amusing to see the two of them side by side, Henry so ridiculously tall and angular, Victor small and increasingly fat. Henry was never anything other than sartorially turned out, in an ironed shirt and a tie even for informal events like barbecues. After work, Victor had adopted the current trend for baggy dad-jeans and bomber jackets that only exaggerated his large paunch. To my eyes, he looked like a prison inmate. Since Grandad's death and his moving in as *de facto* man-of-the-house, Victor had effortlessly adopted the role of "mine host" towards Henry and now Henry responded by nominating Victor for membership in his golf club and taking him as a guest to Masonic dinners and meetings of the local Chamber of Commerce. I don't know how Dad felt about that. Surely if anyone represented Salad Days it should have been him? If Dad minded, he didn't say so. Perhaps he was too wrapped up in Blanche to care.

There were many evenings when I heard Victor stumbling back into the house the worse for drink, and then a tirade of abuse from Isobel as she lambasted him for being so late, so drunk, so fat and useless.

Poor Victor. If he was a drunk he was a happy one, unlike his sister, who had been maudlin in her cups. I wondered whether alcoholism ran in the Bracewell genes and whether you'd fall foul of it one day.

I never saw Henry drunk. If he returned from those sport's dinners and gentlemen's evenings the worse for wear, as Victor did, he would certainly have been over the limit, as the two generally travelled in Henry's flashy car.

As 1978 dragged to its dreadful end and we gave a half-hearted welcome to 1979, I continued my work in the café and the shop, in the production area and increasingly—in an excess of Isobel's vim and to make good for Victor's frequent absences—in the dairy, but I was never permitted to see the accounts. Blanche kept those jealously to herself.

I was seriously afraid that my depression was upon me again. I felt trapped and anxious, as though the invisible force that kept all the Days at Broadacres had ensnared me. I'd never be able to leave. My year of travels was a long-forgotten pipedream, and even my place at university sometimes felt like a chimera, as ridiculous as unicorns.

As much as I felt constrained by obligation to the family, when the time approached to begin my course I deferred for another year. I was less sure that it was what I really wanted and less confident that I *could* cut the cord with Broadacres, which sometimes felt like a noose and sometimes like a life-supporting oxygen tube. Who would I be, away from my family and everything that was familiar to me? Zhi's letters from Oxford University spoke of parties, of lectures, of late nights spent arguing about E.M. Forster and Virginia Woolf, of long essays and short love affairs. I couldn't see myself in that milieu. I'd be a fish out of water.

We received postcards from you from Paris, Berlin, Sienna, Naples … the list went on, a Cook's travelogue. I liked to imagine you as a character in a Henry James novel, lounging in *piazzas*, strolling round galleries, meeting influential men and wealthy women and indulging in erudite conversation with both. Your cards suggested a twentieth century equivalent of a Victorian grand tour. You described getting work in restaurants, as a tour guide, as a companion to some wealthy American widower, as a ski instructor, as a curator of artefacts at a castle on the north bank of the Rhine. Your one year abroad extended to two.

I don't know if it was a comfort to me or a disappointment that where *I* had been caught, *you* had escaped.

You were less one of us than I'd thought.

1979 passed in dole and doom. Grace lost a baby. Hester found a lump in her breast and had surgery. Kath fell in love and had her heart broken by the lead singer of a local band. Henry turned fifty and we held a party, more for Verity's benefit than anything else. We hired the function room at the pub and invited ever so many local dignitaries, businessmen and golf club members—the people Victor said Henry hobnobbed with on a regular basis. I must admit I backed the idea with enthusiasm. I thought you'd come home, Arthur. I so wanted to see you. I thought if anyone could help me out of the doldrums it was you. I asked Blanche again and again if she'd written to make sure you knew about the party, but the day came and went without you. You were not alone. Barely a quarter of the people we'd invited showed up. I can't tell you how disappointed I was—not about them, but about you.

We were glad to see the back of the year and hoped that the new decade would bring better things.

One afternoon, walking aimlessly through the woods as an early spring squall shook the trees, I found myself at the five barred gate into the meadow. I looked over it morosely towards the grey chimneys of Glenister Hall. By the end of the year I'd be twenty-one, truly adult, and yet I'd done nothing, been nowhere, was no one. I was lonely, stagnating. Surely my only option was to take up my university place at the end of the year. But I'd be three years older than my peers by then, the age when most students graduated. The idea of staying in halls with giggling, immature eighteen-year-olds didn't appeal at all. I doubted my ability to relate to them on any level.

On impulse I climbed the gate and crossed the meadow to Glenister Hall.

Everything in the library appeared just as I had left it a day or so before Dad's marriage. Then I saw that the typewriter had seized up, the ribbon bone dry. Some draught must have disturbed my stack of typescript. It was scattered across the desk and onto the floor. I got it back into order and seated myself to read through it. The wind scoured the house and moaned in the chimney. It was cold. The story was as flimsy as the tissue-thin paper it was written on, the characters wooden, the plot predictable. I threw the whole lot into the fireplace and set fire to it. It burned sullenly and the library filled with smoke. I suppose the chimney was blocked.

Afterwards I wandered round the rooms of Glenister Hall. Shuttered and shrouded, its historic issues remained unresolved and its future—if any—remained seriously in doubt. Caught between the past and the future, it was the perfect metaphor for my life. I was unable to undo the past and I was afraid of the future. Wouldn't the best course be to settle for what I had, which was the here and now? Broadacres, Salad Days, the Day family and our unfathomable connection to the Glenisters which, to me, seemed to colour and complicate every aspect of my existence.

I hadn't seen Henry's car on the drive so I mounted the grand, gloomy stairs and knocked on the first door to the right, not expecting anyone to answer, surprised when I heard a key turn and the door swing in to reveal Verity.

'Oh, it's you,' she said, seeming neither shocked nor pleased by my appearance. 'What do you want?'

She looked nothing like the woman-about-town she normally projected. She wore a pair of track suit bottoms and a thick pullover, socks but no shoes or slippers. Her hair was scraped back in a scruffy bun. I thought she looked so thin as to be ill.

'I thought I'd come and say hi,' I said.

We stood either side of the threshold. I peered past her into a drab little vestibule. She searched the empty landing for some reason to send me away, but finding none said, 'Oh. All right then. You'd better come in.'

She and Henry lived in a little set of rooms that I guess at one time was a master suite: a bedroom; a dressing room; a room where I speculated a maid or valet had slept and a small sitting room where the lady of the house might receive visitors before she was dressed. Now the dressing room had become a bathroom, and the other small room had the rudiments of a kitchen within it, although no meal worth the name could have been prepared there. There was a table with a kettle and toaster on it, a small refrigerator, a shelf with a little medley of mis-matched cups and plates. I remember thinking that the student accommodations I'd signed up for were better equipped. There was no sink. She must wash up in the bathroom. But clearly she lived on snacks. I saw a partly used packet of sliced bread, a jar of jam, a box of cornflakes and a bowl with a couple of wizened apples in it. The bedroom was the largest of the rooms, containing an ornate bed and some other probably antique furniture including a large desk on which were scattered various documents and manilla files that really intrigued me. What *was* Henry's business? What schemes did he have afoot?

The window of the room looked out to the front of the house, the driveway and the view of the coast beyond; his domain, I thought, witheringly. The day was already closing in. I could barely make out the curl of coastline that was the focal point of Glenister Hall's principal rooms.

Verity took me into the other room, a small sitting room. It had a settee in it and a coffee table, a television and an electric fire which was on, but emitted a meagre heat. There was a strew of magazines on the coffee table but no other sign of useful occupation: no books, no sewing or knitting.

'Aren't you bored here all day, on your own, with nothing to do?' I burst out. 'For God's sake, Verity, why don't you come home? You're needed there.'

'I'm needed here,' she said, but without conviction. 'Henry wouldn't like me to work. I'm not bored, anyway.'

'Which of those three things is true?' I asked nastily. 'Isn't the truth that he won't *let* you?'

She gnawed at her fingernail.

'Where is Henry, anyway?'

She gave a little shrug. 'I'm not sure. I think he had a meeting. He won't be long.'

'And why do you keep the door locked?' I wanted to know. 'Are you afraid? Don't you feel safe?'

Fleetingly, Verity's face showed a beleaguered expression, her eyes turning involuntarily to the ceiling, as though expecting a manifestation of ectoplasm. The house certainly was very noisy, considering its emptiness. Wind whistled beyond the windows and strange creaks and groans emanated from the floors above us. But then she shook herself. 'Anyone can come and go here,' she retaliated. 'Look how *you've* just breezed in. We have had strangers wandering around. It's just a sensible precaution. Do you want tea or something?'

'Okay.' I sank down on the settee. 'At least he doesn't lock you in,' I said under my breath. 'I'd believe it of him.'

Verity turned in the doorway. 'Of course not. I'm free to come and go. It's just that I choose to stay here most of the time.'

'Why?' I gave her a straight look. 'You *are* free to leave. It's not as though you're really married to him.'

She blanched at that. 'Who told you that?' she croaked.

'Arthur. He was there with you in France, wasn't he? He knows the marriage was a story Henry cooked up.'

My words clearly cut Verity to the quick. She looked really frightened. 'Does Arthur know *why?*' Her voice was barely a squeak.

Given Verity's haunted expression of only a moment ago, I was hardly going to mention mad wives. 'Not that he's told me,' I prevaricated. 'What *is* the reason?'

She seemed to relax a little. 'Oh,' she said, 'marriage is so old hat, isn't it? Who *does* bother nowadays? Mum and Dad virtually bullied Henry into an engagement. Talk about being outdated! It wasn't what we wanted at all.' She flounced out of the room and I heard her filling the kettle for tea.

When she came back, she brought two mugs of tea and a plate with some stale digestive biscuits on it. We chatted about the house, and where you had slept as a boy.

'*This* was Arthur's room, next to Henry's,' Verity told me. 'But he's made it clear he won't be returning.'

'He'll have to, one day,' I put in. 'It will be his inheritance, won't it?'

'I don't think Henry will saddle him with it,' Verity said. 'It's a dinosaur, isn't it? Henry has other plans. If all goes well, Arthur will be very nicely set up.'

At Broadacres, I thought, but didn't say aloud, contenting myself with an interrogative, 'Oh?'

'He doesn't confide in me,' Verity said, but I didn't believe her, and the geyser of distrust that erupted every time Henry Glenister's name was mentioned threatened to erupt once more. What *was* his scheme? Could he have *deliberately* thrown Blanche into my dad's arms in order to secure for you, Arthur, a share of the Day fortune? Was his liaison with Verity just an alternative route to the same destination? If so, why had he stopped short of actual marriage? Was Blanche complicit in some way? She was certainly very cagey over the business accounts. Was it possible she was cooking the books—diverting funds to her own account, or to Henry's? The questions burned my guts like an ulcer, and I put down my half-drunk tea.

Verity said, 'You've got that funny look again, Prue. Are you getting ill? Is your old trouble coming back?'

I knew she was right. The whole subject was a spark to the touch-paper of my neurosis.

For all the fraught nature of my historic relationship with Verity, I felt suddenly overcome with affection for her. I said, 'Why don't you come home, Verity? This place is depressing. You *can't* like it. And, like I said, you're needed. Isobel needs careful handling and Victor's likely to drop dead of a heart attack. Granny's getting less reliable. As you said yourself, everyone *does* come back eventually.' I considered telling Verity about Henry's attempt to entice me into an affair but decided against it. My loose lips had caused Verity enough trouble.

'I can't,' she said.

We sat in silence for a while, then I rose to go. 'Come with me, just for an hour,' I pleaded. 'You look like you need some fresh air.'

She sighed. 'Oh, alright,' she said at last, unfolding herself from her chair. 'I'll go and get changed.'

When we left her rooms I noticed that she locked the door behind her and placed the key in a large Chinese *jardinière* that sat on the landing.

We walked through the woods together. The timber shivered and complained as we passed by, but the place soothed me, as it always did, and I shook off the angst that had gripped me in Verity's depressing little sitting room.

I held open the gate that gave through to the plantation and as she passed through Verity said, 'I read your book. It's very good, as far as it goes. What's going to happen to the woman in it? Will she get her man?'

'I don't think so,' I said, and thought ruefully of the ashes in the library grate.

We got back to Broadacres just as the shop was closing and the day's work was finished. It was the family's habit to gather in the kitchen at Broadacres for an hour after work to exchange news and arrange the schedule for the following day. It was a bridge we crossed every day, beginning as bright, cooperative, helpful colleagues and ending as bored, cantankerous, tired family. Despite—or maybe because of—the sniping, Grace often joined us, knowing the children would get something to eat and that she could exorcise her own angst while others dealt with her kids' squabbles.

But in fact the kitchen was cosy that afternoon as Verity and I entered it, the atmosphere fairly benign. There was a pot of fresh tea and freshly baked scones on the table. The chat of the family as they caught up on the day was surprisingly genial. It couldn't have been a better demonstration to my sister of what she'd forfeited by throwing her lot in with Henry Glenister.

Granny was dewy-eyed with pleasure at seeing her oldest grandchild. She reached out and folded Verity into an embrace murmuring, 'Oh … darling …' She groped, failed to find Verity's name and gave up. 'How lovely. I've missed you so much.' She beamed around the table. 'The whole family,' she sighed happily, but then her smile crumpled. 'Well, nearly.' She winkled a tissue from her pocket.

Because Verity was with us, we lingered over our tea as we would not normally have done, putting off our showers, our quick trips to the library or the out-of-town shopping centre or just a return to our own rooms for some rest—the various ways we would fill our time until supper was served at about half past seven. Hester would normally spend an hour at the dining room table with stock lists and seed catalogues. Blanche would go back to the shop to write up the day's takings in the account ledger. In an effort to lose some weight, Victor had bought a bicycle and tended to wobble off on it most evenings after work for a pedal round the lanes. The twins were often booked at pubs or other venues to sing—their musical duo had gained popularity, and they had a considerable local following. They tended to grab a cup of tea at the big house before heading off to a gig, picking up whatever food they could on the way. But none of these things occurred on that occasion. The atmosphere was warm and upbeat as it hadn't been since we lost Erin. Someone opened a bottle of wine.

I eyed Blanche narrowly, reviewing my earlier suspicions without allowing them to consume me. Was she really capable of such deception? I could hardly believe it as I watched her serving tea and helping one of Grace's boys with his new reading book. I could see that she had the vegetables prepared and a pie ready to go in the oven for supper. She did virtually all the family cooking. Her repertoire was small but she produced plenty of hearty—if bland—meals. Her concerns were all for the family's comfort and prosperity. I'd been wrong to suspect her.

More wine was opened, and I saw that Verity drank more than her share. At last—well after seven—Blanche said, 'I ought to get supper in the oven or it will be midnight before we've eaten. You'll stay, girls? Verity?' and they all said, yes please, they'd like that very much.

I'd promised Verity I'd run her back to Glenister Hall in the car, so I refused wine. I looked around the table and recalled my determination earlier to focus on the here and now—what I had, as opposed to what I'd lost, or the future, which was unknowable. The present was a safe—if mundane—place to be, free of scepticism and distrust, of remorse and regret. It wasn't half bad, I thought, as the twins discussed cover versions of Abba hits they could add to their playlist, Granny leafed through knitting patterns with Hester and Grace, as Jack played with the puppy that had finally replaced Podge. Isobel washed the tea things and Dad talked to Verity. Victor and Blanche bent over something at the sideboard. We were a family. All right, we weren't complete, but even with the gaps—possibly *because* of the gaps—we were whole. We worked.

I don't know if it ever happens to you, Arthur, but just for that moment I gained that sense of distance that sometimes comes when you can look at things with a proper perspective. I thought, this will go on, in some form, for as long as we're here. What Granny and Grandad began forty-five years before would continue. One day Dad would go on with it, Hester, Isobel and Victor beside him, and then the next generation, into the new millennium and *ad infinitum*. I could see myself at Granny's age presiding over this same table with my own kids or my sisters' kids, Jack's, the twins'. What more did I, or any of us, need?

I'd been waiting to strike again with my suggestion that Verity move back to Broadacres, but I saw that I wouldn't need to. Surely *this* would be enough to convince her.

Of course, I hadn't reckoned on Henry.

There was a kerfuffle in the hallway and he burst into the room, treading on the puppy, which gave out a shrill yell.

Conversation stopped abruptly and we all turned to look at him.

He looked accusingly at Verity. 'There you are,' he barked out. 'I've been looking everywhere.'

'Where else would she be but here?' I said, rising and facing him, the only one to do so. 'This is her home. This is where she belongs.'

Verity said, 'I left a note on your desk,' in a pitiful, cringing voice.

Henry waved that away. 'Have you seen the time? It's pitch dark outside. I don't know how you thought you'd get home.'

'I was going to drive her, when she was ready. *If* she wanted to,' I said defiantly.

Verity glanced at the place where the kitchen clock had always hung until Isobel decided to move it elsewhere. She was deathly pale. She lifted an anxious finger to her mouth and chewed a nail.

'And *stop* biting your nails,' Henry roared out, extending an arm and smacking Verity's hand.

My dad stood up abruptly, but before he could speak Granny said, 'Oh George. Don't be so hard on the girl. Take your coat off and we'll have supper.'

They all looked at Granny then, a mixture of amusement, concern and indulgence on their faces. But I did not waver in my fixed regard of Henry. His expression was extraordinary—moved, affected, struck to the heart. His eyes pinkened as he fought back tears. His lower lip trembled. Ah, I thought, so there is a heart in there! You *do* have feelings and they can be plucked.

Verity said, 'Granny's getting everyone's names muddled, Henry.'

George had been my grandfather's name.

And I would have brushed it off as yet another sign of Granny's confusion, if it had not been for that look on Henry's face.

Chapter Twenty-Nine

It was Easter before I had an opportunity to go back to Glenister Hall. Henry had taken Verity to St Moritz and I knew from Granny that the colonel was away at a regimental reunion.

Glenister Hall would be empty.

My inquisitive gland had been working overtime since that strange episode in the kitchen of Broadacres, fully alive once more to the mystery that had plagued me about our two families from the very first day you and your parents had turned up and insinuated yourselves into the Day family. Granny did now muddle our names, or forget them altogether, and we could forgive her because she was getting absentminded, but also because we did all bear a striking resemblance to one another. We Days were pretty much out of the same mould and that mould was Grandad. Of middling height and a medium build, he'd had a fairish complexion and hazel eyes. All his children had the sandy coloured hair they'd inherited from him, as did some of the grandkids. Mine was autumn gold, the twins a strawberry blond. Jack and Erin both had the more original auburn tint, but that was from their Bracewell genes; Victor and Blanche were both redheads, which I suppose is where you got your bright ginger shade. Verity and Grace both had Mum's hair—chestnut—but even that had the Day reddish tone in some lights. All our eyes were brown or hazel. We all had Grandad's build apart from Grace, who had obscured hers with overindulgence.

So why, of all of us, had Granny mistaken Henry for Grandad?

Henry's hair was a dun brown colour, without any fiery highlights at all, and by that time was beginning to turn a dirty shade of grey. His face was thin and his nose beaky. He was excessively, awkwardly tall and he certainly had none of Grandad's genial, easy manner. Henry's eyes were blue.

It was a mistake that would have been quite laughable if he had not reacted to it so oddly, with that stricken, afflicted look.

What was he hiding?

I convinced myself that if I was going to stay and make my life at Broadacres, then I *must* understand things properly. I couldn't go on with the query hanging above my head like the sword of Damocles.

Discreetly, I rummaged through the storeroom at Broadacres—the room that had once been Grandad's office—in search of family archives, photographs, bank statements … anything that would solve the conundrum by explaining the link between your family and mine.

A box of photographs showed Granny and Grandad in their younger days. I hadn't seen these before. The only snapshots on display in the sitting room and at other locations throughout the house were of the younger generations of the Day family. The photographs of my grandparents were old and small, grainy. It was hard to make out their features. And of course they were in black and white, or even sepia. In one picture they stood before the newly built Broadacres house. I recognised the lintel with its date and the side of the dining room window. A weedy stalk snaked a few feet up the brickwork, the first thrust of the luxuriant wisteria that now smothered the front of the house. Grandad was much taller than Granny but nowhere near as tall as Henry. Grandad had a plentiful head of hair—unlike Henry. Granny's was long and of indeterminate colour, styled in what I believe was called a 'victory roll.' That dated the pictures to the early forties.

Delving deeper into the box, I searched for photographs of Grandad and Colonel Glenister together, in uniform perhaps, but found none. Neither was there any pictorial record of Grandad's time as the Glenisters' woodsman. There were some very ancient and fuzzy shots of groups of young men dressed twenties style in baggy trousers and double-breasted jackets, with identical straw boaters. I recognised Grandad, his head thrown back laughing, and Mick Pullman, our erstwhile worker on the property. His livid scarring was unmistakable. It was possible that the man next to him with the walking cane was Bradley Fox. Maybe one of the other men—the taller man at the rear of the group—was Polly Tindall's henpecked husband. I wasn't sure. Without knowing why, I slipped the photograph into my pocket and continued my search.

A top shelf held a row of ancient account books, carefully arranged by date. I pulled out the one dated 1932. A shower of grey dust and desiccated flies came down with it. I recognised my grandad's handwriting, page after page, columns of figures added up in pounds, shillings and pence. In the debit column were sums for purlins, joists, floorboards, bricks—they must relate to the period when Broadacres was under construction. Also listed were seed stock, manure, grit and compost—the building blocks of Salad Days' business. In the credit column were the names of local green-grocers and hotels—Grandad's early customers. And yes, every month, a payment of twenty pounds from "G." Glenister? Only twenty? You'd said it was a lot. But then I supposed twenty pounds *was* a lot in the thirties.

The financial records were interesting, but they only confirmed what I knew already—that the colonel had made regular payments to Grandad for about ten years after he'd ceased to be employed on the estate. But no—it hadn't been the colonel. He'd been in the Rhineland and then in Abyssinia.

Mrs Glenister had made those payments. A business arrangement then, or an agreement between friends? But what was it *for?*

In the hope of answering this question I walked across to Glenister Hall one Tuesday afternoon just before Easter. Easter was late that year, the first week in April. For the school holiday we'd inaugurated an egg hunt amongst the raised beds and in the plantation even though technically it was still Lent. Parents had signed their kids up in droves, happy to let them scurry around collecting chocolate eggs while the adults browsed the trays of annuals, selecting plants for their summer displays. After the egg hunt, and in spite of their excessive chocolate consumption, the children clamoured for Victor's new ice cream flavours. Sales in the shop had increased exponentially and we'd all congratulated ourselves on our brilliance—apart from Hester, who complained at the damage rampaging feet had wreaked on seedbeds and new cuttings.

It had been fun, but also challenging, and I was glad of my afternoon off as well as excited to put my investigative plan into action.

The floor of the woods was already glossy with bluebell leaves. In another couple of weeks the place would be an ultraviolet carpet of bobbing, dancing blooms. The canopy above me was the brightest green, fresh with new-furled leaf. Birds twittered and swooped, gathering nesting material or already feeding their first brood. I climbed the gate and crossed the meadow, entering the overgrown jungle of Glenister Hall's garden.

As I'd expected, Polly's ancient Austin was absent from its place in the rear courtyard. She'd taken the opportunity of the Glenisters being away to allow herself some time off. The house was empty.

It was unlocked, however, and I pushed open what you'd called "the tradesmen's entrance" and, by force of habit, removed my shoes.

I made my way upstairs straight away. I wasn't sure I'd be able to hold my nerve if I delayed. The key to Henry and Verity's apartment was in the *jardinière* as I'd hoped, along with a dead spider and the wrapper of a Mars bar. I grasped the key with fingers slippery with guilt. I had a story ready. If anyone were to surprise me, I'd say Verity had telephoned from abroad, worried that she'd left the iron on. But the vast house echoed with emptiness. Only the faint, rhythmic drip of water broke the silence.

I let myself into the apartment.

Verity had left things in a terrible state. The bed was unmade. Dirty clothes were strewn across the floor. There were mouldering toast crumbs on the table in the kitchenette and the toilet had been left unflushed—the whole place reeked of ammonia. The bedroom was only dimly lit as they'd left the shutters closed. I groped my way across to the desk and switched on the desk light. The surface of the desk was empty, the letters and files cleared away. I tried the drawers and they yielded to my tug. One held only random stationery supplies—fountain pens, a stapler, rubber bands. Another contained Glenisters letterheads and envelopes. A third contained chequebook stubs. I riffled through one of them. It looked like Henry wrote few cheques. The first one was dated over two years ago, the most recent one just after Christmas. The cheques were for ordinary things like petrol, visits to the barber, a bill for newspapers at the village newsagent, and none of them for more than twenty or thirty pounds. I picked up another chequebook. This was quite different, cheques made out to cash on the first of every month, and all for two hundred pounds. Comparing the two, I saw that the two books were for two separate accounts. I rummaged in search of bank statements. What was the source of this considerable income? Frustratingly, I found none.

In the final desk drawer I found the manilla file I'd seen on my previous visit to Henry and Verity's apartment. I leafed through its contents. Every letter was a statement of account for monies overdue. Car repairs, a subscription for a London gentleman's club, a Savile Row tailor, even your school, Arthur. Even with the contribution you'd told me your mother had made to the school fees, there was an overdue amount dating back almost two years.

How could a man drawing two hundred pounds a month be so in debt? It didn't make any sense.

I cast around the room, careful to make sure I hadn't disturbed anything, although the room was in such disarray I didn't know how anyone would be able to tell. I switched off the lamp and let myself out of the apartment, replacing the key where I had found it.

I felt thoroughly discouraged—more confused, and with more questions than ever. I descended the stairs and, on a sort of autopilot, made my way to the library. I packed up my typewriter—I wouldn't be needing it again. I doubted I would ever go back to Glenister Hall after this abortive visit. I looked around the room. I'd become familiar with it in the weeks I'd spent closeted there. It felt a terrible shame that the beautiful books and the antique furniture would, in all likelihood, succumb to damp or worm. I crossed the carpet and was standing in the doorway with my hand on the light switch when my eye lit on the drawers beneath the window. Your words came back to me. 'Help yourself,' and 'The place is full of history.' Likewise, that loaded look you'd given me.

I shut the door again and turned the key to lock myself in. Silly, really, Who would have disturbed me? There was no one in the house but me.

In the drawer, the account books were on top of everything else, and I easily found the debits that coincided with the credits in Grandad's ledgers. The handwriting was quite different though; clearly, he hadn't helped Mrs Glenister with her accounts. Interestingly, where Salad Days' balance sheets enumerated prosaic purchases of fertiliser and rat poison, creosote and bamboo canes, the Glenisters hadn't been buying much at all—far less than I would have expected for a large house with staff, even if—as Polly had told me—Mrs Glenister had lived as a recluse.

Alongside the account ledgers I found the maps of the estate and plans of the house that you'd already shown me, housed in a leather folder. I hadn't examined them carefully before, but I did now. I looked for the gardener's cottage that Polly still inhabited and found it, way down the formal driveway. Right at the end of the drive was a lodge. Who lived there? From what I could see, grooms and other household staff had been accommodated above the stable block. What a teeming, busy place it must have been in its heyday!

The next thing in the drawer was a large scroll. The paper was thick, like blotting paper, rough at the edges. I unfurled it gingerly to reveal a Glenister family tree, generation after generation. The writing was ornate but varied in style. I supposed successive Glenisters had extended the tree as the years passed. The ink of the earliest entries was terribly faded but I made out dates as long ago as 1650. Against some of the names were illustrations in what must at one time have been colour but was now faded to a rusty monotone. I scanned down the branches to find the colonel. His name was illustrated with what I took to be his regimental insignia. His wife's entry was ornamented by a tree—stylised, set within a circle—a cypher I saw repeated against some of the other Glenister women higher up the tree. There was something rather lovely about their design and execution. Was there something special about the ink? They seemed to shimmer, almost burn, defying the dimness of the room. I reached out a curious finger to touch one of the pearly, iridescent symbols but drew it back sharply. The place was warm and left a distinct tingle on my skin. I rubbed my glowing finger against my thumb thoughtfully, as my eye skimmed the rest of the sheet.

Henry's name had been added, and his marriage to Blanche recorded. And there was your name, Arthur, right at the bottom, the last of the Glenisters … except … What was this? I tilted the paper. The light in the room was so poor. Was there the faintest sign of another name there? And the palest, pearly glow … I squinted, but it was no good. I gave up. The scroll was an interesting artefact, but it threw no light on the Glenisters' relationship with the Days and I rolled it back up carefully and put it to one side.

The last thing in the drawer was the hinged wooden box, its lid decorated with marquetry. I lifted the lid.

Letters.

They were bundled and bound with string, the paper yellowed and stiff, the elaborate penmanship quite hard to make out. Each envelope was addressed to your grandmother. The stamps were old and exotic. I hesitated. What right did I have? I prevaricated, the letters weighing heavy in my hand. But then I put them in my typewriter case.

I fled the library, and the house, hearing remonstrating ghosts at my back.

Chapter Thirty

When I returned to Broadacres there was a crisis, and in its aftermath, all thought of the letters went out of my head. Granny had put a pan of soup on the stove and forgotten about it. A pall of foul-smelling smoke met and half-choked me as I entered through the back door. I clasped a hand to my face while I fought my way to the source of the smell and grabbed the pan off the light using a tea towel. I dropped it into the sink where it spat and sizzled, and then ran cold water over my hand, which had burned even through the towel.

The time was about a quarter past five, and thankfully folks were beginning to arrive from the property in search of tea. Jack set to opening the doors and windows so that the fug could disperse. The day had remained fine though chill, and a through-draught soon began to clear the air.

Hester reached for the first-aid kit to treat my hand while Isobel filled the kettle. Dad went in search of Granny and found her in the garden, tying in the rambling rose that climbed over the end gable of the house, quite oblivious to the near catastrophe within. It was unusual for her to have been left alone in the house. Blanche had been at the accountants', the others about their work on the property. I had the distinct impression of accusatory eyes on me as I sat and had my hand bound up.

Hester was efficient but not very gentle. She said, 'This will prevent you from doing anything in the dairy or the production area. I'll have to put it into the accident book. Really, how inconvenient, with Easter upon us!'

'I didn't do it on purpose,' I remonstrated. '*I* didn't leave the pan on the stove!'

Isobel assembled the tea things for an *al fresco* meal in the fresh air of the terrace where, by good fortune, the outdoor table and chairs had been brought out and cleaned the previous weekend. Her mouth was pressed into a censorious line. I could clearly read the thought bubbles above her head. Where had I been? Why had I left Granny on her own?

'It was my afternoon off,' I exclaimed, answering indictments that hadn't been voiced, even though they were all too evidently being entertained. 'No one asked me to stay at home.'

Unintentionally, that put the blame on Blanche, who had just entered the kitchen. Never very resilient, she gave a strangled little cry and rushed from the room.

'It isn't Blanche's job to watch Granny,' Victor said sternly. 'The accounts are a full-time role. She saves us hundreds of pounds. To employ a bookkeeper would be—'

'—out of the question,' Isobel interrupted. 'I'd never agree to a stranger knowing our finances. This is a *family* business.'

She picked up a tray loaded with cups and plates and carried it out of the room.

The stink of burned vegetables and charred metal remained acrid in the kitchen and my eyes stung with it. They began to water.

'Don't *you* start blubbing,' said Hester, finishing the bandage and putting the bits and bobs back in the first aid box.

'I'm not!' I spat back. 'You know I never cry!' But everyone had gone onto the terrace for their tea, and nobody replied.

My hand throbbed terribly, and early in the evening I went to bed with some strong painkillers. At breakfast the following day it was evident that a family conference had taken place without me. The informal understanding we'd had—that Granny needed a careful eye kept upon her—had metamorphosed into a formal rota. Since I was unable to do my shifts in the shop for a few days I found I'd been assigned Granny-watch for the whole of the Easter weekend.

I shouldn't have felt at all troubled by this but somehow I did. It felt like a punishment. Ridiculously, Blanche was in the house for almost the whole time but pointedly refused to help.

'I usually make Granny a cup of coffee at about this time,' she said, looking up from her account books and calculator.

And, 'Since it's such a nice day, your granny will enjoy a walk to the village, I should think.'

I couldn't help myself. 'I'm sure she knows the way,' I retorted.

But in the end I did go with her, and she treated me to afternoon tea in the little café that had opened where Isobel and Victor's shop had been.

I found Granny easy company, especially if I encouraged her to talk about the past. She could reminisce for hours about the early years of Salad Days: the late snow in April of 1950 that had decimated seedlings, frost-bitten new shoots and damaged the blossom in the orchard; the drought of '53 that had resulted in Grandad drilling his own borehole as the Water Board had rationed water even for businesses like ours that depended on it; the big freeze of '61 when snow had covered the ground for two whole months. I found her memory to be crystal clear on events that were half a century old even if they were mazy about things that had occurred just that morning.

I pulled the photograph I'd taken from Grandad's office from my pocket and laid it on the table.

'Who are these people, Granny?' I asked casually.

She pulled it towards her and peered through the bi-focal part of her spectacles. 'Where did you find this?' she exclaimed. 'Oh, look at your grandad, Grace. Wasn't he handsome?' She pointed to the man I'd correctly identified.

'Yes!' I said, passing over her use of my sister's name. 'And this one. Is this Bradley?'

She nodded. 'And poor Mick, look! He never was any oil painting, but the war ruined him, didn't it?'

I pointed to the taller man at the back of the group. 'Is this Polly Tindall's husband?'

'Oh no,' she said, indicating instead the chap to the left of Grandad, a diminutive, heavy-browed man. 'That's Arnold Tindall. Polly ruled him with an iron fist. He and your grandad were friends from school, I think. Well, they were all pals, this whole group. I gather they got up to some mischief in their youth. No, those two at the back are your grandad's brothers. I wonder where this was taken?' She turned the picture over. 'There look, Ayr, 1926. They must have been having a day out by the sea.' She handed me back the picture.

'Why didn't you go with them, Granny?'

She looked at me then as though I was a stranger. 'What do you mean?'

'Well.' I crinkled my eyebrows. 'You were one of the gang, weren't you? You knew all these chaps from way back.'

'Oh no,' she said, a wary, distracted look in her eye. 'No. I didn't move here until much later.'

I was never more astonished in my life! I'd pictured both my grandparents as being as indigenous to the locality as the rocks and trees, born and raised side by side like two seedlings in the poly tunnel.

I thought she must be confused. Perhaps being in the little tea shop that she'd known all her life as the village store had disoriented her. I put my hand over hers. 'No, Granny, I think you're mixed up. You've *always* lived here.'

'I drove an ambulance in the war,' she retorted. 'That was in France. And afterwards I went to Germany.' She was becoming agitated.

I swept the whole subject away. 'Let's go and see the children, shall we?' I suggested brightly.

Her brow cleared at once. 'Oh yes,' she said. 'Verity and Grace will be home from school by now.'

We called in at the pub and spent an hour with Grace and the children. Granny called the little boys Trevor and Eric, and once even Henry, but they didn't seem to care, just rummaging in her handbag for the sweets she always carried.

During the Easter weekend I kept Granny within the confines of the garden. The garden centre was rammed with people coming to buy annuals, although in truth it was much too soon—frost could strike in those northern climes as late as halfway through May. The café sold out of simnel cake and those little chocolate Krispie cakes with a tiny egg on the top. Isobel was bad tempered and Victor's precarious lightness was further eroded at the end of each day; they both resorted to gin as soon as the tea things had been cleared. Again I felt indicted, that I'd in some way deliberately let them down. My hand was improved but still required its bandage and so I couldn't have operated the till or done anything to help in any other department.

I'd quite enjoyed helping Granny in the garden, as far as my bandaged hand permitted. It reminded me of the old days, when work on the property was fun, a family affair, without the public to consider, health and safety strictures, food hygiene regulations, squeezed profit margins and troublesome employee relations. It also recalled the high-spirited atmosphere of our family get-togethers—surely now a thing of the past.

With the stark contrast of the then-and-now so vividly in my mind it was hard to resist picking up the yo-yo of my indecision. I'd all but resolved to give up my university course. Broadacres and my work at Salad Days was familiar if it wasn't always very enjoyable. It felt important, a continuation of the past—however impenetrable some aspects of it were—and a tangible waypoint towards the future. It meant something. At the same time, in the larger scheme of things, it felt like a backwater, far from the exponential progress that was taking place in the rest of the country and the wider world. My friend Zhi had almost completed her second year of university and was beginning to apply for jobs with big corporations and governmental agencies. She would be a high-flier. I could track the trajectory of her progress in my mind. In contrast, I would be an insignificant speck, doing and being nothing.

You didn't help, Arthur. Your postcards made your life seem so glamorous. I found out that after skiing in Switzerland, you were bound for the Adriatic where you'd got a place as a crew member on a private yacht. How small-town and humdrum my little life seemed in comparison. You wouldn't be home for the summer. It felt like a nail in the coffin of my life, Arthur. You'd left me behind.

That left me—again—stuck right in the middle, tangled in the loose threads that constituted the here-and-now.

It was Monday evening before my hand was declared sufficiently healed for me to begin work the following day. My penance of looking after

Granny—if it had been penance; in truth, I'd rather enjoyed it—was done. After supper, Hester helped Granny through to the sitting room where she had laid out the pieces of a jigsaw, making a gesture with her free hand that indicated I was free to do as I pleased.

I went up to my room, locked the door and brought out the packet of letters I'd purloined from the library at Glenister Hall.

Chapter Thirty-One

The envelopes had been superior quality paper at one time, but were now brittle and yellowed with age. The stamps—clearly German—were overlaid with numerous franks. These might have been dated but were so smudged that I couldn't arrange the envelopes in date order.

Of course the envelopes had already been opened, by their recipient and also, I suspected, by you Arthur. How old had you been when you'd stumbled across this parcel? How much of their contents had you understood? Had you gone back afterwards to reread them in the hope that your advancing age would help you make better sense of them?

I withdrew each letter from its envelope, but carefully, making sure I would be able to reunite them correctly when I was done.

Most of the letters were a single sheet, headed simply "Köln" and dated. There were fifteen or so letters spanning a period from 1922 to 1929. They were all addressed to 'My dear Bee' and signed, 'Your affectionate Edward.' Edward, I knew was Colonel Glenister. Bee I assumed to be his wife, the woman in the woods.

I scanned the letters. They were not—as I had half-feared—love letters. Indeed, they were fairly innocuous, describing the weather—generally cold— the colonel's state of health—generally good—and his diet—generally bland. There was no mention of his activities as part of the occupying force in the Rhineland. I supposed that it was forbidden to divulge any details. He mentioned some of his fellow officers but by their nick-names—Bunny, Whizzo, Jock and Pug. He referred in glowing terms to an aide who'd been assigned to him and proved particularly useful. Bill clearly operated as a general factotum, driver and fixer. It seemed to me that Bee had either tried to send her husband supplies or asked if he needed anything, but apparently there was nothing that Bill couldn't get hold of—I presumed via the black market—and the colonel declared himself plentifully supplied with soap, razors, cigarettes and Scotch. It looked like the colonel had made it home on furlough about once a year. His letters touched on parties he and Bee had attended together as well as arrangements he must have made on his few visits home—the sale of a mare, the leaving fallow of a particular field—enquiring about the outcome of these things.

Colonel Glenister responded to information Bee must have sent him. He was 'happy' that the fire in the salon had ceased to smoke, 'delighted' for the safe arrival of Lady Bilton's baby, 'pleased to know' the roses in the sunken garden were so prolific. He made polite enquiries as to her health. The only reference to the Days was in one of the letters dated 1928. He urged her to consult my grandfather if she was in difficulty. 'A good man,' he wrote, 'capable in all areas, locally connected and very discreet.'

I stared at the letters in disappointment. There was nothing in them at all. Had I missed something? I re-read them, more carefully, looking for veiled hints, anything that might have a double meaning, any allusion at all to money. No.

The final letter was dated April 1929, when I knew that the occupation was winding up. The colonel announced that his leave had been cancelled. He must have anticipated his wife's disappointment at this news and sought to soften the blow with the promise of a gift, to be delivered by the redoubtable Bill who, his tour of duty complete, would return to Blighty and call at Glenister Hall. I wondered what the gift had been. Wood carving? Pottery? I knew both were crafts local to the Rhineland because you'd sent your mother gifts of regional handicrafts while you'd been at the castle. It was hard to imagine what artefact the colonel might send that would be at home in the rarified environment of Glenister Hall. A typical man, I thought, sure to send something hideous or useless, or both.

Whatever it was it can't have been much of a substitute, I thought, refolding the letters. They'd got me nowhere at all and now I was left with the problem of returning them to Glenister Hall. Verity and Henry were due back from St Moritz the following day. I'd entered and left Glenister Hall many times without being seen but it would be just my luck to encounter one of them this time, and I didn't have the excuse of collecting my typewriter. I'd brought that back with the letters. I supposed I could pretend to be restarting my novel—take the damned typewriter back to the library. But why would I do that? Now that poor Erin had died there was no one to annoy with the clickety-clack of the keys.

I put the letters back into the typewriter case and went to run myself a bath. Both the bathroom and hot water were always at a premium at Broadacres. There were so many of us in residence and we all did quite hard, physical labour during the day. We needed plentiful baths and showers, but it was not unusual to find the hot water tank empty.

That evening though, I was in luck, and I ran quite a deep, hot bath and lowered myself into it for a long soak, aware that there would probably be hell to pay afterwards.

My mind reviewed the letters as I wallowed. What a sad marriage the Glenisters had, compared to my grandparents, who had built a house, a business and a family together. I didn't know when the Glenisters had married, but poor Mrs Glenister had been left alone for years. No wonder she'd gone a bit cuckoo. Or maybe she'd been cuckoo right from the start—the cause, rather than the effect of the colonel's absence for so many years. I posited the idea that he'd placed my grandad within the grounds of Glenister Hall so that he could keep an eye on the errant lady of the manor. The colonel had certainly praised Grandad and fulsomely recommended him to Mrs Glenister, but that went nowhere towards explaining the outlay of money beyond the period of Grandad's employment.

The more I thought about it the more certain I was that those payments had nothing to do with the colonel at all.

I gazed around the bathroom. It was terribly old-fashioned, probably original to the house. The bath was cast iron, deep and wonderfully comfortable. It was long. I recalled being put into it with both my sisters, the twins and Erin. Jack, the only boy, had luxuriated in solitary baths until you'd joined him. How typically prudish of my grandparents, I thought, to separate the boys and the girls at bathtime. And how hypocritical too, when we'd all shared the same attic room. There had been talk amongst the family of some alteration or improvement we could make to Broadacres to commemorate Granny's wedding anniversary. She would have been married fifty years in October. Personally, I thought the various suggestions were quite self-serving. Granny, bless her, would hardly live long enough to enjoy the refurbished kitchen or bathroom or the central heating upgrade that had been suggested. In truth, these were just ways to get Granny to pay for improvements that the rest of the residents wanted. On the other hand, God forbid we should throw another party. Henry's disastrous fiftieth had been quite enough. Dad would be fifty the following year. What could we do that would be different—better—for him? We were *all* getting older, apart from the ones who had ceased to age at all: Eric, Mum, Grandad, Erin.

I yanked my thoughts back from this maudlin theme.

Something tugged at me, some idea, some notion … I couldn't catch it, like a tune you've heard on the radio but can't quite recall. I retraced the steps of my thoughts. The letters. The bathroom. Granny's anniversary. Henry's party.

I shot out of the bath, slopping water over the edge and almost slipping on the slick linoleum. I grabbed my towel and yanked open the bathroom door. In my room I brought out the letters again. My hands were shaking. I had to check the dates. If Henry was fifty in 1979 then he was born in 1929. His birthday fell in October which meant he'd been conceived in January.

But Colonel Glenister's leave had been cancelled. I found the relevant letter and checked it again. There it was. He didn't go home at all in 1929 and, that being the case, he couldn't possibly be Henry Glenister's father.

Chapter Thirty-Two

I hardly slept that night. The ramifications of my discovery went round in my head until I thought it would burst.

Colonel Glenister wasn't Henry's father. So, who was?

Oh! Believe me, I tried to pin the deed on other men: poor scarred Mick Pullman; Bradley Fox; even Arnold Tindall, notoriously under the thumb of his redoubtable wife.

It was no good. In my heart I knew there was only one answer. Who had been in a position of trust at Glenister Hall in 1929, particularly recommended for his reliability and discretion? My God! Mrs Glenister had been all but thrown into his arms! Who had received substantial payments long after his employment was completed? And why? To keep him quiet about the baby he'd sired on his employer's wife. But no. That cash had been much more than a coldly calculating pay off. I brought to mind Mrs Glenister's expression that evening at the woodsman's cottage. She'd been emotional, her eyes brimming, her hand pressed to her heart. She'd loved him.

And who had welcomed Henry Glenister into Broadacres—the oddest thing, out of the blue—and treated you, Arthur, as another grandson. Which you are.

My grandfather.

And Henry knew it! His scheme to free you of the burden of Glenister Hall? No less than the appropriation of the entirety of the Day property! He'd claim it all! Where would any of us Days be when Henry Glenister walked away with all we'd worked for?

And no wonder he'd persuaded Verity that they needn't get married. He was her uncle! It would be illegal, wouldn't it? At the very least it was … I couldn't find the right word to describe the curdled, nauseated feeling that churned in my bowels. Did Verity know the truth? I thought she must suspect it. It explained so much; her hiding away at Glenister Hall, for one thing, and her sycophantic behaviour towards Henry—she was as vulnerable to exposure as he was. The queasy feeling in the pit of my stomach increased. The idea of the two of them, uncle and niece … It was as repulsive and shocking and just impossible as the idea of Victor and one of the twins, or my dad and Erin. The age difference between them had been hard to come to terms with, and the creepy way Henry had wormed his way into Verity's pants had sickened me, but my parents' acceptance of it had stopped me from thinking of it as outright "wrong." Now, I knew it was wrong, morally and legally, not in a self-righteous or judgemental way, but rather from the way my conscience flinched. What else would I expect of your father? He might be a Day in blood but in every other way he was all Glenister. Hadn't Mrs Gibbs told me, all those years ago, of the Glenisters' propensity to marry "too close?"

I sat up in bed and switched on my bedside lamp. There was more, and worse. The consequences of the situation were so far-reaching I'd have to squint to make them out. I hesitated to bring them into focus, afraid of what they would look like, afraid at the prospect of what would have to be done once I'd brought them into the light.

You were as much a Day as I was. I'd spent years making us both miserable because I'd believed you to be an interloper … It had made me ill— my hatred of you—but now, Arthur … now I hated myself.

How could I have been so cruel?

Or so stupid?

The churned-up muddy waters of my understanding were beginning to clear, but I struggled to make sense of what I saw in their depths.

I might have begun by resenting you, but those feelings had been replaced long ago. More recently, since Dad and Blanche's wedding, I'd been conscious of a different thread in the fabric of our relation, in my side of it anyway. Sisterly friendship had given way to feelings that had a distinctly romantic weft.

I was falling for you, and it wouldn't have taken much to have pushed me headlong in love.

In fact, the truth of it was I'd always loved you, Arthur. I'd misunderstood, misconstrued, perhaps wilfully ignored what my heart had been telling me. I'd been green. As green as spinach, as lettuce, as the cabbage and kale we sold in the shop. Green in judgement. Because what I'd felt for you all along was love. *Real* love. *True* love.

But now, in the very instant of its recognition, it was *wrong* love, tainted and unhealthy, as Henry's was for Verity. I couldn't separate them. In my mind, what was wrong for them could not be right for me and I shuddered at the idea of being anything like Henry. I was to discover—because yes, I looked it up at the library—that although it wasn't strictly unlawful for cousins to wed, it was frowned upon and discouraged, and this accorded with a subliminal but overpowering sense I had that it was dirty; that no good could come of it. Ironically—because you weren't actually a Glenister at all—the fact that I loved you, my cousin, made me feel stained by all the Glenisters stood for, of which I disapproved. My conscience and my lifelong antipathy for Henry made me shrink from it even as my heart reached to embrace it, creating a schism that threatened to tear me in two.

I loved you, but it half-sickened me. I wish I could explain, but you can't hear me or, if you can hear, you can't respond. Oh Arthur! How I wish, how I *wish* you would make some small sign so I can know you understand.

PART FOUR
1980 – 1990
Chapter Thirty-Three

The trees are beginning to turn, Arthur. I always like this time of year. Everything has worked hard all summer and now the time for repose has come. Creatures hibernate or fly to warmer climes. The rest of us hunker down, bank up the fire and retreat to what small and cosy places we have for respite. The forest sleeps, seeds slumber, old things decompose and feed the new ones that are to come. Some old things never die, though they might wish to; and for some, death is no reprieve.

The 1980s was a terrible decade, both for me and the country. Margaret Thatcher crushed the unions and unemployment became a lifestyle for millions of people. At one end of the scale people were angry, hopeless and trapped. At the other, business, entrepreneurialism, tech and the financial markets made a few people fabulously wealthy. You were on one plane, I was on the other. I suppose you looked back at us from such a lofty height that we were barely visible. If you had any feelings at all I imagine them to have been nostalgia, well-seasoned with a sense of a lucky escape.

We lost sight of each other over the abyss, which was layered—for me, anyway—with loss and disappointment and with what I can only describe to you as a nagging consciousness of transgression. I fully acknowledged my feelings for you but, because in my mind they made me the same as Henry whom I despised and reviled, they felt sick and wrong. My old rage had returned but now *I* was the object of it, rather than you.

All my old trouble would have come flooding back, but my discovery about your father and the likely future of Salad Days acted as a catalyst, shaking me out of the slough of indecision that had paralysed me for the previous two years. I didn't know when Henry planned to drop his bombshell, but I was determined not to be around when he did. By June I'd confirmed my place on the university course at Birmingham, bought my books and secured a single room in a hall of residence. I had my student rail pass in my purse. I was ready to shake the dust of Salad Days and Broadacres from my feet once and for all.

But, in its usual way, life had other plans.

Victor fell off his bike as he pedalled home from the golf club one evening in August 1980, where he'd been carousing as normal with Henry. Victor broke a hip so severely he was in hospital for weeks, his recovery hampered by previously unsuspected complications with his heart. No one but me could replace him in the dairy—the time I'd spent in there after Erin's death now more than qualified me to do so. Isobel, torn between the hospital ward and the business, looked likely to make herself ill if I didn't agree to postpone my departure for the midlands. Hester added her voice to the Day chorus that clamoured for my aid. Then, the final straw came: Blanche announced she was expecting a baby. It felt as though the universe and the Day family with it were conspiring to prevent me from pursuing my own course in life but, once more, Henry Glenister seemed to me the most to blame. Hadn't he been the one to encourage Victor's excesses?

I was so laden down in those days with the hopeless sense that there wasn't any point to anything pertaining to the family or the business that I almost told them everything. 'There's no point,' I wanted to say. 'All this has been a waste of time and effort. In just a few years it will be taken from you, and you'll be left with nothing.' But I couldn't do it. Granny's face, so trusting and hopeful, stopped me. How could I tell her that Grandad—her soulmate, her friend, her partner—had deceived her? It was too hard—as hard as facing the awful reality that *my* soulmate and friend could never be my partner.

I looked around the ever diminishing circle of faces as each person stepped forward to offer their plea, and felt the noose tighten with each one.

Dad said, 'I know the timing's awful, Prue, but you've already delayed a year. Will a few more weeks make such a difference?'

Isobel, pinch-lipped, said, 'I can't see why you want to go at all. You've a job-for-life and home here. You're a natural in the dairy. I always thought you'd take it over when Victor and I retired.'

Hester, the only one amongst them who'd had a university education, said, 'I can see the point of study. But literature? Where's that going to get you? You can do a food science degree with the open university. The business would pay for that.'

'Or an accreditation with the cheese academy,' Isobel put in. 'I quite fancied that, but there was never time.'

What? Swap my degree in English literature for a cheese accreditation? Oh Arthur, I wish you'd been there. How we would have laughed.

Blanche stroked her barely-there baby bump and simpered, 'You wouldn't want to be a stranger to your little brother or sister, would you? And I must say, at my age, I'd welcome the help.'

The twins thought it would be 'much more fun' if I stayed around. Jack boasted that it wouldn't be long before the whole shebang passed on to the next generation—meaning himself, the twins and me. That idea made me almost breathless with hysterical irony. If he only knew! The idea of working alongside Jack—however temporarily—was particularly appalling. He had lately become entitled and dictatorial, lording it over the employees while lounging around himself and doing little work. I'd heard the twins complaining about his attitude—he was spoilt and overbearing, they said.

It was Granny who finally persuaded me, not by anything she said—in fact, she alone offered no entreaty—but just her figure in the chorus. She stood amongst them and her attention seemed to follow the course of the discussion, but her eyes were curious, wary and bewildered and I saw that she was lost. Those hands—so capable in the past when I've felt their soothing coolness on my feverish brow, their gentle probing at splinters or grit in a wound, watched them plant seedlings and ease puppies from their mother. But those hands also wielded an axe and wrung the necks of chickens. Now she clasped them before her as though they were the only solid things in a world of shifting confusion. I could see the whiteness of her knuckles, the way the fingers of one hand pressed into the flesh of the other. It was indeed, perhaps unconsciously, an attitude of prayer, but it spoke to me more eloquently of Granny's need for us all. Even for me. One by one her precious family were falling from her world: Eric, Grandad, Mum and Erin. Victor might soon follow. Grace and Verity were daily more absorbed by their own lives. We would all be victims of the great revelation to come but Granny— please God—would be beyond betrayal then. She was the innocent and the injured party even if she did not know it.

How could I desert her?

In the end, I compromised, agreeing to remain at Broadacres but insisting that I pursue my literature studies with the Open University. I was hedging my bets, reasoning that when Victor eventually recovered and I reapplied to Birmingham or another university, the modules I'd covered with the OU would mean I wasn't too far behind.

I'd hated the Salad Days dungarees, but the hairnets and protective overshoes required by the dairy were even worse. I ended each day stinking of sour milk and ripe cheese, my hands chapped and raw, my back aching from bending over the cheese vat. But a quick shower and I'd be ready for my books. I devoured *Pamela, Robinson Crusoe, Moll Flanders, The Life and Opinions of Tristram Shandy, Gulliver's Travels* and *Pilgrim's Progress* and wrote an end of module essay that passed with distinction. I'd fall into bed exhausted but be up at three in the morning for the OU broadcast, and often went straight to the dairy before the sun was fully up. I had in my mind at all times that while doing my duty by the family I must also prepare myself for a life independent of them. It was like walking two roads to entirely different destinations at the same time, and I lived with a sense of continual compromise.

Now, looking back, I recognise that my obsessive study was just another coping mechanism. I escaped into it as I had escaped into books in my youth. Or possibly I can argue that it was just another waypoint to a higher, freer consciousness where all my life's tribulations would disperse into the ether.

A spring storm early in 1981 damaged Glenister Hall's roof, rendering the house unfit for human habitation and necessitating, at last, the commencement of some interim repairs. Knowing the parlous state of Henry's finances, I wondered who would pay for these. It was agreed that the colonel, Henry and Verity should remove to the little cottage, displacing the twins, who would return to their room at Broadacres. That ousted me, but I moved into the downstairs room formerly used by Erin. This had the advantage of allowing me to get up at ungodly hours to watch the OU broadcasts of lectures without disturbing anyone else.

What happened to Mrs Glenister during the repairs to the big house I did not ask. No one mentioned her at all. Perhaps she was dead, mouldering into the forest floor, never to be discovered. Perhaps she was snugly accommodated at the woodsman's cottage. Mindful of the unholy serendipity of my meetings with her and the demise of my family members, I kept well away from there.

The house was overcrowded and often noisy—hardly conducive to study—and characterised by grouch. Victor returned home but was unable to resume work. What remained of his good humour was soured for good— perhaps by pain, perhaps by frustration—and he became querulous and difficult. He took up a position in an armchair in the sitting room from where he hollered for food and drink and for someone to change the TV channel. He became so corpulent he couldn't manage the stairs and I had to vacate my ground floor room before I'd fully settled into it, so that he and Isobel could sleep there. We all tiptoed round him except Jack, who seemed to use his father's incapacity as an excuse to step up his gambits to take control of the business. The two frequently rowed, poor Isobel caught helplessly between them. Jack wanted to expand, to become more commercial, to add a children's soft-play barn and a petting zoo. Victor was adamant that things should remain as they were. Hester frequently weighed in. She wanted to apply for soil association certification—she was sure organic food was the thing of the future. Power struggles erupted at mealtimes and sometimes over the raised beds and plant displays. My father played no part in the argument. Blanche unfortunately lost her baby at six months gestation, a terrible tragedy for the whole family and one we feared would send her running back to alcohol. Dad dedicated all his care and time to her wellbeing.

Thankfully, Granny seemed oblivious to the acrimonious atmosphere at Broadacres, either because her capacity to understand the different factions was impaired or because she was often away from the house, taken off on jaunts by the colonel. The two were increasingly pally, glad of each other's company I supposed, tolerant of the memory lapses and physical frailty only to be expected of people in their mid-eighties. They seemed to spend most of their time happily reminiscing of times gone by. I had nothing against Colonel Glenister and was only too happy to see Granny taken out and treated to afternoon teas and tours of stately homes, trips to the theatre and strolls along the promenades of nearby seaside towns. She'd worked hard all of her life. Why shouldn't she have some fun?

Chapter Thirty-Four

We rarely saw you, Arthur, in those days. I was both happy and wretched about that.

When you did come home it was always *en route* to somewhere else more exciting. Your course in classical architecture gave you behind-the-scenes access to some of the grandest houses in the country—Wentworth, Blenheim, Chatsworth, Burleigh—and your circle of friends seemed scarcely less well-connected. Your former school friends now had jobs at the stock exchange, the foreign office and various banks. Christmases, Easters and summers passed by without you. Your letters spoke of sojourns at friends' villas and ski lodges. How very far away you felt then, Arthur. And on those rare occasions when you did grace us with your company, an unbridgeable gulf separated us. You would arrive in a fancy sports car, the tyres spurting gravel, and leap out wearing clothes that seemed freshly laundered or even freshly acquired, unsullied by hours spent in the plush and no doubt air-conditioned interior of the car. You yourself exuded health and wealth, your hair ablaze and always cut in the latest style, your skin often tanned from a recent trip, your body increasingly honed and toned. You'd taken to wearing Aviator sunglasses even on quite cloudy days and so I could never tell whether your broad, white-toothed smile encompassed your eyes. You looked glamorous and handsome all right, Arthur.

If that was your aim, you nailed it.

There'd be a flurry of welcome as family members hurried from the house and the garden centre like hens at feeding time, clucking and exclaiming, flapping around you proffering drinks, food and questions. How long were you staying? Where had you come from? Granny would become teary at the sight of you, reaching up her arms to be held in the way that, way back when, you had reached out to her. Blanche positively glowed with pride in you. Dad would be hardly less pleased. The only person who was not happy to see you was Jack. Beside you he was pathetic and homespun, a small fish in a small pond, whereas it was apparent to everyone that you, Arthur, were on a trajectory to a success we parochial Days could only imagine or dream of. The family milled around you and eyed the back seat of the car where there were always gifts from your different trips, from Harrods and Fortnum and Mason. You liked to tease us, strolling around admiring the house and garden, enquiring about the business, teasing the twins that they'd soon be on *Top of the Pops* before opening the car with a flourish and handing out all your intriguing and exquisitely gift-wrapped parcels.

I'd linger on the edge of the circle, conscious of my lank, greasy hair and my skin—pale and washed out from too many hours in the dairy and too many nights spent studying. I had nothing to offer in answer to your anecdotes of bumping into Prince Andrew and Fergie in Klosters, of being inadvertently locked inside High Clere, or being—wrongly—arrested after you'd tried to break up a fight in an exclusive West End night club. Often I'd slope off before you'd even finished your rendition. The chill, sour atmosphere of the dairy was the physical manifestation of my chill, sour state of mind. I'd pretend to resent your thoughtless arrival in the middle of the working day. Did you expect everything to stop just because you'd decided to pay us a visit? Like father like son, I'd fume. Inconsiderate. Self-absorbed. Entitled. But in reality, I was eaten up with shame and a sense of crippling inadequacy. You were out of my reach, in every way. Like Jack, I was pitiful and plain, totally eclipsed by your glory; and in any case my feelings for you were iniquitous—they made me as bad as Henry; I was ashamed of them.

The eighties stumbled on. Charles and Diana married, there was war in the Falklands and famine in Ethiopia. Andrew and Fergie got married, the Duchess of Windsor died. I completed more modules in my course: Shakespeare; the romantic poets; the nineteenth century novel; American literature; English Modernism. I immersed myself in the written word and lived for the three or four times a year when I would travel to Milton Keynes for face-to-face tutorials and meetings with others on my course. For those few days I was a different being, in my proper element. My tutor expressed delight in my progress and even held up one of my essays as an example to the other students. I felt vindicated as never before.

I met a post-graduate student named Jonathan. He was ten years my senior and, like me, was tied to his family, prevented by his elderly parents' dependency from cutting the filial ties. The English Literature course was his second Open University degree. He already had a master's in history. He said learning was his escape from life and I knew just what he meant.

He was nothing like you physically, Arthur. He was tall but thin boned with dark hair that was often scruffy and in need of a cut. He wore a short beard and utilitarian but utterly anonymous clothes from Marks and Spencer's. But he had the kindest smile and a gentle, unassuming manner, a dry sense of humour and a patient, listening ear. We spent several evenings over cheap meals and cheaper wine discussing post-modern literature, structuralism and James' *The Art of the Novel* while the others went off in search of action in seedy clubs, bored by our scholarly erudition. After two or three of these encounters I found myself pouring out my woes to him one evening in the student bar, and when he walked me back to my budget hotel I asked him to go in with me. He made love to me with tenderness, consideration and with a selfless generosity that astonished me. I cannot in all conscience say my virginity was 'taken' because the word implies the removal of something, whereas I felt Jonathan gave far more than he took.

We did not speak of love or affection, or of the future, but fell back into what today would be called friendship-with-benefits every time the student cohort convened. Between times we wrote occasionally, recommending obscure articles of literary criticism we'd unearthed for the various texts on our module, but not speaking much of ourselves. From time to time we spoke on the phone, but there was no privacy at Broadacres and I gathered the demands of his increasingly confused parents made telephoning awkward for Jonathan too.

I was not the only member of our family to be exploring relationships. Kath recovered from her broken heart and took up with Aidan, a singer-songwriter she met at *Live Aid* in 1985. By coincidence he was also a twin, with a brother, Aamon, who played percussion and functioned as Aidan's manager and general dogsbody. Aamon and Karen hit it off and by 1986 the four were romantically attached and collaborating musically, the girls branching out into Aidan's original material rather than the cover versions of popular songs they'd had in their repertoire before. The appeal of two sets of twins on stage immediately grabbed the attention of venue managers and the girls were increasingly away, pursuing their musical careers. Hester took on students from her former college for work placements 'in the meantime,' but as far as I was concerned the rot was setting in at Salad Days. Before long Jack and I would be the only Days remaining. The business would devolve onto strangers and whatever Henry eventually inherited it would not be the strong, cohesive family business it had been in the past.

Jack had a string of girlfriends, mainly sourced from the Young Farmers' group. They varied in type. Some were broadly spoken and broadly built girls from local dairy farms who, however thoroughly they might have scrubbed up to meet the Days, still had the whiff of the slurry pit about them. Others were shy and simpering, the daughters of farmers rather than actively involved themselves, biding their time until they could escape from the farm altogether. He brought home a veterinary nurse we all rather liked, Chloe, but she soon tired of Jack's bullish and often misogynistic attitude. A relationship with a shepherdess, Patsy, lasted longer, mainly because she was so busy with the flock that she had little time to spend with Jack at all. Hester tried to interest Jack in some of the horticultural students—who would be much better in terms of the future business—but his dismissive attitude towards them queered his pitch there. I think he didn't like the idea that at least in terms of horticultural theory, they knew a good deal more than he did.

And then there was you. It was inconceivable to me that you did not attract scores of attractive, intelligent and well-heeled young women: the impoverished and not-so impoverished scions of landed gentry; the positively prosperous sisters of your high-achieving friends. You were not so crass as to mention any of them on your infrequent visits home but Arthur, you were *so* attractive—as well as charming—I'm sure you could take your pick. Or maybe it's just that I loved you so much that I couldn't imagine any other woman not feeling the same.

Chapter Thirty-Five

You came home in the summer of 1987 for an unusually protracted stay of a week. By then you were attached to an architectural practice that specialised in the renovation of historic buildings. It was perfect for you, absolutely in line with your degree, and building on the work you'd done for your post graduate diploma. You were between projects, I recall, having just completed the restoration of a nineteenth century Wesleyan chapel, and before commencing work on a derelict eighteenth century orangery attached to a Palladian mansion in Northumberland.

We ate on the terrace for the first evening of your stay, Blanche and Isobel going all-out with the food, the twins especially requested to delay until the following day their departure to a fringe festival they were booked to play. Victor was helped from the sitting room into a seat at the table where he dispensed wine with a liberal hand—especially into his own glass. Jack joined us too, and behaved mulishly throughout the meal, interrupting the conversation of others to raise matters pertaining to the business and causing his mother to scamper in and out of the house to fetch condiments. Grace came over but Gary could not be spared from the pub.

Henry and Verity were there, of course. It was the first time I'd witnessed the two of you together since the day of Dad and Blanche's wedding and Henry's attempt to ensnare me beneath the rose arbour. Since then, I'd avoided gatherings where your father was present if I could, but it wasn't always possible. He'd made no further advances towards me and yet I was perpetually conscious of his eyes on me, a cynically raised eyebrow and a slightly lascivious curl to his thin, cruel lips. I wondered if you'd spoken to him. Warned him off? There had never been much in the way of affection between the two of you, but now I thought I detected a distinct coolness. I inferred that you hadn't forgiven him.

The colonel was also present, treating Granny with his usual gallantry and consideration, but also clearly immensely proud of you as you described something of the difficulties and also the successes of your recent project.

The twilit garden looked particularly lovely on that June evening, and when we'd eaten and cleared the plates away I took the remains of my wine and drew my chair apart a little to admire it, making myself peripheral to the conversation but at the same time hanging on your every word as you spoke—confidently but without the least degree of arrogance—about the artistry required in restoring crumbling cornices and the engineering exigencies of supporting glazed roofs threatened by damp and decay. You raised the possibility of one day restoring Glenister Hall. Half of me thrilled to learn that you planned, one day, to come home. The other half shrivelled—you'd be so near and yet, so very far. I cauterized both emotions by reminding myself that in all likelihood it would be Day money you'd use to restore your ancestral pile. I fixed a look of haughty indifference on my face and stared fixedly at the moon, which was just rising above the tree line. Against my will, my wayward eye watched you pull a paper napkin towards you to sketch out an illustration. Everyone except me leaned close to see, intrigued by your theme. Even Jack deigned to take a sneering interest. Then I noticed Granny—a diminutive figure in those days, so shrunken and reduced from her former indefatigable strength and competence—weeping silently. The table was lit by candles and two dim electric lanterns that hung either side of the French window, but the overhanging clematis cast Granny's face in shadow, and it was only the slight sheen of the wet tears on her cheeks that glimmered sufficiently for me to see them.

I rose without a fuss and crossed the terrace, taking Granny's elbow and lifting her gently to her feet. At the same time, I rummaged a clean handkerchief from my pocket and pressed it into her hand.

'Let's take a turn in the garden,' I said softly, guiding her past the backs of the others. 'It's so beautiful at this time of year. The smell of the roses in the arbour is intoxicating.'

I had unhappy memories of the rose arbour, but I led her in that direction, out of earshot of the table before I bent to ask, 'What's the matter, Granny darling? Why are you crying?'

She sniffled into the handkerchief for a few moments. 'I mustn't be a cry-baby,' she said at last, 'but it's *so* lovely to see Henry, isn't it?'

'Do you mean Arthur?'

She frowned and pressed her lips together. 'Do I?'

'I think so,' I said lightly. 'Henry's here most days, but Arthur's just come home for a visit. We haven't seen him for …' I tried to calculate it but abandoned the attempt. Granny wouldn't remember anyway. '…ever so long,' I concluded.

The shadow of confusion that had clouded Granny's face suddenly passed and she resumed her usual serenity. 'He's so naughty,' she said, but without any trace of censure. 'He got up to all kinds of mischief in the garden. But it wasn't his fault. He was left alone so much of the time.'

That didn't sound right to me. In my recollection, Granny would neglect her work if you needed to be entertained, but that wasn't very often. Usually there had been all the rest of us to play with. 'Arthur was?'

She gave my arm an admonishing little shake. '*Henry* was.'

We generally allowed Granny to persist with her muddle-headedness. Unless it was really important to put her right, what was the point in upsetting her? So I didn't correct her again.

I said, 'He always loved playing in this garden. We all did. Do you remember the day we made a den in the compost heap?'

'Not *this* garden,' Granny said, a little shortly. 'The garden at Glenister Hall. I watched him often there. Sometimes for hours at a time. Poor little mite. Sometimes it would be full dark before anyone indoors thought to take him in to supper.'

Suddenly I doubted my certainty of only a moment before. Maybe *I* was the one who was muddle-headed. Did she mean you? Or your father? Had she really walked to Glenister Hall and watched you playing alone on those few occasions when you were not here with us? Surely not, although the idea of Blanche forgetting all about you did ring true. Henry, then? Was it possible she'd known all along that Henry was my grandad's child and for that reason had taken an interest in him? It would explain her easy—even eager—acceptance of Henry at Broadacres. I looked down at her. Her hair was thinning. Her shoulders had more than a suggestion of a widow's hump. How large-hearted she was. How forgiving and kind.

We made our stately progress around the garden, flooded now with the light of a gibbous moon. From the terrace I heard the strum of a guitar, and the past came flooding back to me—those carefree evenings of our childhood. Eric accompanying the rest as they sang the songs of the day. My mother—still alive and happy. Grandad—the undisputed but oh-so-benevolent patriarch. Erin—serene even though her penetrating eye saw what was to come. I had the most powerful sense that they were there, their shades distinct in the moonlight.

I opened my mouth to say something, but Granny pre-empted me. 'I'll see them soon,' she said, reaching out with an automatic finger and thumb to tweeze a wilted rose head from its stalk.

I saw no point in pretending to misunderstand her. 'I hope not too soon,' I murmured, taking the rose from her and inhaling the scent, which was still sweet.

Granny looked up at me, one eye narrowed quizzically. 'Well, *you* must know,' she said. 'Don't think I don't see you. I know who *you* are.'

I began to say, 'I'm Prudence,' but just then Isobel bustled across the lawn towards us, bringing a cardigan to put around Granny's shoulders. 'It's time you were indoors,' she said a little crossly. 'It's getting cool and damp out here.'

She took Granny away, leaving me alone on the lawn, the smell of roses suddenly cloying and unpleasant in my nostrils. I looked across at the terrace. The party was breaking up. Henry, Verity, the colonel and Grace were calling their goodnights as they rounded the corner of the house. Hester, Blanche and my father gathered up the glasses while the twins put away their guitars—they had arranged to meet Aidan and Aamon at the pub. Jack had already sneaked off, leaving Victor marooned at the empty table.

Then you emerged seemingly out of nowhere, materialising from the shadow cast by the house on the dewy lawn. You took a firm hold of my arm. 'Come on,' you said in a low but urgent voice. 'Let's get the hell out of here.'

I was overcome by shyness, but you seemed completely unfazed by the fact that we'd hardly seen each other for years or spent any time alone. You strode across the garden and through the gate to the plantation. The soil was dry and powdery beneath my feet, seeping into my sandals and beginning to rub, but you set a brisk pace and I kept up with you stride for stride. I didn't need to ask where we were going. The Christmas and fruit trees stood in their ranks like enchanted knights awaiting a call to action—there was no quiver of wind to shiver their branches. Likewise, in the woods, all was still and breathless, the trunks of the trees standing sentinel, dark columns in the silver moonlight that filtered down through the canopy and lit up the undergrowth in shades of pearl and pewter.

You let go of my arm and we took the narrow path towards the cove, your steps not faltering although it was goodness-knew-how-long since you'd walked that way. It was still as familiar to me as it always had been. I often walked that way, taking secateurs in my pocket as Grandad had done, to snip away inveigling bramble vines and leaning nettles. From nearby an owl hooted, and at a distance its mate answered. Something scuttled across the path in front of us, a dim streak against the dun brown of the path.

We got to the boulder steps and descended them to the cove, which was bright with moonlight, the pebbles like opals, still wet and glowing from the just-receding tide. You scrunched across the shingle towards the water and then I did struggle to follow you, my sandals inadequate to cope with the shifting stones. I recalled Verity on that fateful day … how long? Twenty years before. How many things had changed and yet, for me, everything was just the same.

All of a sudden you swivelled to face me. You had your hands thrust into your pockets and your voice was grim and accusing. 'You've been avoiding me.'

I couldn't deny it. 'We left things so awkwardly. That night of the wedding … your father … we never did clear the air about that. And then

Erin died.' There were so many other things I could have listed, but they were too awkward, too painful, too shameful to broach.

You shook your head. 'That was nothing. No excuse. But every time I've come home you've slunk off to the dairy or your room … you hardly looked at me.'

That wasn't true. I'd feasted my eyes on you when you weren't looking, despising myself the while. 'I …' I faltered, wondering how much—or how little—to say, but just a little comforted to know that you'd noticed my reticence; that it had bothered—even wounded—you. You cared. 'I hadn't anything to say to you,' I blurted at last. 'My life was so … while yours …'

That, too, you waved away. 'You and me, Prue … we've *always* had things to say.' You took hold of both my arms above the elbow and dipped a little so that you could look me straight in the eye. 'Haven't we? *Haven't* we?'

Your intensity left me gasping, cornered, even perhaps a little threatened. Instinctively, I countered, 'Some things are better unspoken.' I regretted it immediately. Did I really want to acknowledge the elephants in the room? Once out of their crate, they could never be put back in again.

Perhaps you felt the same. You stepped away and bent to pick up a stone then hurled it into the sea, which was sheer and shining like burnished silver; barely a ripple broke its surface.

Your sinking stone created a sort of vortex I felt compelled to fill. Words spilled out of me. 'Your life has seemed so wonderful and exciting.' I was whining but couldn't help it. 'I suppose I've resented it. You've left me behind … in every way. I don't just mean geographically. Whatever we had as children has been stretched so thin it's like gossamer now.' I knew I sounded spoiled and sulky, and that's just how I felt. 'And in any case …' But I left the end of that sentence hanging because we'd arrived again at that topic of no return.

You wandered along the beach scanning the ground for more stones, appearing to find—in all the millions there—none that would quite serve your purpose. I trailed after you, my sandals slipping, threatening to wrench my ankle. Presently we came to the rocks at the base of the cliff.

'I climbed that cliff, the day of the picnic,' I declared, to veer the conversation from dangerous waters.

'I know,' you mumbled, head still down. 'I watched you do it.'

'*Did* you?' I cast my mind back. Hadn't you been digging your stupid hole in the sand? 'And you didn't tell anyone?'

'No. I thought you'd wave from the top and give everyone the shock of their lives. But you just squirmed over the lip and disappeared.'

'I thought about waving,' I mused, remembering. 'But it seemed that no one had missed me, so I thought I'd teach them a lesson.'

'You did that!' You looked up and grinned. 'You were gone ages.'

I decided to pursue what felt like the lesser of two evils. 'Why did *you* go into the woods?'

You looked at me with the expression I've seen on your face a hundred times; the one that tells me I've asked a stupid question. You indulged me, though. 'Why do you think?'

I didn't need to ponder it. Of course, I'd always known. 'To find me?' My voice was small. I felt myself blushing.

You nodded. 'Why else?'

Tears pricked my throat. Oh, Arthur! Even then, when I was so awful to you, you were my best—my only—friend.

I lifted my gaze to you. Your eyes shone in the moonlight; their straw-coloured lashes darkened by moisture. You took a step towards me and reached out a hand. A bolt of electrical energy shot up my arm and set fire to something in my stomach.

'But instead of that you found Eric.'

'Not until much later. I left the cove long before he did. I went to find Grandma.'

'You knew where to find her?'

You nodded. 'And I knew that she'd know where to find you.'

'She *did*.' I was hardly breathing. You were so close to me, Arthur. I could feel your breath on my face, the warmth that exuded from your body. It brought with it the faint whiff of washing powder and some manly scent that was spicy and exotic, but also toxic. I mustn't, I *mustn't* go there.

'I got lost on the way back. I must have taken the wrong path. That's how I happened on Eric.' Your mouth was next to my ear now, but a sliver of space remained between us. Oh! Just the finest membrane. How I longed—and feared—to pierce it.

'He was looking for us,' I murmured, but you drew back and gave me a straight look.

'He was looking for *you*,' you corrected me. 'Nobody noticed *I* was missing until much later.'

That broke the spell, reactivating the guilt I'd quashed and bundled from view since that fateful day. I slipped my hand from yours and turned away.

Presently I picked up a loose—less barbed—thread from our earlier exchange. 'How did you afford to go abroad, Arthur? And your lifestyle since? I mean, I thought that summer of 1978, we were as broke as each other. I couldn't have afforded to go away, even if it hadn't been for Erin. But you …'

'Mum paid,' you said, leaning against the flat face of the rock and gazing over the water. 'She said she didn't want to see me tr …' you stumbled, readjusted, '… miss out, on all I had planned. And then, when I was twenty-one, I inherited from Grandma.'

I stepped in front of you. 'Your grandma has died?'

Again, that puzzled, slightly disappointed expression, telling me I'd missed some crucial point. 'Well, yes. Years ago. Do you mean to tell me you don't know?'

Years? How many years? When had I last seen the peculiar green woman? 1978, just before Erin's death. Eight years then, at most. But I'd been at Broadacres that entire time and recalled no funeral, no notice in the local paper. And Colonel Glenister was making himself at home before Erin's final illness.

Your gaze bore into me, the question you'd posed still live and crucial in a way I didn't understand. I returned your stare helplessly.

'Oh Prue,' you said, regret and recrimination vying. You reached your hand up and cupped my face. 'Don't you *know*? Surely, surely you must *know*.'

Know what? I was clueless, but too ashamed to admit my patent failure to understand this vital thing, so instead I asked a crass, indelicate question.

'And she left you …'

You made an exasperated exclamation and removed your hands from my face to hold them up in surrender. 'Oh yes,' you threw out. 'A good deal. But not as much as there might have been at one time. However. I have friends who are stockbrokers in the City. So, all in all, I'm pretty well set up.' You pushed yourself away from the rocks and began to trawl the beach for driftwood.

'How ironic!' I barked out after you, my resentful demon in the ascendant. 'We always remarked on the curious see-saw of our family's finances. As the Day family went up in the world, so the Glenisters declined. Well! *That* trend will soon be reversed, won't it?'

You squatted to arrange the wood in a pyramid. The curl of your shoulders told me you were angry at me, but I didn't know why. You said, 'Can you find any dry brush, Prue? What about over there under the trees. Any pinecones or dry grass?'

Automatically, I did as you asked, raking round the area you'd indicated to find kindling. When the fire was built you drew a lighter from your pocket. The fire flared immediately, the smoke rising in a steady column, aromatic, smelling of pine sap. I lowered myself onto a flat rock and hugged my knees. You stretched yourself out on the sandy shingle, propped on one elbow. We didn't speak for a while, watching the sparks rising like fireflies in the night, listening to the crack and spit of the wood.

Then you clasped your hands behind your head and lay back to look at the stars, which were visible now the moon had disappeared behind the cliff. 'Did you ever search those drawers in the library, Prue?' you asked conversationally.

It wasn't an accusation and yet I felt stung. 'You said I should make myself at home,' I threw back. 'But yes. I found the letters.'

You frowned. 'The letters? Oh! Yes. I wasn't quite sure what they meant. I hoped we'd work it out together.'

I waited. And you waited. Our toes were on the boundary again. Maybe the best thing for both of us would be to move the conversation along to another subject. If we didn't speak it aloud then we could pretend it wasn't true. But then, I knew—I thought I knew—what Henry's plan was. One day, perhaps one day quite soon, there would be no room for pretence. There was no point in starting what could not be finished.

'But you worked it out in the end, right?' I ventured.

You answered my question with one of your own. 'What else did you find in the library, Prue?'

I cast my mind back. 'The accounts. And in Grandad's study I found the corresponding payments in his ledgers. Those maps and plans you'd already shown me.'

You rolled onto your elbow and looked at me through the leaping flames. 'What about the scroll?'

'The scroll?'

You gave an exasperated sigh. 'I left it right there in the drawer. You couldn't have failed to see it.'

'What scroll?' I did remember it now though. The family tree. 'That was important?'

You threw yourself back in a sort of anguish and wiped your hands over your face. I could hear the faint rasp of stubble. 'Oh yes,' you groaned.

Up in the woods I could hear the crash of stumbling footsteps, suppressed shrieks and guffaws of laughter, the clink and chink of bottles.

'Here are the twins,' you said with bleak despair.

Kath, Kaz, Aidan and Aamon appeared at the top of the boulder steps, clearly the worse for wear, Jack following in their wake. He pushed past the others and descended to the beach, crossing the shingle with rubber legs towards our little camp.

'Call *that* a fire?' he crowed.

Chapter Thirty-Six

For the rest of your week at Broadacres you were kept busy by Blanche, who delighted in taking you out and about to meet her friends from the WI, the accountant and the proprietors of the shops and cafés she liked to frequent, even her hairdresser. She inhabited a small world, like we all did, but she took you into every corner of it to exhibit her son—her clever, successful, handsome son. I didn't begrudge her your company. I knew your visit would soon be over and who knew when she'd see you again?

It took that visit from you to help me see how bad Granny had become though. We were all used to what we described as her 'funny little ways' of putting dirty dishes into the fridge or the tumble drier instead of the dishwasher and sometimes coming downstairs dressed in two skirts. Being called by each other's names was so commonplace that we'd even started jokingly doing it to each other. Within the confines of Broadacres' house and garden we felt she was pretty safe, although one of us was generally deputed to keep an eye on her and make sure she had food and drinks at appropriate times. The colonel took her further afield and never expressed any concern that her slightly odd behaviour was a difficulty. But you, who hadn't seen her for so long, were appalled at the deterioration of her mental capacity.

'She calls me Henry, Eric, even George,' you complained one day. 'But that's better than when she doesn't recognise me at all.'

'I know,' I said. 'I think we're just all used to it.'

'And I think it's too much responsibility for Grandfather,' you said. 'He's older than she is. He shouldn't be left in sole charge of her.'

'We do our best,' I almost snapped back. 'She enjoys their outings.'

'I don't wish to deny them the pleasure of those,' you said churlishly. 'But someone else should drive and supervise.'

'Who?' I turned to face you. 'You?' You'd waylaid me on my way back from the dairy. My hair was knotty and unkempt from where it had been stuffed into a hairnet all day. One of the staff had labelled a whole batch of yoghurts with the wrong date. I had an essay to complete on Blake's *Songs of Innocence and Experience*. 'Don't you see how busy we all are here?' I asked, exasperated. 'The twins do less and less, so caught up with their music. Jack's a waste of space. Poor Hester is worn to a frazzle and Isobel has her hands full with Victor. Dad works all hours, and your mother has the whole house to run. She feeds us all every night and does most of the laundry. Who do you see at liberty, Arthur, to squire the old folks round the countryside?'

'Verity,' you rejoined quickly. 'And Henry.'

'Well,' I raked my sticky hair out of my eyes. 'You've got that right. They don't seem to do anything, do they? Perhaps you ought to suggest that there is a way they could make themselves useful, before you leave us.'

'I will,' you asserted.

The solution was too simple to disperse the air of antagonism that had curdled between us, and we continued to stand at loggerheads—brows furrowed, hands in pockets.

Then your shoulders relaxed. 'Where are you on your way to?' You put out a hand, indicating that, wherever it was, you'd come with me. I resumed my walk back towards Broadacres and you fell into step.

You might have moved on, but I hadn't. My spleen was not quite exhausted. 'Do you think they'll *ever* move back into Glenister Hall?' I asked. 'The roof must be repaired by now. It's been five years! If Glenister Hall were mine I'd sell off the lodge and any other supernumerary cottages you've got lying about, and convert the stables into dwellings. That would release plenty of capital, wouldn't it? You could divide the whole house into some very elegant self-contained apartments. But I suppose you won't want to pollute the shades of Glenister Hall with in-comers and riffraff. What about holiday lets? They're all the rage nowadays. Polly might still be up for the laundry. What do you think?'

You gave a wry smile. 'One day, Prue, when Glenister Hall is mine, I'll employ you as a consultant. There are specialists who charge thousands of pounds for that kind of advice, and here you are giving it to me for free!'

'Oh well!' I laughed, released from my angst. 'I'm afraid my suggestions are entirely self-serving. If Henry and Verity vacated the cottage I could move into it, all its unhappy associations notwithstanding. At least I'd get some peace there. It's so difficult to get my studying done.'

'The house is all shut up,' you said. 'But having said that, you know the servants' door is always open. You could use the library, if you wanted.'

I considered the idea with a heavy sigh. I felt like a hamster on a treadmill—always moving but forever destined to remain in one place. Why did my life take me round in circles? Broadacres, the dairy, the pond, the library at Glenister Hall—they were all waypoints in the ceaseless loop that had me in its thrall. Your mention of the library though, brought to mind that scroll you'd seemed so keen for me to see.

Immediately, you seemed to reconsider the offer. 'It's damp and dreary—hardly conducive to study,' you said quickly. 'Structurally, I'm told its sound, but there was an encampment of travellers in the grounds a couple of years ago. I wouldn't want you going there, Prue. Forget I mentioned it.'

I shrugged. 'Okay.'

Apparently satisfied, you strolled alongside me, hands in pockets, whistling tunelessly, but I wasn't fooled.

'I'm leaving tomorrow,' you said heavily. 'The new project starts on Monday, and I have to find some digs and get the drawings completed.'

How can one person hold such equal and opposite feelings, Arthur? Your announcement slayed me, even though I'd known all along that your week with us would come to an end. At the same time, I was engulfed in relief. Your leaving would not withdraw the thorn from my side, but it would ease the unbearable agony of it. 'This is the orangery?'

You nodded, but then grasped the nettle you'd been dodging around, stopping abruptly in your tracks. 'I don't want to leave things unsaid, Prue. The other night, on the beach …'

'I know.' There again we'd circled the issues without broaching them, wary of trampling over virgin territory, seeing no navigable route across those untried lands.

We'd both ended up getting a bit drunk. I'd stumbled home too late for my OU broadcast and had barely two hours sleep before my shift in the dairy.

We were at the corner of the house. The ground was powdered with wisteria petals, brownish pink and papery. They lay in drifts against the cornerstone of Broadacres and across the gravel of the drive. 'Come with me, Prue,' you blurted out, taking hold of my arms as you had done on the beach. 'Just come. I can afford to take care of you. I *want* to take care of you. You don't belong here …' You trailed off, as though conscious that this wasn't true. 'You … we … we don't have to have our future dictated to us. Things are *not* set in stone, Prue. We can forge our own destiny.' Your eyes bore into mine. Your expression was so earnest, I could see a sheen of sweat on your forehead. I searched for words but found none. 'Don't you want to?' you urged. 'I do. It's all I've ever wanted, Prudence. You, *you,* are all I've ever wanted.'

You clasped me to your body. Your arms strong and urgent, your hands in my hair. I wished you'd waited until I'd washed it. I wished we could stop speaking in riddles. Didn't you know that it was impossible? My heart clamoured, 'Yes! Yes! Yes!' even as my instinct protested, 'No! No! No!' There would be something stained and invidious about it. It would make us like Henry. My destiny was *here,* at Broadacres. I couldn't escape it.

Oh, Arthur! I wished you could see the longing in my heart, quite equal to anything in yours—or probably stronger, given the bleak alternative before me. No travel, no absorbing architectural projects, no well-heeled chums or impressive portfolio of stocks and shares would salve *my* broken heart.

Gently, I disentangled myself. 'It isn't in the stars for us, Arthur,' I said. 'However much we might both wish. You said just before that you didn't want to leave things unsaid. So let's be crystal clear. It can't be, Arthur. It just can't. I'm sorry, but something in …' I tried to point to it, the place within me that rebelled. Where was it? In my head? My heart? Or somewhere in between— wherever the soul, the conscience resides. I gave up. 'Henry is my grandad's son. I believe that when Granny dies Broadacres and Salad Days will be Henry's. I don't know what will happen to me or to any of us after that. We'll be at the mercy of Henry's good nature, such as it is. And then, presumably of yours. So, ironically, you will get the chance to look after me, if you choose. But Arthur …' I shook my head sadly. 'Not in *that* way.'

You took a step backwards, your face utterly stricken. You stared at me aghast and then slid your eyes away. Your gaze raked the front of Broadacres, then turned to look over the garden to the woods beyond. While your back was turned to me, I saw you dash a tear away.

I was deluged with compassion. It was my turn to take your arm and steer you to a garden bench that sat within an enclave of shrubs at the side of the rockery. I pressed you into it and then perched beside you. 'You didn't know?' I breathed. 'I thought … I thought you'd understood, from the letters …'

'It wasn't the letters! It wasn't the letters!' you cried out, mashing your hands in your lap. Then, with a shuddering sigh, 'I told you. I wasn't quite sure what the letters meant. Something didn't add up, but … for God's sake, Prue, I was a child.' You brought a handkerchief from your trouser pocket and blew your nose.

Of course, I thought. What age had you been when we'd first spoken of the matter? Eleven? How could you have understood?

You spent a few minutes composing yourself and then said in a voice that was hollow, 'So, how did that come about then? How do you know Henry is your grandad's son?'

I explained about the letters and the dates. 'The colonel wasn't in the country when Henry was conceived,' I concluded. 'Believe me, I've considered every other likely suspect. I asked Polly whether your grandma had guests, house parties and the like, but she says not. She says your grandma was a virtual recluse all the years the colonel was away. I don't know if you remember what was in the letters, but the colonel specifically recommended your grandma to turn to Grandad for any help she might need. He as good as threw her into his arms! It explains those payments that so intrigued us. They were to keep him quiet about Henry in the hopes that no one else would twig that the dates don't add up—as if they needed to! Didn't they know Grandad at all? He'd never …' but my spleen evaporated. What was the point in being angry? 'But I'll tell you this, Arthur,' I went on, more calmly, coldly, even, because if I couldn't get mad I sure as hell could get even. 'I believe Henry knows. I think he found out, possibly by reading those self-same letters, or maybe your grandma told him. But I think he found out and that's why he started coming here and why Grandad welcomed him … into the family.'

You considered that; your gaze fixed on a little crop of daisies in the lawn. 'It makes sense,' you allowed at last.

'And it explains why Henry and Verity never actually got married,' I went on, treading tentatively on very tender ground, 'although everyone here thinks they're legally wed. Verity said it was just too old hat, so they hadn't bothered, but I think she suspects the real reason. I mean, I don't know if you can get sent to prison for incest …'

You recoiled at the word 'That's disgusting,' you said through clenched teeth, and there was just the tiniest part of me that was glad that you felt as I did: instinctively repelled.

I said, 'I'm sorry, Arthur. I've had a few years to get used to the idea I suppose, and to come to terms with my disappointment. If it's any consolation at all …' I reached out a hand to take yours, but you leapt up as though stung. 'Don't make it worse,' you said hoarsely.

From the house I heard our names being called for tea. The longest day was almost upon us—the sun was still quite high in the sky. It would not go dark until well after ten. It would be hours before I could retreat to my room and cry.

You paced on the grass, and I saw you take several deep, ragged breaths and I was powerfully reminded of the lost little boy who had pushed me into the rockery twenty-odd years before.

'I think I'll take a walk,' you said abruptly. 'Will you make my excuses?'

'I will,' I said, but you'd already turned and walked away.

You were quiet at dinner—another meal taken on the terrace; the whole family gathered to bid you *adieu*. In his usual way, Henry attempted to monopolise the occasion, lauding your success, making pompous speeches. You could barely look at him or Verity, horrified and revolted by your new understanding of their liaison. You did raise your voice sufficiently to suggest that Henry and Verity ought to accompany your grandfather and Granny on their various jaunts, but in the manner of someone speaking a script, enumerating your points wearily: so much more traffic … parking can be tricky … the drink-driving laws so much tighter. You raised your eyes with an effort to look through the French windows, where the two old folks were absorbed in a game of Scrabble in the room beyond. 'It isn't safe,' you said in a heavy but still emphatic tone. 'He's ninety-one and his eyesight is failing.

Granny needs close supervision. No one else here,' you indicated the rest of us at the table, 'has time.'

To my surprise, Henry raised no objection.

Your point gained, you relapsed into silence, and when the time came to say goodbye to Henry you did so stiffly, with hardly a murmur of farewell.

The next day you left very early. I watched your car reverse from the drive, the top down—it was to be the last warm, sunny day of the entire summer. The passing tyres stirred a flurry of wisteria petals into a cruel facsimile of confetti. Your copper-coloured hair was a bright helmet in the morning sun. I think you must have known I was at the window. You raised an arm in solemn salute, and then you were gone.

The day dragged by. I worked, then showered, ate dinner and finished my essay in the small hours. Even so, it was hardly dark beyond my window, and I don't think the birds quietened for more than a couple of hours. I was shattered but sleep evaded me. My mind rehearsed all you'd said to me there on the drive, about our fates not being set in stone, about choosing our own destinies. And it was only as my eyes were finally closing that the thought occurred to me. If you had not known about Henry's parentage—if that was not the kismet you wished us to circumvent—then what was it?

Chapter Thirty-Seven

The rest of the summer of '87 was poor. Our sales of plants saw a reduction, but the café did a roaring trade as families sought entertainment indoors. Jack sawed on about the profitability of a children's soft play barn. It would be an enormous outlay of capital, but the wildflower meadow would be the perfect situation for it—an area of land currently yielding no return. Personally, I was reluctant to see the meadow ploughed up and the construction of another ugly building. It would be visible from the house, a real blot on the landscape. But on the whole I had a fatalistic view of the whole enterprise. I knew what was coming down the tracks.

Victor was vociferous in his opposition to Jack's scheme. Not, I think, for any commercial reasons but simply to assert his dominance over the business. Isobel tried to be the peacemaker but only succeeded in annoying both husband and son. Hester was adamant that we should pursue our organic soil certification. My dad didn't even pretend to take sides and I rather despised him for that. I knew that too soon he'd have to fight for the business against a far more intimidating opponent than Jack.

Our mealtimes were fraught with argument once more. That, and my heartache over you, Arthur, caused my eating disorder to rear its head once more and I began to lose weight at an alarming rate.

Jonathan, my university friend, remarked on it particularly. 'You're skin and bone, Prudence,' he said, drawing a soft but admonishing finger across the concave space between my hipbones and then up over the ridges of my ribs. 'What's going on with you?'

'Just the family,' I said.

I tried to break the impasse by calling a business meeting. This was an unusual step. In fact, in the past it had been unheard of. The family had always been on the same page and our trust in Grandad to steer the right course had been absolute. Now we had too many chiefs and not enough Indians, as the saying goes. The meeting convened in the dining room while an early autumn storm threw pebbles of rain against the windows. The first twenty minutes was wasted in a debate over who should take the chair. At last, in an extraordinary turn of events, Granny suggested we call Henry in 'as a disinterested party,' a motion seconded by Verity. Naturally, I objected volubly to this, but I was overruled, and Henry was duly summoned. Jack called on Blanche to give us a summary of the accounts and in particular to name the amount of cash on hand available for capital investment. Blanche blushed and fumbled and made excuses. The accounts were not complete, the accountant would need to sign them off. The only opinions she would venture was that it would be reckless to take on more debt before the original loan for the farm shop and café had been paid off. She kept the manilla file before her firmly closed. It occurred to me that I had never been shown the business accounts. Had anyone? I posed the question. Blanche's flush slid from her cheeks to be replaced be a deathly pallor. My dad threw me a look that was positively venomous. Isobel said she was appalled at my question. The entire meeting bristled, and I had to let the matter go.

Jack brought out a set of schematic plans he'd commissioned in spite of the family's reservations and laid them out on the table. He circulated various leaflets from other soft play facilities and a business plan projecting enormous profits. This had the effect of stopping even Hester—the idea's most obdurate critic—in her tracks.

I was disgusted with them all. What would Grandad think? The Salad Days of his conception was lost in the ball pit of profit. I don't think anyone even noticed when I rose and left the room. It was my day off and I was blowed if I was going to waste it.

The rain continued to fall relentlessly, laying flat the last leggy stalks of the year's perennials and battering the petals of the annuals in the tubs and baskets to mush. I grabbed a coat from the boot room behind the kitchen and thrust my feet into my wellingtons. Piglet, the little Jack Russell that had replaced Podge, whined from her basket by the Aga and I took pity on her. 'Come on then,' I said, 'if you really want to. It's pouring with rain.'

She surveyed the scene carefully from the doorstep but then gave a little wag of her tail, so I clipped her lead in place, and we set off.

We passed the premises where Hester's students, clad in Salad Days oilskins, were arranging a display of asters, peonies and zinnias as well as vegetables that could be planted presently to provide winter greens. Sacks of spring-flowering bulbs were heaped beneath a galvanised metal shelter. A few hardy customers toured the displays, trundling trolleys filled with wares. I could see the windows of the café were steamy, every table busy. It was a long time since I'd operated the till, but anyone could see that the business was a roaring success. We must be making money hand over fist. So why was Blanche so reluctant to show us the balance sheets? What had she got to hide? Old suspicions began to raise their heads again. Was she creaming off profits? Was *she* the source of Henry's monthly two hundred pounds? I didn't even know how the business was organised. Were we all Directors? Shareholders? Or did the whole shebang still belong to Granny? However it was, it was obvious to me that Henry would appropriate it. He'd need to keep the family on side, though, if he wished the goose to continue to yield her golden eggs.

Piglet and I walked up the plantation and when we got to the gate I let her off her lead. She shot through the gate and into the woods, a streak of brown-and-white against the dark green of the foliage on the forest floor.

The last time I'd walked that way had been with you, Arthur, the night we'd gone to the beach and lit the fire. How much we'd talked, and yet how little we'd managed to say, talking at cross purposes, skirting the issues. I can't tell you how it soothed my soul to know that you felt as I did. That connection between us, it *had* been a two-way affair. For so many years I'd been oblivious to it, blithely ignorant of the true nature of my feelings for you. And then, when at last the scales had fallen from my eyes, I'd thought it was only me. By then you'd existed on a higher plane—out of sight. Way, way out of my league. But no, all those lovelorn days you'd felt as I did—that we were made for each other. My heart sang, but its song was so sad my throat constricted with grief. I pushed it away. I couldn't think about it. It hurt too much.

I sought an object for the pain and found it all too easily in its usual guise. Henry. It was Henry and the curse of his heredity that stood between us. That, anyway, had been my understanding. But you'd seen another obstacle, Arthur, hadn't you? The curious anomalies in our families' accounts and the unaccountable assimilation of Henry and Blanche into the Day family circle— these had exercised *me* and I'd thought *you* were on the same page. The letters had answered all my questions, but you'd said it *wasn't* the letters you'd wanted me to see.

What then? Clearly, I'd got things wrong—again.

As far as I recalled, the first time we'd discussed the matter was that day we found the walled graveyard. Perhaps instinctively I bent my steps in that direction. The canopy dripped water on my head but shielded me from the worst of the downpour. The brackens and ivy were beaded with moisture and the earth path beneath my feet was sticky and slick. When I came to the little stream, I could barely see the stepping stones, but I forged across, following Piglet, who barked at me from the other bank, hock deep in mud and wet to the skin but having a deliriously happy time of it.

When I got to the place where the path ran beside the old wall, I had to snip my way through a tangle of encroaching bramble vines. No one had been that way for a long time. At one time I'd needed you to boost me up to get over the wall but now I found I could easily climb to the top. The stones were soft with dark green moss that oozed when I pressed it.

The graveyard was much as I remembered it. The grass—full of seeds— was so high it would have obscured many of the memorial stones, but without the shelter of the trees the stalks were bent over, weighed down by water, bowing to some deity I couldn't see. Likewise, some of the statues and obelisks had fallen over, as though in homage. The notion amused me, and I perched on the top of the wall for a while heedless of the rain that plastered my hair to my head and ran down the collar of my coat. Piglet leapt and scrabbled at the bottom of the wall, barking to be lifted up. Then I saw her squirm beneath the old gate in the bottom corner of the cemetery. She half-leapt, half-burrowed through the thick undergrowth to where I sat, then leapt and scrabbled as she had before.

'You stupid dog,' I admonished fondly, and lowered myself down into the burial ground.

Once I was on the same side of the wall, Piglet seemed to relax. She snuffled off in search of mice while I swished through the thigh-high, saturated grass that soaked my jeans. As all those years before, most of the tombstones' engravings were too old and weathered to make out. I drew my fingers across the lichen-encrusted surfaces, deciphering a date here, a name there, but the memorials—like the people beneath them—were decayed and lost. I stumbled over the tumbledown mausoleum and was about to turn back. What was I even looking for? Then I saw it—a fresh grave; or if not fresh, at least much newer than the rest. It was situated in the far corner of the plot. The grass was shorter there, as though scythed, but not recently, and the little hummock of the grave had not had a chance to sink. A small stone stood erect, its legend quite clear to see. *Beatrice Glenister. 1890 – 1975.* Your grandmother—poor, lonely old soul. Henry hadn't even mentioned she'd died. He hadn't mourned her at all.

Beneath the inscription was a pretty emblem denoting a stylised tree. That rang a bell, but I couldn't think where I'd seen it before.

I gave a sudden shiver. I was getting cold. Piglet had ceased to explore and was beginning to jump up at my legs, whining. She was ready to go home too. I hoisted her over the wall and she pattered behind me as we retraced our steps towards Broadacres. My head was full of Mrs Glenister and the strange, almost surreal nature of my various encounters with her: the day of the dreadful summer storm; the Christmas Day of Grandad's stroke and again at his funeral; the evening of our misadventure in the pond; and then last of all, the day that Erin died.

I stopped so abruptly that Piglet ran into me.

If Mrs Glenister had died in 1975, how *could* I have seen her on the day of Erin's death in 1978?

Chapter Thirty-Eight

When I got back from my walk the business meeting had broken up and the house was suspiciously quiet. I was conscious of echoes of argument; the ragged remains of angry altercations drifted like greasy cobwebs just beneath the ceiling. I was only vaguely curious about what—if anything—had been decided.

There was no sign of Blanche in the kitchen, so it looked as though tea was some way off. I put the kettle on to boil while I dried and fed Piglet and settled her into her bed. She sank into sleep with a contented sigh. I made my tea and looked into the sitting room as I passed it. Victor was asleep in his usual chair. Granny and the colonel were seated close to one another on the sofa. A black and white film flickered on the TV but the volume was so low I doubted the old folks could hear it; they chatted conspiratorially.

I mounted the stairs to the room that was now mine—one of the larger, bay-windowed rooms—and got out of my wet clothes. Then I stood at the window and drank my tea. By coincidence, my window gave me the same view of the garden and the woods beyond that I'd had the day Erin died. I could see the place where the green woman had appeared to me. She hadn't spoken. I'd been struck by how indigenous to the woods she'd seemed. There'd been a strange aura about her—and no wonder, I thought. She'd been dead three years!

It may seem really odd to you, but I didn't for a moment question my memory. I *had* seen your grandmother that day. Her being deceased did not alter my certainty, but as I stood and looked out of the window, I tried to rationalise it. I'd always viewed her as in some way touched with the otherworldly. To my mind, to appear *from* there was only the smallest step. The old myths about the Glenister wives were part of my childhood lore, and all my encounters with her were of a piece with those. And then, her habit of appearing at times of death and tragedy—I could easily believe her to be imbued with a knowledge of things beyond the temporal sphere; a wise-woman in the ancient tradition. And last of all, hadn't I been peripherally, if only half-consciously, aware of *other* ghosts? How many times had I sensed … felt … *seen* the shades of my mother, grandad and Eric? My experiences as a reader and as a writer had put me in touch with some alternative level of consciousness. Fiction, the power of the imagination—these things had sustained me through some awful times. They were a comfort, vivid and real. I *believed* in … not an afterlife, exactly, because that would imply that it didn't begin until this one was done. No, I believed in something other, bigger. A sixth sense, a sentience that was part of this life and also went beyond it. I didn't believe I was a medium, but I thought I might be intuitive.

Once I'd satisfied myself on that point, my mind returned to Mrs Glenister. What did I really know about her? That she'd been monied in her own right, and that her eccentricity had fed into the local superstition about Glenister women. And that she was dead.

I'd kept the packet of letters I'd purloined from Glenister Hall in the zipped compartment of my typewriter case. I hadn't used the typewriter since I'd invested in an Amstrad word processor earlier that year. All my fellow students had them. They made writing and editing essays so much easier. Jonathan had one and he'd taken me through the set up and workings so that when I got mine I'd got going fairly easily. I'd shown it to Blanche thinking it would make the bookkeeping much simpler, but she'd flapped her hands in panic at it.

Anyway, the letters were still in my possession. I unzipped my typewriter case and brought them out. The colonel had called your grandma Bee—short for Beatrice, presumably. I wondered how long they'd been married before he'd gone away to war. He must have been incredibly young—I worked it out. Only nineteen. He'd turned ninety last year. And he'd been gone for over twenty years with only the occasional leave. They must have been strangers to one another. If she had been what Polly Tindall had termed 'a queer fish' to begin with she must have appeared completely batty by the time her husband returned—all but an itinerant, spending more time in the woods than she did in the house, perfectly enacting the characteristics of local folklore whilst in fact pursuing an affair with my grandfather—very *Lady Chatterley*. I speculated that the "mad' Glenister wives of history had been nothing more than abjectly lonely. If they'd suffered from anything it was simply the condition of being women—subjugated, suffocated, stymied. No wonder they had sought some alternative spiritual connection.

The colonel's letters lacked any but the most formulaic affection towards his wife, and I could get no sense of her character at all from them. I had only my recollection of her that bizarre evening at the woodsman's cottage. She'd been kind, caring, childishly pleased to have company. I felt a clutch of anger at the colonel for spending such a lot of time abroad—not just professionally but afterwards too, playing golf, sunning himself, leaving poor Beatrice all alone so long as her money lasted.

The idea of money brought a sudden flashback of that day's meeting, and my clamouring suspicions about Blanche. What had been in that manilla file she'd guarded so jealously? Why even bring it if she had no intention of sharing its contents?

I've never made any secret of the fact that I'm nosey by nature, but the more I considered it the more I felt as though I had a right to know how the business stood. I didn't see why Blanche should be privy to details that were denied to me. Now that I'd given up all my hopes of a life beyond Broadacres it seemed only reasonable that I should be aware of what I was committed to. And still, Arthur, a worm of suspicion niggled at me. Those payments Henry received—could they be from Salad Days? Had Henry made a secret stipulation in their financial settlement, that Blanche should cream funds from the Days? Why was she so cagey about the accounts if she had nothing to hide?

Chapter Thirty-Nine

The opportunity to look at Blanche's closely guarded accounts came just a few days later. I was working in the dairy as usual when a loud clatter and a child's scream from the café alerted us to an incident. I sent one of my assistants running to the house to find Isobel, who was our designated first-aider, and went into the office to suggest that Blanche should leave her desk to see what had occurred. There was a one-way mirror between the office and the café and so I'd be able to keep my eye on Blanche while I had a quick rifle through the filing cabinets.

I was only halfway through the second drawer when the office door opened and Jack stepped in.

He raised an eyebrow. 'You had the same idea then?' he said. 'Found anything yet?'

I shook my head. 'No. Just invoices so far. Why don't you try the desk?'

He nodded and began to open the drawers of Blanche's desk. 'Cheque books, petty cash tin,' he enumerated. 'Who needs this many rubber bands?'

'Someone with lots of ten-pound notes to bundle up?' I murmured. I thought I'd found something, but I wanted to scan the sheets before I let on to Jack. They were profit and loss accounts. I'd done the day-to-day bookkeeping in the past, but I wasn't familiar with the accountant's version of the figures. Things looked extremely healthy, as far as I could make out. It looked like we'd paid off the capital outlay of the farm shop and café. I flapped the sheet at Jack and he came over to look at it.

In the same folder was a copy of Granny's tax return—eyewatering—and her personal bank statements. My eye travelled down the columns. She paid all the household expenses, by the looks of things; what did Dad, Hester and Isobel spend *their* money on? Not utilities or insurance—these were covered by regular standing orders. And there was another: on the first of every month, two hundred pounds was paid out to Henry Glenister.

'What's going on in here?' Blanche's voice shook me rigid, but I gathered myself and swung to meet her eye. 'Why does Granny pay for *everything?*' I demanded, using attack as a form of defence. 'And why does she pay Henry two hundred pounds every month?'

Jack waved the profit and loss accounts. 'Why did you imply that we were still paying off the business loan?'

'You shouldn't be in here,' Blanche said, crossing to her desk and fussily restoring things to order. I saw that her hands were shaking.

'Why not?' Jack and I spoke together.

I said, 'I'm not clear whether we are directors of the business, or shareholders, or just employees. But we are members of the family and we've committed ourselves to the business, like the twins, for the long term. I think we all have a right to know the state of things. We're not children anymore.'

'You must ask your grandmother,' Blanche said. 'This is her business.'

'Like *that's* going to shine a light on things,' Jack sneered. He flapped the paper again. 'But you lied about this at the meeting.'

'I didn't,' Blanche replied, her voice a strangled squeak. 'I said it would be reckless to take on a further loan, and it would.'

'You implied the old one wasn't paid off, and it is,' I asserted.

Blanche's face was as pale as ashes. Her mouth flapped uselessly for a few moments, then, 'I just do as I'm told,' she got out. This statement was the first that had the ring of truth about it.

'By whom?' Again, Jack and I spoke in concert, and it felt uncomfortable. Of all my cousins, I had always liked him least. It was unfortunate that I'd found myself allied with him in this escapade, like being stuck in a lift with your least favourite colleague.

The office door opened and Isobel came in. She had a smear of blood on her face. She said, 'Call an ambulance, will you? The child's going to need treatment for a scald, and possibly stitches—she's got a cut on her leg from a shard of broken teapot. Her mother's in hysterics. She says she'll sue. I need to fill in the accident book. What time was the floor mopped this morning, does anyone know? She says it was wet. Why on earth she allowed the child to carry the tray, I'll never know.' Then she seemed to assimilate the standoff in the room. 'What's going on in here?'

'I found them rifling through the accounts,' Blanche said quickly. 'They came in while I was trying to smooth things over in the café. I … I didn't lock the door.'

'Oh Blanche,' Isobel cried crossly. 'How many times have I told you? It's basic security protocol.'

Jack and I exchanged a look. Isobel, clearly, was Blanche's puppet-master. How could I not have realised?

She turned to Jack with an unctuous smile. 'Darling, if there were things you wanted to know about the business, you only had to ask.'

'I *did* ask, at the meeting,' he said, but less petulantly than before. Whatever Isobel's scheme, Jack would not be the loser by it. 'I just didn't believe what I was told. And with good reason, it seems.' He proffered the document, but more in the manner of someone offering a sandwich than a smoking gun.

Isobel plucked it from his hand and passed it to Blanche. Then she turned to me; her sycophancy replaced by naked annoyance. 'And what's your excuse?'

'Like Jack, I wasn't satisfied. I want to know where I stand. And I want to know why Granny pays Henry a monthly allowance.'

Isobel waved my reply away. 'That's Granny's affair,' she said. 'Now, I have to call the ambulance. You'd better get back to the dairy.'

I know I was bad-tempered for the rest of the day, snapping at the assistants and giving short shrift to a would-be supplier who knocked on the door seeking an opportunity to show me his wares. I didn't join the family for tea, taking a shower and then going down to the pub by myself. Grace was behind the bar and I took the opportunity between her serving customers to unburden myself. 'I was all but blackmailed into staying on,' I moaned, guzzling my second large glass of wine. 'I was all set for university, if you recall. Then Victor had his fall. And that was the second time! I stayed behind the first time after Erin died. I think I'm owed *something*, don't you?'

'I have no involvement in the accounts for this place,' Grace replied, irrelevantly I thought, but I was already pretty sozzled. 'Gary could be gambling the profits away, for all I know. But it's a matter of trust.'

'Oh.' I saw her point. 'But that's just it. I don't trust Blanche. I never have done, if I'm honest. Look how she manipulated Verity all those years.'

Grace frowned. 'You've got that wrong,' she said. 'It was Verity who did the manipulating—buying Blanche off with vodka.'

I waved this away. 'And then I've always had the idea that Blanche set her sights on Dad right from the start,' I said drunkenly. 'Poor Mum never stood a chance.'

'You mustn't think like that about Blanche,' Grace warned me. 'She was Henry's victim as much as …' she stopped abruptly, suddenly aware of what she'd said. The bar was quite busy. It was neither the time not the place.

But I went blithely on. 'Oh yes. There's something very dodgy about him. Has he ever made a pass at you?'

She poured a customer a pint with a whisky chaser and rang the money into the till. I thought she hadn't heard or refused to be drawn, but she leaned over the bar, pretending to wipe it with a cloth and said in a confidential voice, 'Not for years. But there *was* a time … you too?'

'Just once,' I said, draining my glass and holding it out for a refill. 'On the day of Dad's wedding. He was disgusting. I think Arthur warned him off.'

'Gary did, too, in the end,' Grace said, pouring my drink. 'Henry's like all bullies—a coward at heart.'

I gave her a narrow look. 'You don't like him either.'

She gave a shudder. 'I don't know how Verity stands it.'

I wondered about telling Grace outright about Henry's relationship to us. I was drunk—I hadn't eaten all day—but I decided to approach it tangentially. 'Why do you think Granny pays him an allowance? Two hundred a month.'

'Do they have a joint bank account? Maybe it's for Verity,' she suggested. 'Does Granny give *you* money?'

Grace shook her head. 'No,' she allowed. 'And I do think she'd be fair, don't you?'

'It's always seemed very odd to me,' I said slowly, 'the way Henry and Blanche just attached themselves to the family.'

Grace dried a few glasses. 'Blanche is Victor's sister.'

I frowned. 'There's more to it than that.' I waited to see if she would take my dangled bait, but she busied herself behind the bar and made no reply. But *what* more, I pondered, as I made my staggering way home later. I had to admit my suspicions that she was funnelling money from the business account to Henry had proved baseless. And now I thought about it, Blanche really didn't have the nerve for such a deception. Having said that, she was clearly in Isobel's sway. What was my aunt up to?

It was dark. The lane was slick and mushy with autumn leaves that stuck to the wet road surface, but it wasn't actually raining. I felt miserable and lonely, full of thoughts and lacking anyone to share them with. I missed you, Arthur. As far as I knew you were still in the northeast, supervising the restoration of the orangery. I had the maddest notion of getting a taxi to the train station and heading over to find you. In my inebriation I felt sure that some homing instinct would guide me to you. I'd step off the train and the hawser that connected us would cause you to be there, waiting.

I had my head down, caught up in a fantasy of what it would be like— your open smile and comforting arms, some cosy apartment or hotel room with dimmed lights and an accommodating sofa or large, comfortable bed, that tangy, washing-powder smell of you, your murmured words of sympathy. Half-mesmerised by the glint of the occasional street light on the leafy mosaic of the road, I had almost passed the little cottage and I didn't see Henry at all as he stood on the other side of the low hedge that separated the cottage's handkerchief patch of garden from the lane.

His voice came out of the shadows. 'Good evening, Prudence. You were missed at dinner.' He stepped forward into what light there was. I mustn't have been walking straight. I was on the verge, rather than the road. Only the hedge separated us, waist-height for me, thigh-height for him. Its leaves were already mostly gone, leaving a skeletal and not very substantial architecture of sticks and twigs.

'I wasn't hungry,' I slurred. 'I've been to the pub.'

'So I see.' His voice was sneering and superior. 'If I'd known, I would have joined you. Dinner was a dreary affair. Jack and Victor at loggerheads again.'

'You could always cater for yourself,' I said mulishly. 'The cottage has a kitchen, I seem to recall.'

He gave a snide little laugh. 'Verity's no cook.'

'And neither are you, I suppose. But then, you've never had to provide for yourself, have you? You've had Polly, or Blanche or Granny to do it for you. Mainly Granny, I'd say. From what I hear, she provides for you in virtually every way. I don't suppose you pay rent, for example, do you?' I gestured in the direction of the cottage behind him.

'She's extremely kind,' Henry said. 'She's always looked after me like a …' but here he faltered.

Drunk as I was, I knew the word he'd cavilled at pronouncing. A son.

I shook myself, trying to get a grip. With dripping insincerity I said, 'Henry, I don't believe I've offered my condolences on the death of your mother.'

Henry breathed in and then out again sharply through his beaky nose and closed his eyes briefly. 'She wasn't my mother,' he said. 'Not in any way that mattered.'

I pressed into the hedge. I'm not sure now if I just wanted to be able to see him properly—the nearest streetlamp was fifty yards away and its light was poor—or if my intention was to face up, even to challenge him. I do know that Grace's earlier words echoed in my mind: "Henry's like all bullies—a coward at heart." I squinted through the gloom of the autumn evening and the fug of my intoxication so that I could correctly read his expression. 'Unlike your father,' I said slowly, my tone still very sarcastic. I conjured Grandad in my mind's eye. 'He stepped up, didn't he?'

I was very drunk. It's possible that I began to keel over and that Henry grabbed me to save me from falling. Suddenly I found myself half lifted over the hedge and carried over to a dilapidated bench that has sat in the cottage garden for as long as I can remember. He sat close beside me, but even so his voice seemed to come from a great distance. 'Ah. You've read the letters. You know all about my ignominious birth.'

I didn't deny it. I said, 'I'm sure they cared about each other, if it's any consolation.'

'Humph!' His tone was cynical. 'Probably just a knee trembler against a wall.'

That was an appalling notion, but I hadn't the acuity to counter it. Henry had placed his arm around my shoulders. I squirmed in protest, but the truth was I was too sozzled to get up and walk away. The trunk of a nearby silver birch swam around me, in and out of focus, its bare branches above me rotating like a record on a turntable.

'I won't tell anyone,' I said through woollen lips.

'Like hell you won't,' he sneered. 'I know you. You'll bide your time and then you'll drop your bombshell. It's what you do, Prudence.'

'No, I won't,' I slurred. 'Apart from anything else, it would kill Granny if she knew you were Grandad's son.'

I felt him stiffen. The hand which had been casually stroking my shoulder stopped abruptly. Then Henry began to laugh, his shoulders shaking, his torso quaking with mirth. I'd never heard him laugh like that before. It was the oddest thing, as though he'd been possessed or was having some kind of fit.

'Me? Old man Day's son?' he wheezed out. 'Oh! That's funny! That's so funny, Prudence.' He continued to laugh, resorting to a handkerchief to mop his streaming eyes. 'Where on earth did you get that idea?' he gasped out after a minute or two. 'From the letters? Oh, but you missed the point. You missed the whole point.'

I was completely nonplussed, but there was no way I was going to explain my rationale even if, just then, I could have summoned up the erudition to do so. His uninhibited glee was utterly humiliating. I sank against the back of the bench, the alcohol, my empty stomach and my complete mortification making vomit rise in my throat. I croaked out, 'What do you mean?'

Henry, still chortling, said cryptically, 'Ask Bill, Prudence. Ask Bill.'

I turned and threw up all over his lap.

Chapter Forty

I was so ill and hung over the next day that I took a day off work, claiming to have caught some bug. I lay all day in the fetid gloom of my room, the curtains drawn across the window, my sheets and blankets in disarray and my filthy, sick-stained clothes in a heap on the floor. I drank glass after glass of water but couldn't entertain the idea of food. The toast Blanche brought me—thin-lipped with martyrdom—went uneaten.

I couldn't sleep, my mind tortured with the events of the preceding day. I was thoroughly ashamed of my scheming efforts to pry into the business' affairs. It would have been so much better just to have *asked*. And I disliked the idea that I'd be connected now with Jack's air of self-importance and entitlement. My easy recourse to alcohol also struck a worrying chord—hadn't poor Mum, in her unhappiness, done just the same thing? Of course, in regard to the scene in the cottage garden, I blamed Henry. He'd humiliated me. It made me feel sick to think of it. I *was* sick, retching and retching, but nothing would come. As much as Henry had cast his long shadow over my childhood and my family, I had never felt as utterly suffocated by it as I did then.

All these things, Arthur, were a chamber of horrors in my mind. But in the midst of those instruments of suffering my tormentor had lit—however unwittingly—the smallest flame of hope. He'd laughed at the notion that "old man Day" was his father. His hilarity at my *faux pas* withered my soul; but if it was true … well—there was no obstacle between you and me.

Bill. Bill. Bill apparently had the proof I needed. But who *was* he, I asked myself, as the spectres whirled around my room. And how could I ask him anything?

My typewriter case with its cache of letters sat in the corner of the room emanating waves of accusation and ridicule at me. Call myself a student of literature! And yet I'd clearly misunderstood entirely the contents of Colonel Glenister's letters to his wife. I'd "missed the point" Henry said.

I tossed and turned in the bed, finding neither rest nor relief, refusing the impulse to get the letters out and read them again but at the same time nurturing the little flicker of hope.

In the rest of the house I heard people coming and going, the clash of saucepans and crockery in the kitchen, the whir of the washing machine, the growl of the vacuum, the tinny theme tune of *The Archers* at two. The day passed without me. My stomach felt raw with being sick, my throat parched and ragged, my head a thundercloud of pain. A hollow well of humiliation churned and scoured my mind—I'd somehow got things so, so wrong. But how?

Eventually, I did sleep. When I was conscious of my surroundings again the faint light beyond my curtains had dimmed. My headache had gone and with it the sour taste in my mouth. I could hear the low hum of chat from the kitchen. Teatime. My belly gave a loud grumble. I was hungry.

There was a soft knock at my door and Dad came in, bringing a cup of tea and a plate with a sandwich on it. I hauled myself to a seated position and reached out for the food. 'I'm ravenous,' I said.

Dad perched on the side of the bed while I ate. 'Feeling better?' he wanted to know when the food was gone.

I nodded. 'Much. Except … I feel bad about yesterday. I shouldn't have sneaked into the office like that.'

He said, 'No. You shouldn't. Blanche is terribly upset about it. She feels that you don't trust her.'

I slid my eyes from his. I *didn't* trust her, but had to admit that my distrust had no basis in fact. I took a sip of the tea.

'The thing is,' I said slowly, 'although I quite see that the way I went about acquainting myself with it was very wrong, I *do* feel that I should know how things stand in the business. I'm committed to it now. It's my future, for better or worse. The decisions that are made now will impact the next generation—me and Jack and the twins. Surely, we should have some say? We should be allowed to see the bigger picture.'

Dad nodded, considering what I'd said. 'I can see that,' he said. 'And I do sympathise. In the early days Mum and Dad took all the decisions and Isobel and Eric and I felt just as you do now. But we were treated as though we were still children.'

'Exactly,' I said.

'I'll speak to them,' Dad said decisively, and I thought the conversation was over, but he sat on while I finished the tea, staring down at his hands, which were folded between his knees. 'The arrangement between Henry and Granny is different, though,' he said, still avoiding my eye. 'It's Granny's affair—nothing to do with the business at all. Private.' He raised his eyes then and gave me a hard look.

I felt myself blush, but curiosity overcame my shame. 'I know,' I said, 'and I'm sorry. But it seems so *odd* to me. It always has, right from the very beginning. And I feel so many of my problems stem from it.'

'Your problems?'

I shrugged. 'Yes. My feelings of resentment; my eating disorder; Mum dying—'

'Your mother's death had nothing to do with the Glenisters,' Dad said sharply.

I thought I knew differently, but I didn't say so, sensing now that my version of events would be dismissed as childish neuroses.

I was right. Dad heaved an enormous sigh and put his hand on mine. 'You were always a troubled child,' he said gently. 'Subject to odd fancies. Lost in your own imagination. Your worldview is … different.'

Tears pressed behind my eyes. 'Maybe different from other peoples,' I said in a small voice, 'but still valid, surely?'

Dad patted my hand. 'It depends. Thoughts, feelings, opinions—these are things that are individual and yes, valid I suppose, to a point. But your feelings have always been so big, Prue, and so deep.' He shook his head. 'Your mother and I didn't know what to make of you sometimes. You were so often off in your own little world. We worried.' He gripped my hand again and leaned forward to look into my eyes. 'You mustn't let it suck you in,' he said earnestly. 'Stick to *facts*, Prue. Things are either true or they're not.'

I nodded, but I wasn't convinced. The green woman, your grandmother, Arthur—I'd swear on my life that I'd seen her the day Erin died no matter what empirical evidence there was to the contrary.

'You *feel* that the Glenisters muscled their way into our cosy family,' Dad went on. 'You resented Arthur, and you were jealous of the attention you thought ought to be yours being bestowed on others. Valid feelings. But the *fact* is that the Glenisters didn't force their way in at all. They were invited and welcomed.'

'Why?' I burst out. '*Why?* That's what I don't understand.'

Dad let go of my hand and stood up. 'That's Granny's affair,' he said, collecting my cup and plate. 'None of our business. Will you come down to dinner? I think you owe Blanche an apology. It might be better if you find a moment to speak to her before we eat. Too many mealtimes have been made unpleasant by a bad atmosphere recently. Better to clear the air.'

I nodded miserably and he crossed to the door.

'Are Henry and Verity coming to dinner?' I asked. The ordeal of facing Henry was far more intimidating than the necessity of apologising to Blanche. I owed him an apology too—my vomit would have ruined his trousers—but I'd be blowed if I would add to my humiliation.

But Dad said, 'Oh, no. They've gone away for a couple of weeks. The colonel has a pal with a big house on the south coast. They've gone to look after the place while this chap's in Florida. I believe there are innumerable golf courses. Nice work if you can get it, eh? Dinner at seven thirty, Prue. Take a shower. You look like you could use one.'

I showered and dressed, changed my sheets, gathered up my stinking clothes and carried my laundry downstairs. Blanche was alone in the kitchen peeling potatoes. I put a load of laundry in the machine and then offered to help—an olive branch—taking the opportunity to tell her I was sorry for my actions the previous day. She accepted with fairly good grace, and I moved the conversation along as swiftly as I could. Wasn't it a piece of luck for Henry and Verity? Wouldn't the colonel enjoy the golf? Had she heard from you recently?

She answered monosyllabically until I turned the topic of discussion to you. She'd received a letter just that morning. She became positively voluble, enumerating the details: the runaway success of the orangery project; a large bonus you'd apparently received in recognition of your contribution; an opportunity to work on an important project in Derbyshire—a tumbledown folly on a remote moor—and, as the cherry on the icing on the cake, a new girlfriend on the scene. I felt sure that she delivered this last detail with spiteful intent, and I couldn't blame her. Of course she'd want to get her own back. The girl in question was a junior partner in the practice, a year or two older than you, alumnus of King's College Cambridge and the younger daughter of a chap who sat in the House of Lords. 'Not an hereditary peer,' she hastened to tell me, 'but one of those knighted for services to the realm.'

'She sounds amazing,' I said through clenched teeth. 'When will we meet her?'

The candle in my heart guttered. Talk about timing!

Dinner was a rather forcedly jolly affair. Jack threw me the occasional wry look, but I ignored him. Halfway through the meal, though, Granny burst into tears, gibbering incoherently about a lost baby. She had to be given two of her tablets and helped to bed. The jovial atmosphere evaporated, and we finished our food in virtual silence. I helped Hester clear away after dinner and then took Piglet out for a walk, but we didn't venture far and I was in bed and asleep by ten.

That year, autumn turned to winter early, with storms that rattled the slates on the house and brought a big tree down on the edge of the wildflower meadow. Jack supervised its cutting up and stacking for firewood. Henry, Verity and the colonel stayed on at the coast far beyond the original two weeks, but that was no loss, as far as I was concerned. The twins' band was booked for several gigs and they were away for half of October. I did miss them, I must say. Our family gatherings were reduced to just the eight of us. As we'd worked together all day there wasn't much to talk about. It was a relief when Grace decided to bring the children over to join us. Pansy was diffident, as usual, but the three boys made up for her detached air. They were chatty and funny—their antics made us all laugh.

I squared my shoulders and got on with life—the life I had—trying to shut out the questions that nagged at my ears, refusing to be drawn back into the vortex of the past. I couldn't trust myself not to misread things—again.

I concentrated on my work, experimenting with and then introducing a new blue cheese and expanding the range of yoghurt and ice cream on offer in the farm shop. I continued with my studies, but in a more dilatory way than formerly and I got such a low mark for my end-of-module essay that my tutor wrote and asked if everything was all right. I told him I'd decided to defer the next module until the spring—a decision he accepted, but with regret. Jonathan tried to change my mind. My deferment would mean our tutorials would be on different timetables—the end to our trysts in Milton Keynes. I said it couldn't be helped. I knew I'd miss his companionship and also the sex, but with the reignition of a possible future with you, I knew it wasn't fair to Jonathan to continue.

A chap called Warren asked me out. His mother had a small business making cakes that he delivered to us as well as various other cafés and restaurants. I knew him by sight pretty well. I went with him to the cinema and for a couple of meals but when he suggested a weekend away, I declined. He was nice enough, local, and I could see that he'd be a perfect fit for the family business, but my heart was as untouched by him as it had been by Jonathan.

Chapter Forty-One

"Black Monday" hit on 19th October of that year, 1987, wiping a quarter from the value of stocks and shares. I worried about you, Arthur—what would the crash mean for your investments? I didn't like to think of your late grandmother's money being swallowed up, shrivelling and shrinking like the woman herself beneath her modest little gravemound. God knew, she'd left little else as a legacy.

I felt a strong affinity with poor Bee. She'd been so isolated, so unhappy. According to Henry she'd been a failure as a mother. How must that have felt? I didn't know then who Henry's father had been—he'd been adamant it wasn't my grandad, however fond she'd seemed to be of him. It appeared she'd had no meaningful relationship in her life at all. Perhaps *that* was the nature of the kinship between us.

It might have been that ineluctable sense of connection that caused me to visit Glenister Hall one Sunday afternoon towards the end of October. What did I hope to find? The old woman's spectre gliding down the empty stairs? The echo of macabre laughter in the upper rooms? Or was it to indulge some fantasy of the two of us living there together, the place restored, a handful of children playing hide-and-seek along the galleried landings? I don't know. My feet just took me there of their own volition and I found myself gaining access via the back door and roaming the corridors in search of … something. The rooms were shuttered and cold. What furniture that remained was piled in heaps and covered with sheets. All the books had gone from the library—had they been sold? But the shallow-drawered bureau was still in place and in it I found the scroll you'd set such store by in our last conversation. I unfurled it and brought it into the light that filtered through the grimy window.

The Glenister family tree was by no means prolific, but it *was* extremely tangled. Marriages between closely related branches were indeed common and commensurately, infant mortality was unusually high. The Glenisters were lucky if one or two of their several children survived into adulthood. Military service seemed the norm for the men, who often died ahead of their time in conflict. I traced down the line of women—desolate, neglected, bereaved, suppressed. Every three or four generations was a "cursed" Glenister wife, denoted by an oddly shimmering stylised tree symbol against their name, the same image that had been appended to Beatrice's gravestone. It identified them as women touched by some queer, mystical intuition and a deep connection to nature, to the landscape, to the trees and rocks of the Glenister estate. Only ignorance had labelled it "madness." I wondered how many of those other illegible memorials in the cemetery marked the final resting places of Beatrice's predecessors.

I peered closely at the dates. None of them had lived to be old women. It looked as though Beatrice, at eighty-two, had lived longer than any of them. How had she managed it, living feral in the woods, foraging for food? I tried to imagine my granny living in a similar manner and gave up. Granny had been strong and resilient in her younger days, working hours that were as long as Grandad's and often doing work that was equally arduous. But for the past ten years she'd preferred a life of comfort—an electric blanket on her bed, a footstool for her feet, the fire lit most evenings. She needed her medication, her spectacles, the thick unguent that soothed her arthritic hands, a hot toddy to take up to bed. My respect for Beatrice Glenister increased. What a woman she'd been!

I turned back to the scroll and saw again—but more clearly this time—right at the bottom, your name in the same beautiful calligraphy of all the rest. And next to it, written in pencil in a childish hand, so faint as to be almost invisible, mine. I had to tilt the parchment to make it out. The light through the window was gilded—it was a rare, sunny day—and filled with motes that hovered like tiny fragments of gold. Tears pricked the backs of my eyes. Is that what you'd wanted me to see, Arthur? That from an early age you'd seen what I'd so manifestly failed to recognise? That we were made for each other, you and I? That you loved me and wanted me for your wife?

I closed my eyes and let the emotion overwhelm me. Tears seeped between my lashes and rolled down my cheeks and I left them unchecked, basking in the weak warmth of the autumn sun and the much stronger glow of being loved by you that flared up from the flame I kept carefully shielded in my heart.

Presently, when the tumult had calmed, I looked down at the scroll again and my eye was caught by something just beside my pencilled-in name. It glinted in the light. Had one of my tears fallen on the parchment? I touched it gingerly. No, it was dry. But something shimmered there, a drop of molten pearl, and as I stared at it, it coalesced into the palest possible representation of that tree cypher. I scrubbed a fist across my eyes but in that second a cloud blotted out the sun and the room was plunged into gloom.

Slowly, I refurled the scroll and replaced it into the drawer. A different possibility suggested itself to me. Was your eagerness for me to see this a warning? A reminder that the Glenister wives were cursed? Were you perhaps asking me if I was prepared to run that risk, for you?

Oh! *Yes,* Arthur. Yes, yes and a thousand times, yes.

October and November passed. Christmas came.
I was almost happy.

Chapter Forty-Two

You didn't return home for Christmas at the end of 1987, instead skiing with your new girlfriend Angela who, according to Blanche, was a paragon of womanly virtues: consummate professional, highly respected in her field; kind and caring; very well-connected and wealthy, and naturally, superlatively beautiful. Blanche claimed to have seen a photograph although she didn't offer to show it to anyone else. She said Angela had melded seamlessly with your other friends and was now quite one of the gang. She and my dad planned a trip to London in the new year so that they could meet her.

I was disappointed that I wouldn't get to see you, but also relieved. I didn't think I could bear to see you if you were involved with someone else.

Henry, Verity and the colonel stayed away too, moving from the impressive home of one acquaintance to the villa of another, then the Austrian ski lodge of a third where they were to *rendezvous* with you and the exemplary Angela for Christmas and the New Year. I couldn't imagine you'd welcome Henry's company on your holiday. Probably he'd railroaded you into it.

Christmas came and went, a quiet affair—the polite exchange of gifts in the morning; a cooperative effort with the meal; the Queen's speech at three; and then a James Bond film before tea followed by a half-hearted game of charades. I felt torpid and detached, as though the whole thing was happening to someone else and I was just an onlooker, vaguely interested as one is at a museum or gallery.

On Twelfth Night I helped take down the tree and put away the cards and decorations. And that's when I saw it. A card from Colonel Glenister to Granny. It pictured a snowy mountain scene with an opal sky above and a smattering of very attractive-looking Tyrolean lodges in a picturesque valley below. Inside he'd written—in a surprisingly firm and elegant hand—'I thought this would bring back happy memories of our time in Germany. With fond wishes from Ted to Bill.'

Oh, Arthur! All the angst came surging back, and the meagre little flame of hope blew out.

I fell into a chair in a kind of stupor, crushing tinsel and angel hair beneath me.

Here he—or rather she—was. Bill! How had I failed to see it? I'd known very well that Granny had spent time in Germany as a driver after the war. And although the family had always shortened Granny's name—Wilhemina— to Ina, it wasn't an enormous leap to see that its diminutive could just as easily be Bill. I'd assumed the Bill in the colonel's letters to be a man—gender stereotyping at its worst!—another member of the Bunny, Whizzo, Jock and Pug fraternity. I was ashamed of myself. And now I understood the "gift" Bill had been commissioned to bring home to Beatrice—a baby. Here, *here* was the "point" Henry had mentioned—the solution, the answer, the crux of the whole affair.

I tried to picture it; the arrival of a young, pregnant but confident, travelled and worldly-wise Granny at the gates of Glenister Hall, coming face-to-face with poor, dishevelled, reclusive Beatrice, expected to hand over her baby when it made its appearance the following October. I was sure that a child out of wedlock would have been an encumbrance as well as a stigma in those days. Granny might have been glad to think the child would have a secure home and find love in the arms of a desperate, childless woman. But knowing Granny as I did—nurturing, loving, selfless in her care for others— I could only imagine the pangs and heartbreak of such a prospect. Had Beatrice already been too far gone in abstraction to care for a child?

Everything fell into place. Granny's clandestine visits to Glenister Hall to watch little Henry at play in the garden and later her eagerness to absorb him into her family fold. Her often overly emotional reactions to Henry's presence or his absence. The close friendship between herself and the colonel—I'd thought it sudden and rather curious, but in fact it was only a resumption of their former association. Her on-going provision of funds to Henry. Her silence on the whole topic—she couldn't have revealed his secret without revealing her own. A child out of wedlock would be considered a disgrace by a woman of Granny's era and moral rectitude; but she must also be plagued by guilt. As things turned out she could have brought Henry up as her own. Grandad would have owned him, I'm sure.

And how had the whole situation impacted Beatrice? Henry was proof of her husband's infidelity. Granny's proximity must have been a daily reminder of Beatrice's own failure—to keep her husband, to produce a child. No wonder she'd failed to bond with the boy, conscious—as she must have been—of the child's *real* mother not a mile away, and—to add insult to injury—now married to the man Beatrice herself had loved!

The money that had flowed from Glenister Hall to Broadacres was hard to account for, unless it was a vehicle to keep Granny and Grandad busy with their own place, family and business. If they were occupied *there,* Beatrice would not have to encounter them. Unless after all it had been at the colonel's instruction, payment in recognition of the great gift of a Glenister heir.

As for the falling out? Well, you only had to look at the colonel and Granny together now to know that their attachment ran deep. Maybe on his return to England they'd been tempted to rekindle things. I could see that a complete severance of any connection between them would have been the best thing and indeed, Granny had called it, "a parting of the ways."

I sat amongst the cardboard boxes and half-packed up baubles and desiccated holly boughs in a room which had gone dark while I'd assimilated all these revelations. I felt no satisfaction in having solved the conundrum at last. A fateful boulder weighed down my heart, a cold, hard stone of disappointment.

When the telephone rang in the hall, I knew it was you. Don't ask me why or how. I knew it in my bones, an in-pouring of sick dread. The ringing went on and on and I wanted someone else to answer it so badly that I even closed the door to give the impression that I'd completed my task and gone away. I didn't know where the others were. Victor couldn't have answered the phone anyway. Perhaps Isobel and Blanche were upstairs with Granny. At last, I could bear it no longer. I flung myself from the room and snatched up the receiver.

I said, 'Hello Arthur.'

Your voice came to me across the long-distance line that fizzed with static. 'Hello Prue.'

We made no pretence that it was a social call. Do you remember? Where were you, Arthur? In a ski lodge? Or squashed into a phone booth while the *après-ski* scene went on hilariously around you? Were Henry and Verity and your grandfather there, pink from the slopes, swigging *schnapps* or *Glühwein?* I thought perhaps you were a little inebriated. Your words were lugubrious. You seemed to drag them up from some deep, unwilling depository in your soul.

Without preamble you said, 'What you told me that day in June. Are you sure?'

I looked around me at the cold, featureless hallway, at the worn Axminster carpet beneath my feet, trying to decide if it was some moral high ground of which I was the righteous possessor, or just a worthless hill I'd chosen to die on. Was I prepared to let it go, the thing I wanted most of all? For the sake of a principle? Just to draw a line in the sand between myself and Henry Glenister? That decided it. The notion of being akin to him in *anything* was too awful.

With the air of signing my own death warrant I said, 'Yes, Arthur. As it turns out I wasn't quite right about the *dramatis personae*—'

'The what?'

'The people involved. Not Grandad, but Granny. Granny and the colonel. They knew each other in Germany. But the consequence is just the same.'

'It isn't illegal, you know,' you said fiercely.

'I know,' I replied. 'But still ...' There was silence for a time, just the buzz and crackle of the line. I heard you sigh. I thought I heard you run your hand over your face, the faint rasp of your unshaven beard—but I might have imagined that. Were you battling your conscience, as I had battled mine? Ah! Arthur. It was a war we couldn't win. After a long time you said, 'It's impossible, isn't it?'

I swallowed a frozen lump in my throat. 'Yes, Arthur.'

'Alright,' you said, very quietly. 'If you're sure.'

'Aren't you?'

You didn't reply.

I made some sound—inarticulate, more of a sob or a howl.

You said, 'Goodbye, Prue.' And then, just before the click of the call's end I thought I heard—but it might just have been the susurration of the line—'I love you, Prue.'

Then the line went dead.

Chapter Forty-Three

Increasingly, as winter took its iron grip on the land, I inhabited another world, an inner realm I'd sometimes glimpsed but now powerfully felt was hovering beyond a nebulous veil. Some cord of darkness connected me to it. I felt the draw of it. Anything that distracted from the physical world—the grind of work, the increasing acrimony of the family, my legion of errors and missteps and, most of all, the doom of loving you—was a sanctuary, and one I craved.

I took to roaming the woods in spite of the weather, which was bitter and bleak. Piglet was my willing companion—she didn't seem to care what the weather was like. I found the moan of the wind in the high canopy a suitable soundscape to my feelings, which were restless and depressed. I spent hours in the cove watching the waves pound the shingle. Endlessly they came, a ceaseless battering upon the implacable shore. I tried to emulate the obdurate rocks, to withstand the relentless assault of disappointment, death and despair that I felt were my lifelong companions. I clambered over the forbidden rocks, daring the gusting wind, almost hoping a wave would snatch me off and cast me into the sea, or hurl me into one of the deep fissures to be broken and trapped past saving, as we'd been cautioned time without number. Piglet— more sensible than I—barked and leapt in alarm from a place of safety as I navigated the treacherous chasms and sheer, slippery surfaces, getting closer and closer to where the foaming sea fizzed and spumed. It was compassion for her that finally drew me back. Why should she suffer because I was miserable?

I was inexorably drawn to the woods, the cove, the pond and the sad, forgotten cemetery. Every night after work I'd walk in that direction, becoming so intimate with the landscape, the pathways and the atmosphere that I could find my way to any location without the aid of a torch. Walking in the woods was like walking in my own soul. *There* was the sanctuary I needed. *There*, I felt different—free, altered, released—part of something that was much bigger than I was, a feeling of belonging I had not experienced since my days at boarding school and, before that, at home, before the family began to disintegrate. I was conscious of being connected to an ethereal ambit I felt shimmering above, around and within me. The very landscape was part of me, an extension of my being. I was bonded to it; the trees and rocks braced and supported me. And the timelessness of it made me feel centred. I was part of the great, inexorable narrative, my role in it predestined from the beginning, a lone character in a story that would go on after me, its chapters numberless as the shingle on the shore. This iteration of myself was so much more comfortable than the drudging, trudging woman I was at Salad Days. There, I was lost and lonely, but in the woods I was … at home. I belonged. And I understood at last the nature of poor Mrs Glenister's "madness." She hadn't been mad at all, just learned and intuitive, grounded. A wise woman in its truest sense. She'd found her place—as I had. It wasn't her fault or the fault of any of the women who had gone before her that ignorant people—men, no doubt—had castigated, denigrated, incarcerated and even burned alive what they did not understand.

Thought of your grandmother led me involuntarily—as though I was in a kind of trance—to the woodsman's cottage and its key, in the hollow of the tree. The interior of the cottage was remarkably simple—just a single room with a rudimentary kitchen on one side and a rustic bed platform on the other. What bedding there was and some ragged curtains had been decimated by damp and rodents. I took it all into the clearing and burned it, having an idea that I would make the place habitable. I spent hours sweeping away old leaves and dirt, carrying water from the stream to boil over the fire, scrubbing the old deal table and the few cooking implements that hung from hooks on the walls. There was a cast iron stove within the main room and I tried to light it, but smoke poured into the house. The chimney was blocked. Nevertheless, I purloined some of Granny's old quilts and blankets from the back of the airing cupboard and transported them down there and made up a sort of bed where I was sure I could sleep comfortably enough. I found an old oil lamp in one of the sheds and bought paraffin and candles from an old-fashioned ironmonger in town.

A few nights, when the house was asleep, I crept out and through the woods and burrowed into my nest of covers. The night sounds of the forest comforted me. I breathed in the smells of damp leaves and old timber and pungent earth and felt as though I had roots that entwined deep within the earth. At the same time, I felt elevated, in some odd way floating and ethereal. It was clean. Wholesome. Healthy. I don't know how to describe it, but the subterranean life force that connects all living things crept into me, Arthur, and a spiritual in-pouring lifted me, and for those few hours I slept dreamlessly and well.

My clothing got ruined, stained by leaf mould, torn by thorn and worn to holes as I hauled logs for my fire, water from the stream and clambered about on the roof to stop up leaks and clear the jackdaws' nest that blocked the chimney. When I looked at my hands they were hard and calloused, gouged by splinters, a wood-woman's hands. Isobel looked at them askance a few times, but I wore gloves in the dairy, so she could not complain.

I felt the family's watchfulness over me. They must have thought that I was on the brink of another of my breakdowns. My long absences went unquestioned and yet I knew that they must wonder about them, and about my general demeanour, which was increasingly shabby and unkempt as the forest absorbed me into itself. I was coaxed to eat, and to be fair I must say that Blanche did her best to tempt me with dishes she knew I liked. I just found it hard to take any pleasure from food or to eat more than the minimum required to fend off hunger pangs. Something closed up in my throat and sometimes I could not swallow at all unless I had a drink to hand. But not an alcoholic one. I hadn't taken a drop of alcohol since the night I'd thrown up on Henry's lap.

Then Granny fell ill and we were all anxious for a few days. She was feverish and confined to bed. We took turns to sit with her and listen to her mumbled nonsense, which was mainly addressed to a corner of the room where a large armoire stood. The doctor visited daily but prescribed no medication other than pain-relief, fluids and rest. He said that only time would tell and reminded us that Granny was incredibly old and quite frail. In fact, in the large bed she'd shared with Grandad, Granny looked so small she might have been a child, not much bigger than Grace's youngest. She lay still and quiet for most of the time, her hands folded on the sheet as though composed for her final resting. But then the fever would grip her again and she'd thrash and complain, her hands surprisingly strong as she fended off cool cloths and proffered sips of water.

Late one night Pansy—fifteen by then, a deep-thinking, rather introverted girl—and I sat beside the sickbed. Granny's eyes opened wide, and she fixed me with a stare that was horror-struck, and called me Beatrice, as she had done once before.

'I see you there, waiting,' she said, very clearly. 'Is it time?'

I looked across the bed at Pansy. I thought she'd be disturbed by Granny's peculiar remark but her eyes—grey, and noticeably clear—seemed only to echo the question.

I said, 'Granny. It's me, Prudence. Go to sleep, darling. You'll be better in the morning.'

But she shrank away from me. 'You smell of the woods,' she said. 'You've been in the woods again. Don't deny it! When are you going to get home and take care of that child?'

Pansy calmly extended her own arm and took hold of Granny's hand.

'I will do,' I soothed, 'when you're better. Try to rest now, Granny.'

Her eyes flickered and half-closed. 'The woods will make you mad,' she murmured. 'You mustn't go there.' And then, whimpering a little as sleep reclaimed her, 'It isn't time. I'm not ready, Beatrice.'

'No, no,' I said. 'Plenty of time, yet.'

After a while, Pansy said, very matter-of-factly, 'You *do* smell of the woods.'

'I know,' I mumbled. 'I like it there.'

She said, 'Me too.'

Granny slept, and after a while Pansy did too, curled in her chair, her head on her arms. She was a pretty girl, slim—as Grace had briefly been at about the same age—with fair hair and a solemn, pensive air that reminded me, worryingly, of Erin. I'd been afraid that Granny's outburst would upset her, but it didn't seem to have done, not at all.

In the morning Granny was better, and I feel sure she had no recollection of our conversation, but I recalled it and thought on it a great deal. Clearly, she'd confused me with old Mrs Glenister, seeing parallels which were ridiculous, but also quite understandable, because, increasingly, I saw them too.

And so, interestingly, did Pansy.

Chapter Forty-Four

We organised a little tea party for Granny's ninetieth, which occurred towards the end of March, when daffodils were beginning to bloom and garden birds began to build their nests. Granny had her hair done in the morning and wore a new frock that Isobel had ordered from a catalogue. We gathered at three—much earlier than usual. We'd had to rota extra staff in the shop and garden centre to cover for us. The reason for this wasn't quite clear to me but Blanche had insisted upon it and in those days, I was little inclined to question or challenge her.

There were a respectable number of cards and Granny insisted upon laboriously opening and reading each one aloud while the tea in the pot cooled and the hot savouries Blanche and Isobel had slaved over grew greasy on the plate. Your card—signed 'Arthur and Angela'—was put in a place of special prominence on the dresser. The colonel had sent a ridiculously large bouquet—we'd need three vases to arrange the blooms.

Finally, we began to pass sandwiches and fuss with napkins. Granny sat and stared round the table owlishly. She said, 'You're all very dressed up for a Thursday. Is something happening?'

It was Tuesday, but that hardly mattered.

'It's your birthday, Granny,' Jack yelled. That was unnecessary. Granny was a bit daft, but she wasn't deaf.

'Oh!' She beamed. 'How nice. Are there any cards?'

I gathered them from where we'd displayed them on the dresser and along the window ledge so that she could look through them again. She began with enthusiasm but soon lost interest and laid them to one side.

'Where's George?' Granny said. 'His tea will be cold if he doesn't come in soon. Oh!' She cocked an ear. 'Is that him now?'

Indeed, there was the sound of arrival in the hallway. I hadn't heard a car, so I got to my feet, expecting one of the assistants from the shop needing help with something.

But Blanche was at the door of the room before me, wreathed in smiles, blushing and wet-eyed with excitement. 'Surprise!' she squeaked, and made a ti-dah! gesture with her hands. You walked into the room.

Oh, Arthur. For the briefest moment I thought I'd melt with happiness. My marrow gave way and pooled in my gut. But immediately it curdled with the half sandwich I'd eaten and I felt the familiar clutch of my throat that presaged sickness. Already on my feet, I took a pace or two backwards from the table, arriving at the side of the French window where the thick drape of the curtain provided a sort of refuge and from where I could open the doors and dash outside if I needed to. Pansy, who sat beside me, pushed her chair back in such a way as to make a sort of screen between me and the room. From behind it I could observe without being seen.

You looked simply amazing; your chest broad, your belly flat, your chin smooth-shaven but manly, your eyes bright and matching a plain but expensive-looking blue shirt. You'd let your hair grow long on top, but it was close cropped at the back—Brad Pitt and Leonardo de Caprio came to mind. You swept it back with your hand as you made a beeline for Granny, who had half-risen in her chair, and scooped her up into an embrace that made her burble with laughter.

She said, 'Oh Henry, darling, I knew you'd come,' and a gout of bile bubbled in my throat.

You laughed off her mistake, smiling round the table at the rest of the family, saying, 'Did we miss the cake?'

We?

I peered through the door jamb, making out a slice of movement as people removed coats and tidied their hair before entering the dining room. Soon Verity and Henry were in the room, tanned and relaxed, and I heard the colonel speaking in a muffled voice to someone before he too made his entrance.

The tea party was utterly ruined as chairs were found, clean cups brought out, food reconfigured on plates to appear less 'left over.' I remained in the shadow of the curtain and shielded by Pansy, who stayed resolutely in place even while the others milled and manoeuvred furniture and made room for the new arrivals. I perched awkwardly on the arm of a wingback chair, pressed right back into the curtain, my cup and saucer balanced in my trembling hand. I was horribly conscious of my tangled hair and shabby clothes, and my thinness, which had crept back upon me since Christmas.

The day was already drawing in. Someone lit a lamp and stoked the fire into greater brightness, but thankfully it didn't penetrate to where I lingered and I found myself in a curiously detached bubble, watching events unfold as though they were on a stage and I a member of the audience, anonymous in the auditorium.

Isobel brought in an elaborate birthday cake—made, I knew, by Warren's mother—and we sang "Happy Birthday to You" before Granny made an attempt at the candles assisted by Grace's boys. The cake was cut and distributed around but no one ate very much of it. It was overly sweet, the icing especially cloying. I doubted it was homemade at all.

All the time I sensed an undercurrent of expectation, some other revelation that would burst out like a geyser, swamping the birthday itself and even the surprise of your arrival here in time for the celebration. Verity wriggled in her chair and Henry smirked and the colonel was puffed up with excitement. Blanche could barely contain herself.

Then you rose from your chair, and I felt the colour drain from my face even as my stomach clenched. I would faint, or throw up, or both. I swallowed hard, and so did you, Arthur, as you lifted your teaspoon and tapped it on the edge of your cup. Inexorably, your gaze travelled the room, but it skipped past me as though there was nothing more in the shadowy corner than cobwebs.

You opened your mouth to speak, but before you could utter a word, Henry was on his feet as well. He was always inflated with pride and self-importance but his hubris on this occasion was insufferable. It bloated and expanded him until I thought he would fill the entire room. Unlike yours, his eyes fixed on me and held me transfixed. They glittered with malice, but then he turned back to the company and laid his large hand on Granny's shoulder.

'I feel a few words are in order,' he said pompously, 'in honour of this remarkable lady, on this very special day.'

Glances were exchanged round the table. Surely, those curious looks said, if anyone were to propose a toast it ought to be Trevor? And in any case, we had only tea before us—and cold tea at that.

Naturally, no one raised an objection and Henry went on. 'I believe I have as much reason as anyone here for gratitude. I owe Ina my life.'

Oh God! Was he *really* going to do this now? Granny would be mortified, to have her past exposed. I looked across the table to where you remained standing awkwardly, your spoon and teacup still held aloft but your eyes, like everyone else's, were riveted to Henry. I read curiosity in them but also anger. In some way I couldn't fathom, Henry had stolen your thunder.

'I am not sure how many of you are acquainted with my history,' Henry began, sounding, I thought, like the opening of a Charles Dickens novel. 'It may be that you have speculated as to my ready acceptance here amongst the Day family. It's possible ...' he gave a self-deprecating chortle, 'that you have even suspected a *closer* connection ...' he waved an airy hand, '... but no. Surely, no one would be *that* obtuse.' I cringed at that, and cut my eyes away in shame, pretending intense interest in the pattern of the curtain. 'The fact is,' Henry resumed, 'and I do not know why it has never been generally discussed—there is certainly no *shame* in it. Family pride, perhaps ... and then one might argue it's no one's business ... but you may be surprised to discover that I was an orphan of the war.' General murmurings of surprise, eyebrows raised in wonder. The family emitted polite sounds of interest, but my heart fell, like a cold dead thing, from my chest.

'Yes, indeed. A German orphan, abandoned in the streets of Cologne. A newborn baby. I would have died but for the great kindness of this gentleman …' he gestured at the colonel, '…and the courage of this lady.'

Granny blinked up at him. The rest of the family continued to exhibit courteous signs of astonishment. Only Verity and Blanche displayed no amazement. They already knew.

I slid from the arm of the chair into its seat, wishing it would swallow me whole. I kept my eyes fixed on you, Arthur. Your tan had disappeared leaving your face white and bloodless, but your eyes did not leave your father's face.

Henry forged on. 'She brought me across Europe,' he said. 'It can't have been easy. A woman alone and a newborn baby. People made assumptions, no doubt … ill-informed, ignorant people.' I felt the malevolence of this remark directed at me like an arrow, but he didn't glance my way again. 'Europe was in the grip of depression. Already, in Germany, fascism was on the rise. There was unrest and violence in France. You don't need me to teach you history. And some of my earliest, happiest memories are of her. She would come to Glenister Hall to check on my welfare. Right up until the time I went to school. So, I wanted to offer my tribute.' He raised his cup, although it was empty. 'To Ina,' he said, smiling broadly, 'a redoubtable woman.'

The others echoed his toast, and he regained his seat, but remained so swollen with delight in himself and his coup that it was as though he floated six inches above it.

All eyes turned to you, Arthur, still standing, but now ashen-faced, your eyes round and staring. I saw your Adam's apple bob repeatedly as you tried to find your voice.

Isobel said, 'So you're not *really* a Glenister?'

Henry said, 'Not by blood. But I hope …' he looked down at his father, 'I hope in every other way.'

'In every way that matters,' the colonel affirmed.

Still you remained, Arthur, fixed to the spot and speechless. I couldn't bear your paralysis any longer, so I said, 'And you're not related to the Day family.' It was a statement, not a question, and Henry did not deign to reply. My voice was dead and flat, defeated; and no doubt lost in the obscurity of my corner, baffled by Pansy's chair and by her slight little shoulders that provided a brave if ineffectual fortification between me and Henry's malicious intent.

Victor mumbled, 'I don't know who'd be crass enough to suspect *that.*'

I shrivelled at that, but not enough. I wished I could dematerialise altogether.

For the duration of Henry's speech Granny had remained in a neutral gear she often adopted these days when events moved faster than her ability to keep up with them. But some circuit must have momentarily reconnected because she said, with great lucidity, 'Oh well, if it comes to that, we should thank *you*. Or at least Teddy. I don't know what we would have done without his generosity. He loaned us … oh! Ever so much.' She turned to my father, who sat beside her. 'Didn't he, George?'

Dad made a noncommittal sound in the back of his throat, and lifted his teacup to his lips, although there was nothing in it.

Blanche said, mildly but pointedly, 'A debt that has now been amply repaid. With interest.'

The colonel raised an eyebrow at this. 'Has it?'

It was Henry's turn to drink from an empty cup.

A small movement out in the hallway—the smallest creak of a board—broke the bewitchment of the moment and galvanised you from whatever hex had held you in its thrall.

You croaked out, 'There's another surprise, although …' you gave a little shake of your head, trying to dislodge your inertia, '… although, in comparison to what we've just heard … but no matter.' I could see you take a grip of yourself. With infinite care, as though handling the finest antique Limoges porcelain, you replaced your cup on its saucer and the spoon alongside it. Your hands didn't shake but once they were empty you clasped them together before you in an attitude of entreaty and also of resolution. Your gaze rose from the table to where I sat and at last met mine. Your eyes were glassy, pools of emotion. I felt as though all the blood had drained from me. I wished it would do. I read volumes of words in your expression—regret, anguish, anger and remorse. I'm sure I answered you, word for word, in the silence that stretched out between us.

Then a small but rather high and strident voice in the hall said testily, 'Arthur,' and the spell was broken. It electrified you. You shoved your chair back and crossed to the doorway.

'I'd like to introduce Angela,' you said with a brightness that was as manufactured as the icing on the cake. You stretched your arm through the open door and she appeared as though conjured from thin air, smiling happily, inserting herself easily into the space beneath your shoulder. 'My wife.'

There were cries of delight as people rose to meet her, and it was easy for me to turn the key to the French windows.

I took a last glance around the room, at all the familiar faces, the furnishings, the well-known china. You were lost amongst the congratulations and so was Angela, enfolded in the embrace of her new family.

No one saw me except Pansy. She turned in her seat and her wise grey eyes met mine.

Her mouth formed the word, 'Goodbye,' and she gave me a sad little smile.

I closed the door without a sound and slipped away into the night.

Chapter Forty-Five

I had neither thought nor plan as I crossed the lawn and made for the woods, for my refuge, for my *alter ego*. It was cold and fully dark by then and I wore only jeans and a plaid shirt. A fine rain fell, and I was instantly soaked. My feet, in light canvas trainers, skidded about on the slick leaves and I threw them off, ploughing up the slope of the plantation barefoot and crossing through the little gate that had felt increasingly to me of late a kindly portal to peace and respite.

I stopped beneath the trees and breathed in the narcotic scent of wet wood and rich humus, sap, earth, ancient rock and the faint, salty tang of the sea. Deep in the undergrowth I sensed the welcome of that indefinable life force, its spirit moving. Sprites and dryads, nymphs and centaurs, the ancient shades of the passed-over. The trees shivered in greeting, and I felt my ragged breathing slow and settle, my pounding heart resume its steady beat.

There was no moon, the sky above the canopy a cloak of cloud, but my eyes soon adjusted to the gloom and I walked without a sound along the meandering pathways through my little woodland demesne.

Arthur is married. Arthur is married. The phrase came to me, but from a distance, an owl's cry across the forest.

And he could have been *mine!* Its mate's response echoed back.

I wandered for a long time, visiting all our childhood places: the pond, green and gently dimpled by rain, my mother just visible to me, a nimbus of light in the dim; the cemetery, quiet and restful, its spirits hovering, unconfined by their earthy mounds; the cove, where the shingle whispered words of comfort and the waves sang their everlasting song to the strains of Eric's guitar. Glenister Hall was dark and brooding but the rain stopped as I stood and looked at it and a moonbeam penetrated the cloud and lit it up, bleached and white as bone. A lone figure in an upper window raised her hand in benediction, and I gestured back.

As I approached the woodsman's cottage I thought I heard the thud of an axe on wood, my grandad at work, and when I gained the little clearing I found a stack of firewood by the door. The circle of blackened stones with its tripod and cooking pot marked the centre of the clearing. A tarpaulin covered a bucket of water to prevent creatures from falling in. The key was in its place and when I opened the old wooden door I felt a sigh of greeting from the scrubbed floor and the neat nest of bedding. I fumbled for the matches and lit the oil lamp. It seemed to me that the shadows shrank like cowering children from the sudden illumination, and I said, 'It's alright, dears. It's only me.'

I was cold, and I considered lighting the fire in the clearing, but the rain had begun again. It made a gentle percussion on the roof of the cottage and dripped musically from the gutters. I decided to try the stove again. The wood must have been damp and the fire caught only very sluggishly. I drew a blanket around me and brought a chair close to the stove, staring into the struggling flames.

Henry was not my uncle. He wasn't related to the Days at all, except that Granny had brought him as a baby all the way across Europe to place into the barren arms of Beatrice Glenister. Doubtless Granny had bonded with the baby on that long and difficult journey … oh! It was all too clear to me. Why wouldn't she take an interest in him? Until he went to Holmewood school. Only that—and nothing more sinister—had been the cause of the separation between the two families.

Henry was the "gift" sent by the colonel, not a child *in utero* but a child in flesh. I allowed myself a little smile. Hadn't I *predicted* the gift would be something hideous or useless, or both? Ah! Whatever else I'd got wrong, I'd got *that* right, at least. It was small comfort, though.

And the money? A simple loan and its repayment. In this as in everything else, I'd twisted a rope that was perfectly straight.

The hollow place where my heart ought to be was cold and aching. I'd lost you—irrevocably this time. And for no reason at all. My fault, my fault, my own stupid fault. The finality of it was terrible, like death. How naïve I'd been, so easily misdirected, puerile, prejudiced. Green. Green. The green woman in very truth.

I had a vague, half-formed urge to stir myself, get out of my wet clothes, put a kettle on to boil. Erin would be there soon, and she'd need tea. But a sort of somnolence crept upon me. My limbs were heavy as though weighted down by earth and the sensation was not at all as you would think—chill, damp and appalling with anaemic, squirming things. No. It felt comforting, and I was reminded of that quilt I'd liked as a child but buried in the compost heap to spite you. It seemed so silly now. Pointlessly destructive, causing thoughtless harm. Like climbing the cliff, making my family panic and sending Eric to his needless death. Like opening my mouth to declare Verity's secret— the shock had brought on Grandad's stroke. Like failing to go home to supper with Mum—the last straw in her wretchedness.

All, all, *all* my fault.

But there, in the whispering silence, I heard no accusing voice but my own. The knowledge soothed me, like Granny's cool hand on my fevered brow, and I felt my lifelong angst ebb away.

I think I must have slept, and when I came to … it was the strangest thing, Arthur, and I'll try to describe it to you because I think that very soon now, you'll experience something like it. I was in two places at once, participating and observing, involved and detached, actor and audience, both. It wasn't alarming but it was very curious for a while.

There was the brightest light. It rippled and rolled across the ceiling of the cabin. So beautiful. Every colour. And I heard the family's voices calling. I was there, somewhere up there amongst them, within the tongues of flame. Oh, it was wonderful, a liquid rainbow. But boiling just beneath the curtain of light there was thick, roiling darkness, acrid—it burned the throat to breathe it in. I was down there too, coughing and choking. And so were you, white-faced, shouting and shouting, but your words were snatched away. You caught me up in your arms, bundled me into the blanket and carried me out of the cottage to where the air was wet and cool, but not dark. I think it must have been dawn. A rosy glow lit up everything. The trees of the clearing were bright like mother-of-pearl, and diamonds festooned the twigs and branches.

The strength and comfort of your arms overwhelmed me, and I cried out in the final culmination of it, but my voice, like yours, was lost in the tumult. You laid me on the ground and then you kissed me, Arthur. Oh, the passion and urgency of your mouth on mine, the love and life you imparted with every breath. You poured yourself into me and I filled myself up to the brim and I thought if I never saw, never heard, never touched you again I'd be satisfied, because what you'd given me in those kisses was enough. It was everything.

PART FIVE
1990 – Present Day
Chapter Forty-Six

I was stretched out, thin and light as gossamer, and floating on a breeze. It was very pleasant. Wind and weather, seasons, sun, tide and time—they all swept past, around and through me for a while. I went where they took me— now caught and quivering on a bright green holly leaf, now meshed into a robin's nest, now angled across a corner of a window. From there I became conscious of movement within the room, and voices, and they brought me to myself again. I reknitted myself into something like my own image, but it was one that borrowed from those who had gone before me and also from the plants and trees, the soil and rocks that were my spiritual home.

I was me, but a new me.

I hovered on the periphery, detached and indifferent, sometimes present but mainly absent, as life—as it always must—went on. I observed. I bore witness. I participated in the shadows. And sometimes I intervened. I *had* volition, but I rarely engaged it.

One thing stayed constant, Arthur, and that was my connection with you. You are my fulcrum, my anchor, my kindred spirit.

And so, here—where you are—is where I have always been. And here I still am.

Chapter Forty-Seven

I must say, I like what you've done with the place. Today's Glenister Hall is nothing like the crumbling wreck of the old days. The gilding and plasterwork have all been restored, the panelling is just beautiful. I love the way the light streams through the atrium now. I don't know if the artworks in the long gallery are originals, but they look authentic to me. The servants' quarters, where Polly Tindall used to while away her days with magazines and the radio, are unrecognisable. The cavernous old kitchen is refurbished; homely but also splendid, with a range cooker and an enormous fridge and copper pans hanging from a rack. It's a place for communal gatherings, with squashy settees around a log-burning stove, and bifold doors leading to steps and a wonderful, sociable terrace. Elsewhere there's a storeroom full of gardening tools—still shiny new, pristine as the day they were bought—and a place for outdoor coats and boots—unused. Did you hope for a thriving community of residents here in your ancestral home, something akin to the old days at Broadacres? Did you envisage folks working in the grounds and then gathering for meals as the sun went down? Ah! They were happy days, Arthur, weren't they? Happier than we knew! But I come and go through those deserted passages and I never encounter a soul. Not so much as the ghost of an echo suggests that the rooms above us are tenanted or that the house is anything other than it always was—empty and dismal, reverberating with the moan of the wind in its cold, cold chimneys.

So, in a sad way, the place is as much a mausoleum as it ever was.

You and Angela never lived at Glenister Hall. Perhaps the place had too many unhappy memories for you, or you feared that she would fall foul of the legendary "curse." How could you have thought so? She was never right. She didn't have the intuition, the imagination, the aptitude for it. She couldn't *see*, Arthur. Not beyond the end of her own snub nose. I gather the two of you formed your own architectural practice. She had the aptitude for *that*, I'll grant you. You specialised in the restoration of historic houses. Is it true that you worked on the rebuilding of Windsor Castle after the fire in 1992? Quite a feather in your cap, Arthur!

In your absence—but no doubt under your close supervision—Glenister Hall underwent its enormous programme of renewal and renovation. As I'd suggested, you sold the ancillary dwellings to private buyers, and these too were extended and refurbished to provide holiday homes or retirement properties for well-heeled folks with a yen for a place in the country. The stables block was likewise converted, and an artist took up residence there.

She was an ill-kempt, straggle-haired woman with neo-pagan, druidical pretensions who had a penchant for wandering naked in the woods at night. We bumped into one another from time to time. She'd frown and do a double take as our orbits passed—what a fright I must have looked, with leaves in my hair and my clothes all anyhow and larded with the tilth of the forest floor! But better than her, I'd venture to say. What a crone, with her flat, empty breasts and mottled thighs! She smoked too much dope, but whether our encounters caused her to smoke more or less of it, I can't say. Her paintings were well-received, I think, but I don't see any of them gracing the walls of Glenister Hall.

The colonel passed away in his sleep a few months after your marriage. His funeral was surprisingly well-attended, but no one cried apart from Granny.

I attended of course, but no one took any notice of me.

I wonder if it saddens you that he never saw the place restored to its former glory. But then it seems to me that the male Glenisters generally had little attachment to their ancestral home. The colonel spent years away from it, and Henry never seemed to have much pride in it. Even you, Arthur, stayed away until the inevitable loop of life brought you home—brought you back—to me.

After the colonel's death, Henry and Verity remained in the little cottage next to Broadacres until the apartments in Glenister Hall were complete, which took five years, all told. They were done on a lavish but very tasteful scale. Clearly, Angela had money. Even with the sale of the cottages on the estate and the stables, Glenister Hall's renovation must have cost a fortune. I realise now what Henry's big plan for your future was: simply, that you would meet and marry money. I met her, you know. I don't know if she ever mentioned this to you, but I found myself with her amongst the scaffolding, the bags of plaster, the long planks of mahogany and the exquisite Italian tiles. I must say she was pretty, Arthur, petite, and no doubt very accomplished. But she had a hardness about the eye and a way of pressing her lips together when she was irritated that gave me the impression of an inner coldness.

Is that why your marriage didn't last?

The room was dusty, the air filled with motes—sawdust, plaster dust— and the light was poor; evening was upon us. She was making notes on a pad of paper, scribbling to get down her thoughts as they occurred to her. Then she shivered and put down the pad to button up her jacket more warmly. Her eye must have caught the slightest shimmer in the ether, or perhaps I caused a tremor in the veil. She gasped and her hand flew to her mouth, but not before she said an unladylike word. Her eyes narrowed into a squint, and the current vibrated again. I smiled at her and then her eyes were wide open. I could see little blobs of eyeliner at their inner corners and her skin, beneath her makeup, was blanched.

I didn't mean to frighten her; and I know that, strictly speaking, I had no right to be there at all. You might accuse me of making mischief. It was quite fun, though, after that—opening windows to cause spooky draughts, and slamming doors so hard they made the whole house shake! Poor woman! I shouldn't laugh, really.

Henry and Verity chose the largest apartment on the first floor of the south wing. It had the best view of the sea and of the sunsets, which can be glorious. The other apartments were bought by a retired solicitor, a former ambassador and a woman who had been famous on TV for a while as a children's presenter before some fall from grace—I can't recall the details. I'm sure Henry and Verity thought these people eminently suitable as neighbours, but sadly they weren't the right types at all for the kind of cooperative, gregarious community you'd had in mind.

They moved in and lived their separate lives, barely exchanging a civil word if they passed on the stairs, making rigid rules about car parking and whether potted plants should be permitted on the communal landings. The superannuated ambassador maintained a feud with the TV presenter over the volume of her television, and the solicitor threatened legal action when the artist in the stable block invited a gaggle of ancient hippies to celebrate the summer solstice. Henry attempted to impose his authority over the other residents but none of them were going to allow him to play Lord of the Manor and he was universally shunned by his neighbours.

I felt a bit sorry for Henry, if I'm honest. My default setting was to blame and suspect him and in my mind he remained culpable for several crimes. He was a manipulator and a bully. His penchant for very young women verged on the criminal. I choose to believe he inveigled his way into the Day family circle the moment he realised there was a seam of kindness to exploit. The Days were well-set-up. There was a historical connection he could use as leverage, and to reinforce it, he married Blanche. Then, with a foothold in the family, he began to make mischief. I don't know if his motivation was financial, sexual, emotional, social … or all of the above. What I do know is that one way or another, we scratched all his itches while he gave us nothing. Nothing at all. His secrecy about his birth is part and parcel of this scheming. When I'm feeling bitter, I think that he did it for devilment, knowing very well it would lead to speculation and muttering, and that Granny's partiality for him would cause division amongst her children that he could exploit.

In my kinder moments, however, I tell myself it was simply a sign of his arrogance, or a result of the fact that he hadn't fully come to terms with his history. I can't blame *him* for the erroneous conclusions *I* leapt to. I know that now. If I'm being really honest, I think Granny and Grandad were complicit in Henry's reticence, but it goes against the grain to accuse them of any wrongdoing. Henry was socially awkward; but that was probably a result of his miserable childhood, so perhaps that isn't to be wondered at. No wonder he was keen to spend time with the Days—a normal, well-adjusted, hospitable family. Who wouldn't?

And there's no escaping the fact that when Henry came, he brought you. That, by itself, might be sufficient compensation for the havoc he wrought, were it not for the fact that I'm convinced we would have met anyway. Somewhere in the woods, or down by the cove, I'd have seen you: a small, red-haired boy with freckles and dreadful hay fever ... I would have befriended you, Arthur, I know I would.

I think that wherever or whenever I met you—in whatever time or place, in whatever life—I'd feel the tug on my soul that says, 'Yes. He's the one.'

I yo-yoed between hating and feeling sorry for Henry, and looked on as the years passed bringing him little in the way of happiness or satisfaction or peace.

December 2000 saw a blanket of snow cover the entire country and arctic conditions wrought havoc. There was a blizzard. Snow hissed and fizzed where it fell between the trees but out across the meadow it gusted like damp sheets ripped from a line.

I met Henry's car as it sped along Glenister Hall's driveway, off to the golf club no doubt, or some other entirely pointless destination. What was he thinking, in that storm? The drive was obliterated by the snow that had already fallen, and drifts made new topography across the grassy areas to either side fashioning a landscape as familiar to Henry as his own hand seem alien. Visibility was dreadful and Henry wasn't taking anything like the care he needed. I stepped in front of the car and Henry slammed on the brakes. The years had not been kind to him, Arthur. Never a very handsome man, too much sun had turned his skin a liverish yellow. His precious hair was all but gone. His face in that instant was a picture—his mouth wide open, a rictus of yellow teeth, his small, rheumy eyes round and starting with astonished terror. He saw me, and he knew what seeing me meant: karma.

The car careered off the drive, spun, hit a tree and landed in the ditch.

He died straight away. I felt him go, his soul a meagre strewing of ashes across the snow, soon caught up by the bitter wind.

Later, it transpired that Verity and the retired ambassador had been carrying on a torrid affair behind Henry's back. I liked that touch, as you can imagine, for her sake. Interestingly, the relationship between Verity and the ambassador didn't continue after Henry's demise. I suppose Verity just enjoyed the thrill of the clandestine. She died of cancer in 2016, aged sixty-four.

Chapter Forty-Eight

The loose ends, Arthur. They're all that remain. But we'll tie them up neatly, shall we? Just while we wait.

Victor died a year or so after the colonel. It was a miracle he survived as long as he did. He passed away in his chair one afternoon. I'm afraid it wasn't an easy death. Some kind of apoplexy. His eyes bulged and his face went very dark. He looked at me as though for some kind of aid, struggling and gasping for breath. But what could I do? It was just his time.

Granny didn't quite make it to her century. She had a fall in 1996 and never recovered. I was with her at the end. She looked me in the eye and said, 'Is it time?'

And I said, 'Yes, darling Granny. It's time.' And she went as meekly and willingly as a child.

Granny's death—or rather her will—took the heart out of the family. She left the house and business to Jack. Isobel—the undoubted author of the scheme—offered the explanation that while my dad and Blanche had the proceeds of her divorce settlement, and Hester had Eric's life insurance, Granny was critically aware that she—Isobel—had nothing at all and wouldn't be able to provide for her sole remaining child. No one saw her point of view and there was outrage that she'd been so conniving as to have Granny alter her will behind the backs of the rest. The scene at the solicitor's office was very terrible, I'm sure you can imagine. My dad, in particular, was utterly broken. Whatever Isobel's reasons for persuading Granny to such a radical alteration of her will, she cannot have foreseen the complete destruction it would wreak. It was the death-knell of Salad Days, of Broadacres and of the Days.

Immediately, the twins quit the business and went to London to pursue their musical careers full time. They were long in the tooth for it—they were forty—but Aidan's big-ballad music appealed to a slightly older generation— adherents of Celine Dion and Whitney Houston—and they did very well for a while. In later years they hosted a daytime talk show and endorsed clothing for the more mature woman, and they both appeared on *Strictly Come Dancing* a couple of years ago. They remain close to Aidan and Aamon, but they never married and have no children, remaining, as always, self-sufficient.

Dad, sixty-five when Granny died, decided to retire, and he moved with Blanche to Spain. He had a stroke the following year and died a few months later, just like Grandad. Blanche remained in Spain, mingling with the ex-pat crowd. She abandoned sobriety and died of cirrhosis of the liver in the spring of 2001.

Hester also left the business immediately the contents of Granny's will were revealed. She returned for a while to the little house she'd kept in town, but soon got bored and lonely and bought an organic small holding on the Isle of Jersey. I heard that she remarried and lives very comfortably.

The wholesale defection of the family left Jack and Isobel to struggle on alone. How Isobel's coup had backfired on her! It's hard to think that she never considered what the outcome of it would be, isn't it? Did she really think the rest of the family would accept being passed over like that? She always did look out for number one without a thought for the consequences. Look how she treated Mum.

Of course, it was unsustainable.

Jack sold the business lock, stock and barrel to a national garden centre chain in 2000. It limped on for a year or two, but the absence of the "family" element and poor management meant it ceased to be profitable, and it closed. The buildings are abandoned now, looted and sprayed over with graffiti. The raised beds are choked with weeds. It's an eyesore, Arthur. Such a waste.

Broadacres was bought by a couple who had won the lottery. They wanted it as a countryside bolthole. They had it all made over, tarmacked the front garden to accommodate their several cars and planted a leylandii hedge to screen the business premises from view. They rarely visit though. I drift through the rooms now and again, reliving old memories, but it isn't the same. The garden has gone to seed.

Jack bought his mother a small house in the village, but he didn't stay around. He moved to London where he spent his money in night clubs and on cheap women. He died of an overdose in 2016. Isobel had his body brought back here to be buried in the family plot, and she visits most days even though, nowadays, her mobility is poor. She likes to keep the graves of Victor, Erin and Jack tidy, tending the plants and clearing away the leaves and litter that tend to accumulate in that corner of the graveyard. If she sees me watching her—which I do from the shadow of the yews or the gloom of the church portico—she never lets on. She can't ignore me forever though.

The village pub closed when Gary drowned trying to rescue a dog that had got into difficulties in a reservoir. Grace had been dead for years by then, from heart disease. Grace's boys left the village and never returned.

All this doom and gloom, Arthur. It can't make for very pleasant listening, and yet what I think I'm trying to say is that everyone dies and there's nothing to fear, especially for you, my love.

I'm here, waiting.

Chapter Forty-Nine

And so we come at last to you, Arthur. You're the end as you were the beginning. The alpha and the omega. My world, my life, my only love.

Of all the grand apartments of the newly restored Glenister Hall, you chose these modest little rooms as your *pied-à-terre*. What were they originally? A butler's pantry? I suppose you didn't expect to be here very often—any small space would do. But fate, destiny—call it what you like—brought you back as inevitably as the tide is drawn by the moon. What *I* think is that it was me who drew you back; the power of our connection could not be fought, even if you wished to.

But you didn't, did you Arthur? You didn't wish to fight it. No. No more than I did.

Once you'd split with Angela I wondered if you'd marry again. I watched you and Pansy working on the repairs to the woodsman's cottage together, and I thought, well, that could work. In the evenings you sat on opposite sides of the fire on the roughhewn benches I presume my grandfather made, not speaking much, just staring into the flames and thinking your own thoughts. There was a peaceful companionship between you, and I wasn't jealous because Pansy is like me—you could say that she *is* me—already marked out and part of this continuum. Like you, she was single, rooted and attached to the locality. She was only twelve or so years younger than you. That was nothing. I waited to see what would develop, but nothing did. You lived a bachelor life, from what I could tell, and I can't say I was sorry.

What clever gismos you've installed at the woodsman's cottage, by the way! The rainwater tank, and the little windmill that makes the lights work, the composting toilet. Lucky Pansy! She's perfectly happy there, isn't she?

Time passed, the seasons' perpetual cycle. Stormy winters and springs that seared the eyes with the intensity of new-furled leaf and bud. Short summers, the slow decline of autumn. Christmas, Easter, harvest. Equinox and solstice. The moon's wax and wane. Time etched your skin with frown lines and furrows, the bright hopefulness of your periwinkle blue eyes dimmed to patient navy. I watched your brisk walk in the beautifully manicured grounds slow to a stately stroll as, in their turn, daffodils and tulips gave way to peonies and sweet peas, roses to dahlias, nerines to chrysanthemums. Equal beauty, but different.

Did it sadden you that you had to employ a landscaping company to keep the lawns in trim and the gravel free of moss and weeds? Did you sometimes fantasise that *we'd* brought those gardens back to life, you and I and our healthy, happy brood of children? *I* did, Arthur. I imagined another life for us, a different life, one that ran in its pre-ordained grooves rather than being contorted out of shape by all my slip-ups and misfires.

Sometimes, when the purple gloaming came, I'd see the shades of them, those never-were children, the dim glow of lives that could have been, that might still be, in a different turn of the wheel. I'd see the slight turn of your head, the wrinkling of an eyebrow. Did you sense them too?

You aged well, I must say that. Even at sixty you were strong and upright, still very handsome, and you kept most of your hair, although its copper fire had turned white. I liked the good-quality but somehow shabby clothes you wore—tweed jackets with patched elbows, roomy corduroys, Aran sweaters. I liked the slow, considered way you toured the estate, the patient conversations you had with the eccentric artist, the irascible solicitor and the alcoholic TV presenter. Did you feel me by your side as you followed the pathways through the woods or sat on the roughhewn benches by the fire at the woodsman's cottage? Did you hear me laugh to see you scale the cliff and append your 'A' to the faint 'P' in the grey trunk of the old holly bush? You old fool! Don't you know you could have slipped and broken your neck?

Sometimes, in the cove or by the pond or in the quiet of the old graveyard, you'd turn abruptly and stare around you, as though you'd heard a sudden noise but didn't know what it was, and I'd hold my breath, waiting for whatever veil separates you and me to shift just a fraction. I was there in the greyish haze, indistinguishable from the shade beneath the trees, the miasma of rain across the cove, the bright shafts of sun that pierce the woodland canopy. I was always there, my heart aching and my arms waiting.

And then, last year, I saw your inner light began to dim; golden sun to silver moonlight, morning mist to evening shadow. It frayed at the edges and was ragged.

I knew my wait was almost over.

You came no more to the gardens. The paths through the woods were untrodden. I looked for you in all the special places, but you weren't there, you were *here*, lying beneath the smoothly ironed sheets, your hands neatly folded, your eyes closed but your face slightly tilted in a listening attitude, a very slight furrow between your brows. And so I have come and gone, and filled the waiting with our story, with *this* version of our story, until the time comes.

This room is lovely, pleasantly warm and tastefully furnished. They keep the lamps low, and the various bits of medical apparatus are unobtrusively masked by a rather lovely screen. It is silk, I think, heavily embroidered with classical scenes: Zeus presenting Pandora with the box; Smyrna's seduction by

Theias, Persephone's descent to the underworld; the doomed love of Theseus and Ariadne.

Nurses come and go at regular intervals. I presume they are accommodated somewhere in the place. Their hands are deft and impersonal. There is nothing to be done but to mark the days, the hours, the minutes. Evening and morning. Dawn chorus and murmuration at dusk. The tide's retreat and return. The beat of the diurnal clock. Tick tock. Tick tock. Tick tock.

In the end it is just the smallest step, Arthur, the space between one second and the next. Don't be afraid. Here. Let me take your hand. Ah! A little twitch of consciousness. You *can* feel it! Is it cold? Yours is warm. Oh! So warm. I can feel your fingers curling. The slightest possible pressure. Yes. Yes. There. My hand in yours, and my voice in your head, telling and retelling our story until the tale is done and the clock … stops.

Chapter Fifty

My earliest memory is of you, Arthur. It was summer and I was playing in the cove, sorting pebbles into groups according to a lexicon of my own—by size, by colour and by shape, but with a special category for stones that shimmered with quartz or mica or seemed to me to have another curious value. My sisters—sour and sulky in flounced frocks and white bobby socks—perched on flat stones and looked blankly at the scene. My father poked about in the rock pools out on the spur that reached into the sea.

I glanced up at the boulder steps that led down to the cove and saw you, dwarfed by the towering cliff to your right and the dense woodland behind; a small boy—smaller than me. You wore a blue sailor suit, and your feet were bare. The sun on your hair made it look like copper wire. Your appearance was so sudden it seemed that you'd stepped through a magical curtain. Your face was so white, taut and ghastly that I thought you must be a ghost. I'd never seen a stranger at the cove or anywhere in the woods before. In fact, I think I had little idea that anyone existed at all beyond my own family circle. Neither could I conceive of a child alone unless it was a sprite, or a changeling like the ones I'd heard of in stories. I waited to see if a grownup would emerge, but when none did, I rose from where I squatted and crossed the shingle towards you, drawn by a power I didn't understand but couldn't resist.

When you saw me, your face crumbled. You opened your mouth into a big square maw and began to cry; huge hiccoughing sobs that made your nose run. At the same time, you began to descend the steps, lost your footing and fell headlong, cutting your lip on a sharp stone.

My father came running and scooped you up, not caring about the blood that dripped onto his good shirt.

We could get no sense out of you—who you were, where you'd come from. We hollered at the tops of our voices, 'Halloooo!' but no answer came from the silent, secret wood.

You blubbed, 'I'm lost! I'm lost!'

But I took your sticky little hand and said, 'No. You're found.'

Dad carried you home through the woods to Broadacres, where the grownups were having tea on the terrace. My mother jumped up and wiped the blood from your mouth with one of Granny's best embroidered napkins, making sympathetic mewing noises in the back of her throat. She said she'd take you indoors to get cleaned up.

Ordinarily I'd have brought home a pocket full of stones, or pinecones, or a wilting bunch of wildflowers, but that time I brought *you*, Arthur. You were the best thing I'd ever discovered in the woods; the foundling friend I'd always wanted.

It was 1964, the summer before I started school, so I was nearly five years old.

It's strange, isn't it? That my first memory is of you. Or maybe it isn't very strange at all.

YOUR REVIEW MATTERS

Thank you for reading this book. As an indie author I don't have the support of a marketing department behind me to promote my books. I rely on you, the reader, to spread the word.

A short review provides great feedback and encouragement to the writer, and is a helpful way for others to know if they might enjoy the book. Please write a few words along with your star rating.

Connect with me on social media: @alliescribbler on X and @allienovelist on Instagram and Threads. Search Allie Cresswell on Facebook or sign up for updates and blog posts on my website at www.allie-cresswell.com from where you can directly buy eBooks for any eReading device.

ABOUT THE AUTHOR

Allie Cresswell was born in Stockport, UK and began writing fiction as soon as she could hold a pencil.

She did a BA in English Literature at Birmingham University and an MA at Queen Mary College, London.

She has been a print-buyer, a pub landlady, a bookkeeper, run a B & B and a group of boutique holiday cottages. She taught literature to lifelong learners but nowadays she writes full time.

She has two grown-up children, three granddaughters, two grandsons and two cockapoos, but just one husband—Tim. They live in Cumbria, NW England.

Salad Days is her fifteenth novel.

AFTERWORD &
ACKNOWLEDGEMENTS

I wrote *Relative Strangers*, my "family" book, almost twenty years ago. I felt it explored and described everything I had to say about the wonderful, complex and sometimes very challenging issues of belonging to a family.

But time moves on, and so does—so *must,* you might argue—our understanding of the world and our place in it. Then, I was in the middle years of life; occasionally bobbing along on the stream, but mainly thrashing wildly against life's currents. Now, I am past those turbulent times. I have more perspective, and I'm beginning to view the years of my youth with a curious sense of nostalgia.

Like Prue, I grew up in the sixties and seventies and so yes, some of her perceptions and experiences are mine. The Days' family evenings of song and laughter were certainly a feature of my childhood, and I hope I've recreated for Prue and Arthur those glorious summers of playing out from dawn till dusk, when there was no television to speak of, a trip to the cinema was a twice-yearly treat, when we had only our imaginations and the landscape around us to inform our play. These form the basis of the nostalgic tone of *Salad Days*, and I hope it will call to my readers' minds their own childhoods and happy family memories.

However, like my protagonists, I was largely protected from the huge social and political upheavals of the period. It wasn't until I got to university that I discovered what a sheltered existence I'd had, and how uninformed I was about so many things. I was ignorant of any sexual orientation that wasn't heterosexual, had no political opinions, didn't know what the word 'apartheid' meant, didn't know why a woman needed a right to choose. The world I discovered was big and scary, ugly and unequal but, crucially, had been there all the time I'd skipped and made-believe my way through childhood. My awakening created a tension between the simplified bubble of my infancy and the reality that existed just beyond its shimmering membrane. I hope the darker, malign forces that operate just beyond Prue's comprehension, and the occasional intrusion of later twentieth century British history, illustrate this dichotomy. I want the tone of *Salad Days* to be nostalgic but I don't want it to be naive.

Prue's combination of innocence and imaginative curiosity are crucial to the plot of the book. She's the latest of the unreliable narrators who clamour to tell my stories. I'm aware that readers don't always feel very empathetic to them, but writing a flawed main character is so much more interesting than writing a goody two-shoes! Jane Austen did it in *Emma,* and so did Charles Dickens in *Great Expectations.* Writers too numerous to name have followed suit. Presenting Prue with a series of conundrums and allowing her to leap repeatedly to the wrong conclusions was rather fun! And while I toyed with a number of potential titles for the book—The Green Woman; The Woman in the Woods—it was Prue's enduring greenness—in all its senses—that brought the line from Shakespeare's *Anthony and Cleopatra* to mind.

My favourite character in this book is Granny. As a granny myself, I can appreciate—as Prue and her cousins do not—the planning and sheer graft of preparing meals for large numbers, the herculean bedmaking attendant on their arrival and the mammoth laundry and housework left behind when I've waved them goodbye. But, like Granny Day, I'm lucky to have children and partners who pitch in once they've arrived, and I adore facilitating the get-togethers and of making, for them, the stuff *their* happy memories will be made of.

This is a book about memory—its unreliable nature, and the way we often shape our recollections to fit a narrative we can live with. Prue has no one to contradict her version of events. Arthur's account of their lives at Salad Days would be very different! So I've made it the reader's job to decide how much of what went wrong for the Days was Henry's fault, as Prue believes, and how much others—even Prue herself—might be at fault.

In this book, place has once again been a huge inspiration. From Yorkshire—in the *Talbot* series—and northwest Cumbria—in *The Cottage on Winter Moss*—here I've moved on to a place I discovered a couple of years ago, on the Scottish side of the Solway coast. The bluebell woods are real, and so is the cove. Also the forgotten, walled graveyard and the woodsman's cottage. But Broadacres, Glenister Hall and Salad Days are all figments of my imagination.

There is always a list of people to thank, without whom this book could not exist. Sallianne Hines of Quinn Editing, who, as always, treated my work with such a deft and helpful touch; Aimee Walnofer (author AE Walnofer) and author Sandra McIntrye for their insightful beta-reading; my sensitivity reader and friend Deirdre O'Grady (www.abilitywise.ie) who helped with Prue's eating disorder and General Anxiety Disorder; Deborah Hubbert, my American pen-pal, who encouraged me throughout, and who inspired the gothic element of this story. Thank you to Alastair Clarke (@tallentireart) for his wonderful original artwork and to Rachael Ritchey (<u>www.rrbookdesign</u>) for her graphic design expertise. Finally, as always, my thanks to Tim, who shoos me up the stairs to write and who knows when that faraway look in my eyes means I'm lost in the world of my fiction and can't be expected to respond like a normal human to questions like, 'What's for supper?'

ALSO BY ALLIE CRESSWELL

Game Show

Relative Strangers

Crossings

Tiger in a Cage

The Cottage on Winter Moss

The Widows Series

The Hoarder's Widow

The Widow's Mite

The Widow's Weeds

The Talbot Saga

The House in the Hollow

The Lady in the Veil

Tall Chimneys

The Highbury Trilogy inspired by Jane Austen's *Emma*

Mrs Bates of Highbury

The Other Miss Bates

Dear Jane

Non-fiction

About Self-publishing: an essential guide for new authors